The Barbed Crown

ALSO BY WILLIAM DIETRICH

FICTION

The Emerald Storm
Blood of the Reich
The Barbary Pirates
The Dakota Cipher
The Rosetta Key
Napoleon's Pyramids
The Scourge of God
Hadrian's Wall
Dark Winter
Getting Back
Ice Reich

NONFICTION

Green Fire
On Puget Sound
Natural Grace
Northwest Passage
The Final Forest

The Barbed Crown

An Ethan Gage Adventure

William Dietrich

HARPER LUXE

An Imprint of HarperCollins*Publishers*

FIRST HARPERLUXE EDITION

HarperLuxe™ is a trademark of HarperCollins Publishers

Library of Congress Cataloging-in-Publication Data is available upon request.

ISBN: 978-0-06-225376-7

13 14 ID/RRD 10 9 8 7 6 5 4 3 2 1

To Molly, just starting her own explorations

The world belongs to him who knows how to seize it.

—CORSICAN PROVERB RECITED BY NAPOLEON BONAPARTE
WHILE MAKING PLANS FOR AN INVASION OF ENGLAND

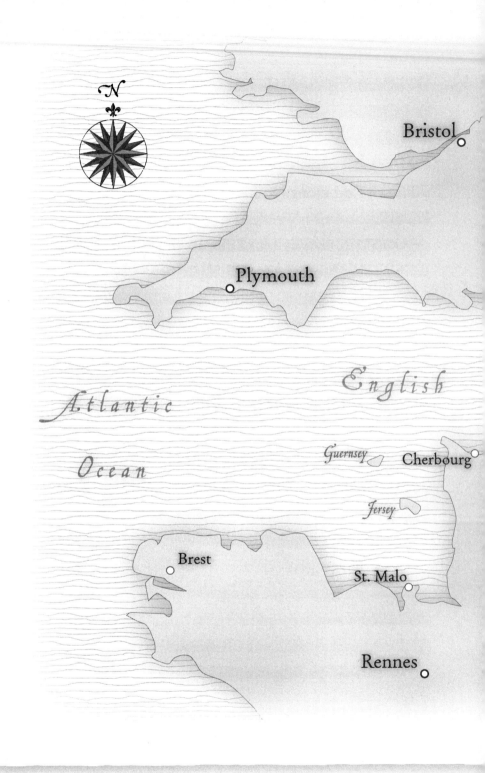

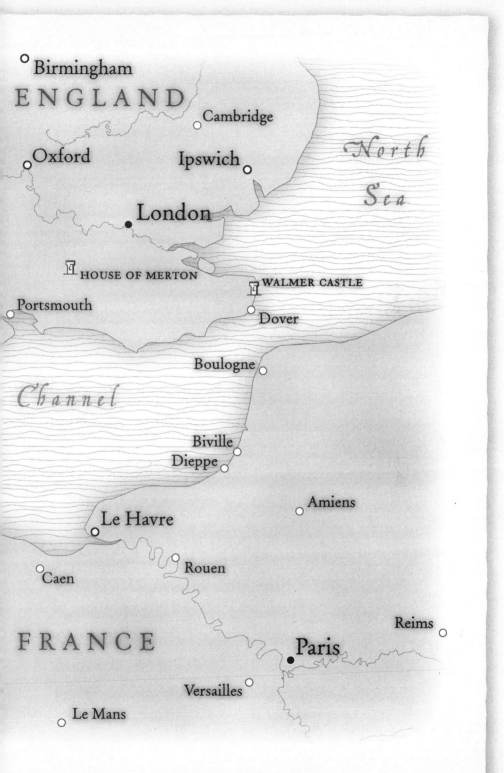

The Barbed Crown

Chapter 1

I was smuggled to France on a moonless flood tide, soaked from rain and spattered with the blood of a sailor beheaded by a cannonball. The Comtesse Catherine Marceau took out a lace handkerchief as Davy Burgoyne's body toppled overboard and was gone with a splash. I blinked and held tight to the tiller of the renegade sloop *Phantom*, more accustomed to carnage than I would have preferred.

In fact, I judged Davy's death an opportunity to engage my aloof yet strikingly attractive fellow spy. "I can offer my arm if it would make you feel safer, Comtesse."

She dabbed her pale face, spotted like measles, and remained resolute in her rebellion against Napoleon. Catherine had witnessed worse sights, watching her parents beheaded before escaping to England during a Reign of Terror that executed forty thousand French and exiled one hundred thousand more. She didn't need comfort from a lowborn and seemingly penurious opportunist like me. "Tend to your tiller, Ethan Gage," she said in accented English. "I am quite capable of completing our voyage if we don't wreck or surrender." She was pretty as a porcelain doll, proud as a toreador, and stiff as whalebone. Spray sheeted across the gunwales, helping clean both of us.

I was recently bereaved, consumed by dreams of revenge against Napoleon, and richer than I appeared. I'd sold a stolen emerald in London so quick that you'd have thought it was a hot coal. I hadn't dared crank up the price because of the jewel's cursed history, lest it cause more trouble. Despite my haste, I'd still netted an astonishing £10,000, enough to keep me a minor gentleman for the rest of my life. I'd prudently invested it all with the financial firm of Tudwell, Rawlings, and Spence, which promised it could double my money, should I survive. My intention was to manage my fortune for my son, Harry, and avenge my missing wife, Astiza, who'd been carried off in a hurricane. Meanwhile, I appreciated the charms of my new co-conspirator I'd been matched with in London, quite the ornament for a raffish adventurer like me. "I'm here if you need me, mademoiselle."

"And I am content to stay where I am." She clutched the gunwale an oar's length away, her demeanor cold as the wind.

The crewmen weren't as entranced with our passenger as I was. "I told you a woman was bad luck," one smuggler muttered to another. "Mercy on Davy's soul."

"It wasn't *my* luck that was bad," Catherine retorted calmly, not pretending she hadn't overheard. "*I'm* still alive."

I liked her spirit, but then I like pretty women even when I'm mourning, or perhaps because of it. My ache and longing for Astiza was a cavity, but one that nature prefers to fill, I guiltily told myself. And what a sally we were on! War between England and France, the English Channel crammed with hostile shipping, and a French cutter stumbling on us this foul night as we tried to sneak into its country. Our captain, the notorious moonshiner Tom Johnstone, gave me the job of steering toward a reef while he manned a swivel cannon. The rest of his crew cranked on sail and fired muskets. Catherine held a pistol in her lap, in case her enemies got close enough to kill.

The French bow gun that had killed Davy fired again, the cannonball screaming as it punched a hole through our jib, slackening our pace slightly.

The thing I don't like about sailing is that there's never a place to hide.

"Hold this course and watch for the white of breaking waves on the reef," our captain instructed me. "Then aim precisely between the two highest fangs when they loom out of the dark. Our hull doesn't draw much water, so with timing we'll scrape across the barnacles while the frog boat tears out her bottom."

"Timing?"

"Need to catch it on a swell, lest we smash and drown."

Our own craft was thirty-six feet on the waterline, with a single high mast, jutting bowsprit, and a lively fore-and-aft rig built for speed and close-haul sailing. *Phantom*'s hull was low and lean as a greyhound, hard to spy, hard to catch, and tilted so hard that one rail was nearly in the water. Johnstone's trade was smuggling contraband English wool to France, and French tobacco, brandy, and silk back to England. Normally, s bunch crisscrossed the Channel without problem, but this time we were pursued by a ship with a longer waterline, bigger sails, and eight broadside cannon. Had our enemies gotten a tip? The greater the conspiracy, the easier to find weak members to turn. With thousands scheming for the first consul's downfall, any number of traitors could have betrayed us between London and Paris.

The cutter was gaining.

"They're setting a spanker," I said, sounding more nautical than I really am. "Or maybe it's a studs'l." I've crossed the ocean several times and acquired some salty vocabulary, but the enemy was actually little more than a gray blur. Our compass gyrated as uselessly as my stomach, I couldn't see a star, and if I remained the helmsman, then my mission to kill Napoleon seemed likely to end before it properly got started. We were looking for a beach north of Dieppe, but damned if I knew whether we were pointed at the North Pole or Tahiti. I just aimed where Johnstone told me.

"A risk for Lacasse in this wind," our smuggler said.

"You know our pursuer?"

"I know his boat. Antoine is an able seaman, but not as able as me." Johnstone aimed his little cannon. It fired a ball too small to sink anything, but big enough to make our pursuers duck. "Maybe I can shoot down some rigging."

"I hope you agree with the comtesse that it's Davy's fate that was bad, not our own."

Johnstone grunted. He was a strapping six-foot-three, dark-haired, blue-eyed brute, with a big-nosed lump of a face from decades of wind and drink. "That lad never had luck since breech birth killed his ma. Clumsy as a mule, dumb as an ox, and happy as a clam, as the slower sailors usually are. Intelligence is the enemy of contentment, Ethan Gage, and Davy's luck was accepting his lot and then finding a quicker way out of it than most of us can look forward to." He cupped his hand to shelter a match near the touchhole, since the gun lacked the newer lanyard. "I've seen men hit by cannon fire take three days to die, screaming till their lips cracked." He lit the charge, there was flare from the touchhole, and it fired. "Now, we Lymington sailors ain't as neat with our round shot, so we'll try to give the frogs some splinters to howl about."

It was too dark to see the cannonball's effect, but I imagined I heard shouts across the water.

I glanced again toward the comtesse, who'd been eighteen when exiled by the French Revolution and was now a Bourbon beauty of thirty-one, her cloak hooding a mass of golden hair as glossy as smuggled silk. I'd too recently lost my wife to be my typical flirtatious self, but it was still male instinct to want to impress a pretty Frenchwoman. We were introduced by the spymaster Sir Sidney Smith in London, united in wanting to do away with Napoleon, and divided by her haughty high birth. Her motives weren't entirely clear to me, but I was happy having company in vengeance. My charm having failed to impress her, I decided to grin fiercely instead. "Win through or die," I growled.

I was rewarded with an evaluating glance of her green eyes.

It was April 3, 1804, and the ashes of my ambition had been rekindled by tragedy and the desire to give payback for my missing wife. A mere year before I'd been hoping for a quiet retirement with my new family, financed by an emerald I'd snatched from the pasha of Tripoli. However, procrastination, greed, and poor vigilance ended up endangering my son and losing Astiza. I chased and lost a fortune in the Caribbean, and because I blamed myself for her drowning, I was anxious to extend the blame to someone else, like Napoleon. Her loss left me the shattered caretaker of little Harry, now approaching his fourth birthday. My enemy in the Caribbean, Leon Martel, had persuaded me that Bonaparte himself was behind this cruel manipulation of my family. So I'd returned with Harry to England, used the sale of the emerald to temporarily establish my boy with a clergy family named Chiswick, and sought the help of Smith to strike back at Napoleon. Much to my liking, he suggested Catherine as a useful partner.

One final quest, and then I'd make Harry and me a home.

A better man might have set aside such self-importance to take care of his son; my sticking him with strangers adding to the guilt I carried like chains. But like so many faulty fathers I let a noble and dangerous mission convince me that the more mundane duty of child rearing could wait.

Sir Sidney enlisted me in an elaborate French royalist conspiracy financed with English gold. That flamboyant officer had been fighting the Corsican since Bonaparte was an artilleryman who drove the British from Toulon and Smith was the English daredevil who burned the French fleet before retreating. The two have been scrapping every since.

I had a belt of francs, Louis, and English sovereigns strapped around my waist and another reserve tucked in my boot. I'd also retained two trinkets from the Caribbean. The first was a pendant with the letter *N* surrounded by a laurel leaf, which had been a gift from Napoleon. The second was a golden Aztec curio of a man astride a delta-shaped object that might be wings, and thus might represent a flying machine from the ancient past. Either or both might win me access to France's ruler, so I could finish him off. There was also a pistol in my greatcoat pocket and a tomahawk in

my sash, meaning all I lacked was a good Pennsylvania
long rifle.

Our strategic situation was building to a climax.
I'd met Napoleon when he was a mere ambitious general. He'd since seized power, gone back to war with
England, and had one hundred thousand men eager to
jump the Channel and reform English cooking. My late
enemy Leon Martel had dreamed of vaulting the tur-
bulent moat using Aztec flying machines. There were
also schemes for balloons, tunnels, floating windmills,
and twenty-mile-long pontoon bridges. Invasion was as
daft as it was daring, so maybe a coven of spies could
discourage it. That was my job.

My feelings about Napoleon were a mix of envy,
admiration, resentment, and knowledge that he was as
human as the rest of us. Bonaparte was a fallible idealist, ruthless as a banker. We'd fought together in Egypt,
fought against each other at Acre, and I'd been his
agent in Italy, America, and Greece in between times
that he contemplated shooting me. Our history was a
stormy one, the loss of my wife tipping our relationship
to disaster.

Now it was time to put a stop to him, or at least his
ambitions.

The Breton rebel Georges Cadoudal had already
been landed with a million francs to prepare revolt. The

assumption in Britain was that the French were restive (the fact I'd seen no evidence of this was met with annoyance) and that eliminating Napoleon was the easiest way to eliminate his army camped around Boulogne. "His imprisonment or death is the road to peace!" exhorted Smith. My job was to utilize my trinkets to get access to the highest circles, find Bonaparte's weakness, and tell royalists the best time and way to strike.

The comtesse had been trained to be a seductress of an agent, and she'd practiced by letting me flirt with her before setting me straight with her political seriousness. Now she would pose as consort to my role as a self-absorbed, pleasure-seeking, politically harmless opportunist: a slander people disconcertingly accepted as fact. Catherine endured more than welcomed our partnership, worrying it would reflect on her own taste. It was too early to link with another woman and impossible not to think about doing so. In short, I was sailing for France with a ragged mess of feelings, not the least of them gloom, desperation, guilt, and suicidal recklessness. Frankly, I never would have hired me, but the British were eager for anyone lunatic enough to thread through Channel patrols.

Johnstone, who'd been transporting contraband since boyhood, had been freed from Fleet Prison to smuggle us in.

Now the black ocean lightened ahead from breaking surf. "I think I see the reef."

"Cheat the rocks like you'd cheat at cards, Ethan," the smuggler instructed as he rammed home a charge. Another French cannonball came our way, skipping like a stone off our stern. "A bluff between the worst pinnacles." I'd inspired his metaphor not only by boasting of my gambling skills but by proving them by cleaning his crew of every shilling in the first ten miles. Accordingly, Johnstone thought me clever, which always results in too much responsibility.

I eyed the boil of foam ahead. "Maybe we should trade jobs."

"I'll give a hand when need be." He sighted along his little cannon. "I do the gunnery because there's an art to aim when rolling. And you're used to risk."

Our smuggler was a charming free-trade runner so fond of luxury and whores that he was thrown into Fleet for running up £11,000 in London debts, or more than I'd gleaned from my emerald. I agreed with Sidney Smith's strategy of hiring a rascal to do a rascal's job, but the foul weather we'd waited for is not the kind I prefer to sail through. Tom and his other smugglers regarded gales as friends, masts bent and lines thrumming. I dislike cold water, as well as jailing, death, or torture. So I steered dubiously toward a great wash of breaking waves, sea stacks materializing out of the gloom like guarding towers.

To take my mind off our peril, I decided to reinforce my reputation as a worldly gambler to impress Catherine Marceau. "To win at cards, you must be able to count, figure odds, and guard against cheats," I pronounced loudly.

Johnstone fired his swivel. "And to win as a free trader you need cool nerve and the trick of concealment. There're twenty thousand Englishmen who make their living evading the Revenue Service, Gage, and the first skill is concealing a false bottom or bulkhead. A customs officer without a tape is like an angler without a hook. He has to calculate if a ship's hold matches the outside of the vessel."

"Then I'll be wary of officers with yardsticks," I replied. "Now in gambling, the way to mark cards is to use your fingernail to notch the edge, or a sander to roughen, or a point to make a blister."

"Old Jack Clancy built an entire double bottom," our captain volleyed. "A false keel and false sides to lay in French brandy that could set him for a year. But you had to beach the beast and pry off its planks. One time the tide swept in and carried off half his cargo." Johnstone laughed.

"I admire such architectural ingenuity." The rocks were looming closer.

"I've seen silks slipped into plaster Mother Marys," the smuggler recounted. "Barrels with secret compartments. Boxes for artificial French flowers with double bottoms just wide enough to slip in a gauzy dress. Hollow iron ballasts to secrete contraband, and tobacco sewn into potato skins. To outfox the customs officer is as much fun as the profit."

"The creativity of the criminal mind is exemplary," I agreed. "Even better than knowing cards is a holdout, where you tuck away a king or ace. Eye a man's cuffs for a silk-lined pocket, and insist on counting the deck. And mind a mirror glued on his inner finger, used for reading cards."

"Wise counsel, American. And if you see a coastal cutter sailing slow, fire a shot, get them to heave to, and look for a tail of contraband underwater."

"Like my friend Robert Fulton's submarine, or plunging boat!"

I gave a peek at our female passenger. She seemed more focused on the flashes of French cannon fire than on our manly brilliance. A waterspout wet us again.

"It's good to have an escape plan at the gaming tables as well," I went on, the rocks looming huge.

"I'm beginning to understand why I lose to sharps," Johnstone said. "One of our cleverest moonshine tricks is to make a rope out of twist tobacco and then wind it into a thicker hawser. You can't see the sot weed inside the hemp."

"And even easier than holding out a card is pocketing another man's winnings," I returned. "When you push a pile of coins or chips, have some gum on your wrist and pick up one or two for yourself."

"You've got the mind of a smuggler, Gage. When you get tired of fighting Bonaparte, come see me for employment."

"I appreciate the compliment, but a gambling den is warmer than a smuggler's smack. And it doesn't sound like you need my advice. It's a wonder the king collects any duties at all."

"The free trader doesn't always win. The sharp, neither, I suppose. We've both spent time in jail." He shrugged. "Time is a tax in itself."

"A gambler who always wins advertises he is cheating," I agreed. "There's a fine art to pinching just enough." The passage looked no wider than a door.

"So I'll run from the king's men, but if they wish to pay me to smuggle you, I'll run from Bonaparte's instead." Another cannon ball sent up a spout near our bows.

"Sir Sidney would call you an expedient patriot, Captain."

"And you, American, a man who doesn't know to leave well enough alone."

"Reef is on us, dammit!" the watchman cried.

A small cannonball clipped our rail, splinters flying, and one of Johnstone's boys let out a howl. Our own swivel gun went off in my ear again. Foam heaved up between the barnacled obstacles like a giant lung taking a breath.

The captain finally slammed his heavy bulk against the other side of the tiller, and our bow swung just slightly. "Nicely timed, Gage, but allow for drift. Steer for the windward rock until the last moment."

We pointed straight at destruction. But no, we were pushed sideways and sailed neatly into the gap, our boom scraping stone on one side and our hull the bottom on the other. No normal skipper would try pinching through, but Captain Tom had studied the intricacy of this coast for years. The hull shuddered, and suddenly, Comtesse Marceau clutched my arm.

"Lantern ashore!"

And as the surf sucked and thundered, the faintest green light shone.

Chapter 2

The French cutter chased us to disaster. It followed through the gap and grounded so violently that its mast snapped, its sails collapsing like an unpegged tent. There were oaths, yells, and a final frustrated cannon shot that passed a good fifty yards off our stern. Captain Johnstone gave a satisfied cackle. Comtesse Marceau balanced to peer backward with a slight smile of triumph. My hand on the tiller was sore and sweaty.

"Will Lacasse sink?" the comtesse asked our captain.

"More likely left dry when the tide drops. Companions will take them off tomorrow, and their government will get them another ship."

She clutched her pistol, a silk reticule with her purse and necessaries tied with a silver cord to her wrist.

"The French navy has been helpless since the officers of the aristocracy were driven from the kingdom. It's one more way the revolutionaries have betrayed France."

"A more prudent commander might have rounded up and given a parting broadside," Johnstone agreed. "Better to lose us than your own vessel."

"Curious luck for them to stumble on us like that," I said.

"If it *was* luck."

We sailed on toward shore. High gray cliffs materialized in the murk. Surf pounded their base. It looked like the devil's worst place to go ashore.

"You promise a way off such a bleak beach?" I asked.

"A smuggler's path," said Johnstone.

Behind us, red light flared. The wrecked cutter had sent up a rocket.

"Be quick," Johnstone added. "Foot patrols may see that commotion and come looking."

"You're very brave, Comtesse," I said, even though she hadn't done anything of note yet. Men make pointless compliments to attractive women out of instinct and vague hope.

"I've no life except France and was dead in England," she replied. "I'm risking nothing except resurrection."

"I suppose we'll have to share quarters in Paris to pose as a couple. More convincing, don't you think?"

"Indeed not, monsieur. You will install me in fine apartments befitting a highborn consort, and I will receive you at my whim. Our friendship is solely political, and we're both mere soldiers in a great royalist army of conspirators already two thousand strong."

"Maybe just arm in arm to the opera, then," I persisted, wondering if we could afford two places. "And elbow to elbow in that new Parisian invention, the dining restaurant. Smarter than an inn, using chefs unemployed by the revolution to make their best for a roomful of strangers. I'm told the Véry offers eight choices of soup, ninety-five main courses, and twenty-five desserts."

"Mercenary, impersonal, and common," she judged. "The modern world is a tasteless porridge of coarseness and mediocrity. We go ashore not just for restoration, Monsieur Gage, but to save civilization from the mob. I will pretend to accompany you, but never forget that birth made us different beings."

Well, her message was clear enough. The truth is that I was less than comfortable throwing in with a bunch of royalists, whatever the excesses of Napoleon. They were a self-satisfied yet needy bunch, and though I'm a bit of a climber, I get tired of their pretensions.

Catherine Marceau's snobbery was only reinforcing my longing for commonsensical Astiza. But if I was going to give payback to Bonaparte for destroying my family, these blue bloods were the only chance I had. War makes strange alliances.

"Captain, they holed our tender," a seaman reported to Johnstone, looking at the dinghy lashed amidships.

"Say what? Damaged our gig? The frogs usually can't hit a thing, and tonight we're cursed with a marksman?"

"We've no means to get these two ashore." The mate looked at us unhappily, clearly not eager to lug us back to England.

"Then they'll get themselves. I haven't come all this way not to get my promised fare from Sidney Smith. Do you swim?" The question was addressed to both of us.

"With reluctance," I said.

"Certainly not," Catherine added. Swimming is what common people did, apparently.

"Then keep her from drowning, Gage. The beach is steep, and I'll get you within yards of the shingle."

"Captain, you can't be serious," she protested.

"Maybe we should take time to patch the launch," I said.

"With rockets lifting up?" Johnstone's sloop slid in under the cliffs, came about, and anchored into the wind, its stern paid off into surf. His crew pushed us to the back rail, muttering about the reforming benefits of a chill dunking for a cardsharp and female curse.

"Smith isn't paying you to drown me!" the comtesse warned.

"One man has died, mademoiselle," a mate said. "Another wounded by splinters. Someone has obviously betrayed you, and we've paid the price. The least you can do is plunge." He pushed us, with Catherine shrieking, into the sea.

I grabbed her as we fell, the cold water knocking my breath away and my heavy belt of gold pieces dragging us to the bottom. Fortunately, the water was so shallow that Johnstone must have scraped his rudder. I felt a mix of stone and sand, shoved off with one arm clutching my struggling companion, and surfaced with a *whoosh*. Bloody hell, the water was bracing! A wave pushed us toward shore and then broke over us, making us sputter. But my legs got a better grip, I held against the suck, and we staggered ashore, half frozen and spitting Channel salt. I gripped Comtesse Marceau like a wrestler, trying to concentrate on our predicament instead of her form. We men inventory the female shape the way a lepidopterist does butterflies. She shivered and pulled away.

Phantom had used her anchor to kedge off the beach. The sloop caught the wind with its jib and began to work into the dark. Above us, chalky cliffs rose into gloom.

"I could have died!"

"You will die, sooner or later, as will we all," I snapped. Women usually find me irresistible, or at least don't keep such wary distance. By thunder, I've had Napoleon's sister, a British aristocrat, and an Indian maiden, so Catherine needn't pretend I'm a leper. "In the meantime we try to defeat Bonaparte."

"Don't lecture me about the Corsican."

"If you're going to be a spy, you really should learn to swim," I retorted.

She lifted her head. "No. I am on French soil now, and don't intend to leave it again. I will triumph, or be buried." She crossed her arms, but then they flew apart. "My reticule!"

"What about it?"

"Lost in the water. You must find it!"

The surf was roaring, the Channel black, and the tide wicked. "I'm afraid that's impossible."

"But my money was in there!"

The lost coins made me hesitate. It was a dark night, but I made a futile grope before a particularly big wave broke, foam swirling against our knees, before admitting it was useless. "An offering to Neptune, I'm afraid."

"This is your fault for letting us make that foolish leap!"

"On the contrary, your fault for not hanging on to your vital possessions. Next time, clutch before you jump, Comtesse." She shivered miserably, sniffling, so I took pity. "I've money enough for both of us."

"I do not like being dependent."

The woman had never worked a day in her life. "Then swim for your savings."

She glanced at the pounding water before replying. "But I will allow you to help me this time."

"We're friends, then?"

"Allies."

"We'd best get beyond the reach of the tide." I turned toward the cliffs, which appeared impassable, and saw that green lantern again. "There. Either our salvation or our doom."

We stumbled up the slippery cobble to a cluster of men in bicorn hats and flapping greatcoats, their lantern hooded once we got near. In the rain the hats formed twin gutters that diverted rainwater from their crown to their shoulders in little rivulets. We were all silhouettes in the dark.

"Good King Louis," their leader said. It was the password.

"By the grace of God may he reign," the comtesse replied, finishing the code.

"They wouldn't ferry you ashore?" the man continued.

"Our launch was holed. We've had storm, gunfire, and a soaking."

"I apologize your return to France wasn't easier. *Bonne nuit*, I am Captain Emile Butron of the Vendée rebel army."

"I thought that force was destroyed by General Bernadotte."

He spat tobacco, which soldiers chew nervously before a fight. "Not entirely. We still have a network of safe houses, once we top this bluff. But we must move quickly; there are spies everywhere. The policeman Réal pays a hundred francs for each report of a royalist, and gets three basketfuls of condemnations every morning. The denunciations cost Bonaparte's government four million francs a year, and they consider it a bargain."

"Once in Paris we'll be hidden among friends," Catherine said.

"Alas, we're hard-pressed in Paris as well, Comtesse. Georges Cadoudal has been arrested."

"What?" Catherine's question was more of a cry. She was having a bad night.

"After a coach chase through Paris, Georges shot one policeman and tried to blend with the crowd, but someone pointed him out. General Pichegru was seized after fighting a dozen men in his sleeping chamber. General Moreau had already declined to cooperate with our plan—he says he is a republican, not a royalist, even though Bonaparte is neither—but they've imprisoned him anyway. Our conspiracy is falling apart before it can get started."

I turned around, wondering if it was too late to get back aboard *Phantom*, but the sloop had disappeared. "They didn't tell us this in England," I said, sounding more inane than I intended.

"They didn't know. A servant was caught, and the network unraveled under torture. Réal is an expert at coercion."

"Perhaps our chase on the Channel crossing also came from betrayal."

"Indeed, Monsieur Gage. It's sheer pluck and fortitude you've come this far."

So I'd sailed into a fiasco. Cadoudal was a burly rebel from Brittany. Former French generals Pichegru and Moreau were military heroes who despised Napoleon. Now they were all in prison? "We should regroup," I said.

"First you must hide."

"We will not give up," Catherine vowed.

"*Oui, mademoiselle.* But only if you can keep from being imprisoned."

This rebel captain had common sense. "And we avoid that how, exactly?" I asked.

"By getting off this beach. Come, there's a slit of a ravine smugglers have used for decades. It's wet, steep, and muddy, but we have climbing staffs." He looked at Catherine. "Some dry clothes soon, Comtesse. And a brandy."

"What would warm me is a regiment loyal to the Bourbons."

"*Oui, mademoiselle.* All in good time."

The cut in the bluffs was almost impossible to spot from the sea, and probably just as invisible above. Storm-gnarled shrub hid us as we climbed steeply toward a plateau of farmland. Mud soon joined the blood and water in our clothes. Fortunately, there were fixed ropes to help. To Catherine's credit, she didn't complain once except to curse the geography. For a lady, she had a rich vocabulary.

We'd ascended halfway, coming out of bent trees to flattened grass and heath, when a shot came and one of Butron's men coughed and fell backward. I'm always amazed at how a musket ball falls a victim, as if a puppeteer cut his strings. One moment a man is thriving, and the next he is a silent sack of meat. And it's dumb chance that you live and he dies.

More shots rang, slugging into the grit around us.

"Patrol! They must have seen their ship's rocket!" Butron's men drew pistols and fired at the flashes. Then silence as everyone reloaded, ramrods scraping barrels. Sword fights don't pause, but a gun battle provides intermissions.

Our comrade was dead, the captain confirmed, so we abandoned him and crawled a few more yards. More shots whined overhead. Shooting high is so common a mistake that soldiers wear high hats and plumes to bait the enemy. Aim low and slow is always my advice; your quicker opponent will likely miss.

"They'll block us at the top," Butron predicted. "We can't descend; the incoming tide will reach to the cliffs." He sounded apologetic. "We may be trapped, monsieur."

"The devil we are. Those soldiers are between me and a warm fire." I had to live up to my reputation for ingenuity, especially if I was going to impress a comtesse. I was a protégé of Benjamin Franklin, after all, and a hero of Acre. There was no time to be truly clever, but perhaps I could be daring.

"Listen: pick up stones or clods of earth. I'm going to draw their fire with the help of rocks you throw my way, and when their weapons are empty, charge. Save your powder until you're right on top of them and then finish with ball and steel."

"You'll expose yourself for us, Ethan?" I detected a slight note of deference from Catherine, and puffed at finally getting proper notice and being addressed by my first name. It's easier being brave with a female looking on.

"I need your coats and climbing staffs. I'll scramble up the side of the ravine and make it look as if we've fled that way. When I shoot at the enemy patrol, throw your rocks at me to make more noise. After they empty their guns, have at them."

"The point of all this is wasted if you, the agent we were assigned to deliver, is shot and killed," Butron objected.

I couldn't agree with him more. "I am rather important."

"And nefarious, we're told. Devious, wily, and unscrupulous."

"Calculating. Never fear, I'll fall flat and trust the inaccuracy of their muskets. I've been shot at before."

"Yes, your reputation is of being everywhere, on every side, and somehow surviving," the comtesse said, a little ardor finally in her tone. "I knew you were brave, Monsieur Gage, but this amounts to sacrifice."

That was more like it. "No sacrifice is too great for a beautiful woman. Captain, please get ready."

So up I scrambled rather ingloriously on all fours, dragging cloaks and staves. Random gunshots banged below. Peering into the dark, I could just make out movement at the head of the ravine.

I balanced on a precarious perch, thrust the staffs into the soil, and draped coats on them. "Now, now, give it to their flank!" I shouted in French, fluent from my earlier years in Paris. I aimed my pistol and pulled the trigger.

It snapped uselessly. Soaked.

"By Franklin's lightning rod," I muttered. I'd dunked the piece in the ocean, hadn't I? I have a habit of not thinking my daring through. The enemy soldiers shouted, trying to spy me, and one musket went off, the bullet buzzing. At least my cartridges and powder flask were wrapped in oilskin. It took what seemed like a century to unwrap, reload, wipe the flint, and add a pinch of fresh powder to the pan.

Another enemy bullet came, striking close.

I pulled again.

The pistol banged, the flash giving my position away. Then a humming through the air as my companions hurled stones and clods in my direction to mimic a rattle of footsteps. One elicited a quite realistic cry from me as it smacked my thigh. I fell.

Just as I did, the enemy patrol let off its volley. Bullets hit all around, and I flinched so violently that I began to slide back down the slope. I clutched at the walking sticks to arrest my fall and instead they pulled free, so I had an armful of canes and coats as I bounced toward the bottom.

"We got one!" the enemy cried.

"Charge!" Captain Butron shouted.

I skittered, bumping and filthy, all the way back to where I'd started. Upslope I could hear shouts, curses, and gunfire as my escort collided with the blocking soldiers. Then a cheer, but from which side I knew not.

Well, it wasn't as if I had a choice. I stood, wincing from a twisted ankle, and ascended the trail with my arms full of coats and staffs, like a limping laundress. Along the way I came upon Comtesse Marceau, sitting in the mud because she was weaponless. "Come, the fight's over," I said, freeing an arm to haul her up.

She didn't volunteer to carry anything. "Is it safe?"

"I don't know if we won or lost, but it's settled in either event."

"Are you shot, monsieur?" Was there at least a hint of concern?

"A sprain from hurrying to reinforce you and our companions."

"You are indeed a gambler."

"When the winnings are enticing." I winked, which she couldn't see it in the dark.

We awkwardly climbed the last slippery yards and emerged on farmland. Butron's smile was a reassuring crescent in the night. Some bodies lay in high grass, but the other surviving soldiers had fled. The comtesse and I were soaked and smeared, the hood of her cloak fallen back to reveal her sodden mass of curls. I put an arm around her waist and gave her a squeeze, hip to hip, figuring I deserved it.

"Well done, Captain," I said.

"And the same to you, Monsieur Gage. You make a splendid scarecrow."

"Did we fight the army?"

"The Gendarmerie Nationale. And the Customs Service."

"I'm afraid your greatcoats have a few bullet holes. Save them to show your grandchildren and embroider the story."

"No embroidery is necessary. But we had some help with this adventure. The Coastal Patrol was assaulted from two sides."

He pointed, and more figures came out of the gloom. Waiting allies! Perhaps the royalist conspiracy wasn't so desperate after all.

And then my world reeled. One of our rescuers had the slimness of a woman and moved with astonishingly familiar grace, and she carried a small child in her arms. The sky was black as Hades, dripping with rain, and she was bundled like a czarina, and yet I'd recognize her form anywhere.

I was looking at a ghost.

Chapter 3

I learned on a Caribbean-bound frigate that the Royal Navy has a toast for each night of the week. Saturday's is: "To sweethearts and wives—may they never meet."

Now they had.

My arm dropped from the waist of Catherine Marceau as if chopped.

"You didn't lose time finding a female companion, Ethan," my deceased wife said. Except that Astiza wasn't dead, apparently, and in fact had accomplished the impossible by waiting for me in France with the son I'd left behind in England. I've always enjoyed interesting women, but the one I married is eight degrees more interesting than I can ever keep up with. Somehow she'd achieved resurrection, reunion with her child, magical transport, and then helped in my rescue by attacking the French from the other side.

By the geraniums of Thomas Jefferson, I hadn't even managed dry clothing.

My heart lurched from bereavement to embarrassment, my guilt at Astiza's drowning replaced with guilt at flirting with Catherine Marceau. I was astonished, reprieved, and defensive, all in an instant. "She's not a woman, she's a spy," I stuttered, my mouth running ahead of my confusion. "Not much of a swimmer, but a genuine comtesse."

"You couldn't find a male confederate?"

"Sidney Smith thought we'd make a team. And we didn't know you were alive." How had this miracle happened? I've yet to summon clever phrasing for momentous occasions and keep a notebook full of things I should have said, had I the wit to think of them. I mentally vowed to jot down a few more for this surprise, once I had the leisure to think of something intelligent.

"I'm not about to let you run off by yourself again," Astiza said. "You get in trouble every time you do. If we're going to be married, we need to have the habit of staying together, Ethan, and devoting our attentions to each other, not highborn espionage agents." She looked at the comtesse with a mixture of skepticism, amusement, and pity. "He would exasperate you, I promise."

"This is your wife?" Catherine asked me.

"Apparently so." I gave Astiza a good squint, just in case I was faced with an imposter, but she has a Greek Egyptian beauty not commonly found in Normandy. "My bride has a habit of surprising me."

Catherine drew herself up. "I can assure you, madame, that I was doing my best to deflect his attention. Our partnership was one of temporary expedience. His manners, after all, are American."

"I entirely believe you, and apologize for any forwardness my husband has exhibited," Astiza replied like a diplomat. "He has the enthusiasm of a billy goat, though his heart means well."

"The shamelessness of a politician," the comtesse judged.

"The anxiety of a treasure hunter," Astiza countered.

"The longing of a lottery player."

"The wanderlust of a minstrel."

"The grace of a plowman."

"Naughty and opportunistic, but with the earnestness of a schoolboy."

I tried to interrupt but couldn't get a word in edgewise.

"Thus I am relieved to deliver him to you, madame," Catherine summed up. "He has élan, but like most men he is in need of great reform."

"I have returned to do just that, and in my trying to do so, he is teaching me patience." Astiza turned to me. "And exactly why are we in France again, Ethan?"

I was flustered, not to mention muddy, hungry, cold, and tired. I cleared my throat. "To avenge your death. Didn't I see you drown in a hurricane?" I had a distinct recollection of watching her be carried off in a great green wave, a memory that had given me nightmares ever since. I'd hoped she hadn't succumbed to the tide, but as weeks turned to months, my yearning had become thin fog.

"I *almost* drowned, but I struck and caught your diving bell. It must have been washed off the wrecked ship and floated because it trapped air when falling into the Caribbean. I swam into it, caught my breath, and suspended myself by its straps."

"The devil you did! How smart of me to build it."

"By the time the atmosphere was stale, I'd recovered enough to swim. I spied a wreckage of hatch and mast, dragged myself aboard, tied myself on with its tangle of rope, and drifted for three days. I eventually was rescued by a French merchantman and spent weeks recovering on Saint-Lucia."

"Harry and I were already on our way back across the Atlantic."

"The French authorities made inquiries, and when reports came that you'd sailed for England with our son, they released me to follow. By the time I arrived, you'd gone with this woman to wait for smugglers' weather on a Channel isle."

"I am the Comtesse Marceau, madame."

"Interception seemed the best strategy, because I've been puzzling over something I read when held captive in Martinique by Leon Martel," Astiza carried on. "The Bibliothèque Nationale of Paris is the best place to research." She shrugged. "So I have joined your conspiracy."

"You rescued me to go to a library?"

"To read about medieval attempts to divine the future."

Being widowed is bad enough, but learning that all the grieving was for nothing is disorienting. Not to mention that my resurrected wife chatted about medieval lore with my archenemy, kept strict tabs on my movements, and got to France faster than I did. I was uncharacteristically incoherent. I was the recipient of a miracle? Who now stood before me like a visiting saint? By thunder, marriage is complicated enough without being confused as to whether your spouse even exists or not. I suppose I should have . . .

What?

"Monsieur, it is your wife who has saved us?" a puzzled Captain Butron finally asked, snapping me back to the present.

"Yes, she turns up like a penny and has a knack for rescuing me from myself. I think my boy is here as well. Harry, is that you?"

Horus, a real armful at nearly four, clung to my bride as if worried I'd leave him with the Chiswicks again. "Mama came for me," he said with reproach in his voice. I'd first given him hope after the hurricane that his mother might live, and then told him she apparently was dead. "After you left me," he added. Hell's fire, now I looked like the world's worst father.

There was an awkward silence that the kindly captain finally broke. "I think, American, that you should take a moment to kiss your reappearing wife."

Of course! I limped forward, with all the grace of a plowman—I hate accurate assessments of myself—took the woman in my arms, Harry mashed between us, and gave her a buss on the lips. Astiza was real all right, warm and ripe, and familiar as a favorite shoe, the mash of mouth and teeth and tongue a brand that brought back sweet memory. I kissed her with relief, exaltation, and near disbelief, positively poleaxed by fate. For all my luck at cards, this was the biggest pot I'd ever won. I thought myself cursed by any number of voodoo, Egyptian, and Greek gods, and yet here was my bride, as beautiful as I remembered and little worse for wear. Her face was cold—it was stormy, after all—but her breath was as invigorating as brandy.

We broke for air, gasping. Catherine gave us a little clap of approval, looking at me with new interest, and Butron raised his sword in salute.

I kissed my boy, too.

"I don't like the Chiswicks, Papa."

"Well, then, you'd better stay with me. Frankly, I didn't like them, either; I should have shopped around. In any event, I'm eager to play with you again, Harry."

His eyes were wide in the dark. "We shot the bad men." My boy had already been in as many scrapes as a Guard grenadier. "And I'm wet. It's raining."

"We'll look for puddles to splash in." I addressed Astiza. "How did you find Harry?"

"I went to Sidney Smith, asking where he'd sent you. He explained that you'd joined his cabal of spies and conspirators and that Horus had been deposited for safekeeping. The Chiswicks wouldn't believe I was his mother, even though he ran to me, because you told them I was dead. So I kidnapped my own son in the night. I hope you haven't paid them yet."

"I gave half in advance. I finally sold the emerald."

"I'm hungry," Harry interrupted.

"The emerald!" Astiza exclaimed. "I thought we'd lost it."

"I swallowed it in the Caribbean for safekeeping. We're rich, Astiza. We can retire because I've invested our fortune with brilliant London advisers who are going to double our money in less than a year. Once we figure out how to return you to England, you can retrieve the fortune and hunt for an estate. Look for something with modern fireplaces and a stable to keep the horses I intend to buy. And you must return, of course. I can't risk the two of you here."

"But I will not risk *you* here, either." She glanced at Catherine, who'd wrapped her arms around herself and was studying us with speculation. "Not without me."

I looked at the bodies. "Our entire situation is dangerous."

"Then why did you come back to France at all?"

"To avenge you by killing Napoleon. I suppose my quest is somewhat obsolete, since you don't seem to need avenging." I struggled for a plan. "Maybe we'll explain the misunderstanding to the authorities and take a holiday in Italy. I'll tell them the reason I helped wreck a coastal cutter and shoot through a *gendarmerie* patrol was love. The French understand these things."

"No, they don't," Butron said.

Astiza looked at me fondly. "I'm flattered you wanted revenge."

"None less than bringing down their government and that Corsican schemer."

"Mama helped shoot the bad people," Harry said. He'd encountered more bad people in four years than most of us do in forty, and each of my attempts to shelter him had completely come to naught.

"Your mother can be quite determined," I confirmed.

"But I think they'll likely guillotine us, Ethan, not send us to Italy," Astiza warned. "You've been as foolish as you've been brave."

She had a point.

"Nor has my survival changed the strategic peril," she went on. "We've allied with both France and Britain at times in the past, as was expedient for love and family, but this time you can't abandon your mission. The French still want to cross the Channel and, by conquering England, conquer the world. Our fortune waiting in England may become a French spoil of war. Napoleon needs to be thwarted."

"Your grasp of the stakes involved is exemplary, madame," Catherine approved. "As is your grasp of both politics and men." The two women seemed to be bonding over my failings.

"Moreover, I see the hand of fate," Astiza said. "I'll search out medieval archives in Paris while you spy." She liked nothing better than a great library with half-forgotten cellars of dusty tomes, spotted with mouse droppings and improperly filed, so she could organize things.

"But apparently, some of our intended allies are already in prison," I said. "Captain Butron here reports there have been arrests."

"This is true, madame." He cocked his head, clearly fascinated by my wife and taken with her beauty. I'm used to men paying her such attention, accepting it with a mixture of pride and annoyance. "Can I ask how you arrived in France ahead of your husband?"

"Smith arranged for the daring Captain John Wesley Wright to bring me with a shipload of rebel arms."

I'd heard of Wright. He'd escaped years ago from a Paris prison with Sidney Smith, making them both famous. He sneaked about like Tom Johnstone, but with a naval commission.

"Wright found fog to hide in and told the rebels receiving the weapons that I needed to meet you here. We've been waiting three days for the storm we knew would blow you in."

"Yet the French coastal guards were waiting, too," Butron said.

"Somewhere there's a traitor," concluded Catherine. "The danger is grave. But now we have new opportunity, too."

"What's that?" I asked.

"It would have been hard to convince Parisians I'm in company with a lowborn opportunist like you. Our habits are too different. But now I've lost my money. To return with your bride is perfect. After this skirmish and betrayal, we must creep into Paris and determine where our conspiracy stands. Having a family makes you less suspicious." She was as brisk as Bonaparte.

"Certainly not. I won't risk Astiza and Harry again. Good heavens, I just got them back."

"Ethan, we have no choice," Astiza said. "We watched Napoleon try to suppress the slaves of Saint-Domingue. He wants to conquer England. His goal is mastery of the world, and he needs to be checked. If we keep our wits, we're in a unique position to infiltrate French society and report what we learn. Let's upset his invasion, win a peace, finish my research, and *then* retire."

"You're a little more martial than I remember."

"The word is payback, is it not?" She looked lovely when vengeful.

"We conspire with Harry?"

"Let's put an end to things and keep together as a family while we do. Napoleon can't last. Meanwhile, we start teaching Harry to read."

"And to spy," I mused. "I suppose it could be a lucrative profession for him someday."

"I think he'll learn to be anything *but* a spy."

"I want to go to sleep," Harry protested. I took him, and he nestled into my shoulder. Good heavens, he weighed as much as a keg of powder.

"All right." I began to cheer up. "And maybe we can make another one or two just like him in Paris. The city is quite romantic, after all." The thought of my wife's flank in bed gave me something to look forward to. And while she'd never admit it, she'd acquired a taste for adventuring. I knew I'd found a keeper when the woman began our relationship by taking a shot at me. Pretty, brave, smart as Franklin, and just as corrective.

"We can practice, but you're not to impregnate me until our conspiracy has succeeded. The last thing I need is to be heavy with child."

I shrugged. Practicing was good enough for me.

"Then we're allied," said Catherine. "I will play your governess, and we will live, all of us, under one roof."

Chapter 4

We crept toward Paris like the spies we were, taking boggy back roads and sleeping on floors and in stables. There's a good toll road that speeds travelers from Calais to the capital in twenty-four hours, each of the privately maintained sections between tollgates called a *stage* and its vehicles *stagecoaches*, a briskly modern word like *cabriolet*. But this technological progress did us no good because our lack of proper papers and rough-looking escorts would raise questions.

"The telegraph will send word of our skirmish," Butron warned. This insidious invention relayed messages by moving fifteen-foot-long paddles on spaced towers in the same way a navy uses signal flags. It seems invasive to me that authorities can waggle information at a hundred miles an hour, speeding up life yet again, but such are modern times. Careers uncertain, privacy under assault, and police proliferating as the nineteenth-century dawns: how grim the future! So we moved cautiously on horseback from one safe house to another.

Harry rode in front of me, hugging my saddle pommel and asking questions about the color of the sky or why horse droppings look different than ours. Astiza mounted sidesaddle at the insistence of Comtesse Catherine, who announced she would prove herself useful by training us to function in society once restoration occurred. I wondered at how swiftly she had migrated from treating me as inferior to treating the pair of us as useful companions who could be trained, but maybe word of the arrests in Paris and the loss of her money had convinced her to be more companionable and expedient. Or, maybe she was warming to my charm.

"Swing the legs from one side of the horse to the other each hour to sustain the symmetry of the derriere," our aristocrat advised my wife. "Don't look backward because twisting your shoulders upsets the set of the cloak behind your saddle. Kid gloves to keep the palms smooth, and creams against the weather. I have egg white to lighten, or a paste of strawberries and fat for blush."

"You both look fine the way you are," I ventured.

"It is not a man's opinion women value, Monsieur Gage. Do not get involved in subjects you know nothing about."

"You have a point," I said agreeably. "'Eat to please thyself, but dress to please others,' my mentor Benjamin Franklin used to say."

"A proper lady eats to please others, too, with restraint and delicacy."

"You believe it's by style that one succeeds in Paris?" Astiza asked. Most people are confused by new information, but my wife absorbs it.

"It's by style that one succeeds anywhere. Presentation implies competence, and manners fortify beauty. A moment's wit can equal a year's labor. Correct fashion can wring salvation from scandal."

Catherine's confidence made us tolerate her pomposity. It's human instinct to abide those who think they know what they're doing, no matter how optimistic their opinion of themselves.

Except for their shared beauty—Catherine's pale glow a complement to Astiza's warmer honey—I could scarcely conceive of two more different women. The comtesse was obsessed with position and power, Astiza with revelation and truth. Our "governess" was born to be a courtesan, my wife a priestess. Any partnership wasn't natural, and yet they seemed to get on. The comtesse seemed relieved that Astiza's presence ended any flirtation on my part, and in fact warmed to me in her presence, regarding marriage as proof I wasn't entirely oafish. My wife recognized that Catherine had expertise in her own vapid way. Our countess was a window to the superficialities of the elite.

"I apologize for bringing her," I initially whispered to Astiza as we clopped along. "She's somewhat imperious and probably unrealistic about getting her lands and titles back."

"How much do we know about her?"

"She's an heiress with a hatred of the revolution and its inheritor, Bonaparte. Catherine is mysterious, but in London she knew table place settings and spring fashion. We thought she could enlist other royalists and seduce a key informant or two."

"But not you."

"Apparently, she concluded more quickly than most that I have little information." My tone was deliberately ironic.

"I've no doubt she can operate in social circles we cannot," Astiza said. "But if we leave her to her own devices by lodging her elsewhere, we'll have no idea what she's up to. So until we repair the conspiracy, we must pretend she's our governess." My wife is eminently practical. "I'd prefer her homelier, however."

"She's a muddy wick next to your chandelier," I lied with husbandly instinct. "It's good you two are cooperating."

"Only because it's obvious she's not attracted to you, Ethan." And she nudged her horse ahead to converse quietly with the comtesse, me brooding about unflattering observations the pair might be making about my character.

France's soil is the foundation of its power. In April, that means mud. We averaged five miles an hour on horseback, sometimes waiting until dusk before approaching the farmhouses of royalist sympathizers that Butron had arranged as safe houses. Then we'd dry out, dine, and plot fruitlessly about the future, each refuge offering a distinct French smell of hay, wine, manure, baking bread, and wood-smoke that is characteristic of rural shelter. We were dangerous to host but a respite from boredom. As firelight flickered and cows mooed, the Bourbon conspirators waxed nostalgic. The French love to argue, and I spiced the conversation by serving as philosophic foil.

"Unlike some Americans, you seem to have escaped the seductions of the revolutionaries," Butron told me.

"They went too far with the guillotine. Tom Jefferson is a kindlier democrat, and good dinner company to boot. France needs moderation, is my advice. Extremism never works."

"The Jacobins governed with atheism, anarchy, and theft."

"The irony is that Napoleon has declared the revolution over, invited the church back, and even welcomed exiled nobles, if they swear allegiance. I want to defeat the bastard, yes, but he's really one of you in believing in order and authority." I'm nothing if not fair, even to tyrants. "Isn't the choice one king against another, the exiled Bourbons or Napoleon?"

"No. Bonaparte the usurper buys people, paying for them with cruel taxes and reckless borrowing. He purchases some with money, some with promotion, and some with promises, be they émigrés or bishops. Then he sets them against one another. He's no right to rule. He doesn't recognize high birth. The result is naked ambition and ruthless competition. Napoleon uncorks the worst in human nature."

"Which of us isn't bought, my friends—with everything from social status to the promise of heaven?"

"You're too judicious, American. It's a weakness."

"I just have the perspective of an outsider who's met the man. Pompous and ambitious, yes, but clever as the devil." My views were tolerated because I could turn a storied ogre into a comprehensible politician. "He

succeeds by merit. Memory like a ledger. He understands soldiers, is a quick study of politics, and naturally commands."

"I hear he's blunt, impatient, and lacks social
grace," said Catherine. "He spies on men and insults
women."

"He outmaneuvers everyone," I said. "When he first
jumped ahead of other generals and was offered command of the army of Italy, disgruntled officers reporting to his tent decided they wouldn't remove their
hats, in order to put this Corsican upstart in his place.
So Bonaparte studied them a moment and abruptly
removed his own. His subordinates had to do the same,
lest they display ridiculous rudeness. He then put his
hat back on, point made, and proceeded to tell his generals what to do."

"But to follow a man who started from nothing?"

"The fact he started from nothing shows how able
he is."

The concept baffled the room. It's really a minority
who want to make their way in the world; most men
are content with taking the place their father gives
them, bowing to this and being bowed to by that, without having to strive too much or think things through.
Everyone knows where he stands when stature comes
from birth. Kings meant predictability, while military

dictators meant reckless adventure, prying policemen, ceaseless taxes, and military conscription. Or so they told me.

"People hate equality because it means they must be equal, too," Catherine added with some perception.

"Which is why Napoleon offers the illusion that everyone might rise," I replied. "You were born into privilege you've lost, yes, but most were born into obscurity that Bonaparte offers escape from."

"Which means they'll feel failure if they don't escape."

"And triumph if they do."

I wasn't defending the fellow, exactly, but for a would-be assassin, my views were definitely complicated. Napoleon and I had a complex history, because he had used me for conquest and I had used him for treasure. Circumstance had made us allies one moment and opponents the next. I envied and admired Bonaparte's success while still believing the story of my enemy Leon Martel, that Napoleon had ruthlessly put my family at risk to manipulate me into hunting for Aztec secrets. The first consul was the architect of a world in which honor was hostage to ambition, and compromise suspended for war. Expediency trumped loyalty, and the kidnapping of my son was a sin too far.

So would I still kill him, if I had him in my sights? The truth is that we were both rascals, and it was suicidal to play assassin. It would risk my wife and son. After reunion with Astiza my new scheme was to redirect Napoleon toward peace or abdication, though just how I didn't know. Maybe I could even persuade him to compensate us for all our troubles; I did have his pendant and the Aztec toy of a flying machine. Why not get paid by both powers? It's always encouraging to get a public stipend for vague advice, and people contend I'm an opportunist.

Or maybe I was just a coward, now that I had my family back.

There was a further consideration: Napoleon gave me importance. British officials enlisted me because I'd been close to the first consul, and French farm-wives listened to my opinions for the same reason. Proximity to power is heady, and vanity is the chink in my armor, or at least one of them. While I resented Bonaparte's bidding, I was proud that great men paid me attention.

So I dithered as we rode.

I wanted time alone with my wife, but no opportunity for intimacy presented itself. We kissed without embarrassment, but Astiza was shy about going further where everyone could hear and see. So we were as pent up as if we'd taken holy orders, adding zeal to the goal of reaching Paris.

"We'll stay anonymous in the capital until we have a better gauge of its politics," I whispered to Astiza as we lay one evening. "These arrests are catastrophic, and being the famous Ethan Gage carries its own baggage. Once I announce myself, a great deal of explaining becomes necessary. Why did I disappear from the negotiations over Louisiana? Did Martel report my presence in Haiti and Martinique? What am I doing back in Paris? We should skulk around first."

"Yes, all of France is waiting to hear the latest of Ethan Gage," my wife said dryly. She keeps me from inflating.

"Just policemen and scoundrels," I said. "I know I'm not really important, but I am occasionally controversial. Or notorious, to unsavory people."

"The gods will give us a sign." Astiza had been raised with Eastern fatalism.

"But the hurricane proved that all wrong. You foresaw doom, and yet thanks to my diving bell here you are, saved from the sea."

"Don't you see fortune brought us here for a reason, Ethan? If we hadn't been separated by the hurricane, we'd have retired in America or England. Instead, we're carried by history's current to Paris and the French archives."

"Yes, your old books. What's all this about telling the future?"

"Just some references I stumbled across that piqued my curiosity. One spoke of a remarkable medieval machine that could answer questions about things to come. It's only a legend, but a legend based on what?"

I don't mind philosophizing when you can cup a breast and wedge against a bottom. "You cite destiny only when it's convenient. Though I will admit that fatalism takes the pressure off. Yet if we're just carried along by fate, then our suffering is pointless, don't you think? I think that if luck put us here, it's so we can choose, not be directed."

"Yes, fate and free will are married. So choose how, treasure hunter?"

"I'm thinking that having seen so much violence and heartbreak, perhaps my real mission is to make peace, either by thwarting Napoleon or calming him. Why were we saved, if not to save the world? And, perhaps, get paid for it."

"You manipulate, and submit an invoice. I'll research."

As you can tell, ours was not the usual pillow talk. But we also kissed, my feeling again the fan of her silken hair and curve of hip, which meant I stayed rigid and sleepless for two hours after.

Accordingly, I was groggy when our gang of conspirators departed each dawn, leaving generous payment. We'd also pay a full franc at ferries, double the usual rate, to purchase silence from the ferryman. We avoided inns, ate in the saddle, and took four long days to reach Paris.

The capital announced itself with a horizon of smoke from the new ironworks and cotton mills of Chaillot, Saint-Lazare, and Saint-Laurent. Before crossing the Seine at Neuilly we transferred to a hay wagon as cleverly constructed as one of Tom Johnstone's smuggling boats. Its heap of straw hid a chamber little bigger than a kennel. Astiza, Catherine, Harry, and I squeezed inside.

"If they find us, we're already caged," I noted.

"They won't, monsieur," Butron assured. "Slipping contraband through the gates of Paris is as essential as drawing water, and ten thousand men are employed to skirt tax collectors. The hiring of more policemen has meant only that there are more policemen to bribe."

"The French are as dishonest as the English? That's hard to believe."

"No nationality likes paying taxes, and smugglers are a lubricant for commerce. Relax, soon you'll be a nobody amid half a million Parisians."

"This is fun!" Harry said. And off we lurched.

Hours later Butron knocked, and we crawled out at midnight inside a barn near the old walls. A hatch revealed an ancient stone tunnel that smelled like the grave, leading under the ramparts to the cellar of the Convent of the Filles Saint-Marie. I carried Harry past a skittering rat or two, our lanterns bubbles of light. He's a brave lad, having stabbed one of the vermin in Sicily, so he watched their scurrying with more curiosity than fear.

At a ladder, a limestone passage branched off. "Where does that go?" I pointed.

"The new catacombs," Butron replied. "The city's cemeteries are so crammed that authorities have been moving bones to old limestone mines to make way for a frenzy of construction under Bonaparte." He glanced at Harry. "Millions and millions of dead."

"Are we going to live down here, Papa?"

"No, your mother wants a proper house, and this place requires too much dusting. Up you go, I'm right behind you."

We climbed to resurrection. A generous donation to Catholic charity, sorely needed after the privations of the revolution, meant the nuns wouldn't do more than whisper and giggle at our emergence. Smuggling kept them solvent.

"Hail Mary, full of grace," I said companionably to the Abbess Marie, looking about for informants or sentries and seeing none.

"You are Catholic, monsieur?"

"My wife is religious." Astiza is an ecumenical pagan, but spiritual as an abbey of friars.

"You follow God, madame?" the abbess asked.

"All of them."

"I believe in the True Church," Catherine chimed in, fretfully beating her gown for dust. The abbess looked at her skeptically.

"We seek the holy," Astiza added.

I suppose the nun could have called down a bolt of lightning on all of us, but the truly good see hope in the least likely. "Perhaps you'll join us for prayers sometime?" she asked my wife.

"I would enjoy that."

The abbess turned back to me. "We know that Napoleon has reinstated the church for his own cynical political purposes, but God works in mysterious ways, does he not? So I advise you, Ethan Gage, to go with God as well."

"Appreciated. Though it's sometimes difficult to understand which way He's pointing."

"*She's* pointing," Astiza corrected. "Isis and Athena."

It's awkward being married to a heathen. "Mary, too," I said quickly.

The abbess regarded us uncertainly.

So I gave her an extra gold piece and hoped she'd choose our side in her prayers, whichever side that was.

Then I set out to enjoy Paris with my family.

Chapter 5

The sound of the guillotine chopping through a rebel neck is exactly that of a cleaver through cabbage, the vegetable in this instance being the head of Georges Cadoudal hitting its basket with an audible thump.

The crowd rumbled as if a bull had been dispatched in the ring. The execution meant stability, finality, and tyranny, all at the same time. History would not reverse. It was June 25, 1804, nearly three months after my family and I had landed in France, and a royalist rebellion was as remote as the moon.

The conspiracy and assassination attempts encouraged by the British had reminded Frenchmen not of Bourbon would-be kings waiting to be welcomed but of the chaos of revolution. The opportunistic Napoleon seized on extracted confessions from Bourbon plotters to fortify his own position. He argued France needed a return to the stability of a monarchy, but a monarchy headed by him, not the ousted heirs of Louis XVI. And since the revolutionaries had pronounced inept Louis "the last king of France," a new title was needed. Accordingly, just one month before Georges's beheading, the French had voted 3,524,254 to 2,579 (by the eventual count of Napoleon's minions, at least) in favor of making Bonaparte—a man who still spoke French with a Corsican accent—their emperor.

As first consul he'd beaten the Austrians at Marengo (with my help, though I never got proper credit), revitalized the economy, reformed the military, restored public works, reworked the law, and kept public order. Three overlapping police services spied not just on Frenchmen and foreigners but on each other. Sixty newspapers had been shuttered, plays were censored, and martial music banged in the streets. By making Napoleon's rule hereditary, the French had made it immensely harder to overthrow him by assassination or coup, since his heirs would fill his empty throne. So while in 1789 the French had risen to eradicate royalty, in 1804 they voted to establish a brand-new one, trading freedom for stability.

I wasn't surprised. We all balance liberty against risk, and are seduced by the safety promised by the strong. *They that can give up essential liberty to obtain a little temporary safety deserve neither and will lose both*, Benjamin Franklin had warned. Like any youth, I ignored his advice while never quite forgetting it. The older I grew, the wiser the words became.

Napoleon's coronation would take place the coming winter. With it, he hoped to be accepted by the crowned heads of Europe as a royal himself, and to bring a French-dictated peace to the Continent.

No one saw the irony clearer than Georges Cadoudal. The Breton royalist and ardent Catholic had fought the French revolutionaries and Napoleon for eleven tumultuous years before being captured, only to see his crusade turned against him. "I meant to give France a king, but I have given her an emperor," he summed up on the way to his beheading.

The counterrevolution I'd signed on for was in tatters. Fellow conspirator General Charles Pichegru had been strangled in his cell by Napoleon's fierce Mameluke bodyguards, or so the rumor went. The four executioners were then killed themselves so complicity could be denied.

General Jean Victor Marie Moreau, the military hero of the Battle of Hohenlinden that had finished the

Austrians after Napoleon's Marengo, and who considered himself superior in generalship, had been exiled to the Americas. He was too popular to be either killed or trusted.

In the frenzy against conspirators like me, an apparently hapless Bourbon royalist named the Duc d'Enghien had been seized across the border in Germany, dragged back to France, found guilty without proper trial, put up against the wall of a dry moat, and shot.

Eighteen others had been condemned with Cadoudal in a sensational spring show trial designed to demonstrate the peril to the government. Subtracting six pardons, the guillotine *schicked* this day thirteen more times, filling five wicker baskets that were shared, for economy. Some victims wept, some proclaimed final loyalty to the Bourbons, and most went with stoic silence.

I'm not a believer in last words, either, since you never get a proper reply.

Rumor held that a composer named Ludwig van Beethoven was so disturbed by Napoleon's suppressions that he'd renamed his new "Bonaparte Symphony" the vaguer *Eroica*, a puzzling title I doubt will ever catch on. The cranky German songmeister believed Napoleon, once the Prometheus of Liberty, was betraying his own reforms.

No matter. Most Frenchmen had concluded Bonaparte was the best thing since the baguette. The audience sighed and applauded every time the blade dropped. It's mesmerizing to watch a massacre.

Astiza kept Harry home at our Paris apartment while I morbidly witnessed the slaughter with Catherine Marceau. She pressed to my shoulder, one of a number of surprising intimacies that made me increasingly uncomfortable, but which I couldn't bring myself to entirely discourage. She jerked slightly each time a head rolled, eyes wide, no doubt remembering the execution of her parents. Since we'd begun sharing an apartment, the comtesse had become inexplicably more flirtatious, as if inspired by the competition of a wife. Women forever confuse me.

"I'm sorry you have to see this, Comtesse," I said.

"On the contrary, it reminds me of my purpose," she murmured.

Astiza considered execution barbaric. "What if the judges make a mistake?" she asked. "The truly secure show mercy."

"Napoleon preaches that killing a few keeps the many in line. He says executions are a mercy for the nation as a whole."

"The creed of the hangman, not the hanged. Wait until it's his turn."

I watched the slaughter to gauge our situation. Even the English captain who had brought Astiza to France ahead of me, John Wesley Wright, had been captured off the French coast and imprisoned. Betrayal had followed betrayal. Sir Sidney Smith's brother Spencer had been forced by French pressure to leave Württemberg in Germany, where he'd served as a spymaster. Another British agent, Francis Drake, had fled Munich. My family was marooned as forgotten agents of a conspiracy in utter collapse. My investments in England were out of reach, and the gold I'd been given as salary had to be carefully nursed because we were supporting Catherine, and communication with Sir Sidney Smith was broken. I calculated we'd just enough to last until the coronation, planned for early December. I could still send messages out to England, using a collaborating priest in the confessional at Saint-Sulpice, but received no word in return.

In short, I'd given up control of my fortune and joined the wrong side at the worst possible time, at frozen wages, with a flirtatious roommate who lost her own money in the Channel, all to avenge a wife who turned out to be alive.

My foresight could be improved.

We also suspected we were being followed. Catherine said men watched her from café tables (a claim I didn't doubt), and Astiza said clerks made notes of books she examined at the imposing Bibliothèque Nationale on rue de Richelieu. These gatekeepers claimed that the records she most ardently sought either didn't exist or were restricted. Harry reported seeing a shadowy giant, though this specter melted away every time I turned, and I knew he might be a product of my son's anxious imagination. He would wake with nightmares. It's natural for a child to have a nervous imagination, but it was with love and guilt that I'd buy him pastries—or an early orange from the Mediterranean—or tell him monsters aren't true.

Police were everywhere. Informers rife. Conspirators bleated under torture. And the most powerful army the world had ever seen was being honed like a knife on the Channel, ready to leap on Britain.

In short, it had been an anxious spring.

After emerging from the convent in April, a royalist tip had led us to a Paris landlord who didn't ask too many questions. Our lodging was a second-floor apartment in the fashionable Saint-Germain neighborhood. The comtesse had insisted upon such an address to avoid complete humiliation, and it was certainly a notch above my earlier hovel amid the furniture workshops in Saint-Antoine. Perhaps I was making progress after all! Our quarter smelled of flower shops instead of tanneries, and we heard church bells instead of hammers and saws.

Status and price were contingent on how many stairs you had to climb, so we, on the second floor, were middle class in a literal way, paying four hundred francs a month. Above us on the third were a coppersmith with his wife and three noisy adolescent children. Tucked under the rafters were four washerwomen, war widows all, who worked on a laundry barge on the Seine. Once a week we gave them a basket of our clothes to clean. If they teased me for being a handsome and dashing rogue, I tipped them.

Bonaparte was restoring order to street addresses, but his committee hadn't completed its reports yet, and so we were No. 1,043 rue du Bac. We were hardly secret. All the tenants used the same central stair, so we could hear the steady troop and quarrels of neighbors going up and down, just as they could see and hear us. But there was nothing remarkable about our household, much to the comtesse's distress, and the presence of my son helped deflect suspicion. Spies don't take rambunctious children along. We lived in obscurity while tracking the fast-changing political situation. My name, if asked, was John Greenwell of Philadelphia. I was in Paris to foster American trade if it could circumvent the British blockade. Since that was unlikely, it was justifiable to my neighbors that I did little during the day.

Catherine, easily bored, was impatient. "Nobody knows who we are. You should announce yourself as the famed electrician and diplomat, back from new adventures in the Americas with a royalist benefactor. Me."

"Pride that will jeopardize my family."

"But as Ethan Gage you would have access to high circles," she persisted. "We could attend salons and balls together. Astiza could look after Harry."

Before I was beneath her dignity, and now she wanted me on her arm? "I thought I was a colonial commoner you wanted nothing to do with."

"I have new respect for you as husband and father." Her smile was sly.

"You know very well that I'm a struggling husband and a hapless father, since I keep misplacing both wife and son."

"I'm intrigued that a pretty woman loves you, Ethan. It makes you more attractive to other women's eyes."

"It's not that unlikely, you know. I *am* amusing."

"That's exactly my point." She touched my hand with dancing fingers. "With my manners and your charm, people might believe we *are* a real couple, if your wife is careful to hide at home. Just as a strategy."

Had her opinion turned so much that she was flirting to separate me from my wife? Or was I a temporary toy to provide distraction? Was she an ardent agent, eager for action? Or was she proposing risks she knew I'd never agree to? I admired Catherine for not scuttling straight back to England, but was puzzled by her, too. It was like analyzing a player's bet in the card game brelan, where one could never be certain if a move was a novice mistake or a clever long game.

"I don't think my pretty wife would agree to that," I said. "And celebrities in France have a way of landing in prison or worse. Let's test the political winds without notoriety. My role as seaborne trader helps explain my exotic-looking wife. You're swank for a governess, but we can say you lost your fortune in the revolution and that we took pity when we found you stranded in Calais."

"Pity!"

"Only as a ruse. We'll write coded messages in sympathetic ink, and await further instructions."

She sighed, looking bleakly at our modest home. "I long for society."

"Well, until Napoleon's overthrow, you just have us."

And we had her. Catherine believed that high birth made her expert not just on fashion and flirtation, but also on finance, espionage, and child rearing. She chafed under my careful budgeting and treated my wife to unwanted advice.

"Harry is entirely too carefree," she informed Astiza one day. "Children need discipline. He should be learning his catechism, music, and the names of the kings."

"Which you can do with your own child, should a man ever give you one," Astiza replied. Their catty bristling made me edgy. "Horus is *my* son, Comtesse, not yours."

"I know you're trying, but you were raised an Oriental slave. I provide perspective you lack."

"As I have a husband, a child, and a home—and you do not—perhaps I have perspective that *you* lack. Here's my advice: keep your opinions and hands to yourself."

The comtesse looked stricken. "I am only trying to help."

"Help with deeds, not words, and maybe we can make this triad work."

I put in that the boy was doing fine, and was rewarded with looks of annoyance from both of them.

Accordingly, I didn't mind getting out of the house. It was on one of my strolls that I confirmed Catherine Marceau's ingenuity.

Against my intention, I was accosted by Edme François Jomard, a companion from Egypt, while shopping for a telescope on the rue Saint-Victor. I didn't know what I needed to observe, but I thought a spy should have a spyglass, and the British had neglected to provide one.

I was weighing the quality of optics against the size of my purse, wishing for the millionth time that I had access to my swelling England investments, when Jomard touched my shoulder. "Ethan Gage, is that you?"

I jumped. "Greenwell, sir." Then I turned and recognized my old friend. Jomard was a mathematical wizard who'd led me to the top of the Great Pyramid. "Except to you, Edme. Keep your voice low, please."

"Mon Dieu, I'd no idea you were in Paris."

"It's something of a secret."

He cocked his head. "But of course. Always attached to one conspiracy or another, aren't you? What a romp your life is." He said it lightly. "Are you on a mission for the United States?"

He'd given me an alibi. "Yes. You may know I was involved with negotiations over Louisiana. Now, with war . . ." I shrugged, as if unable to share more information.

"I quite understand. No doubt it involves ladies as well! My own occupation is scholarly; I'm working on presentation of our discoveries in Egypt. A lost world, Ethan, and we're making new calculations about the pyramids every day. How I long to go back for more measurements! The English block us. Still, human knowledge will leap when we publish. Savants are thinking of coining a new term, *Egypt-ology.* Clever, don't you think?"

"I'm in awe of your intellect, Jomard."

"But where are you staying? Can you visit?"

"I'm not really here, I told you. Is it possible to keep this encounter quiet?" I glanced about. "It would be a pity to upset affairs of state."

"But of course! You must be working with Napoleon."

"Jefferson, actually." That tidbit seemed innocent enough.

"It's genius how you insert yourself. Without academic degree, birth, station, appointment, or accomplishment, you remain indispensable. I don't pretend to understand it, but certainly you're an inspiration."

"It's you who are the vanguard of knowledge." I put the spyglass down and eyed the door. As much as I'd enjoy chatting about old times, this encounter could spoil everything.

"I suppose you're rich, Ethan."

"An investment here or there."

"Do you need help? I have many contacts."

"No, I'm fine." I decided not to mention Astiza or Harry, in order to protect them. "A young woman is sharing my quarters."

He smiled. "I am not surprised."

"An aristocrat, actually. A comtesse, if Bonaparte brings back titles from before the revolution. Catherine Marceau must remain as secret as I am."

"Marceau! But that's genius. How clever of her."

"Clever?"

"To use a name wiped out in the Terror."

"She's quite real, I assure. More than I can handle at times. Her parents died, but Catherine fled to England and has returned to see to her affairs."

"So you say?" Jomard was turning the matter over in his mind. "I thought her dead. Did she fool us all? What a happy miracle! And now she's back? No wonder you want to keep things quiet."

"Indeed." I was confused and wary.

"I remember her story of youth and beauty, throttled in her cell."

"Throttled?"

"There was even a headstone before the cemeteries were emptied into the catacombs. But obviously it was a ruse to smuggle her to freedom."

Had Catherine survived by faking her own death? Or was the comtesse in my apartment pretending to be someone she was not? "She's very adroit," I said, pretending to knowledge I didn't have.

"Attractive?"

"Bewitching. So please, Jomard, not a word until I complete my assignment for Jefferson. I can succeed only if no one in Paris knows I'm here."

"Your secrets are safe with me. You were never here, and Catherine was never alive."

Chapter 6

"Of course I'm dead," Catherine told us later that day. "I have to be."

"Do you mean you're not really Catherine Marceau?"

"I mean my coffin was as empty then as my purse is now, but I depended on evil men thinking it full. Ethan, the only way to escape was to erase all record of myself. I used my beauty in ways I'm embarrassed to remember in order to persuade my captors to slip me across the Channel. It was planned so that I could return to Paris to conspire without family and friends seeking me out."

"You faked your own death?"

"I faked my burial. It's a shame the gravesite is gone. I heard strangers wept and left flowers." Catherine turned to Astiza. "I assure you, madame, that my untimely death a dozen years ago protects your family today. I'd never insert myself into your home if old enemies could bring risk. The police won't look for me because I don't exist."

"Why didn't you tell us this before?"

She blushed, which was most uncharacteristic. "I admit to vanity. My titles were erased since I was believed dead, and so regaining them will be more complicated than I've admitted. I *am* truly a comtesse, but will have to prove it eventually."

"Then you're not really gossiping with royalist con-spirators?" I asked.

"But I am, under any number of names. I've lost my outward identity but not my inner character and train-ing. Please, life has been a struggle."

I felt sorry for the girl, though I'm not sure my wife did. "I think it's rather clever," I said to encourage her. "Brave, too."

"Don't betray my secret. As long as I'm safely dead, I can move about the city before returning to shiver here."

That was another complaint. Like all French apart-ments, ours was drafty, poorly heated, and ill designed, since builders refused to learn the superior carpentry of the Dutch and Germans. Our antechamber had to serve as our dining room, and it was so tight that the front door scraped our table. Our drawing room had a largely heatless fireplace that smoked—on chilly spring nights we drew chairs around like a campfire until our eyes watered—and our kitchen was little more than a cubby with a brick oven, a bowl for washing, and a tin bathtub shaped like a sabot shoe. We usually ate out, with a meal costing thirty sous.

On the other side of the antechamber were three bedrooms, each leading into the other since only palaces have that expensive waste of space called a *hallway*. The comtesse demanded the front sleeping chamber, Harry we put in the middle, and Astiza and I took the rear. There we reconsummated our marriage while trying to muffle the noise as much as possible, though I suspect Astiza didn't mind if an audible cry or two escaped to annoy Catherine.

I prudently bought some sheaths at a barber since it would be reckless to impregnate my wife while spying. I blew into the intestines to make sure the condoms didn't have holes. "Once we're done with Bonaparte we'll have a bigger family," I said.

"When we're done with him? Or he's done with us? With peace we'll add a daughter."

"And little Harry?"

"He fits into tight places, like you said he did in Syracuse. So he remains a partner in adventure until we're finished here."

"It's a curious occupation we have, Astiza."

"True. We're qualified for not much besides spying, treasure hunting, war, and sacred mysteries. Yet somehow we make a living. It makes you enviable to men who don't know better. You're a hero, Ethan."

Some hero. It was my job to empty the chamber pot in the cesspool that led to the sewers. I also pitched our dirty wash water out a small rear window into the courtyard below, and then closed the glass against the smell. Water, at three sous per bucket, was delivered twice a day, but I had to carry it from our stoop up the stairs. We bought from a waterman who drew only from fountains, not the polluted river, so each bucket cost an extra sou.

With forests cut back for centuries, firewood cost thirty-eight francs a cart, and there were stories that cold snaps forced veterans of Napoleon's Egyptian campaign to burn the mummies they'd brought home as souvenirs. Astiza pronounced such sacrilege mad with magical risk, but I thought it eminently sensible since the market for powdered corpse tissue as an aphrodisiac had collapsed, given the disappointing results. The newest enhancement for lovemaking was asparagus. Men ate it manfully when fed by their wives, but it accomplished little but to change the color of pee. In any event, we nursed our fuel, donned nightcaps, and argued over candles, which cost four francs a pound.

"Our domestic situation is entirely too cramped," Catherine would complain. "I'm embarrassed to be governess in such a frugal household."

"Franklin said it's easier to build two chimneys than keep one in fuel."

"He also said wealth is not his that has it, but his that enjoys it."

I was surprised. "You're a student of the sage of Philadelphia?"

"No, but I bought his almanac so I could counter your tedious quotations with my own. He also said to lengthen life, lessen meals, but *he* looks quite well fed in every portrait I've seen. Your philosopher is inconsistent."

"True, old Ben flirted and fed too much, but that doesn't mean he wasn't right. When I reform, I'm going to write my own book."

"Eagerly awaited, I am sure."

"It's the sinner who knows what it means to be holy. That one I made up myself."

"Birth makes character. That one is mine."

So we lived as a den of spies. Harry was thrilled to have both parents again, and we began teaching him numbers and letters. He was fascinated by carriages, wary of dogs, and delighted by pigeons. On June 6 we celebrated his fourth birthday, buying a cake in the shape of a horse and giving him new shoes and a wooden sword. I also made a toy boat we sailed at Luxembourg Gardens. Out of boredom, Catherine instructed him on the ranks and proper greetings of the aristocracy. When our son wasn't drilling imaginary troops he would sweep off his cap and bow gravely, pretending we were kings and queens.

Our in-house aristocrat also made lists of how she'd furnish her own salons, once the counterrevolution triumphed. She wheedled as much money from me as she could to update her wardrobe.

"Our stipend is melting like snow, Comtesse."

"Contemporary dress means we can circulate without suspicion," she argued. "Do you want us to look like bumpkins?"

"You mean clothes from one season ago?"

"Exactly."

With espionage difficult, both women became addicted to the new romance novels that had exploded in popularity. The chief duty of the protagonists in these stories was to tragically die, preferably by killing themselves. Long lines of females waited at bookstalls to buy the latest title.

"If real love went the way of novelist imagination, the species would have vanished aeons ago," I pointed out. "Suicide seems extreme, not to mention selfish and cowardly."

"And if men understood that the heart weighs more than a purse or a sword, they'd have more success with women," Catherine replied, leaning against a window to read by its light.

"Soldiers say that the danger of combat makes survival sweet," Astiza added. "For women, the prospect of tragedy makes love more exquisite."

"But it's a jolly wedding that makes the story work, right? Just in case our money runs out and I need to write one myself."

"Nobody wants to read about happy people," Catherine said.

Their fascination made me so curious that I took to reading the romances myself when no one was looking. It was purely for research, you see, so that I could better understand the fairer sex. I doubted any damsels had killed themselves over me.

While we idled in conspiracy, Paris meanwhile cast its usual spell, smelling like bread, tasting like chocolate, and moving like a dance. Trees leafed along the Seine. Fresh oysters dripped from baskets on the walls. Dice rattled and billiards clicked in shadowy gambling salons I avoided to preserve anonymity. There's nothing like winning to make strangers wonder who you are.

The French capital, the British complained, had "the conceit of being Athenian," but its pride was justified. Conversation was sharp and gay, history palpable, ideas in ferment, glamour revered. I slipped into a reception at the salon of the famed beauty Juliette Récaimer, the crowd so thick that musicians had to pin their scores to the backs of listeners because there wasn't room to erect their music stands. Juliette had the face of an angel and the neck of a swan, and if she stood in a garden with Astiza and Catherine you'd have the Three Graces come to life. Her fame was heightened by her reputation as a virgin, an illegitimate child who during the Terror had dutifully married her own father—thirty years her senior—so she could inherit should he be executed. Scandal made her tragic.

The city never slept. The day began as the salons and taverns emptied, when the gates opened at one A.M. to allow carts to resupply the markets of Les Halles. Sometimes we'd hear the clatter and lowing of cattle and sheep being driven down the dark streets for slaughter. The bells for first Mass for the reinstated Catholic Church would ring at five (reminding the empire's late-sleeping atheists why they'd been glad to be done with religion in the first place), and by six o'clock laborers and craftsmen, including our coppersmith neighbor, were clomping noisily downstairs to work. Flower markets blossomed on both banks of the Seine with the rise of the sun—Astiza bought a fresh bouquet for our apartment every three days, despite my scolding about the expense—and stalls and carts jostled for the best places to begin selling tobacco, brandy, ribbons, and crucifixes. You could get your portrait painted, a sonnet composed, or a uniform ordered, in minutes. Laundry would be unreeled across streets and court-yards like signal flags, and crepes would sizzle on irons. By nine the wineshops were open, and by ten the Palais de Justice on Île de la Cité dispensed deci-sions. Workboats swept up and down the Seine and, as the weather warmed, youths dove naked into the Seine. Mothers hid their daughters' eyes while peering themselves.

"Invitations must be interpreted," Catherine explained to us. "To be asked to a dinner at five o'clock means it is perilous to arrive before six."

"Then why not say six?"

"That is just the kind of question an American male would ask, which is precisely why you require my instruction." She turned to Astiza. "'Five precisely' allows you to appear at five thirty. Only 'Five very precisely,' which you are unlikely to hear from anyone except ministers and police, means five. Even then, a quarter past will not provoke comment, even from a prosecutor."

"It *is* humiliating to arrive too early," Astiza noted.

"This is just the kind of irrationality supposedly eliminated by the scientific precision of the revolution," I said.

"It requires a minimum of sixteen dinner courses to impress," Catherine went on, "and something more to be talked about. The new grand chamberlain searched days for the biggest and most spectacular salmon available, had it baked to perfection, flanked it by vegetables carved like rosettes, sprinkled the fringe with silver, and had it presented on a golden plate. Guests gasped; such a fish had not been served since the fall of the king. Then the servant carrying it tripped, and the glorious meal crashed onto the Oriental carpet, ruined for all time."

"I suppose the poor man was whipped," I said.

"Such a supposition shows how naive you truly are, Monsieur Gage. All was staged. Talleyrand waited several seconds of dread silence, timing it like an actor, and then said, 'Bring the other one.' And that is how you become talked about in Paris."

By day the narrow streets were so jammed that we went almost everywhere on foot. At night it was so dark that a cabriolet at twenty sous was justifiable, even on our budget. I read with considerable interest about experimental gas lamps by Philippe Lebon, mirrored lamps by Sauer, and "parabolic reflectors" by Bordier the engineer, but never saw any on an actual street. In my experience the French are the cleverest, the English quicker to put ideas to use, and the Americans the likeliest to steal from both and sell it cheaper.

Progress threatened jobs. Streetlamps jeopardized the employment of lantern bearers, who waited outside theaters to escort patrons home. Road repair ended the livelihood of men who rented levers to pry wheels out of potholes and planks to bridge puddles. Entire industries were built on inefficiency, and Napoleon had to pound for reform as patiently as attacking a fort with siege artillery.

Another modern oddity was the abandoned steamboat built by my friend Robert Fulton and demonstrated the year before on the Seine. At sixty-six feet long and eight feet wide, the *Vulcan* had hips made of two enormous paddle wheels connected to iron machinery. It had no deck, and no cover for the wheels, so one had to walk a plank over its exposed skeleton of rods and gears to get from stern to bow. While the boat had managed a brisk walking speed when demonstrated, that meant it barely made headway when going upstream against a strong current. Gaudily painted, it floated forlornly next to the downstream corner of the Louvre after its dismissal by French authorities drove Fulton to the English side. I jumped aboard without challenge, curious about its engine since I remembered how hard it was to hand-crank the propeller of Fulton's plunging boat, the *Nautilus*.

This craft was steered by a tiller and, despite some rust and pooled water, looked capable of running again. A canvas tarp concealed enough coal to burn for hours. There was also a set of instructions wrapped in oilskin against the damp. I carefully refastened the tarp and went home to read.

With our conspiracy in disarray, I had time to practice being a father. I took Harry to the Promenade de Longchamp at Easter, where we watched helmeted cavalry clatter in parade between wagons holding images of the pacifist Jesus. Gas balloons hung above the city, and fireworks exploded at dusk. At a toy booth I bought him a leather sack of marbles that he enjoyed rolling on the sloping floors of our apartment. Catherine grumbled after slipping on them twice.

Other days we'd wander through the entertainers on the Boulevard du Temple. We watched Indian sword swallowers, the famed tightrope walker Mademoiselle Saqui, jugglers, tumblers, dwarves, and a bearded girl who let Harry tug her whiskers. Munito the Wise Dog told fortunes by cards, pawing them one by one after payment of a franc.

Mine was a watery trip, and Harry's a secret prize.

Carnival booths displayed five-legged sheep, two-headed calves, and races in which tiny chariots were drawn by fleas. Pug dogs fought across a pie baked in the shape of a fortress. We'd watch the rich parade in the Tuileries, the aged relax in the Luxembourg Gardens, and African animals pace morosely in the Jardin des Plantes. I wouldn't take Harry to the notorious Palais Royale after dark, but he pleaded relentlessly for the cannon clock that was fired by sunbeams. At noon the sun focused through a glass, ignited its powder, and set off the gun.

"Boom!" he shouted as we walked back home. "Boom, boom, boom!"

I had him promise not to tell his mother.

Chapter 7

In sum, I rather enjoyed being a conspirator, since there no longer was much of a conspiracy to attend to. Yet our idyll grew grim as the execution of the royalist plotters approached, and our claustrophobic lives complicated my relationship with Catherine, who became evermore familiar and imperious.

"Ethan, I don't understand your choice in marrying a slave," she challenged once when we were alone together. "Your wife is intelligent, yes, but wholly unpresentable."

"That's as silly as it is ungrateful. Napoleon and I captured Astiza to be a translator, and she helped get me inside the Great Pyramid. Good swimmer, too."

"It may be too late for annulment, but certainly you should explore divorce. The revolutionaries have made changing wives as easy as changing shoes." The cheapening of marriage was another royalist lament, although they took advantage of the laxity as quickly as anyone. Since the revolution, a couple living together was as likely to be unmarried as wed, and few brides came to the altar as virgins. Census takers estimated that up to a third of the children in Paris were illegitimate.

"On the contrary, Comtesse, I'm desperately in love with my wife. You may recall I came to avenge her."

"That was for honor. I'm talking about standing. Your faithfulness is entirely out of step with the times."

Certainly the era was licentious. A former priest named Banjoir had organized saturnalias under the guise of his newly invented religion. Audiences wore masks to watch naked actors in the play *Messalina*. Police confiscated pornography from the Barabbas Bookshop to share with their own dinner guests. Even with a swelling police force, Paris still had ten thousand prostitutes. It also claimed six thousand writers, the consensus being that the scribblers were considerably less useful than the trollops.

"Bonaparte is trying to reestablish propriety."

"Bah. He fornicates like a sultan. And love has nothing to do with marriage. A wedding is a contract of rights, property, and reproduction. Sleep with whomever you want, but marriage requires a strategy as careful as a military campaign or the seeking of court favor. It's true you had limited prospects, but an Egyptian serving girl? My poor American, I shudder at the advice you were given."

"I didn't have advice at all. She's gorgeous." Why did the comtesse obsess about my marriage? Ladies do find my company irresistible (given enough time, and convincing) but I was not about to swap wives. Catherine seemed to be prying us apart when we should all be pulling together. But then the female heart could stampede heedlessly, I'd learned from the romance novels, so maybe the girl simply couldn't help herself.

"Beauty can be rented," Catherine said.

"And she's wise," I defended doggedly. "Astiza knows more than any royalist I've ever met."

Catherine was oblivious to my comparison. "Hire expertise. Blood, you must marry."

"You're living on our charity while insulting my wife?"

"I'm helping you face the truth. She *is* wise, since she married a handsome rogue who also claims to be an electrician, a Franklin man, an explorer, and a soldier. You're common, but a commoner of an interesting sort. It's only *your* judgment that is faulty. A proper comte would make Astiza a courtesan, deny paternity of any offspring, and cast her off before she begins sagging.

I entirely understand her determination to follow her husband to France; it's unlikely she'll do better. But you need to marry breeding if you're ever to rise."

"Which you could supply," I said dryly.

"Certainly not." The comtesse sniffed. "It would be as foolish for me to marry down as it was unwise for you not to marry up. Only in an exigency do we cooperate in this hovel. We're pretending to be democrats until natural order is restored. You cannot aspire to me, but you need a powerful father-in-law. I'm saying all of this to be helpful."

"It's you who doesn't understand marriage," I countered, truly annoyed now. "It didn't matter that Astiza had no property, and I no title. Have you ever looked at the half moon and seen the dark wedge that blocks out the stars and completes the sphere?"

"We're talking astronomy now?"

"That was me before my wife. Astiza came in and began to lighten my dark half, day by growing day, as I came to love her, until the moon was full—representing not one of us, mind, but both of us combined. I fear that's a completion you've yet to understand."

A shadow passed then; she looked stricken for just an instant at my jab, and even vengeful. There was some wound on her that I didn't know. Then she gave a short laugh, forced gaiety. "And you've yet to understand how big your moon could be with the right person. Or listen to realism."

The odd thing was that Catherine could be as charming as she was maddening. She actually warmed to her governess role, playing with Harry when we went on errands. "He listens to me better than you do." She also confessed that she regretted that her crusade to restore the monarchy and avenge her parents was postponing her own marriage, household, and children. I'd actually catch her with a look of pensive sadness at times.

The comtesse could also be a witty dinner companion, sharing gossip of fallen aristocrats struggling desperately for new positions. She'd compliment as deftly as insult, and sought my wife's suggestions of classic books to buy besides romances. Not that Catherine actually read such books; she simply enjoyed dropping the imposing-sounding titles into conversations.

She was mercurial toward me, disdainful at one moment and flirtatious the next. Catherine found an excuse to touch me when my wife wasn't around. She'd propose that we go together to the arcades of the Palais Royale to listen to Parisian gossip and street speeches. Even when I kept saying no, she somehow appeared on my arm. When I was a widower, she'd treated me like the plague; when convinced I was married, she found it amusing to tease me.

An example is a time I came home when Astiza and Harry were at the fruit market and Catherine called for help from the kitchen. I found her bathing in the tub in a linen shift, as is the female custom. The fabric was transparent from the water, however, one arm only half concealing her breasts.

"Fetch me more hot water, Ethan," she commanded. A golden necklace and bracelets accentuated her near nudity. A sheet lined the tub to insulate her from the metal.

"I'm not a maidservant, and this is inappropriate." Not that I turned away.

"You don't want me clean?"

"I don't want to watch you get that way."

"Then you're a very peculiar man."

I should have fled, but found it more enjoyable to debate the issue. "Comtesse, I'm happily married, as you've sourly observed. This is inappropriate."

"And I'm not embarrassed at our lack of privacy after so many weeks together. I've heard your love-making with your wife and applaud it. What a stallion you are! Now, don't stint me the pleasures of a bath."

I didn't miss the compliment. "I'm just saying you can bathe yourself."

"Ethan, we've no maid because as spies we must be careful. That requires expediency. Please, warm water!"

So I poured some in, pretending not to look and looking plenty. Her nipples were pinker from the heat of the water, and there was a flush around her neck, tendrils of hair curling there. I retreated in embarrassment while she laughed.

But the comtesse also had a morbid interest in the guillotine, which is how she and I came together to watch poor Georges lose his head. There was a great slop of blood, the fiery color exciting the crowd, and a mix of cheers, curses, and weeping.

"If the Corsican is confirmed emperor, the whole world will be like this," Catherine muttered.

"Not necessarily," I said, being the judicious sort. "He's strict, but not cruel like Djezzar the Butcher, or Omar the Dungeon Master, or Red Jacket the Indian, or Rochambeau the Slave Hunter. The useful thing about knowing horrid people is that they put everyone else in perspective. Even Napoleon."

"We have to stop him from being crowned."

"What chance do we have of killing him?"

"Not killing. Turning people against him. Breaking the spell he's cast. We can't mount a coup, Ethan, but we must mount an embarrassment."

"But how, Comtesse? Word is that he's seeking no less than the pope to crown him this winter. He's determined to win over your class."

"Then we have to act before winter, and before our money runs out. You've a reputation for being clever. Live up to it."

"And your job?"

"To goad you."

We turned to go, the crowd milling. She tugged my sleeve and nodded toward a gigantic dark-clad spectator.

"He's been watching us instead of the executions. It's the policeman Pasques, I think, as strong as he is tall. You've heard of him?"

"No, and nor do I want to. He looks big enough to cast shade for a picnic." Had Harry seen something after all? This fellow was somber, with a great mustache that drooped to his chin. He had a dark suit, a cloak like raven wings, a battered and dated tricorne, and the bulk of a dray horse.

"Quick, to the left. We'll melt into the street crowd."

But other police materialized to block that way, and the giant proved surprisingly adroit. He used his muscle to part dispersing spectators like a buffalo through corn. Quickly, he loomed over us. "Monsieur Ethan Gage?"

"John Greenwell, of Philadelphia."

"No. You are Gage of Egypt and Marengo, Mortefontaine, and Saint-Domingue."

"You're entirely mistaken." My heart was hammering, given the chop of the blade we'd just seen. "If you'd please stand aside, monsieur, we're late."

He shook his head. "The notorious American is too well known and remembered to remain unnoticed. We've been following you since your arrival in Paris and puzzled only over how little you've seemed to accomplish."

This was unsettling and insulting to boot. "'We'?"

"The police ministry. Do you know that your household has led us to three royalist cells?"

Catherine gasped, and I struggled to pretend calm. "I'm sure you're confused."

"And I'm sure that Police Councillor Pierre-François Comte Réal, administrator of northwest France, requires a meeting. You'd be wise to cooperate, since you'll meet regardless and he has ways of forcing conversation." The other police surrounded us.

"He couldn't send an invitation?"

"Your invitation is I."

"This lady plays no part in this."

"On the contrary." He inspected her, his gaze lingering longer than it had to. She looked flattered and fearful.

I sighed, wishing I'd brought a weapon. "You'll tell my wife what has happened?"

"Tell her yourself. Your wife and son, monsieur, are already in custody."

Not again. "But wait—didn't you say I've accomplished little?" I'm used to arguing incompetence. "Why would the councillor want me?"

"He has a present for you." Pasques shrugged, as if this was as incomprehensible as my own sorry performance as a spy.

"A gift?"

"From Napoleon Bonaparte."

"From the emperor?" While I echoed him with my own stupid questions, the comtesse looked at me with surprise and suspicion.

"Yes. From a man who gives nothing without expecting something in return."

Chapter 8

I've described Police Minister Fouché as a thin-lipped lizard, and renegade inspector Leon Martel, safely dead, as a rodent. Councillor Réal I'd call a forbidding French father-in-law: handsome, distinguished, and naturally stern, with a long Gallic nose, searching gaze, and a mouth pinched with habitual disapproval, its corners rising just enough to betray weary amusement at the fables and lies of the prisoners he interrogated. It was this man who'd traced the horseshoes of the animal that pulled the huge bomb that almost killed Napoleon in 1800. He'd broken assassination conspirators Louis-Pierre Picot and Charles Le Bourgeois with torture so relentless that they begged for death. More recently, royalist conspirator Jean-Pierre Quérelle betrayed Georges

Cadoudal after Réal let the man watch preparations for his own execution. Terrified of eternity, Quérelle confessed all.

I knew vaguely that Réal was considered a moderate, had gambled by throwing in with Napoleon for the coup of 18 Brumaire, and now oversaw the policing of the Channel coast facing Britain. He received me in the cavernous police headquarters off rue de Jerusalem, its hive of cubicles wormed into a decaying pile of a palace. Posts and beams had been inserted to keep the edifice standing, and mezzanines had been built on these to stuff in more policemen, the new floors reached by stairs as steep as ladders. The result was a gloomy maze. Réal's own office was a stony corner suite overlooking a stone courtyard with stone walls beyond. He wore a severely black civilian suit without insignia, the color the perennial favorite of my police acquaintances. It makes them a dour lot.

High collar and cravat reinforced Réal's formality, but five gaudy rings hinted at worldly pleasures. I tried to analyze him as annoyingly as he was analyzing me. Perhaps he was not the humorless puritan of reputation, but rather a man who enjoyed profiting from power. I pictured a rich house and family gatherings with laughing children and amber-colored spirits, Réal serenely presiding over bourgeois pleasures, not speaking of the day's routine of firing squads, weasel informants, and tenacious torture.

Now Réal splayed his fingers on his massive maple desk, as if considering whether to spring. It was said he'd made a study of the interrogation techniques of the Ottomans and the Spanish Church and was a student of the criminal mind, particularly those with shifting causes and irregular employment.

I, in turn, have become something of an expert on ambitious policemen.

"Monsieur Gage, so gracious of you to visit." The tone was ironic.

Guest I technically was, since the giant Pasques had explained that I wasn't really under arrest so long as I visited the police inspector "voluntarily." I was unclear as to the distinction. "I'm flattered by your invitation," I lied, "though I'm not really Ethan Gage."

"Amusing fiction. Impostors and aliases have become a fixture of our age. During upheaval, everyone can pretend to be something they're not. It's what makes revolution so popular." He gave me a nod. "It's an honor to meet a hero of the Pyramids."

I do have a weakness for flattery, and it seemed futile to pretend I was Greenwell. "Hardly a hero, Councillor," I said. You have to decline compliments if you hope to get any more. "When the Mamelukes charged, I was safely inside an infantry square." It was a subtle way of confirming that, yes, I'd been an aide to Napoleon in Egypt. I'd put Bonaparte's pendant around my neck, in hopes it might prove as potent as a crucifix in a situation like this.

"You're too modest. You've had many adventures since, on assignment for Talleyrand and Jefferson in North America, Bonaparte in the Mediterranean and"—he picked up a folder to peer at it—"Jean-Jacques Dessalines, the black revolutionary who defeated Rochambeau in Saint-Domingue. You've also fought with the British general Sir Sidney Smith, against Pasha Yussef Karamanli in Tripoli, and"—here he squinted at his folder again—"done both with former police inspector Leon Martel in Martinique." He put down the document. "I envy your worldliness, while remaining baffled by your causes."

"My cause is my family." I was wary. "It's actually quite the trouble bouncing from one belligerent to another. Labors of Hercules, and all that."

"Your wanderings are suspicious."

"I always come back to Paris."

"Under an assumed name." He tapped his file. "Most peculiar, no? The young general you rode with in the Egyptian campaign rises to emperor, and you hide in his capital like a thief?"

"I didn't want to bother him."

"Your obscurity aroused our curiosity, especially since Britain has employed half the scoundrels of Europe to spy on France. You fought at Acre with the spymaster Sir Sidney Smith. And every man in Paris seeks advantage from his personal acquaintance with Bonaparte—every man except the famed Ethan Gage."

"I'm just avoiding responsibility. Being important is tiring."

"I don't believe you." Réal's gaze bored like an auger. Smart policemen make you feel guilty no matter how innocent you are, and of course I was a would-be Nathan Hale or Benedict Arnold. Yet except for my wife recently sweeping a deck clear of roguish French with a grapeshot-loaded swivel gun, I couldn't think of anything in particular to confess to. I was a spy, yes, but not a very good one.

"And how is our old comrade Martel?" he went on.

"His name reminds me that the other half of Europe's scoundrels are working for France." I was stalling; I'm so honest by nature that I'm a poor liar, making it a habit only because of the bad company I keep. "Is Leon missing?" As I said this I pictured him cutting our rudder cables and dooming our ship on a reef. I'd later found his corpse on a beach, and when inspecting his body found a tattoo marking him as a henchman of Napoleon.

"'Disappeared on a peculiar mission, according to the governor of Martinique,'" Réal read.

"If I remember correctly," I tried, "Martel had left French government service and had his own background in crime. Pimp, slaver, thief, and rogue. If he was on a mission for the governor, it must have been of the most disreputable kind." Which was working with me, but no need to call that out.

"Perhaps." The councillor stood and moved to his window, looking at a courtyard crisscrossed by gendarmes on urgent, silent missions. Under Napoleon, seriousness meant advancement. By rumor, Fouché was about to be appointed police minister again, and other police chiefs like Savary, Dubois, and Réal were competing over who could catch the most traitors to win favor.

"Martel's mission was quite important," the policeman went on, "and we were informed he'd united with you after Dessaline's victory in Haiti. Two adventurers, pursuing ancient Aztec knowledge for France! And then Martel and an entire bomb vessel vanish, as well as the notorious Ethan Gage. So mysterious and tragic. Until you're smuggled back into France, arriving from England with your wife and son, and accompanied by a comely governess with royalist background. Perhaps, Monsieur Gage, you've become a spy for the British side." He said it sadly, as if greatly disappointed.

"Then why would I bring my family? It would be lunatic risk." I wondered where Astiza, Harry, and Catherine Marceau waited in prison.

"Bonaparte tells me you're clever without sense." He turned back and sat down behind his desk, as if weary with disapproval. Then Réal gave a Gallic shrug. "So I suppose we'll start with the comtesse."

It took me a moment to realize what he'd said. "Start?"

"If she doesn't talk, and she won't, some bad food and complete isolation will prepare her for torture. No word will leak of our cruelties. It's hard for the ministry to know what happens to prisoners when our jailers are their only contact with the outside world. And if she remains silent, then scientifically applied pain."

"But she's just a governess. A silly one at that."

"I've found the garrote is an effective tool that leaves little lasting damage. Experts strangle the interviewee to the point of near unconsciousness, revive them, and then strangle again. You had something of the same experience, I believe, with drowning." He made a temple of his hands.

I had a frightening mental picture of my beautiful comrade with contorted tongue and bulging eyes. "She's not up to anything, except gossip, fashion, and spending too much of my money. I can show you my ledger book if you don't believe me. She's as profligate as Josephine and flitty as a swallow."

"Then your wife, Astiza, before we start on your little boy, since I have a soft spot for children. I understand she's part Oriental, and the conventional wisdom is that hot tongs work on them. It would be an experiment on her race. There'd be no need to use instrumentation on Horus until I was certain the adults wouldn't cooperate. Then you could watch . . ."

"Napoleon would never tolerate such monstrosity."

"Napoleon, like all leaders, makes a point of not knowing everything done to keep him in power."

"You're a wicked man."

"I keep order."

We stared at each other. "There's no need for barbarism, Councillor. We both know I'm a spy, and that my family and companion are innocent."

"I doubt that, but admitting you're a spy is the first encouraging thing you've said."

He kept me off balance. "Encouraging?"

"We *like* English spies, Gage, so long as we know who they are. In fact, we want you to continue spying for Sir Sidney Smith."

"Councillor?"

"So long as you also spy for us." His tone became almost cheerful. "That will allow your wife and son to escape torture, your governess to keep her pretty neck, and yourself to once more play a role in great events, as you so like to do. No, don't protest Gage, you're a lazy layabout who pursues his own ends in a troubled world, but you're as driven as a soldier aspiring for a marshal's baton. It's simply that in your case, you're driven by greed, lust, and vanity."

"I think of it as trying to get ahead." Napoleon had just appointed eighteen generals to "marshal of the empire"; I was no different in ambition. "You want me to spy for both sides?"

"I didn't invite you here to discuss the weather. And if I wanted you out of the way, you and your family would already be dead, as you well know."

The threat, while accurate, irritated me. "I'm afraid I'm disappointed by your new emperor, Councillor, because of exactly this kind of threat. It's the boast of a bully, and I don't want to spy for bullies."

"Why not?" Another Gallic shrug. "Your royalist conspiracy is a ruin. Do you know we've arrested three hundred fifty-six people to date who played a part in it?" He recited the statistic with satisfaction. "You'll be tortured and executed if you don't cooperate. If you do, you could earn money for your family. What does it matter if you like our emperor? You must provide." He said this matter-of-factly.

I stalled, trying to calculate what I *should* do while also realizing I had little choice. "I *am* a man of political principle."

"No you're not, American wanderer. Like most spies you're an opportunist and schemer. Besides, your country has more in common with French revolutionary fervor than British royalism."

I glanced at Pasques, who guarded the door as still as a statue. There's a time for heroic defiance, and a time for calculating the odds. "You have a point."

"As a double agent you'll tell Britain what France wants it to hear, which is that invasion is imminent. This is nothing less than the truth. And you'll tell *us* what they think about it. Telling the truth again. I realize that's a novel idea for you, but you can be paid well for doing the right thing."

"Paid well?" It's best to pin these elusive promises down.

"Four hundred francs a month."

"That covers only my rent."

"Five hundred, to supplement what you already have in English gold. Not as generous as Smith, perhaps, but I don't have his resources."

I hadn't expected this, and acceptance sounded like a quick path to being caught in a crossfire. On the other hand, I'd completely failed to deny my connection to the British, and playing along with Réal might give us a chance to escape.

I shifted in my chair, trying not to sound too eager. "I *am* a moral man. Isn't working for two sides unethical?"

"Unethical compared to the espionage and assassination cabal of Sir Sidney Smith? Who is a man with no ethics of his own? Do you know that his heroic escape in 1798, celebrated in song and novel, was in fact the product of bribes to French officials who wanted him gone?"

"Certainly not. We're told he wooed comely women from his Temple Prison window, got word to royalist agents, and made a daring escape with the help of my late friend Phelipeaux, hero of the siege of Acre. People treat him like Robin Hood."

"History is just that, Gage, a story, and nothing is more fanciful than a man defying impossible odds. No one escapes Temple Prison without connivance." That had certainly been true in the case of Astiza and me, when we did so in 1799. "The Directory couldn't prove allegations of espionage against Smith and found his imprisonment an embarrassment. Yet they couldn't release him after authorities ballyhooed his capture. Easier for both sides were British bribes to key French jailers, who became conveniently stupid when agents arrived with forged papers. This is how the spy game works. A great deal of skullduggery, and then a satisfactory conclusion for everyone involved. Our business is happier than people think."

I conceded the argument. Espionage was like juicing cards, and was all the sneaking about simply a scheme to divert some English gold into everyone's pockets? I tried to work out my chances while deciding if at least temporarily joining the French as well as British was expedient or suicidal. I do have principles: namely, to protect my family from torture. As government, armies, and businesses become ever larger and more implacable, I'm a leaf in a hurricane, a man among millions trying to make my way home. So I take opportunities as they come, and revise strategy as I go along. "How did you know I was in Paris?"

"We knew everything, Gage, including when and where you'd land, though we didn't expect the coastal ambush that allowed you to escape capture. We knew your address shortly after you arrived in Paris, and we've followed with curiosity the little you've been doing since. As an agent of the British Crown, you are remarkably unproductive. I'd suspect it an American trait, but your mentor Franklin accomplished a great deal."

"Ambitious as the devil, and a clever conversational-ist. It's not a fair comparison."

"We know what you eat, the romance novels your wife reads, and the box under your son's bed where he keeps his toys. This is not the chaos under the Directory you once knew. This is the empire. France is organized now."

There's no privacy in our new nineteenth century, it seems. I twisted uncomfortably, trying to figure what I might bargain for. "If you've found me out, I'm indeed a poor spy. The British would do the same, would they not, and dismiss my reports as useless? Maybe you should just pack us off to Italy."

"Of course they'll discern you've been turned, and like us they won't care. They're as conceited as we are, and will believe they can skim useful observations from your abominable character. The fact that every-one treats you like a puppet is your only hope."

"It's being a puppet I'm trying to get away from."

"All of us are puppets, Gage. Even an emperor has strings pulled by the millions under him, a mob he must ceaselessly placate. But perhaps a better descrip-tion is that you serve as a go-between, diplomat, to improve understanding. Do you have a model of a flying machine?" The change in subject was abrupt, and his knowledge disconcerting.

"Perhaps."

"Monsieur Gage, I'm inquiring to save your neck."

I cleared my throat. "Then yes, I do. It's a little golden toy, actually, and not much to learn from in my opinion. I might just melt it down."

"France is a ferment of ideas about how to cross the Channel. Martel was working on this. So are many others, including some of our most esteemed savants. Bonaparte is open to each, and thinks that while your character is threadbare, your ingenuity might prove useful."

"I *am* an electrician of sorts. A Freemason, too, though I can never remember the ceremonies."

"Listen. I don't know precisely what happened to Leon Martel, and I don't care, but don't pretend he didn't disappear while in your company. He was a rascal but a useful rascal, so you can save yourself only by taking his place. Every attempt you make to wriggle from Napoleon's control will only enmesh you deeper. And don't pretend you don't know a great deal about flight and firearms. You escaped Egypt in a balloon, worked with Martel to find this Aztec flying machine, and there are even stories you befriended an English scholar of flight named Cayley. Not to mention the American inventor Robert Fulton."

"I like smart people."

"Bonaparte wants your expertise again. He says you've occasionally been unwittingly inspirational, such as provoking his brilliance in crossing the Alps for the Marengo campaign."

"He gives me too much credit." Requisite modesty again. "I did remind him about Hannibal." Napoleon wanted to see me? And would I accuse him of jeopardizing my family if I did? Should I shoot him and be done with it? Every time I stayed in Paris, life became more complicated. "He's a difficult chap. Napoleon, I mean. Hannibal, too, I suppose."

Réal was impatient. "Should we guillotine you instead?"

"I *am* a fount of intriguing ideas. You know, your emperor once gave me a mark of favor." I pulled the pendant out like a trump card. It was a golden *N*, surrounded by a golden wreath. "I worked on negotiations for Louisiana and kept pirates from a dangerous weapon." The trinket glittered.

"So you're warming to my proposal."

"I'm just trying to save my family."

"Napoleon doesn't fear that you can provide anything truly useful to the British. But he does want your thoughts on military matters. He said you're a thinker when pressed."

"Then perhaps I should earn a thousand francs."

"Be prudent, not ridiculous."

The trouble with hurling yourself into a conspiracy is that once it collapses, you have few options. I stewed only because my weakness was so humiliating. Then I remembered another possible sign of favor. "By the way, Pasques said Bonaparte wants to give me a present?"

He scowled. "Yes. A joke of sorts, from one soldier to another. But not a joke, as well." He picked up a twin-bladed dagger on his desk of the kind a murderer might wield—had it been confiscated?—and used the blade to ring a small brass bell. Another policeman entered, carrying a long package bound in a cotton sheet.

I perked up. Everyone likes a gift.

"The emperor said you claim you lost your long rifle to a dragon, a story that has provoked a great deal of amusement at dinner parties."

"Well, I did."

"He's decided to offer you a replacement."

"A gun?" It was the last thing I expected.

"More than just a gun. It is, after all, from an emperor."

I was presented with a German Jaeger hunting rifle, which had been the Old World inspiration for the Pennsylvania long rifle I'd once brandished.

The Prussian weapon is grooved in its barrel like the American version but is shorter, making it easier to carry in brush or on horseback.

"More indeed," I admitted. This particular piece was gorgeous, its stock carved with stags and unicorns. "The brass plating is really quite brilliant," I said. "The entire piece is pretty as a Spanish saddle."

"Not brass. Gold, like your pendant." He watched me like a horse trader.

Good heavens. A man I'd vowed to kill had just given me a weapon perfectly suited to do it with, and worth a diadem besides? "Solid?"

"Plated. But more than you could afford."

The rifle had the same *N* with engraved laurel wreath, I saw. The generosity was embarrassing, the bribe clear, and the arrogance annoying. Pure Napoleon. "You first have me followed and then trust me with this weapon?"

"Rest assured it's unloaded." The tone was dry. "And men like Napoleon never give without expecting something in return. You know that. The emperor actually does want your advice about tactics and aerial maneuvers. And he thinks you've become confused about what each side stands for. Therefore, he commands you and your wife to attend him in the first public display of imperial ceremony."

"Astiza as well?"

"He's created a new Legion of Honor to which every Frenchman will aspire, and he's betting it will remind you of what the new France is all about."

"And what is it you are about again?"

"Reforming Europe, restoring honor, and institutionalizing ideals. This country is the future, Monsieur Gage. And despite your transgressions, you're still invited to be a part of it." He looked stern. "The British are about to be conquered. You would do well to ponder which side you want to be on when the tricolor flies over London."

Chapter 9

The unveiling of Napoleonic pomp and glory came with the smell of sawdust. Adjacent to the gigantic Invalides—the Bourbon hospital for wounded soldiers that was also a church, then a "Temple of Mars" under the revolution, and now a marble stage for national pageantry—was a new, makeshift shipyard for boats being built for the invasion of England.

While larger craft were under construction on the Channel, the Seine was being used to build the *péniche*, sixty feet long and ten wide, which was capable of carrying sixty-six soldiers and two howitzers. The completed vessels would be floated down the river to Le Havre, then up to Channel ports to join the armada being assembled for attack. On July 15, 1804, when Napoleon's Legion of Honor was ceremonially inaugurated, many of the boats were still half planked, ribs jutting like combs and guards posted to prevent thievery of firewood. Royal woodlands were being cut to build an invasion fleet of at least two thousand landing craft, fifty of them here.

The line of cradled *péniche* was a fist of war made visible. War's glory was a bombastic parade of flags, military bands, saluting cannon, church hymn, and tramping boots on a scale Paris had never seen. As first consul, Napoleon had taken care to appear as a modestly uniformed democrat, a Gallic Thomas Jefferson. But France was not Virginia, and French passion isn't ignited by modesty. So while it was still half a year before Bonaparte's papal coronation would give the general a crown, the newly elected emperor put on a show.

"*Vive l'empereur!*" came the answering roar.

Napoleon rode across the Seine in an open golden carriage, Josephine in a white coach behind. Plumed and helmeted cuirassiers rode escort while infantry lined the route with bayonet and banners. Cavalry breastplates shone like mirrors. Sabers were blades of light. Pennants bobbed as chargers trotted. A hundred drummers thundered welcome. Field gun salutes covered the river in a fog of smoke.

No would-be assassin could come near the elevated warlord. I watched Napoleon approach our crowd of dignitaries at the Invalides with wonder and envy, mystified that Astiza and I had been invited at all. The policeman Pasques was our towering escort. Catherine had reluctantly agreed to watch Harry in return for my bargaining to spare her from torture and prison. "I'll take you to the next one," I promised.

"They put me in a cell and peered at me as if I were an animal," she recounted. "They treated me as if I were common."

"But now they want something, and our fortunes have turned," I said, secretly doubting my own optimism. When authorities notice, trouble sticks like tar.

"You see how France loves our new emperor?" Pasques now asked. "Conspirators fear his genius, and the people adore his ambition. If you can persuade the British of his popularity, they'll give up on the Bourbons and avoid a lot of killing. It's a noble cause you've enlisted in, Monsieur Gage."

I avoided responding. "It looks damn costly to have a king back," I said instead. Napoleon was already reputed to have 250 servants, including 64 footmen. "Jefferson is cheaper."

"On the contrary, Bonaparte saves money by preventing chaos."

"He provides spectacle like the pharaohs and Caesars he hopes to emulate," Astiza assessed. "Bread, circuses, and a new trinket for his soldiers."

Pasques frowned. He trusted my wife even less than he trusted me.

When I told Astiza of my uncomfortable interview with Réal, she'd been sober and realistic, advising me to play along until "fate shows a way." While Comtesse Marceau had been given the taste of a cell, Astiza and Harry had been detained in an office. Far from threatening Harry with hot tongs, a police recruit gave my boy a top to play with and let him keep it. I realized that Réal's threats had probably been exaggerated.

Astiza said our invitation to the Legion of Honor was as intriguing as it was unavoidable. "I'm as curious as anyone."

So how was I to regard the godlike Napoleon, who'd once chatted with me on an Egyptian beach and given me my future wife after bombarding her house? He seemed as remote as a deity now. His Mameluke bodyguard Roustan Raza, a gift from Egypt, was proud as a centaur as he trotted behind the carriage in turban, Greek costume, and curved scimitar. An entire company of these Oriental warriors followed. There were Georgian giants from the Caucasus, Abyssinian blacks, expert Arab horsemen from Syria, and sharpshooters from Malta, all recruited in Egypt and sworn to defend Napoleon with their lives.

The emperor's real protection wasn't his soldiers or bodyguards, however. It was the cordon of cheering French who lined the parade route in relief and hope. The long dark years of the revolution were over. I saw not a single jeering or sullen face amid the masses chanting *Vive l'empereur!* As intended, the conformity was intimidating. I'd been conspiring against a man who'd just won more than 99 percent of the popular vote. Still only thirty-four years old, he wasn't just the most powerful man in France, he was the most powerful man in the world.

Madness.

It didn't help that Napoleon's appointees were making the order of things clear. "Severity but humanity!" Dubois had proclaimed in writing when appointed Paris prefect of police five days before. "My eye shall penetrate the innermost recesses of the criminal's soul, but my ear shall be open to the cries of innocence and even the groans of repentance . . ."

My old foe Fouché had been reinstated as head of the national police that same day. He'd first been reminded by Napoleon that he could fall, and now was reminded that, under Napoleon, he could rise again.

So be it. I wasn't about to martyr myself and leave my family bereft; that's for men with greater conviction than me. So I'd convey news to England they already knew by reading French newspapers: namely, that the man they feared most was the most popular French hero since Roland and Joan of Arc. I'd once more play the murky role of double agent, never quite belonging to anyone but myself, and deciding at each crisis which path to take. My wife would search for tidbits in the ossuaries of musty records. And we'd wait for opportunity to . . .

What? Somehow undermine Napoleon's legitimacy, as Catherine had urged. It seemed a futile goal.

I glanced at Pasques, but he wasn't even watching us. Like everyone else he had eyes only for the emperor.

The triumphant procession commemorated a new medal of merit. The Legion of Honor was roughly modeled on the Roman legion, but it was an honorary fraternity of the best of France, a pantheon that all men could, and should, aspire to. Inductees had to either achieve something outstanding or serve the state for at least twenty-five years. It was open not only to soldiers but to scientists, inventors, artists, writers, entrepreneurs, and explorers. No women, of course.

Today was public demonstration of the society of merit Napoleon had in mind for France and Europe. Granted was prestige without the requirement of high birth. I've never seen a more baffling juxtaposition of symbols. Here crippled veterans and bright young scientists alike would be given democratic honor by a man more absolute than former kings. *All human situations have their inconsistencies*, Franklin had observed.

With Napoleon's arrival we went inside the Invalides, its brilliantly white arched church a sumptuous backdrop for political opera. Dark-suited senators and deputies occupied the front rows of temporarily erected tiers of seats, as if elected representatives still mattered. Colonels, society ladies, contractors, savants, and artists sat in rows behind, looking down as if on an athletic contest. The main floor was jammed with the new legionnaires and the most favored generals, bishops, and ministers. An altar was ringed by Catholic clergy with splendid gowns and mitered hats, demonstrating Napoleon's astute recruitment of the Church. The prelates were led by ninety-four-year-old Cardinal Jean-Baptiste de Belloy, who won the post by supporting the new regime and who'd moved into the Archbishop's Palace next to Notre Dame.

The Invalides church was dominated by Napoleon, not God. Green-carpeted steps, the color of Corsica, led to a scarlet-and-gold armchair that was the day's throne, the elevated perch canopied by a red awning gaudily crowned with ostrich plumes and a gilded imperial eagle. Standing below on the nave floor were the milling honorees. Grizzled grenadiers boasted imposing mustaches. Rising generals sported mutton-chop whiskers. Courtiers and diplomats sneezed bits of snuff into lace handkerchiefs: Napoleon himself used two pounds of the inhaled tobacco a week. Male hair was in transition from powdered wig to the revolution-ary pigtail and on to the newly fashionable "Titus cut" of short curls combed over the forehead. Napoleon's youthful curtain of shoulder-length hair had been clipped to this Roman fashion to disguise a prematurely receding hairline.

There were also enough epaulettes, medals, velvets, silks, and leathers to outfit a dozen American armies. Here in Paris men could be peacocks, strutting in uni-forms costing a year of laborer wages. How brilliantly they would ride into battle! They had the gusto of sur-vivors from the catastrophe of revolution. It had been computed that of the original 1,080 members of the Convention after the fall of King Louis, 151 revolution-aries had been executed or murdered, had committed suicide, or had been driven into exile. Those remaining felt reprieved.

The few women present were just as glorious, hair pinned into towers roofed with slanting hats and color-ful plumes. My wife, on the advice of Catherine, had parrot feathers. To revive the silk and velvet industries that had gone moribund in the revolution, Napoleon was encouraging a move away from gauze and muslin, meaning dresses had become more opaque, with higher necklines and longer trains.

The air was rich with Catholic incense, tobacco, and perfume.

The crowd clustered around the empire's new nuclei, the eighteen marshals Napoleon had appointed on May 19. Some generals I remembered from the Egyptian campaign. There was the handsome and redoubtable Lannes, the gloriously black-curled Murat, the stern and balding Davout, and the severe Bessieres, who commanded the Guard Cavalry. Their uniforms were outrageous rainbows of blue, red, white, green, and yellow. Murat by rumor had spent one hundred thousand francs on his. There were buttons enough to require half a morning of fastening. Sabers clanked and rattled. Boots creaked from polished leather. Spurs jangled.

"The French can be governed through their vanity," Napoleon had reportedly said.

The marshals also represented a new tangle of marriages, appointments, and opportunities as complex as a medieval court. Catherine recited this new order with envy. Murat was married to Caroline Bonaparte, Napoleon's sister, and rumor was that both thought the cavalryman would make a more able emperor—or at least a more dashing one—than his shorter brother-in-law. Lannes, the farmer's son turned warrior, had returned from a profitable tenure as ambassador to Portugal with enough pocketed bribes to purchase a Paris mansion. Davout had married the sister of Charles Leclerc, and thus was brother-in-law to Leclerc's widow Pauline, Napoleon's sister. Massena had evolved from Italian smuggler to French military hero. Bernadotte was married to Desiree Clary, the beauty who had once been engaged to young Napoleon. Bernadotte's sister-in-law Julie was married to Napoleon's brother Joseph.

Napoleon was building a clan worthy of Machiavelli. A study of the army lists and genealogical tables showed France boasted 240 generals in some way related to one another. Half a dozen were publicly known to have conspired against Napoleon, and their new emperor needed war to keep them campaigning instead of plotting. The French victories at Hohenlinden and Marengo were four years past, and there was hunger for new glory. They swaggered. If they could come to grips with England's small army, they'd rip it apart.

I was surprised to have been given gold tickets that admitted us to the main floor, since I'd little chance of being inducted into anybody's legion of honor.

I had a different kind of celebrity and was both flattered and frightened when the odious and limping Charles-Maurice Périgord—better known as simply Talleyrand, or the "lame devil," and the foreign minister of France—approached. His narrow head was erect, as if braced, with the limpid stare of a fish, and lips tight as a virgin. It occurred to me that the towering policeman Pasques served as a useful lighthouse in this jammed church for any official trying to find the politically compromised Ethan Gage.

I was wary. Prevented by his childhood limp from entering the military, Talleyrand was instead ordered by his family into the priesthood, where he rose to the position of Bishop of Autun despite his opinion that the entire Christian catechism was nonsense. His atheism, greed, and cynicism eventually resulted in his being defrocked. He'd also betrayed both the Bourbons he once served and the revolutionaries after by throwing in with reactionary Napoleon.

Yet Talleyrand was also credited with being the slyest foreign minister since Cardinal Richelieu. He'd spent two years in American exile at the height of the French Revolution, living as a houseguest of future vice president Aaron Burr. Later he helped embroil France in an undeclared naval war with the United States that I'd played a small part in ending. Now he'd been named grand chamberlain of the empire. He studied the map like a chessboard and manipulated kings like pawns.

His handshake was soft and without conviction. "The American electrician," he greeted with the unction of the highborn. "You were honored for your service at our celebration at Mortefontaine."

"I'm flattered you remember, Grand Chamberlain. My role was brief."

He managed a thin but wooing smile, the effort seeming to pain him. "I don't remember your being modest and, at age fifty, I remember far too much." He turned and bowed slightly. "This is your intriguing wife?"

"Astiza, from Egypt."

"I'm honored, madame. I understand you are an intellectual, a remarkable achievement for your sex."

"Someday men will recognize that gender has little to do with the mind," she responded. "Just as stooping to help a child makes a woman stand tall as a man."

Now his smile widened, his eyebrows elevating. "Your reputation for wit and perception is deserved. And you study the ancients?"

"Yes. You're a student of history, Grand Chamberlain?"

"Of power, for the good of mankind." He looked about. "Ah, Monsieur Gage, how triumphant this all is, and how anxious! Napoleon is out to create a new court in order to be accepted as an equal by royal houses that despise and fear him. It's a longing that will bring much blood, I predict. No new emperor can compete in stature with an ancient line of kings. I'm his servant, but I'm also nostalgic for the less complicated past. Before the revolution men knew their place, beauty was worshipped, and life was refined. Now everyone is sweaty and striving. Those who didn't experience the security of a king will never know the full sweetness of living."

"Sweetness for a few," Astiza said. "Most were starving." My wife is disturbingly honest.

"True, true." His agreement was judicious, as if we were discussing insects. "Still, there was a civility that was lost forever. Ask your governess. She'll tell you."

So he knew Comtesse Marceau's background as well. A fine hive of spies we were. "She already has," I said.

His hand fluttered. "So many swords, so many uniforms! This is a masculine age, Madame Gage. The years of the king were a feminine era. Marie Antoinette was slandered, but the truth is she was kindly, sweet, and deserved veneration, not beheading. I believe ages come in cycles, the wise domesticity of women alternating with the heroic aggression of men, peace cycling with war, and grace followed by grandeur. Both, I believe, are necessary for human progress."

"You're a philosopher, Grand Chamberlain," my wife said. "And a believer in progress?"

"Progress that always comes at a cost."

I felt rustic next to this worldly adviser, chaperoned by a giant, and surrounded by men who might kill me if they knew all my alliances. In a crush of five thousand people, I felt lonely, save for my wife. "This gathering sparkles," I said without conviction. "And congratulations on your own elevation, Grand Chamberlain." Compliments are never wasted.

"Regimes fall, but I do not." He said it lightly, and then regarded me more intently, suddenly all business. "I was disappointed not to have more correspondence from you on our strategy for the American frontier."

That hapless adventure had been three years before. "Again, I'm surprised you remember. In any event, I didn't find a postal system among Red Indians. But as you're no doubt aware, I came back to help with the sale of Louisiana to my own country. I was delighted it was successfully concluded last year."

"Yes, a bargain for both of us. I understand an exploration of it is under way by Jefferson's secretary, a man named Lewis, with a frontiersman named Clark."

"Clark, too? I've met both. An able pair, but then Jefferson is a good judge of talent." I implied we could include me in that roster.

"A Frenchman joined them, my correspondents tell me. A voyageur you knew by the name of Pierre Radisson."

"You follow the travels of Pierre? You are remarkably well informed." So my old friend was off with Meriwether Lewis. The West was where he belonged.

"It's a small world," Talleyrand said. "And will they succeed?"

"They are very capable. But the United States has become very big."

"I'll be interested to hear what they discover. We've little idea what we sold you." That thin smile again.

What was this about? We were spies, not ministers, and the business of police, not ambassadors. Why was Talleyrand bothering with us? "You're working, I trust, for an end to the present war with Britain?" I said in order to say something. "The United States wishes to resume trade with both sides." France was under British blockade.

"The United States spent money for Louisiana, borrowed from a bank in Britain, that the emperor intends to use to conquer England. A small world, indeed. As for me, I'm always working for my country at great sacrifice to myself." It was a sardonic lie, given that the man made a fortune from every office he touched, be it religious, revolutionary, or imperial.

"Councillor Réal told me the tricolor will soon fly in London."

"I expect stalemate, Monsieur Gage. France is the elephant and England the whale, and each is struggling to come to grips with the other. Which is why Councillor Réal and I agreed that, rather than just jail and shoot you, we would ask you for advice. To help persuade you to truly help us, you've been brought here to see the future of Europe."

"I doubt the emperor really needs my advice. Nor, might I add, does he need to shoot me."

"Never forget that he could do so; the Jaeger rifle is to remind you how powerless you are to a man surrounded by an army. I'd hate for you to make a misstep. So tragic for your wife." His glance at her was now cold. "She, too, must help us as we help you."

"Am I to speak to Napoleon?" I could barely see the new emperor. He had on a bicorn hat with cockade, pivoted so that the ends pointed toward his shoulders, as he preferred. But at five feet six and sitting, he did not tower like a Charlemagne. He'd lost some of his campaign leanness, too, and was thicker than

I remembered. His coat was military blue, his stockings and breeches white, and he wore only a few simple medals. The simplicity marked him apart. A man is truly important when he doesn't have to show it. "I'd have to tunnel or vault just to get to him."

"The meeting is not here, but at a later time and in a place of his choosing. Today is just to remind you of his power."

"I am reminded."

"Are you willing to contemplate what Réal suggested?"

I had to be careful. "I'm doubtful of the utility of such a course, but I'm also trying to save my family. I become ever more confused as to which side I'm really on."

"That just means you're able. Napoleon says all intelligent men are hypocrites."

"Half a compliment, I suppose."

"And I think Napoleon is not only intelligent, but a genius."

I was surprised. Talleyrand by reputation had a cynical view of the abilities of everyone, especially those he had to answer to. But he was serious.

"Yes, I respect and fear him," the chamberlain went on. "Like me, he has no friends, but he buys loyalty with reward and keeps his marshals off-balance by setting them against one another. His policemen spy on one another, don't they, Pasques?"

"No good policeman trusts another," the giant grunted.

"His ministers compete for favor to get their budget. Every decision goes across his desk. I've never seen a man work harder. Reward, divide, control. He understands power better than any politician I've met."

"But to what purpose, Grand Chamberlain?" Astiza asked.

"That is a tremendously insightful question. Too few ask it."

"I hope you're sharing your own wisdom with him."

"I share my experience. History will decide if it's wisdom. Ah, it's beginning."

The drama unfolded as scripted. There were hymns and patriotic songs. A parade of flags, including banners captured in battle and tricolors impressively shot through by bullet and shell. Octave-Henri Gabriel, Comte de Ségur, was master of ceremonies. The Comte de Lacepede was inducted as the Legion's first grand chancellor. He gave a windy speech, a roll call of the Legion's grand officers was read, and then the chosen legionnaires came forward to receive their medals. The first, a wounded and crippled veteran of the revolutionary wars a decade earlier, had to be helped up the stairs for Napoleon to tenderly pin on the medal. It was a touching sight, even to me.

The requirement was service, the motto "Honor and Fatherland," and the pay to Legion members ranged from 250 francs for an ordinary legionnaire to five thousand to Lacepede. As usual, the less a fellow needed the money, the more they gave him.

The bauble itself had a noble look. A white radiating star had the head of Napoleon in the center, pinned on the breast as a mark of distinction. No one would accuse the Corsican of false modesty.

"Civilization works through information, Monsieur Gage," Talleyrand murmured as we watched. "That's all we're asking from you, that you convey what you see. As courier or go-between, you can make history."

"So long as it safeguards my family."

"Your family will safeguard itself. I'll pay your new French stipend while you and your family attend Napoleon at the army camps on the Channel coast." He turned to Astiza. "It was to be five hundred francs a month, but for your cooperation, let's make it six."

"You can simply pay the money to my wife here in Paris," I said.

"But Napoleon wants her, too, along with the boy and the comtesse."

I was surprised. "For what?"

"He'll tell you in due time."

The oath was to both France and emperor, the roars of *Vive l'empereur* shook the church, and at last we were released, long lines of men lining up at temporary privies to pee.

As the mob slowly carried us outside, I put a question to Talleyrand. "To a realist does such ceremony matter? I mean, a trinket and a ribbon? It's like trade goods to the Indians, isn't it?"

"Napoleon heard the same doubt in his Council of State. To which he replied, 'By such toys are men led.'"

Chapter 10

Napoleon watched England from a gray wooden gallery with glassed oval ends, nesting on a bluff above Boulogne. The pavilion was built near the legendary site of Caligula's Lighthouse, erected when that mad Roman emperor dreamed of conquering Britain and fired catapults at the water when storms dashed his chances. Soldiers called the one-hundred-foot-long aerie "the Big Box." When Channel squalls blew, the pavilion was a cozy refuge. On clearer days, a telescope gave a view of the white cliffs of Dover and the British navy between. A long table inside was strewn with maps of England and its shoaling shores.

There was only one chair. Attending generals were required to stand in order to keep meetings short. When Napoleon launched into monologues, they leaned on the hilts of their sheathed swords to give their legs relief.

The emperor's panorama was like that of a giant child with an unlimited supply of toy soldiers. The Channel shore had been dubbed the Iron Coast for its menacing artillery batteries. On the sloping meadows around the French seaport was a vast military city of eighty thousand men, living in mud-and-wattle barracks with thatched roofs and smoking chimneys. It was no secret that there were thirty-five thousand more drilling in Saint-Omer, fourteen thousand at Dunkirk, twenty thousand at Ostend, and ten thousand at Bruges, along with ten thousand horses and hundreds of field guns. All of this I had duly put in coded messages with sympathetic ink and passed to Sir Sidney Smith, as Réal cheerfully suggested.

Waiting to take this army across the Channel were thirteen hundred boats classed as *prame*, chaloupe, bateau, or péniche, with another thousand under construction.

The quest was hung with history. Napoleon had displayed the famed Bayeux Tapestry in Paris the previous winter, reminding the French of their success with the Norman conquest of England in 1066. And William the Conqueror had led a platoon compared to this lot.

But patrolling offshore, like sentry dogs, were scores of English ships.

Elephant and whale, indeed.

My family and Catherine rode in a coach from Paris to Boulogne on the swift stage roads we'd avoided before, us chattering and our escort Pasques as mute as a mummy. Since the royalists had been crushed and I was supposedly working for both sides, I didn't understand the need for a watchful policeman, but at least the giant was useful in getting men to slide out of the way at an inn table. He tended to get faster service and hotter food, too, with less need to check the arithmetic of the bill. I like large companions.

It didn't require a spy to know we were approaching military encampments. Even in summer the roads were churned to wallows from a constant stream of supply wagons. The outskirts of Boulogne had a new tent city of sutlers, prostitutes, moneylenders, horse traders, food wagons, and casinos. As we rode past we were offered pigs, chickens, pastries, bare breasts, campaign equipment, loans, and gypsy fortunes, Harry taking in more of life's realities than I would have preferred. He was most mesmerized by the uniforms and guns. Cannons thudded in practice drills. Muskets crackled on the firing range. Newly purchased mares were commanded and spurred next to a deliberate cacophony of cannon blast, bugle call, gunshot, drum, and practiced screams from a chorus of village women hired expressly for the purpose, to mimic the cries of combat.

"Why are they yelling at the horses, Papa?"

"A mount is useless if panicked by battle, and so horses have to be trained not to bolt when the noise starts. They have more sense than people and want to run away."

"Aren't the horses brave?"

"Nobler than their masters."

We settled in Boulogne, a small port with cobbled quays and a new stone basin shaped like a half-moon. This was filled with the moored invasion fleet. Larger warships, floating batteries, and underwater chains formed a protective hedge beyond to deter British attack. Four gigantic army camps squatted upslope, three north of the city and one south. A letter from Réal directed me to seek out General Phillipe-Guillaume Duhèsme, to whom I was to offer my eccentric expertise. While the women and Harry explored, I went looking for him.

The scale was imposing. Men of an *ordinaire*, or squad, were housed fifteen to a hut in rows more than two miles long. Soldiers did their best to make these hovels a home. Some were whitewashed, had wooden floors, and some even had secondhand carpets. Next to each were plots for vegetables, flower gardens, and chicken coops. Officer villas were in a row beyond, and kitchens and latrines beyond that.

There were street signs with the names of French victories, such as Valmy, Fleurus, or Marengo. Veterans of the Egyptian campaign set up miniature pyramids or obelisks made of clay and seashells. Pet cats that helped keep away the vermin prowled longingly beneath the birds in the officers' aviaries.

There were cheerful oddities everywhere. One hut I passed had a pilfered chandelier, another a pair of Spanish bull horns, and a third chairs fashioned from driftwood. Two veteran sergeants occupied these seats, smoking clay pipes and calling out advice and insults to all who wandered past. A garden statue of Venus was festooned with bawdy notes, and another hut had a mast and boom on the roof, with a rotating sail like a weathercock.

Duhèsme was a tall, thin, and restless officer with an anxiously friendly face; his head tended to bob when talking, like a rooster. He wore his bicorn hat at a jaunty angle, and muttonchops held his chin like calipers. His headquarters were in a requisitioned stone farmhouse, staff offices on the ground floor and sleeping quarters above. Three farmwives had been hired to keep house, and two hunting hounds lay like lazy sentries.

"Ah, the American. Did you bring the Jaeger?"

I'd wrapped the rifle in oilcloth to discourage thieves from its gleam of gold. It was opulent enough to be embarrassing. "I haven't had an opportunity to use it, General." I untied the bundle.

His eyes gleamed at its craftsmanship as he reached out. "May I?"

"Of course."

He turned it and sighted. "Pretty as a woman. And worth a small fortune."

"A present from the emperor." The rifle gave me more credential than a satchel of medals.

"An impressive patron to have in imperial France, though exactly where our empire is—a grand claim for a nation ringed by enemies—has eluded my discovery. I suppose the emperor is an optimist." He grabbed a tin plate from the table by the house's kitchen. "And you're curious about your pretty gun, no? I certainly am. Do you have powder? No? We'll requisition some. Come, come, let's give it a try."

We trudged up a long sweeping hill with the general pointing out Napoleon's pavilion. "He has an iron bed with a horsehair mattress there, but usually sleeps on feathers on the other side of town, in a mansion called Pont-de-Briques. That's when he sleeps at all. Mostly he prowls from six in the morning until five in the afternoon, at which time he returns to headquarters to do paperwork, dashing off a hundred orders to all corners of France until midnight. It keeps men at their jobs, I can tell you. He'll pinch your ear if you displease him, and give you a silver snuff box if he approves."

"I'm not sure why he brought me here. Perhaps to meet with him?"

"Not today!" He laughed. "Our *petit caporal* took it in his head to be the first to shoot the mighty mortars we've installed to hold off the British ships. The monsters fire sixty-pound shells, and a single hit would be enough to sink a frigate. But as a former gunner Napoleon was too confident, and he stood so close that the roar and concussion deafened him. He's had cotton in his bleeding ears the past two days and is sour as bad milk."

An injury report from famed spy Ethan Gage was something Smith could use, I thought. "You mean he can't hear?"

"Temporarily, the doctors say. Meanwhile, he shouts because he thinks we can't hear him." Duhèsme laughed again, an officer of rare good humor. His face was weathered from coastal duty, pockmarked from some earlier disease, and handsome in the lean way of a hound. "His enthusiasm is always getting him into trouble. He's fallen out of boats and had to swim for his hat, and been thrown by his horse while crossing the river. But his frenzy produces respect. He's caught sentries napping. He also came upon one soldier they forgot to relieve and took his place on a blustery night, saving the man from freezing. Or so the story goes. Bonaparte is as much legend as fact anymore. What do they think of him in America?"

"The hope was that he'd sustain a democratic republic."

"Copy the chaos of your United States? I think not."

"Then what was your revolution for?"

"Liberty. But people in France are tired of freedom. It's when people can vote that they realize how catastrophic and stupid are the opinions of their neighbors. Better to have a Bonaparte in charge whom you can never remove, and always blame." He laughed again.

There was a thunder of hooves behind. The general jerked me off the track, and a captain of the Hussars rode past, whooping drunkenly and holding a champagne bottle. Duhèsme gave him a wry salute.

"Your officers gallop intoxicated?"

"It's his initiation after a promotion. To confirm his new rank, the cavalryman is given three horses and has three hours to gallop a twenty-mile course, all while drinking three bottles of champagne and rutting three whores. The order with which he accomplishes these tasks is entirely up to him."

"And they accomplish it?" Even I was astounded, and a bit envious.

He winked. "We're a highly trained army. Are you a military man, Gage?"

"Not by profession. Armies seem to scoop me up."

"You've seen action in the Orient and the Americas, I understand, and by reputation are quite a shooter."

"I learned on the American frontier but am out of practice."

"Let's see you practice now." We reached a camp firing range set against a dune. Duhèsme placed the plate a hundred paces away. "Show me what your pretty gun is capable of."

I loaded the Jaeger. Unlike a soldier's musket ball, a rifle bullet is tightly squeezed in the barrel so it can grip the grooving and spin for accuracy. That means ramrodding takes care, strength, and time. I spent a full minute inserting powder cartridge, ball, wadding, and primer.

"My God, the battle would be over by now," Duhèsme judged, looking at his pocket watch. "This is how you won the American wars?"

"For speed, use a musket. You can almost drop the bullet in. But to actually hit anything, use a rifle." I primed the pan, cocked, aimed slowly, and squeezed the trigger. There was a bang, kick, and a puff of powder smoke. Through its haze, the distant tin plate twitched. I felt satisfied. I was rusty but could still shoot.

The general snapped open his telescope. "Just centimeters off the center. Impressive, American. Try again."

I shot five more times. Every bullet pierced the plate. Then Duhèsme followed, hitting three of four shots.

"Impressive, Frenchman."

"It's the gun. The inaccuracy of firearms is the intriguing dilemma of the battlefield. We've run tests with our infantry firing at targets the size of horses. With a musket, just half struck the target at a hundred yards. At three hundred, the accuracy dropped to one hit in four. Charging cavalry can gallop that distance in half a minute."

"Meaning your soldiers get off just one or two volleys."

"And that's on a firing range. Put peasant boys on a smoky and hellish battlefield, men bleeding and horses screaming, guns going off in their ears, and we're fortunate to get them to point their muskets in the enemy's direction. It took more than four hundred shots at Marengo to produce each Austrian casualty."

"You might as well wait for them to keel over from consumption."

"Our soldiers stagger from sixty-five pounds of gun and kit. You need bright uniforms to tell friend from foe in the murk of powder smoke. Drums and bugles because no one can hear their officers. And should the rank be one deep, two, or three? It's not uncommon for the third rank to shoot the ears off those in the first."

"The British stand two deep, I'm told." This was no secret.

"All those men must be fed. A cannon requires ammunition and gunners, and the gunners food, and so a battery of field pieces requires a hundred horses that need to eat in turn. Any economy saves lives and francs. What if our army was armed with Jaegers?"

So that was in it. This Frenchman wanted to mimic Daniel Morgan's frontiersmen in our Revolutionary War, picking the British off from an impregnable distance. "Rifles are fussy," I warned. "They take too long to load, are more apt to foul and misfire, and are easily broken. Muskets can take the abuse of an oaf and be loaded by a village idiot."

"An elite rifle unit, then. Lafayette brought back enthusiasm for skirmishers from your Revolutionary War."

"Red Indians are most expert, so perhaps you should go back to arrows. They're silent and don't emit smoke."

The idea was meant as a joke, but he took it seriously. "Do you know how to shoot a bow?"

"Regrettably, no. Years of practice are required, I'm guessing."

"Crossbows, perhaps. Let me ponder that." Duhèsme had more imagination than most army officers I've encountered.

"For every advantage there is a disadvantage."

He nodded. "You understand war, Monsieur Gage. People think generalship is arrows on a map, but it really is difficult choices, and getting men to function when they're hungry, thirsty, and exhausted. They seldom know exactly what they're fighting for, so they fight for friends and flag. Their reward is proof of their own courage."

"Men fight wars to become men."

"Indeed." He cocked his head. "So why are you here, so far from home?"

"My goal is peace, which no one seems to share."

"You're not loyal to a flag?"

"I understand being loyal to yourself, your family, and even the country that protects them. If that's represented by the flag, then of course. But if the flag represents a king's quest for glory, or a vainglorious general? Then I'm loyal to reason. I'll retreat or desert if it will save my life."

Duhèsme was disappointed in me, as so many people are. "You're missing the meaning of life, Monsieur Gage. You need a cause and companions! Someday, perhaps, you'll experience the exhilaration of dedicating yourself to a banner, melding with your unit, and feeling as one. It's transforming: a touch of the Divine."

"The transformation comes when a cannonball shreds your extremities. And I hope the Divine is dedicated to beauty, not butchery. Yes, I know my selfishness makes me a poor soldier. But a sensible man, don't you think?"

"A morally impoverished one." He shook his head.

That's the nut of things, isn't it? Do you live for yourself or your country? For reason or passion? Are you responsible for your actions, or do you hand responsibility to an army and commit glory and crimes on its behalf?

"I mean no insult," Duhèsme said, "but one's country is all. And unity is what we're drilling here, and why we'll cut through English militia like a knife through butter if we can cross the Channel. Nearly half our number here has already seen combat. No army in history has the preparation of Napoleon's Army of

England. But we constantly seek advice, even from independent Americans, to improve even more."

"I'm flattered but mystified, General. You already know the advantages and disadvantages of rifles."

"I'm asking if they are practical."

I rummaged for something useful. "In America the colonials fought from behind trees and rocks. The British regulars couldn't close without breaking apart their lines in rough terrain. Washington wanted to fight on level fields, but I never understood the point of it. Fight like Indians! The English called cowardice what I call cunning."

"I want you to work with us on tactics, Gage. And when you're finished, go tell your British friends they can't stand against us. Your incorrigible character will convince them you're betraying us, so they'll believe you."

I sighed at this assessment. For all my skepticism of following a flag, I had effectively been drafted into the French army. Some spy! "This is what Napoleon called me here for?"

"Napoleon called you for a different purpose. When his ears heal, he'll give you your true mission."

Chapter 11

What Astiza calls fate I call luck, and Napoleon has bad luck with the sea. He lost an entire fleet to Nelson at the Battle of the Nile. He'd turned his back on Fulton's nautical ingenuity. And I reunited with him on a day that was stormy in more ways than one.

It was July 20, 1804, the kind of sullen summer day that promises thunder. Our audience with the emperor had yet to be scheduled, but General Duhèsme sent word that Napoleon had ordered an invasion exercise in Boulogne's harbor and suggested we might enjoy viewing the rehearsal.

My relationship with the leader of France was complicated. Other English spies had been summarily shot, and yet our family of agents, Harry and Catherine included, was invited to review invasion preparations!

I knew enough to be insulted. Napoleon judged me liable to seduction and meant to win me over by a combination of flattery, reward, and demonstration of France's inevitable victory.

Why he cared about us at all I still didn't understand, but would shortly.

First, though, we witnessed disaster that provided opportunity.

Bonaparte had gone on his daily inspection ride and would return to Boulogne in time for the review in a galloping column of aides, bodyguards, and couriers. We waited for him at a harbor overlook amid a cluster of generals and admirals. The officers kept peeking at my lovely wife and governess while Harry crawled between their boots, impish mischief that they found amusing and I found embarrassing. "Harry, stay with Papa," I'd commanded.

"He has his father's restlessness," Duhèsme observed.

"And willfulness," Catherine said.

The day was humid, pregnant with storm. Word came that Admiral Etienne Eustache Bruix had canceled the maneuver. Bruix was a quietly self-possessed officer as popular with the navy as Napoleon was with the army, and he had a seaman's caution. Black clouds were building to the northeast. We were about to return to our lodging to stay dry when Duhèsme put his hand on my arm.

"Don't leave yet. Napoleon is approaching, and Bruix is as stubborn as the emperor is adamant."

"They don't get along?" Another possible note for my spy book.

"On the contrary, the emperor respects the admiral. But Bonaparte is as impetuous as Bruix is judicious. Napoleon loves to leap aboard boats and be recklessly rowed around the harbor flotilla. In a recent skirmish with the British navy he insisted that he round a point to see the action. Bruix countermanded the order. You can imagine the plight of the sailors, their emperor pointing one direction and their admiral the other. They finally obeyed their own officer, to Bonaparte's fury, and he became even angrier when a boat that ventured where he'd proposed was blown to pieces by English gunnery. There's nothing worse than being proved wrong in front on your entire navy and army. Rather than thank the admiral for saving his life, the Corsican stalked away, seething with anger, and then challenged a gun crew to shoot the bowsprit off a British ship to divert attention from his folly. They actually did so, skipping a cannonball across the water to clip the spar like a twig. The emperor gave the crew some gold pieces. Now he's given a naval order again, and once again Bruix has countermanded it. Let's see what happens."

As he spoke, Napoleon's column rode into town in a blue serpentine line and reined to a halt at our overlook, hooves clacking on cobble. Seated on his gray mare, face flushed from the exertion of riding, the newly elected emperor looked more the hero of the Pyramids and Alps than he'd seemed at the sumptuous ceremony in Paris. His bicorn hat was set to emphasize the width of his shoulders, and under a dusty overcoat a plain green chasseur uniform with two medals again stood out for its martial plainness. He swung off his horse without help, the turbaned Mameluke sentry Roustan keeping a protective eye. Then the emperor strode to a low parapet to survey the harbor.

He'd already achieved a miraculous transformation. Boulogne, formerly a muddy estuary home to a few fishermen, now had a gigantic stone harbor filled with hundreds of boats that were crammed with thousands of soldiers.

Nothing was moving.

Thunder growled, dirt swirled in the wind, and the tails of his officers' coats lifted like bird wings poised for flight.

"Where's my review?" Napoleon held a riding crop in his hand.

"I'm very sorry, sire, but the review can't be held today," Admiral Bruix replied. The two men looked somewhat alike, but while Napoleon was fiery and brittle, Bruix was stolid and calm.

"What?"

"The review cannot be held. We sailors are captives of the weather, and the weather is threatening indeed." He pointed to the thunderheads sweeping down from Belgium. The afternoon sun lit them to imposing blackness, and trees rustled warning.

Napoleon's face also clouded. This was the second time the admiral had publicly countermanded him, and the emperor had become accustomed to sycophantic obedience. His voice rose, pale eyes as cold as a glacier. "You won't carry out my orders?"

"A terrible storm is preparing. Your Majesty must see this as well as I do. Surely you'll not risk the lives of so many brave men unnecessarily?"

The Napoleon I'd met six years before might have yielded at that point. He'd learned from a hasty and stormy landing at Alexandria. But power gave him omnipotence at a time he felt threatened by conspiracies and coups. "Sir, I gave my orders. Again, I ask, why do you not obey them? Their consequence is my affair, and mine only. Obey at once!"

"Sire, I cannot obey."

The rest of us had frozen. Watching a quarrel is never pleasant. Napoleon had rank and temper, but Bruix had experience and pride. The emperor stepped toward the admiral and raised his riding crop.

Bruix stepped back and put his hand on his sword hilt. "Sire, take care!"

Their eyes locked, Bruix firm, Bonaparte volcanic, and then at last the emperor realized the embarrassment a fight would cause and turned away, hurling his crop to the ground. Bruix turned his back, too, trembling, while Napoleon was rigid and fuming. Then Napoleon wheeled and snapped an order to Admiral Charles René Magon de Médine, who jumped at the crack of his voice. "Magon, get the review of boats under way!"

This junior admiral had neither the rank of Bruix nor his respect. He glanced at his naval superior, but the senior wouldn't look at him. Magon had no choice but to obey. "At once, Your Majesty."

Bruix stalked away, shaking with anger.

Signal guns fired. Bugles called. Flags ran up, shuddering in the rising wind. Drums rolled. With shouts, cheers, and soldierly curses, the French invasion boats and barges lumbered away from quay and mooring and began to maneuver claustrophobically between the shore and the line of protective French ships at the harbor mouth, like a nautical ballet in a bathtub. Then with a hard pull of their oars, a line of boats crawled into the Channel proper, like rodents poking out of their hole.

The wind grew chill, and people slipped on cloaks and coats, their hems dancing. The black clouds mounded higher, a dark awning pulled across the sky. Napoleon ignored the approaching gale as if he could will it away by not looking. The sea turned choppy, the blockading British ships were lost in haze, and the rising gusts pushed patterns of gray and silver across the water like spilled paint.

"Ethan, this is madness," Astiza whispered. "How can he be so obstinate?"

"The less sure you are of your authority, the more you try to exercise it. He's emperor now but remembers, even when everyone else forgets, that he was too poor to buy a new uniform little more than a decade ago. In 1792 he pawned his watch to the broker Fauvelet."

"So he proves triumph with idiocy?"

"It isn't the first time great men have done so. When the Persian emperor Xerxes was thwarted by a storm when crossing the Dardanelles, he lashed the waves with whips."

For one last moment the review played out as intended. Boat flags stuttered spritely in the wind.

Oars dipped with synchronized precision, the splashes confirming months of practice. Troops sat with muskets erect, fixed bayonets shining. A hundred cannons fired blank salutes.

Then the gale fully struck.

We snatched at our hats. The wind hit like a wall, buffeting the high command, and dust and leaves whirled. There was a boom of cacophonous thunder and lightning blazed overhead, lifting strands of hair from Astiza's and Catherine's necks. Bonaparte cursed like a corporal. Then rain shot sideways, and the harbor was lost to view.

We could faintly hear shouts and cries of alarm over the roar of wind and rain. Most of the army generals ran for nearby houses, but the admirals and captains dashed toward the water to help. Napoleon, to his credit, ran with them.

"Take Harry to our rooms," I told the women. "I'm going to lend a hand."

The harbor had turned white with foam. Scores of invasion boats scudded before the wind with infantrymen shouting in terror. The furthermost were pushed parallel to the Channel beaches. Napoleon ran along the shore after them, his aides and bodyguards strung behind. I ran, too, matching the bodyguard Roustan pace for pace, and both of us caught up with France's ruler at the same time. We'd passed the quays and were on a sand and shale beach where surf boiled, the men at sea pulling frantically for land.

As the boats reached the breakers the invasion craft began to flip, spilling hundreds of men into cold water.

Other sailors were dragging down skiffs that could be used as lifeboats. Napoleon ran for one. Was he mad?

Roustan, turban soaked and mustache streaming, tried to restrain the emperor, who shook him off. "We must get them out of that!" With surprising agility he leaped into a lifeboat like a hurdler clearing a fence, stunning the sailors with his sudden appearance and famous hat. "Row, row, to rescue those soldiers!" I leaped aboard, too, not thinking of anything but to try to save lives. I'm a better swimmer than most. Roustan stood helplessly on shore. He couldn't swim at all.

We made perhaps twenty yards before a huge comber crashed down on our lifeboat, filling it with water. We foundered. The water was just as freezing as when Catherine and I landed near Biville, and I felt the familiar sting of salt in my nostrils as our craft went under. As we sank we were buffeted by surf. I reached to grab Bonaparte's coat collar.

I could have had revenge in that instant. Hold Napoleon under the sea, punch his gut to make him suck in water, and an emperor's death would be blamed on his own folly and obstinacy, with no risk to my family or me. I might even wrangle a medal by pretending I'd attempted a rescue instead.

Yet I couldn't bring myself to do it, which suggests I would make a poor assassin. Murder wasn't my style. When lightning turned the sea surface into a golden mirror and showed which way was up, I hauled the ruler of France with me. Napoleon had the swimming skills of a Corsican boy. We broke for air, gasping.

"The damned coat," he choked. We sank with its weight. I helped pull his arms free of the sleeves and it fell away. Then I seized his uniform jacket and kicked upward again, breaking to the surface. The surf, fortunately, pounded us toward land.

One moment we were alone, struggling against drowning, and the next twenty pairs of arms reached to drag Napoleon onto shore. I was left to my own devices, which was just as well since the rescuers were half trampling their emperor in their zeal to save him. I staggered out of the water and numbly fell upon the beach to spit and gasp. Hundreds of other capsized men were also crawling from the waves, while scores of drowned bodies floated like driftwood logs.

It was the disastrous landing at Alexandria all over again.

For several minutes Napoleon stood bent, with his hands on his knees, sucking great shuddering breaths as chaos continued around him. A blanket was thrown across his shoulders. Someone handed him a flask of brandy. He took a swig, coughed, and straightened. His hat had disappeared, the sea pasting his thinning hair to his forehead. He looked out at the Channel with grim fury. Then he snapped an order. "Fires for the survivors."

Any normal ruler would have retreated to his bedroom at that point. Bonaparte did not. He began striding up and down the sand, shouting commands, and erected order in his wake. A more systematic rescue was organized. Some of the hundreds of dead, their faces bleached of color and eyes wide from the drowning, were dragged out of sight. Beach fires flared and shivering survivors huddled around them. As night fell the bonfires helped orient the helmsmen, and most of the boats eventually made it back to shore intact. Twenty did not, however. The waves pounded them to fragments.

Bonaparte spotted me, gave a nod of acknowledgment, and offered me his flask. The brandy was welcome heat.

"Go to your wife, American. You've witnessed enough catastrophe for one evening."

"And Your Majesty?"

"A soaking for my body. A worse pounding for my pride. Go."

So I did, but then he called after me.

"Gage? Thank you for saving my life. The ledger of accounts between us is getting complicated, is it not?"

"More than you know."

"And more to come. We'll talk soon."

I learned later that Napoleon didn't leave the beach until dawn, his clothes crusted with sand, salt, and bonfire smoke. Sunrise revealed horror. The smashed remains of the capsized boats and drowned corpses marked the high-tide line.

By official French count, fifty men needlessly drowned. Duhèsme told me privately the toll was actually two hundred, and the British would publish accounts claiming twice that. And this had been a summer storm in a harbor! What would happen to these elite legions when they tried to row across the entire Channel?

Two final things washed ashore.

One was a half-frozen drummer boy, kept afloat by his drum. He lived.

Another was Napoleon's bicorn hat.

Every soldier in Boulogne applauded the emperor's courage. And every soldier muttered that the disaster was a bad omen for an invasion.

For me, the event had a different outcome. "It is even more imperative that I see you and your wife," Napoleon wrote two days later. "My pavilion, at ten o'clock tomorrow, very precisely."

I decided not to be late.

Chapter 12

The Big Box had a floor of black enamel, silver wall-paper, and an azure ceiling painted with a golden eagle hurling thunderbolts at England. No wonder the French were interested in flying machines; Napoleon could be inspired by the idea every time he tilted his head. There was also a large oval conference table covered by felt cloth like a green England. A huge map of the Channel hung on one wall, and there was an ink-stand with sheets of paper and quill pens cut ready for use, should Bonaparte need to dictate an order.

Pasques pushed Astiza and me through the pavilion door and took up sentry duty outside with the body-guard Roustan. We'd been searched for weapons.

The new emperor was standing at a window, feet planted, hands clasped behind his back, to stare into the Atlantic haze toward Britain. His uniform coat was his favorite chasseur green again this day, boots bright as obsidian, and vest buttoned tight across his stomach. The foul weather had at least temporarily scrubbed away the habitual yellow pallor that new acquaintances commented on, giving him a ruddy flush of health. He turned and smiled, reminding me how capable he was of mercurial charm. "Ethan, my savior! And your lovely wife. Welcome."

We'd left Harry with Catherine, the two planning to stroll the port boatyard. My son liked to watch the men hammer and saw, and the comtesse enjoyed the glances and catcalls of brawny carpenters.

"I'm honored, sire." I suppose an American should have sought a democratic alternative to such honorifics as "sire" and "majesty," but I no longer knew what else to call my old friend and enemy. Since I well remembered the crunch of the guillotine blade, I'd call him anything he liked, until either he was dead or I was a safe ocean away.

"The honor is mine. You saved me from the surf." He addressed my wife. "I made a fool of myself, I know."

The confession had the intended effect of thawing her. "You cannot fight heaven," Astiza said.

"It's stubbornness I must master. From my will comes success, but it also tempts danger." He turned to me. "I find it very odd, Gage, how you circulate in and out of my life to cause trouble and then rescue. I'm inclined to suspect you're a Little Red Man yourself."

Napoleon had a firm belief that a peculiar French gnome unpredictably appeared in the night to make murky forecasts of his future. He was as superstitious as the black rebels of Saint-Domingue, scoffing at religion one moment and crossing himself the next.

"Just an American trying to make my way with my family."

"And a spy." He said it matter-of-factly.

"For both sides." I shrugged as though this were the normal state of affairs, even though my heart hammered.

"Yes, the perfidious British. Why are you working for that devil Sidney Smith again?" He sounded genuinely puzzled.

Since Napoleon was in my debt for saving him from the surf, there was no better time for the truth. "I feared I'd lost Astiza in a hurricane. A renegade French policeman with your secret tattoo blamed you for the circumstances that put us all there. I wanted revenge, and the British offered a way to achieve it. Except that it turns out my wife miraculously survived."

"Blamed me?" He struck a pose of injured innocence but also seemed amused, as if the suggestion that he could influence anything was absurd. This from a man who had cut down a Paris mob with grapeshot, abandoned an army in Egypt, and tried to reinstate slavery in his colonies.

So why not make the accusation and hear his defense, since I seemed to have little aptitude as an assassin? "The former policeman Leon Martel said it was your idea to steal my son and hold him for ransom. He said you knew about an emerald I'd found, and used it and my boy to manipulate me to search for an Aztec secret of flight."

Bonaparte looked genuinely puzzled. "Ethan, I'm trying to govern a large, intractable nation surrounded by ruthless enemies. Employ you, yes. Extort you through the theft of your son? *Mon Dieu!* I've no time for kidnapping children. I truly have no idea what you're babbling about. Come, we're old campaigners. Remember the Alps?"

I was sweating from making accusations to a powerful man. "I know what I heard. He made you a monster. I called him a liar, and he called me naive."

"Did he, while wearing my tattoo?" He wasn't in a rage at my accusation, so he wanted something. "And do you have the golden pendant I gave you?" He knew the answer, of course, since I'd already shown it to Réal.

I brought the trinket out. There was the *N*, for Napoleon, circled by a wreath. "It's proved useful at times," I admitted. "I saved it through a hurricane."

I didn't tell him I'd ripped it from my wife's throat to cast aside in the ocean, and that it had floated unbidden back into my pocket.

"Saved a monster's pendant? Perhaps you weren't sure this renegade policeman was telling the truth. Perhaps, Gage, I don't have time to make plots with henchmen I've never heard of. I thought you were helping me make the bargain for Louisiana. The next thing I know, you're missing for months and then reported hiding in Paris as a British spy. It makes no sense."

Should I believe his denial? Maybe he really didn't know of Martel's manipulation of my family. Maybe he did but hadn't played a direct role. Maybe Martel had exaggerated events in order to torment me, and divert blame from himself. Or maybe, like so many things in our histories, the entire scheme was one more misfire on all sides. In payback I'd broken into a prison, helped win a slave revolt that robbed France of its richest colony, and sent Martel to hell, so by that measure accounts were settled. Napoleon was ambitious, I was an adventurer, and our relationship was a complicated mess of debts, appreciations, and slights.

"Neither did it make sense to save you from drowning," I said, "but I did so, even after your order forcing my family to come here. An order that makes no sense, either. You're emperor. Why do you need us in Boulogne?"

"I need every soldier you can see from these windows. And I invited you here to explain our cause and get you and Astiza to help. France is going to win, Ethan, and when it does the world will be a better place, unshackled from moribund royals and medieval prejudices. Parliaments and Congresses don't work. You can't get two ambitious rascals to agree, let alone two hundred. But a single great man of ability, not birth, can accomplish something! I mean to allow trade between all nations, instill public instruction, open Jewish ghettos, reform the courts, and build canals and bridges. Does that sound like a monster to you?"

I have cheek I learned from him. "Accomplished at the point of a bayonet."

He barked a laugh. "What an idealist you've become, gambler and scamp! You know as well as I that it's only by bayonet that *anything* gets done. But my bayonets are propelled by ideas. I worry about newspapers, philosophers, politicians, and, yes, spies, but only because they influence opinion. And I worry about opinion only because I need it to accomplish my task on earth, which is to turn slogan into law and mobs into armies. So: I could have you shot in an instant for treachery, but instead, I invite you here to consult, observe, and, if you wish, pass on the truth to the British. I'm a general, yes, but a man of peace forced into war."

"With a hundred thousand men," I persisted.

"Two hundred thousand by next year, and the boats to carry them. All to end, once and for all, a contest that has dragged on for centuries. The British have tried to assassinate me a dozen times, Gage. They're implacable and conspiratorial, a cabal of cowardly plotters who buy Austrians and Russians to do their fighting for them. England is a wretched nation of shopkeepers, a global bully, and the world will be better when France scrubs their grubby island clean as the Normans did in 1066. Tell me, what's the name of that water out there?" He pointed out the window.

I was puzzled by the question. "The English Channel."

"No, Ethan. La Manche, the Sleeve, the name given by France, and yet the world sees it as the property of the English. Soon that will change. My own generals are skeptics, but the reason I'm emperor and they are not is that I have the vision to imagine a better world, while they have the perspective of pygmies."

"You do understand that Sidney Smith has a different view." My tone was dry. Every nation edits history, and no one likes to be called a pygmy.

"I understand that as a neutral you see both sides, which only confuses you." He moved to look at the map. "And I understand that in your adventures with this Martel, who has completely disappeared"—he cast a glance in my direction—"you did find an Aztec artifact that looks like some kind of mechanical bird."

"I don't think it's of practical use."

"Show it."

So I took the curious object out. A helmeted man on a delta-shaped machine, but with no detail on how it might work. The solid gold was heavy and smooth. I handed it over. Good men had died to retrieve it.

Napoleon rubbed the ornament with his fingers. "A pretty toy."

"Maybe they did fly, but I think you'd have to find the actual machine to copy them, not this representation. To learn from this is like trying to build a Napoleon from the image on a Legion of Honor medal."

He smiled at the analogy. "Is there a different place we should search?"

"This came from an underwater cave, but there were no other clues. Maybe the Spanish know more in Mexico."

"Perhaps I should ally with Spain." He handed it back. "Men are beginning to dream of flight. Have you heard of an English inventor named Cayley?"

I was sweating again. Did he know of our insane escape from Fort de Joux? "Never heard of him," I lied.

"He's trying to emulate birds. Well." Napoleon looked at me skeptically. "Show this to my savants; maybe it will inspire them to leap the Channel. In the meantime, I want to put you all to more immediate work."

"All?"

"Confer with Duhèsme this summer on skirmishing tactics. I know you're not an officer, but you've observed fighting prowess from the Mamelukes to Red Indians. You're worldly, and you can share some of that wisdom with my officers."

"Betraying England." It's damn hard feeling noble about yourself while working for both sides, and I felt like a fly in a European web, trying to negotiate my way under constantly changing circumstances. I admired Napoleon, and feared him. Smith was my ally, but England was America's frequent foe. I needed a chart to sort my sentiments out.

"Hardly. Send them coded letters from inside our camp about exactly what we're doing. Emphasize the quality of our regiments, which I'm certain you'll find impressive. Confirm my popularity, which will be repaired from the recent gale. We simply ask to read your letters first, and suggest amendments that might make Britain sue for peace."

Napoleon took pride in finding the special utility of each man, and each man's weakness. He took comfort in judging me an opportunistic scoundrel because he was one himself. Napoleon liked me because he thought I was so incorrigible that I couldn't judge him.

But I'd changed. Mostly.

I cleared my throat. "Advise Duhèsme for how long?"

"A month or two, and then back to Paris to confer with my savants. Monge, you know; he continues to improve my artillery. I fired a monster mortar myself the other day."

"Your hearing has recovered?"

He ignored this. "The mining engineer Mathieu has proposed we dig a tunnel to England. My adjutant Quatremère Disjonual has proposed we train dolphins to carry sharpshooters across the Channel, or infiltrate saboteurs by diving bells."

I didn't say anything of my own diving bell experience.

"Jean-Charles Thilorier," he went on, "has an idea for gigantic balloons."

"Franklin had the same notion."

"All I want is your habitual skepticism, married to your considerable imagination. Your mind works in strange ways. The notion that men flew in ancient times makes it possible we'll fly again. Share your bauble with my scientists."

Since I constantly question my own worth, I am susceptible to flattery. We all wish to be useful. I glanced at Astiza, who had an expression of careful neutrality. She was more suspicious of the Corsican and yet said nothing, because she was still wondering why she was here at all.

"I'm hard-pressed," I said, to say something. "Réal mentioned a salary?"

He waved his hand. "Yes, yes, you're on his payroll—take up the details with him. I'll give you a letter testifying to your mission."

"I appreciate your confidence, Your . . . Majesty."

"I'm not confident in you at all, Gage, but you have a knack for strange success." He rubbed his hands. "Now, your royalist conspirator, Catherine Marceau, must also work for me if she wishes to live. She doesn't have to betray her friends, but I want her to advise on my coronation to give it royalist endorsement. The whole point is to demonstrate that my ascension can never be reversed, and so its symbolism must include the reintegration of royalist émigrés like her. I understand Marceau is a student of fashion, so she can confer on gowns and protocol. Do you think she'll be willing?"

"She loves opulence. As long as you can persuade her that she has no choice but to work on your coronation, what you're proposing will entirely seduce her."

"Good. Now, the most important member of your triad is your wife. And how do you regard me, my dear?"

"Competent, but too quick to risk your men." She glanced at the shore. The girl is honest to a fault, as I've said.

He colored. "You began our relationship by shooting at me in Egypt."

"And you killed my Alexandrian master with a cannon blast."

"You and I are not so different, madame; we are both fond of the desert. If the entire world was land, not water, I couldn't be stopped. But the sea frustrates me."

"Controlled by gods instead of men."

"Controlled by weather: we're not in the Dark Ages. Yet from our blustery beginnings, Astiza, things can only improve, no? Was I really so bad for Egypt?"

"A better question is whether Egypt was bad for you. You fled when you could."

"I didn't flee, I was called to duty by the plight of France. And you ask that of me, a Corsican? I'm not a man confined by borders. Perhaps I'll return to Egypt someday. In any event, my invasion there is history, and it is because of history that I've asked you here." He straightened to emphasize he was brisk and commanding, but he was still only her height. "You're a historian. I understand you've been frustrated in getting access to archives in Paris."

She was surprised. "You know about that?"

"My agents haven't just followed you, they've thwarted you, because I was wary of what you were searching for. I remember the Book of Thoth and your skills as a scholar." He glanced at me. "Yes, Ethan, I learn everything, and forget nothing." Then, to her. "But now I promise unlimited access to the records of church, state, and university—if you do something for me in return."

"Sire?" She used the word before thinking about it.

"Have you heard of the Brazen Head of Albertus Magnus?"

Astiza was cautious, but not surprised. "A very odd legend. The machine was destroyed by Saint Thomas Aquinas, according to the same stories."

"Perhaps." He began to pace in front of the bank of windows, lines of troops marching far below like blue centipedes.

"The Brazen Head?" I interrupted. "What the devil is that?"

"Tell your husband, madame."

She was looking at Napoleon warily, and replied slowly. "Albertus was a Dominican friar who lived in the thirteenth century," she began.

"About 1200 to 1280," Napoleon put in, pacing back and forth.

"He was a German, educated in Italy, who came from Cologne to Paris, and became the foremost scholar of his age. Albert was appointed chair of theology at Saint James. Like many learned men he sought the Philosopher's Stone, that alchemist's grail with the reputed power to turn lead into gold and grant immortality. He never found it. But unlike others, he didn't just yearn, he built. Legend says he spent thirty years constructing a manlike figure that could speak."

"The Brazen Head," Napoleon said. "A mechanical head made of brass. Not so different from the clever automatons craftsmen make today, which seem to talk, eat, or play chess. Except those are toys, and this was not."

"Some say Albertus Magnus built an entire body," Astiza went on, "and one account holds that it was made of iron, not brass, and was called the Iron Man.

Still others contend it was wood. About eighty years ago, a new name was suggested for this being: An 'android.'"

"By Samuel Johnson's dictionary, what does that mean?" I asked.

"It's coined from Greek, meaning 'in the likeness of man,'" she said.

"How do you know all this?"

"Ethan, it's what I do." She addressed Napoleon. "Your agents told you I was attempting to research that subject."

"Yes, and I became intrigued," the emperor replied.

"The Brazen Head was designed not just to talk and possibly walk, but—according to legend—to answer peculiar questions."

"Questions about the future. It could forecast events."

She cocked her head, as intrigued by the emperor's curiosity as he was by hers. I have a bad habit of being jealous, and that prickly emotion stabbed again. "But legend says Albert's protégé, Thomas Aquinas, was horrified and destroyed the android," she said. "He thought the machine infused with Satan. No one can truly know the future, he said, or should know."

"But wait," I objected. "You try to see the future all the time."

Napoleon smiled. "As do I. Predicting the future is what makes us human. No other creature records its history, tries to learn from it, and anticipates what might come next. I want a reliable fortune-teller of my own: not a sideshow charlatan but a real machine of uncanny accuracy. Can you imagine knowing disaster before it occurs, and avoiding it? Or knowing of fortune before it occurs, and investing?"

I agreed with Thomas Aquinas: this was wicked. "Surely no such thing ever existed."

"Just like the Mirror of Archimedes or the Book of Thoth never existed." He watched me.

Since I'd found both those things, and Thor's Hammer besides, I understood Napoleon's real reason for offering alliance. He didn't want sharpshooting tips. He wanted my expertise, or luck, as a treasure hunter. He wanted us to find this Brazen Head, just as he'd wanted an Aztec flying machine. My wife said the head had been destroyed. But she clearly didn't believe so, or she'd never have researched it to begin with.

"We're hundreds of years too late, aren't we?" I tried.

"Perhaps," Napoleon said mildly. "Or perhaps it wasn't burned but instead secreted in a castle deep in Austrian territory."

"And you want us to get this devil's tool for you."

"Just locate it, my armies will do the rest."

"In the Austrian Empire?"

"Looking into the future, again."

His army was pointed west, not east. Had I learned something of importance for Smith? Or, knowing me a spy, was Napoleon misdirecting me? "But a machine that predicts the future would give you unprecedented advantage."

"Put to unprecedented good use." *A man wrapped up in himself makes a very small bundle*, Franklin had remarked.

"No, this is another of your goose chases," I said. "You're as mad as Sidney Smith. The Brazen Head? How could Albertus construct such a thing? And even if he did, why would we find it for you?"

"To avoid the massacre of your own family." He walked to plop down in the sole chair, a portable wooden one with a green cushion. His threat was given plainly, without drama, as something so obvious as not to require repeating. His level tone emphasized his power more than a shout would have done, and his lack of emotion was as cold as a bayonet. "To solve a scholarly puzzle, which your wife loves to do. But most important, Gage, to cement your own place in history."

"I don't want a place in history. People who do have a tendency to be dead."

"If I know the future I can outmaneuver my enemies and defeat them without war. You will end this
conflict by helping me checkmate the British and their
European allies with perfect foresight and, by so doing,
save thousands and thousands of lives." He set his fists
on the green table. "If the android of Albert the Great
still exists, we're going to find it, harness it, and usher
in a glorious new age of unity in Europe. Under my
leadership." His look was commanding. "Tell Sidney
Smith anything you like about my army in Boulogne,
but this is a mission you will keep from him, on pain
of death." He stood again, restless as a rabbit, and
addressed my wife. "I was defeated by the sea, but the
response to any defeat is a different attack. Come see
my legion ceremony if you doubt *my* future, Ethan.
And then attend my coronation, both of you. Your governess should make it quite a show."

Chapter 13

Three weeks after his disastrous swamping of boats in the summer storm, Napoleon restored morale with a gigantic Presentation of the Crosses, a larger repeat of the ceremony I'd witnessed in Paris. This time expansion of the Legion of Honor would occur outdoors so that England could watch as well as France.

The rest of my household had already returned to Paris. Astiza left with letters of recommendation to begin researching in earnest. Catherine departed to excitedly consult on the coronation even while protesting that she did so under duress, "to protect little Horus." My son said good-bye with tears in his eyes. He cried not so much from leaving me as for having to trade the excitement of tramping soldiers for the company of women. I presented him with a miniature drum, and he rattled it mournfully as Pasques boarded the coach to escort my family out of camp. Harry had the instincts of an adventurer, and I was pleased and appalled that at age four he was taking after his father.

Lingering in the Boulogne camp, I consulted with Duhèsme on skirmish tactics and had fun with an antique crossbow he conjured, "So you can play Red Indian." I decided it could theoretically work from ambush to slay an enemy scout silently, but was otherwise too cumbersome, slow, and short-ranged. David's sling could still slay Goliath, too, but I wouldn't equip a regiment with that weapon.

I also toured the shipyards. Napoleon said crossing the Channel was but a jump, and yet without naval superiority the task was impossible. Even if the French controlled the water for a week or two, they had to transport not only a huge army, but all its powder, shot, food, and horses. England's beaches were fronted by shoals, fringed by cliffs, and pounded by waves, and reports came back that its government had enlisted tens of thousands of militia to defend its shores. British authorities were constructing a string of Martello towers to give warning, and laid plans to drive away all the livestock and burn all grain.

French generals were confident of the outcome of any battle, but skeptical of the chances of getting one.

La Manche might be tantalizingly narrow, but it was still a tide-wracked, stormy moat.

The soldiers were drilled incessantly to avoid boredom, and found the usual ways of amusing themselves between marches. Besides making visits to tent brothels and gambling dens, they scavenged for food, forcing Bonaparte to distribute a steady stream of gold to complaining farmers. His troops also did their best to seduce farmers' daughters, dueled illegally in copses of trees, and had rowdy rowing competitions in which the chief object was hurling buckets of water at one another.

The troops were frequently entertained by troupes of actors imported from the Comédie-Francaise. The men also put on their own productions, playing female parts as well as male. At frequent dances, the soldiers took turns in the woman's role, a handkerchief tied to their heads identifying them as "ladies."

Their most popular game was loto, a simple contest of matching announced numbers on a card that even near illiterates could play. Bouts were made more competitive by giving each number a colorful name such as "the little chicken" for number two and "the gallows" for number seven, all the way up to eighty-nine. Players with faulty memory who called out the wrong name were penalized with great hilarity.

Regiments formed choirs and bands that sang and played in noisy competition. The faithful marched to the local fisherman's chapels on Sunday. While some soldiers plagued civilians, others repaired churches, schools, and roads. England's small army was a criminal depository kept in line with the lash. France's conscripted force boasted educated men of the middle class. Officers had chess clubs, philosophic societies, and astronomy lectures. There is always more song and laughter in French camps than English or Prussian ones.

I enjoy this masculine company but periodically sought solitude. I was flattered one day while out on a picnic and saw a young redheaded woman on a horse picking her way toward me on a bluff trail overlooking the Channel. I was seated with bread and cheese and guessed even at a quarter mile that the approaching rider was pretty.

She rode to me and reined up: a Norman *fille* with hair like flame, a dusting of freckles, and a saucy look. She wore riding boots, gloves, and had a small pistol tucked in her waistband.

I stood. *"Bonjour, mademoiselle."*

"Good King Louis," she replied in English.

I was startled, accustomed as I was to speaking French. Then I remembered the password on the beach

where we landed. "By the grace of God may he reign."
An English spy?

She slid from her horse and reverted to French. "My
name is Rose, monsieur, and I've deliberately followed
you here."

"Mademoiselle, it's dangerous to talk to me."

"Yes, the famed Ethan Gage, collaborator with generals and emperors. I've been admiring your ability to
insert yourself into high places. No one understands
how you do it."

"It would be more correct to say I'm inserted,
sometimes against my will. They think me useful."
Sometimes modesty works with women, not that I had
anything to work, being married and all. "And you
are . . ."

"A rare survivor in a conspiracy gone to ruin.
I provide help for agents traveling between Paris
and the coast, and socialize with the officers here.
Sometimes men tell a woman things they'd withhold
from a man."

"I can see why."

"I've taken the risk to tell you two things, Ethan
Gage."

"Would you share some wine first?"

She shook her head. "First, you may encounter an
opportunity to affect history more than you think possible. Many people are watching you."

Was this a trap or test? For all I knew, this woman was Réal's agent, not Smith's. "That's rather vague."

"Second, your mission may someday require you to escape from Paris and France in a hurry. If you do so, go to the Inn of the Three Boars in Argenteuil and ask for the cook. Without anyone seeing, present him with a rose. A dried one will do. I will come, and I will help."

"But how do I know to trust you?"

"When desperate, you have no choice. Don't worry, monsieur, I've helped many travelers before you. Play along with the Bonapartists, but strike for Louis." She clicked her tongue to beckon her horse and swung back into the saddle.

"Wait, please. Have some cheese. Let's start a friendship, at least."

"Friends are dangerous, and lovers can be deadly. You'll not see me again until you have great need. But I was told to tell you one more thing in case you doubted my sincerity."

"What's that?"

"The Chiswicks have filed suit against your money." And with that, this "Rose" gave a little kick and trotted off.

Damnation. Which side was I on, again?

Napoleon understood that men are led by example and inspiration, and so the ceremony of August 16 was designed to restore the mantle of invincibility that had been dented by the drownings. The day picked was the anniversary of the repulsion of British Admiral Horatio Nelson from Boulogne three years before. The place was a natural amphitheater, a swale near the town that swooped down to low bluffs and the sea. At cliff's edge, a stage was built to hold throne and banners, the emperor facing France but so near the precipice that British captains could watch from spyglasses offshore.

Streamers bearing the names of French victories fluttered, flags flapped, and new regimental standards topped by polished brass eagles shone like torches. A loose phalanx of several hundred opulently uniformed officers surrounded Napoleon. His Imperial Guard in imposing bearskin hats was drawn up around this assembly, the ranks taut as a bowstring and their bayonets a silver picket fence. To one side regimental bands combined to create blaring music, banging away at anthems such as "La Victoire Est à Nous," and "Veillons au Salut de l'Empire." On the other, two thousand drums provided a thunderous roll. How little Harry would have loved this show! From his perch Napoleon could turn right to see the neat avenues of his vast camps and Boulogne harbor. To his left he could look up the coast and across the Channel to England.

One hundred thousand infantry in full dress uniform jammed the amphitheater's bowl, with tens of thousands of cavalry poised in the wings to clop by on cue. Field guns were parked hub to hub, barrels gleaming. Uphill of the soldiers were tens of thousands of civilian spectators like myself. The men smoked, drank, and played amateur general from camp chairs. Ladies sipped cider in shady white tents or strolled the perimeter with parasols.

I looked for flame-haired Rose but didn't see her.

The ceremony began at midday with a thunderous salute from the coastal batteries. As the shots echoed away the Corsican was lent celestial help by the skies parting to let down beams of light, as if God were stage lighting the army. The Channel wind rose to make banners snap and whitecaps dance. "Napoleon weather," men whispered, forgetting the storm of a few weeks before. A choreographed review of regiments began.

All of us gasped and murmured; even I, the jaded Ethan, understood again the dangerous allure of war. It gives men an excuse to dress up, to carouse as boys, and to make friends through shared hardship. The brilliant splendor gives pathos to the inevitable destruction and turns the plod of life to poignant tragedy. Men will kill and be killed to escape boredom. War is also a way to arrest the tendency of the rich getting richer and the poor poorer; the looting redistributes wealth to the ruffians of the infantry. Gambling does the same, both more efficiently than taxes.

Napoleon stood, two thousand drums beat a charge, and the columns marched and reformed with mechanical precision. I didn't detect a single misstep. Then the noise and marching stopped, noise grumbling away, and Bonaparte began speaking. I couldn't hear his words but was told the emperor was reciting the oath of the Legion. When he finished, there was a roar of *"Vive l'empereur!"* so volcanic that it hurt my ears.

Next, thousands of new medals with Napoleon's image were carried out for presentation. They were heaped on the medieval shields and helmets of French heroes like shoals of Spanish doubloons. The recipients filed forward, hundreds and hundreds of them, to receive the honor individually from his hand. I was told he greeted each by name and achievement in a procession that took hours.

How easily are we seduced by pomp and glory! Women wept, civilians lifted their hats, and soldiers roared themselves hoarse. To complete the triumph, the rising wind forced the English ships to beat farther offshore, providing an opening for a sailing convoy of supply from Le Havre that was six months overdue.

The weather that had betrayed Napoleon before was his ally this day.

I found myself unexpectedly invited to his Pavilion for the celebratory banquet when the columns finally marched away. I was seated at the smallest and farthest of the tables. Men looked curiously at me, and there were murmurs that I was a great and ruthless spy, an idea I did nothing to discourage. The room was set with linen, silver, flowers, and paper regimental flags. Toasts were raised so often that all of us got drunk. The coastal artillery continued to boom salutes, the setting sun ducked in and out of clouds, and fireworks came at dusk, the exploding stars promising eventual victory. The scent of gunpowder blew back over the beaches and filled the room with its smell.

How odd to celebrate a man whom I knew believed in gnomes, shot at his wife's swans, pinched ears like his Corsican mother, and whom I'd seen in his bath and in bed with his wife. So ordinary, so extraordinary! The writer Goethe had put to poetry last year the tale of the Pied Piper of Hamelin, and now France followed its own piper like those German children. Maybe all future kings will be in Napoleon's mold, rising from obscurity to make their ambition that of their nation. Stature will come not from birth but from pageantry, men staking their lives on political opera. Truth will be defined by illusion. People will rally around lies.

We filed to go out, congratulating the emperor, and I gave him my hand in a daze of wonderment, apprehension, and calculation. This Brazen Head: did it really exist and, if so, was it something we should find and control to keep it from misuse, like the Book of Thoth from my earlier adventures? Could Rose be trusted? Did I belong with France or England?

"My star is ascending, Ethan," Napoleon told me quietly, grasping my hand in both of his own. "Do not betray me." His bright gray eyes had seduced every man in the room.

"I'm dazzled, Your Majesty." This was true, though that didn't mean I wanted him to succeed. "I'll return to Paris to consult with your savants."

"Listen. You are ever the outsider, so become part of France. Surrender to history. The feeling is electric."

He meant surrender to him. "I envy your rise."

He nodded, and then suddenly flashed that soldierly smile. He could be as earthy as his soldiers. "Don't envy me too much. The worst thing about these ceremonies is that you can't break for a piss, and I have had to hold my bladder for four hours!"

Chapter 14

So I returned to Paris as a dubious double agent, armed with the Jaeger rifle and ancient crossbow. Both fascinated Harry. I continued to leave reports for Smith in the Saint-Sulpice confessional without police interference. It was unlikely that anything I reported would frighten the British to sue for peace, but my cooperation with Napoleon allowed me to stay in the capital until the emperor's formal coronation. As usual I got no reply from my English spymasters, and no money, either. Réal's police had destroyed royalist communication, allowing my missives to go out but nothing to come in.

As compensation, we now had a French stipend. My wife plunged more deeply into her studies in the archives. And Catherine, our ardent royalist dedicated to Napoleon's overthrow, seemed more than willing to help with the winter's coronation, since I'd persuaded her we had no choice. She came back from a meeting with Josephine positively giddy at her brush with celebrity. "I can spy from inside their family!" she justified.

The latest gossip was that Napoleon's sisters had refused to carry Josephine's coronation train and didn't relent until their brother threatened to cut them off. More than pride was at stake; the coronation would put Josephine ahead of the emperor's blood relatives in honor and inheritance. Napoleon was also replacing the fleur-de-lis, the lily symbol of French royalty, with the bee, emblematic of his own industry and hive-like order.

"He says the Invalides presentation in July was entirely inadequate, and that he wants a coronation more magnificent than any in history," Catherine reported. "No expense is being spared. The coronation costumes for the royal couple will each exceed one hundred thousand francs. The jeweler for the crowns is Marguerite, with Nitot jealous he's contracted for lesser ornaments. There are companies and platoons of costumers, tailors, and embroiderers. Nuremburg, Aix-la-Chapelle, and Saint-Denis all offered what they claimed was Charlemagne's original sword, so to avoid choosing one and insulting the others, Napoleon is having a new one made. The planned music consumes 17,738 pages, and if every oath, prayer, and hymn that people propose is offered, the coronation will last until the Second Coming."

She gave these breathless reports with censor and envy. "Napoleon has had dolls made of the invited dignitaries, and he and his wife move them around on a plan of Notre Dame like toy soldiers."

"Astiza and I kept our shipboard wedding simple. A scrap of sail for a bridal train and 'Yankee Doodle' as wedding march."

The comtesse shuddered. "I'd seek annulment. Or stab you in your sleep."

Both women were so busy that more of Harry's care fell to me. I was proud that even at four he could puzzle out some words in books, convinced that his genius reflected the supple seed of his father. All parents hope their children will prove, in the face of contradictory evidence, the brilliance of themselves.

I met again the mathematician Gaspard Monge, who'd made himself an expert on cannon and who lightened and simplified the French artillery train. Monge was one of many savants employed in state service. While Fulton's experimental steamboat sat abandoned on the Seine and his submarine rested at the bottom of Tripoli harbor, resulting in the American decamping for England, different French schemes were being pushed to dig tunnels under the Channel or lay a pontoon bridge across it. Another proposal was to drift in vast "floating forts" that would fight off English ships with stupendous batteries of artillery. I was directed to contact Jean-Charles Thilorier, who proposed balloons that could lift three thousand men and horses.

It was at the end of September that I introduced myself to Thilorier with a letter from Napoleon's staff that described me as a Franklin protégé, expert in electricity, military consultant, and scholar of Aztec flying machines. I showed him the gold model.

"It clearly shows the ancients were masters of the air," he told me. He turned it about. "Unless this is merely one of their gods, like a winged Mercury. Or a bird. Or an insect. Or a child's toy. Or something entirely else altogether."

"The ancients did do a poor job of leaving explanatory notes."

"Was the past more advanced than the present, in your opinion, Monsieur Gage?"

"One would hope so. And that the future is not even further downhill."

"You and I are men of tomorrow, so we must invent devices to make life better, not worse."

"I'm not sure aerial machines will accomplish that."

"Perhaps your electricity?"

"It will get hair to stand on end, and can make a magnet out of a spike wrapped with electrical wire. I invented an electric sword, but it was the devil to keep powered. It's difficult to see how electricity will ever be practical, though it's great fun at dinner parties. I smack the ladies with an electric kiss."

He looked at me warily. "Perhaps we'll have more practical success with balloons. Here's my idea: why spend hundreds of million of francs trying to defeat the English navy when we might fly over it? If we simply scale up existing hydrogen balloons, I calculate we could transport a regiment at a time. Wait for a favorable wind, hoist them aloft, and descend on London."

"So long as the wind doesn't shift and carry them out into the Atlantic."

"If they landed anywhere in Britain, they'd cause chaos. The first step, of course, is to test the idea with smaller models. Can you help?"

"My son can load them with lead soldiers."

I learned that an aeronautical device that looks logical on paper can prove maddeningly difficult in practice. Even on calm days our experiments tended to drift unpredictably. One ran into a church tower, and another exploded in a bright ball of flame from a cause we never discovered. A line broke on a third balloon, its basket tilted, and Harry's toy soldiers tumbled out in a distressing dribble that extended across three cow pastures. I spent an afternoon helping him look for his little army. He still cried when seven stayed missing. Astiza decided she didn't want my son around eccentric inventors and kept him with her.

Next, Thilorier and I built a one-third-scale mock-up, a project still so vast that it required a silk bag twice as big as those usually sewn. To test its lifting capacity, we invited cadets from the École Militaire to climb aboard, but their professors wouldn't let us risk them. Instead, we flew ourselves with two hobbled donkeys, a pig, and fifty bags of millet. The combination was a poor choice because the animals kept trying to get at the grain.

It was a fine October day, the last leaves turning, and initially I found it fun to drift over farmyards and wave at pretty milkmaids below. But the sun on dark harvested fields created a thermal of rising air that lifted us higher than we planned, and when the savant released gas to bring us down, we plunged once we drifted out of the updraft. We eventually crashed into trees and had to hire three farm laborers to help lower the terrified animals with a rope. The bag was ruined.

When Thilorier asked for more money to try a full-scale version, he was turned down. "We do not believe your experiments are sufficiently advanced to chance the fortunes of a regiment," the War Ministry informed us.

I was relieved. I'm happy to lend ingenuity, but Thilorier was balmy.

Astiza was having better luck.

A peculiarity of Paris, and a sight that added to the nervous edge of the times, was the constant cortege of funeral wagons taking exhumed bones from city cemeteries and dumping them into new catacombs. These underground ossuaries were established in the tunnels of limestone quarries that ran under the capital. More than a millennia of burials had crammed city churchyards so full of remains that there was no room for either the dead to sleep or the living to redevelop, so more than a million corpses had already been dug up, dusted off, and wheeled through the streets for quick reinternment, the skulls anonymous as cobblestones. Authorities said there were famous people in the bunch, but you couldn't tell their notoriety now.

Harry asked about the funeral wagons with detached fascination; while he understood in theory that he would someday die, at age four the prospect is an abstraction. He liked the way men doffed their hats as the big black dray horses plodded by, and the rattle of their cargo.

One day my wife proposed that we descend to this bizarre new crypt.

"All in good time," I tried to joke.

"The catacombs are deserted at night. Even after the rationality of the revolution, men fear spirits. But that gives us privacy. A chemist asked that we meet him there."

"A chemist? Do we need drugs?"

"We need his guidance, and it was mere chance I stumbled upon him. In the Bibliothèque Nationale I finally got access to some archives from the sixteenth and seventeenth centuries, which, as you know, were the height of religious conflict and philosophic speculation in Europe."

"I didn't know, but go on." People are always fighting and always speculating, it seems to me, and I'm not certain why historians bother to keep track.

"From those books in the Mazarine Gallery I descended to the library's crypt, a warren of shelves stuffed under low Roman arches. Candles dimly light it, the shelves are dark oak, and the heavy leather-bound volumes have the scent of age and lost wisdom. It's called the Saint-Denis scriptorium, named for the patron saint of Paris, the early Christian martyr."

"The stink of lost wisdom," I corrected. "Mildew."

"I was searching for histories of the monk Albertus Magnus, looking for references to this Brazen Head. One tome had mention of an automaton, calling it no more than a legend, but said it was part of a wider quest for physical and spiritual alchemy. Wizards of the time didn't just want to make lead into gold, they wanted to lift the soul into heaven. As such they were trespassing on church prerogative and were hunted down as heretics. But curiously pressed on that page, as if left as a message, was this." She held up a dried rose, stem and thorns squashed flat. It was brown as paper.

Rose, the name of the redheaded spy and the symbol she'd said to use to signal her. Odd coincidence. "What does a flower have to do with the catacombs?"

"Why would it be left in a book of ancient wisdom? No lover would be likely to find it there. No, it was a message for someone seeking knowledge. I took the stem with hope and foreboding."

"You stole this from the library?" She was so virtuous that this act of thievery surprised me.

"This was left as a sign. For a week or more I pondered what it might mean, and then one day I acted on the name of the scriptorium and walked the length of the rue Saint-Denis."

"Known for its ladies of the evening."

"So was it coincidence to happen upon an apothecary that had a red rose on the swinging sign above its door?"

"A common enough decoration, surely."

"I went inside, not at all certain what I was looking for, and then saw a wizened chemist with a bent back and shuffling gait. He reminded me of Enoch in Egypt, and he wore a most unusual symbol in revolutionary France: a wooden crucifix."

"Religion is making a comeback, apparently."

"The juxtaposition came to me instantly: Rosicrucians."

She'd intrigued me. The Rosicrucians are a secret society seeking ancient wisdom that is tied into any number of others, including my own Freemasons, Cagliostro's nefarious Egyptian Rite with which I'd tangled, the Bavarian Illuminati, the Scottish Rite, and so on. There's a lunatic lacework of all these groups, and I've been tangled in their nets in my travels. "The rosy cross, symbol of their order," I said. "It stands for knowledge, sacrifice, and redemption."

"Exactly." My familiarity with such things made me suitable as her husband. "So on a hunch I took out the pressed flower and said I'd been told that with the right alchemy, the petals could bring great power. His old eyes glimmered, and he studied my face carefully. 'You're not French,' the chemist said. 'Egyptian,' I replied, 'but a member of all nations, and all races.' After consideration he beckoned me to a back room with shelves of chemicals and asked where I'd found the blossom. I said in an old book. And he said, 'A rose can prick and a rose can seduce, and sometimes a rose can also lead to foresight and immortality.'"

"The promise of the Rosicrucians, and the Brazen Head." I felt a chill, as if once more we were being led on paths winding and perilous. We're all puppets, Réal had said, and not just of each other but some higher power. Napoleon had told me several times he felt driven by unseen forces, and my own life had become nearly as strange as his.

"I said yes," Astiza recounted, "and he said that we must meet to discuss possibilities further. He invited us to the catacombs."

"Like being invited for dinner in a dungeon, by a dragon."

"He wants to learn what we're about and decide whether to help us."

"What's this chemist's name?"

"He gave it as Palatine, the noble title given to the famed alchemist Michael Maier by the Emperor Rudolf II of Bohemia, two centuries ago. Maier was a German doctor who studied the teachings of the rosy cross."

Yes, I'd certainly married a pretty bookworm. "And this Palatine left his flower in a dusty book and then waited for someone to bring it by years later? That's more patience than a fisherman throwing a line into the polluted Seine."

"Perhaps it was left by others. Perhaps the Brazen Head prophesized when it would be found, and Palatine set up shop accordingly."

"To wait for us."

"To wait for whoever found it. We're to find something more, I believe, which disappeared in Germany or Bohemia during the Thirty Years' War."

"Good heavens. So instead of toppling Napoleon we're on his errand, instead of quietly retiring we're spying for all sides, and instead of setting up a home like a normal married couple we're lusting after a lost object of supernatural power. Just to be clear about the mess we've mixed for ourselves."

"We're reconstructing a lost history, first in Egypt and the Holy Land, and now here in Paris and central Europe. We're seeking not for Bonaparte but for ourselves, and not for treasure but for wisdom." She took my arms. "I've felt directionless since we returned to France, Ethan. Now I realize we've been put here to participate in great things."

She was as balmy as Thilorier. I gave her a kiss.

Chapter 15

Catherine and Harry had warmed to each other, since she had maternal instincts and enjoyed the chance to lecture anybody, even a four-year-old, while he regarded her care as a novel break from his parents. Still, the comtesse was suspicious when we left our son in her care after supper, since that wasn't our habit. We told her to put him to bed at the usual hour and that we'd be back before dawn after urgent business.

"What urgent business?"

"For your safety and that of our son, it's better that you don't know. Tell him about the coronation, tuck him in, and enjoy this new romance Astiza bought."

"Don't do anything to jeopardize the way I'm infiltrating the Bonapartes!" she begged. "They're beginning to trust me."

"We're doing this *for* Bonaparte," I said, which was slightly the truth.

Not wanting the police to know where we were going, we slipped out through our rear yard into an adjacent alley, crept along in the dark, and came out on rue de Bac two blocks from our residence. Rather than risk the chance that a cabriolet driver would talk, we decided to walk the gloomy streets, my opening my coat to display my tomahawk to discourage thieves or pickpockets.

"People will think you're a savage," my wife said.

"You don't hear of the Iroquois being robbed, do you?"

Palatine had directed us to a catacomb entrance just outside the city's southern walls, in the sprawl of housing that had leapfrogged those fortifications once the economy recovered under Bonaparte. Half a dozen black wagons used for delivery of excavated bones were parked near a worker's enclosure at the mouth of the Port Mahon Quarry, guarded by two sentries we marked by the glow of their pipes. Our secret way was several hundred yards farther, through a utility hatch and down stone stairs to sewers awash with two feet of filthy water. I used a tinderbox to light the lanterns I'd carried in a bundle on my shoulder. Their glow chased rats into the shadows.

"So romantic to have an evening together without our boy," Astiza remarked.

"I'll speak to Napoleon about the accommodations."

"Palatine advised us to wade quickly to avoid vermin. There's a tunnel to the quarries not far downstream."

Cities are built of stone, and Paris has ninety miles of limestone quarries mined for monuments above. I feared we'd be lost in a maze, but my wife had a map provided by our wizard. So we entered the mines, wove this way and that, and eventually saw another glow like a welcoming window in a snowstorm. We came to a chamber of bone.

The ceiling was barely six feet, meaning my hair scraped. Candles flickered on a stone altar. To either side, femur and humerus had been stacked like cord wood with courses of skulls between. This made a retaining wall that held a jumble of ribs behind. The result was a pattern of balls, sockets, craniums, and mandibles.

Waiting for us was a living gnome: a bent, short, wrinkled specimen of a scholar in a dark robe and sewer-spattered boots who'd beckoned us to this spooky chamber. He had a wild mat of gray hair, ragged beard, and scholar's stoop. Wise men often seem stumpy and homely, in my experience, and perhaps they became scholars because no one would pick them for team sports.

"So you brought the great Ethan Gage," the fellow greeted with a voice coarsened to a rasp.

"You recognize my husband?"

"I recognized you in the apothecary, madame, or rather was told who you were by compatriots after your visit. You have a certain exoticism, as fascinating as a Negress, so you're not anonymous, even in a city as big as Paris. Your husband has his own reputation, though whether wastrel or warrior seems in dispute."

"I'm an electrician," I said. "Military consultant, explorer, diplomat, and confidant of the emperor himself."

"Gambler, spy, treasure hunter, fugitive, and Barbary slave," Palatine completed. This fellow knew his history.

"And you're named for a hill in Rome?"

"For an alchemist in the employ of Rudolf II. 'Palatine' is a title from Roman through medieval times, for experts in law and history. I'm a member of the Invisible College, that brotherhood that seeks truth in a world of lies and illusion. You can see I'm old; it's been a lengthy pursuit."

"I've known seekers who tend to shoot or torture folk who don't agree with them on what the truth is. Like Cagliostro's Egyptian Rite."

He gestured toward my waist. "I believe in tolerance. And it's you who are armed, not me."

"My tomahawk? For firewood and home repair." I glanced around our morbid meeting room. I've camped in ruins, hidden in a sarcophagus, and shoved aside skeletons, but this dump of the dead was the most macabre meeting place yet. Every skull here had thought itself the center of existence in its day, and now it was all black sockets and toothy grins. Would a man like Napoleon be chastened by bones that mocked ambition, or driven more than ever to escape their anonymity? "You've an odd way of communicating, Monsieur Palatine, if you rely on flowers found in books and rooms stuffed with the dead."

"Not odd if it works. And what if you had a means of foretelling just what messages would work and which would not?"

"You mean the automaton of Albertus Magnus," Astiza said. "Surely you don't already have it."

"Alas, no. Legend among legends. But those legends suggest that seekers shall find the rose. What would you say, madame, if I told you what I was really interested in was not the flower, but the stem?"

"I don't understand."

"It has thorns, does it not?"

"Yes."

"So we're going to make a bargain, you and me. I can start you on your quest for the secrets of Albertus and the rosy cross, but only if our purposes are aligned."

"Meaning?" I asked.

"To thwart Bonaparte, not aid him. Isn't that what you really seek?"

We had to be careful here. "Perhaps."

"You can have my help to seek what Napoleon has asked you to seek only if you ensure that it never falls into his hands, because he is entirely too dangerous. He's capable, but dedicated only to his own glory. So I'm going to tell you of a relic that can spoil his coronation, if you promise to keep the alchemical magic of Albertus Magnus out of reach of his marching armies. I don't know if the Brazen Head exists or not, but there are enough stories to make me fearful."

"What's wrong with telling the future?"

"Controlling it. Chaos can result. Such a machine belongs with scholars, not soldiers."

A thousand skulls were staring at me. "Spoiling a coronation sounds risky, if not impossible."

"So does knowing your own future." He gave a grim smile. "We all think just one more discovery will enlighten us, while actually it deepens the abyss of incomplete understanding. Each answer poses more questions. Still, we're humans: it's what we do. So my order is well aware of your reputation, Ethan Gage, and we are nothing like the heretic Egyptian Rite. The Invisible College simply wants your mission for Napoleon to give you the ability to carry out the same mission for us; to probe old legends and decide if any are true."

"And the legends are what, exactly?" Astiza asked.

"Well back in the thirteenth century—"

"The time of Albertus Magnus," I interrupted.

"The castle of Gemelshausen stood in the middle of Germany's Thuringia Forest. The family that inhabited it had the reputation as grim pagans who made their living as brigands. By rumor, they worshipped an eroded statue of an old goddess set in the castle courtyard. Athena, perhaps."

"A guise of the eternal goddess. Isis and Mary as well," Astiza said.

"A Dominican friar named Tors was on a rampage to root out unbelievers, aided by a one-eyed henchman named Rollo who claimed to be able to detect heretics at a glance. The two decided Gemelshausen was a fortress of evil, and they convinced Count Conrad of Thuringia to raze it. A siege commenced, culminating in a bloody massacre in which almost the entire Gemelshausen clan was slaughtered. The only survivor was a five-year-old boy, rescued by a monk and carried out from the flaming castle through a secret cave. This monk, a guest of the castle, studied ancient mysteries like us. He took the boy for safety to the refugee survivors of the Albigensian sect in southern France."

"The Albi-what?" I asked.

"They were also called the Cathars," Astiza explained. "A twelfth- and thirteenth- century mix of Eastern and Western religion that sees life on earth as hell. The world is a struggle between good and evil, or light and dark, reflecting the dualism of Persian religion. Jesus was a spirit instead of Son of God, and thus his sacrifice was only symbolic. Human redemption could be achieved by one's own spiritual growth instead of through the clergy—redemption could even be achieved by suicide! The Church declared the movement heresy and crushed it all, massacring followers after horrific sieges."

"Why do you know so much of other faiths, madame?" Palatine asked.

"By studying the linkages between the ancient Eastern religions and the new Western ones, I hope to discover universal truths." Which sounded considerably more ambitious than my own goal of retiring on the sale of an ill-gotten emerald, but then I was a good shot, and she was not. We all have our talents.

"This five-year-old survivor . . ." Palatine went on.

"Little older than Harry!" I interjected, feeling a little left out of the conversation.

" . . . was raised in the aftermath of the war against the Cathars and became interested in ancient knowledge. He set out for Damascus, crammed with learned men from Persia who were fleeing the invading Mongols under Hulagu, grandson of Genghis Kahn. Our hero took an allegorical name, Rosenkreutz, which is German for 'rosy cross,' the flower being a symbol of knowledge and the cross for spirit and sacrifice. Then on to Arabia, Egypt, Turkey, and Spain, each time seeking out scholars and spiritual masters. In Spain he learned from the Alumbrados, another secret society ultimately wiped out by the Inquisition."

"What has all this to do with the Brazen Head?" I asked impatiently.

"Rosenkreutz had experienced firsthand, since childhood, the mob's persecution of people who think for themselves. He formed a secret brotherhood of eight members to pass on secret knowledge. They were sworn to use it only for curing the sick and helping the poor. Like many holy men, they did their best to avoid the sins of vanity, lust, greed, pride, and gluttony, committing to chastity."

I can never understand such a commitment.

"From Spain, Rosenkreutz traveled slowly through France on his way back to Germany, and it is in Paris that he met the German scholar Albertus. It is legend that Albertus worked on some kind of automaton around 1260, and legend that a horrified Thomas Aquinas destroyed this mechanical seer, and competing legend that the head was *not* destroyed, but rather completed with the contribution of Rosenkreutz about that time. It was taken to central Europe and hidden away until mankind has the maturity to master its awesome powers of prediction."

"Where in central Europe?" Astiza asked.

"That, madame, is what you and your husband must learn. I'm going to suggest you begin in Prague, a magical and mystical city where the greatest alchemists of the age gathered for experimentation and philosophy. I think Napoleon chose you not just for your research abilities, but your abilities to cross borders and meet with all sides. Your husband's reputation has its advantages. Since no one is certain what he believes, all think he can be employed in their cause."

"I believe in love and family," I said. This fellow seemed entirely too convenient to me, with his rose sign and crypt of a meeting place. "And why are you sharing all this information, eh?"

"Pamphlets revealing the life of Rosenkreutz and promising secrets of lost knowledge began appearing early in the seventeenth century. Since then modern Rosicrucian groups have sprung up. I belong to one. We're as interested in the truth of the Brazen Head as anyone. We're also disturbed by the idea that a newly created emperor might misuse its powers for his own ends. We'd prefer that people of wisdom find it first and decide whether its powers should be harnessed or hidden."

"People like us."

"People like your wife. If she found that book in the library, it's a sign she has official support and freedom of movement. She fits our needs."

"If the head is in German or Austrian territory, Napoleon can't get it anyway," I said.

"Unless his armies march that way."

"They're on the coast planning an invasion of England."

"An invasion? Or a feint before a strike to the east?"

There it was again. Were the Boulogne camps nothing but a sham? As usual, I had no idea.

"Napoleon may loot all of Europe if he's not stopped at his coronation," Palatine went on.

"You're asking for assassination?"

"That would make him a martyr and elevate his inept brothers. No, we prefer humiliation. Which brings us to the real reason I'm meeting with you. Does the Brazen Head exist? I don't know. Where is it? I've suggested where you should begin, but not your final destination. Napoleon's ultimate strategy? We're guessing. But this man is seeking power greater than Charlemagne, harnessed to supernatural secrets. Men of learning are concerned. So you came to me with the rose, and I'm here to remind you that the rose has thorns."

Mystics love to make things as obscure as possible, I've learned, and never use a sentence when a paragraph of riddles will do. Priests, savants, politicians, and barristers are much the same. The ambitious believe that if you want people to think you're smart, pose as pretentiously as possible and charge a premium for confusion and wasted time. "Can we get to the point?"

"When the Church was banned and Notre Dame designated a Temple of Reason at the height of the revolution, a number of sacred religious objects were removed to the Bibliothèque Nationale. With Napoleon having reached a concordant with the Church, some have now been repatriated to the Archbishop's Palace next to Notre Dame, inhabited by Cardinal Belloy.

One of those is the most famous relic in Christendom."
The druggist paused, for dramatic effect.

"Which is?" I finally prompted.

"The Crown of Thorns, allegedly worn by Jesus Christ
at his crucifixion. It came to Paris in 1239 when Saint
Louis paid the Venetians for twenty-nine relics that the
Emperor Baldwin of Constantinople had pawned to raise
money to fight the Turks. Can you imagine pawning
eternal salvation for a war nobody remembers? Among
the objects were a nail from the crucifixion, a fragment
of the True Cross, and the crown, all traced back to the
Holy Land in the centuries after Christ. They'd been
moved west to Byzantium to keep them safe after the
Muslim conquest of Jerusalem. Our glorious Parisian
cathedral of Saint-Chapelle was built as a reliquary for
these objects, and later the Crown of Thorns was displayed for years in the church treasury at Notre Dame.
Its seventy thorns were gradually removed and shared
among the royals of Europe, a prick of Christ's agony for
each. But the vines the thorns were attached to remain
and are instantly recognizable by the faithful."

"What's left is a wreath of old brambles?"

"A crude and irreverent description, but yes. My
proposal is that when the coronation occurs, Napoleon
be crowned with that relic." He said it as casually as if
suggesting we meet for a drink.

Astiza gasped. "But that's blasphemy! To put the crown of Jesus on your own head? Even atheists would riot. Bonaparte would be condemned as a sacrilegious usurper by every Christian in Europe."

"Exactly." He smiled. "His rule would be wrecked before it properly began, his assertion of regal power would be destroyed, the pope would be furious, and excommunication might follow. The coronation would not be confirmation of Napoleon's power, it would be a mockery. It would make him impotent, and it would likely end any chance he could ever seize the Brazen Head."

"So why would he select this Crown of Thorns?" I asked.

"You will pick it for him."

"Let me review. You want us to somehow put this instrument of Jesus's torture on the head of Napoleon Bonaparte?"

"I want Pope Pius to do it, and upend the Corsican's entire regime." He nodded, already seeing the tumult in his head.

"But the pope would never do that. Would he?"

"He would if the Crown of Thorns was substituted for Napoleon's coronation crown without anyone's knowledge. Even if the pope dropped the Crown of Thorns in shock before actually lifting it to the dictator's head, the effect would be the same. Napoleon would be accused of insane hubris."

I tried to imagine the scene. "Perhaps. It could certainly confound the coronation, but why would Cardinal Belloy do such a thing?"

"He wouldn't. Catholics are grateful to Napoleon for inviting the Church back. Someone else must steal the crown from the cardinal, substitute it for the intended one, and take everyone by surprise."

I had a sinking feeling. "Someone?" The plan sounded blasphemous even to me.

"A man with access to Napoleon and his coronation preparations, allied with a comtesse advising Josephine on fashion, and with an Egyptian bride who can research the object and speculate where it might be hidden. A man, Monsieur Gage, with a reputation as one of the greatest thieves of France and America. You."

Chapter 16

The Archbishop's Palace is a venerable medieval heap of a chateau adjacent to the rear quarter of Notre Dame, with tower, steep roof, and stacks. Therein was our opportunity. I strategized to send Harry down the cardinal's chimney.

Astiza wasn't happy with my idea, given that our mission was sacrilege, government sabotage, trespass, and theft. But I thought my son's small size represented the only feasible way to break into the guarded clerical palace an alley's width from the church, and that the adventure could be fun besides.

Harry was enthusiastic. "Like Sinterklaas!"

"Yes, like Sinterklaas." From my time in New York I was familiar with the Dutch version of the Father Christmas fable, and had promised Harry that if he was good, some version of Saint Nicholas in a green coat would creep down our Paris chimney and bring him presents in the depth of winter. "You're small, like an elf. Out you'll pop to open a window for Mama and Papa. We'll have a treasure hunt."

"What if there's a fire?" My four-year-old thought seriously ahead, which is more than I can say for myself sometimes.

"We'll be sure to pick a chimney with no blaze burning. Even with autumn advancing they don't keep all of them lit the entire night." Wood was expensive for cardinals, too.

"No doggie?" Harry had been afraid of dogs since his introduction to the beast of Aurora Somerset. When we retired to an estate, I was going to get him a puppy, but meanwhile, he was fearful of the mutts that barked from farmsteads, snarled from alleys, and snapped at wagon wheels.

"No dogs." Why would there be a dog in an upstairs clerical council room, which was the intended landing place for my son?

"Ethan, it's a filthy idea," my wife said. "Chimneys are foul, and the boys who sweep them are gutter-snipes." She could be snobbish about who befriended her son.

"Boys love to get dirty."

"It's terribly dangerous."

"Not really. I'd try it myself if I were small. Rather a clever way to gain entry."

She sighed. "In Egypt we didn't need chimneys. The water was warm, and everyone was cleaner."

"Yes, and in Egypt there's so much religious bric-a-brac lying about that we could just scoop some off the sand, instead of having to creep into an archbishop's palace and tiptoe around a snoring cardinal. You're the one who confirmed by research and queries that the Crown of Thorns is almost certainly in his private chambers. We're in France, there's a precious circlet of brambles to be snatched, and once more we're on a mad errand."

"What if Horus gets stuck?"

"I'm going to lower some crossed sticks to confirm the dimensions before sending him down."

She bit her lip. "He's my only child."

"Harry did a fine job crawling inside the Syracuse cathedral, and he speared a rat. Didn't you, son?"

"I don't remember."

Well, he had been only two. From necessity I'd been exposing him to adventure from a very young age, after getting embroiled with a temptress and pirates. "If we spoil Napoleon's coronation and royal ambitions," I reminded patiently, "maybe the Corsican will have to trim back and avoid a monstrous war. We'll be heroes, even though we never get a sou of credit. We're thieving for world peace."

My wife is more intrigued by religious relics than I am, so her objections were halfhearted. She finally agreed that she herself would assault the Archbishop's Palace from the Seine side, helping to establish our escape by shooting up a rope with my crossbow. That was after she used her womanly charms to lure away guards, priests, or gendarmes.

"If we're guillotined, at least we'll all be guillotined together," she said.

Is it any wonder we married?

I picked a moonless November night since we'd be crawling on the clerical palace roof in full view of central Paris. We kept this business of Brazen Heads and thorny crowns secret from Catherine, telling her the family was going to a comedy and not to wait up. She looked disbelieving, but I told her it was a good evening to stay longer at the Tuileries to work on coronation preparations. She had stopped her flirting since our arrest by Pasques, and had been happier and preoccupied working on the coronation. What had seemed mysterious about her was apparently a temporary lack of purpose after the collapse of the royalist conspiracy. Now she was employed and less quarrelsome because of it.

It never occurred to me that in fooling everybody, we risked being fools.

The coronation was near. Pope Pius VII had arrived from Rome to stay in one wing of the Tuileries after a carefully calibrated, first comic meeting with Bonaparte. The collaboration between general and pontiff was a calculation between Paris and the Vatican, the pope wanting to play a role in European politics and Napoleon craving legitimacy. Every detail was a ticklish dance. It took months of negotiation to make Pius agree to the arduous journey to crown a man with a cynic's view of religion. Nor could their meeting be simple. The egotistical emperor didn't want to appear to be obsequious by waiting for the pope like a petitioner, and the pontiff didn't want to have to knock on one of Napoleon's palaces like a supplicant. Accordingly, Napoleon pretended to be out hunting—an activity that usually bored him—when the papal coach approached the palace at Fontainebleau. The two "accidentally" met on a country lane that avoided either waiting for the other. The French general timed his dismount to match the pope's exit from his coach, they greeted one another as equals, and then went to either side of the vehicle so they could step back inside at exactly the same time.

So is status shared and measured.

I encouraged Harry by promising that we might find some candy on our expedition, and brought some for him to discover later. Astiza and I practiced by cranking, aiming, and firing the crossbow at one of the cemeteries being excavated, since the grim task of transferring bones kept the superstitious away at night. She proved a good shot.

On the evening of our attempt, Astiza put a length of rope, a crossbow bolt tied to thin line, and the weapon itself in a shallow wicker basket, disguising her load with baguettes and bread cloth. She temporarily hid the basket near the Seine and waited to play alluring decoy.

Horus and I didn't dare take ropes on our mission lest we arouse suspicion. Since we were already breaking a commandment or two, we'd steal the lines we needed from the cathedral. We crossed to the Île de la Cité as if we were religious sightseers and ate supper at a small café, my treating us to pastry at the end.

"I get to stay up late," Harry boasted.

"And eat sugar and get dirty in a chimney. It's fun to hunt for treasure."

Our problem was this. The Archbishop's Palace was set between Notre Dame Cathedral and the Seine, security was tightening as the coronation neared, and it was easy to be conspicuous. A large number of houses had been torn down around the church to heighten its grandeur and accommodate crowds expected to total half a million. A temporary gallery and tent were being built alongside the transept doors as a private way for dignitaries to enter and dress: the coronation robes were so heavy that no one wanted to bear them more than a few hundred feet. Accordingly, hammering went on day and night. Torches burned. Guards strutted across the new plaza

Harry and I entered the soaring cavern of Notre Dame at sunset, its western rose window on fire atop a nave of shadows, and the church strewn with heaps of lumber for the coronation stands being built for spectators. The church was a cavern of Gothic gloom, smelling like a cave. There were just a scattering of old women worshippers in a monument in sad disrepair since the revolution, and one desultory priest shuffling toward the confessionals. He looked bored. In Astiza's novels, beautiful young women whisper of stolen hearts and sexual indiscretions to wise parish counselors. In real life it seems to be women of sixty relating that they're tired of their husbands and cross with their grandchildren.

We hid in the shadows by a chapel altar until the cathedral was shut for the night. Then, using skills my

British spymasters had taught me, I picked the medieval lock on a heavy wooden door and entered the north bell tower. The trick impressed my son.

Circular stone steps worn by centuries of sandals ascended. Harry led as we steeply climbed to where the bells were hung, a timber framework inside the outer stone of the tower. Just two bells remained; the others had been melted down to make cannon.

We caught our breath as we took in a grand view of Paris. Then we settled in. A ghost of twilight came through the apertures, enough that Harry could use chalk I'd brought to draw pictures on the plank floor while we waited. Once it became completely dark he began squirming, so I whispered to be patient and told him stories, half true, about Red Indians and Nordic treasures. He finally nodded off, while I waited impatiently for midnight.

When it was time to finally assault the Archbishop's Palace, I lit a candle with my tinderbox and used a knife to saw rope from the bellpulls. I made two coils, one for each shoulder. I tied off the remainder to be discovered by puzzled priests at dawn when they found that there was no way to signal for Mass. Then I woke Harry, and we stole partway downstairs to a child-size door giving access to a narrow balcony. It led across the front of the church, around the south tower, and to the eave of the steep slate roof. There was a wide gutter we could follow.

The height made me dizzy. Below, jutting out into space, were flying buttresses that arched down into the dark.

"Cling like a squirrel, son."

"This is fun, Papa."

I looked down the precipitous drop. "Yes, it is."

Harry again led, me watchful to catch him if he should start to go over. But instead of looking at the gulf of gloom, my boy was more intrigued by the gargoyles that jutted over each buttress. "Monsters, Papa."

"Gargoyles. They catch the rain and spit it from their mouths."

"I want to see them chase it."

Children are like monkeys, and the entire expedition was the type of naughty thing mothers never allow. The gutter walkway was wide as a ship's plank.

"We should do this at our house."

"Quiet like a gargoyle."

The floor plan of Notre Dame is like a cross, and now we had to negotiate our way around its western arm on a narrow balcony. We crept on all fours so as not to be spotted, passing under the cathedral's enormous rose-shaped window.

Rose. The rosy cross.

Then we were creeping the gutter along the rear third of the church, above what was called the choir. Once again the buttresses fell away and gargoyles spat.

"I'm getting tired," Harry whined.

"We're almost there."

Each buttress was a pitched beam that rested on a column, giving the high walls a sturdier stance. Gargoyles spat rain into a channel grooved into each one, and at the lower end a companion gargoyle collected this stream and spat toward the river. Atop this lower junction jutted a decorative stone tower like a little chapel, spiked with a cross, Gothic gables, and studded with gewgaws, knobs, and fantasy creatures from the imagination of the masons.

"Now we're going to swing," I whispered to Harry. I peered into the pit between cathedral and Archbishop's Palace and caught the glow of a pipe. Yes, a sentry was down there.

So I briefly lit my candle again, letting it signal.

On cue, Astiza called from the dark. The sentry hesitated, the ember of his pipe lowered a moment in perplexity, and then he walked toward the feminine voice.

"Now, comes the tricky part. You'll mind Papa, yes?"

He looked down. "I don't want to fall."

"Which means you must sit still as stone while I rig a rope. Then we're going to have very great fun indeed."

I slid down the buttress gutter as if it were a leaning log, climbed its decorative tower at the lower end, and tied off my rope on the neck of a snarling gargoyle that pointed sideways. This would give us swinging room.

I quickly looked around.

Across a yawning gap was the steep slate roof of the cardinal's quarters. A tower and steeple jutted from one corner. Beyond the palace were the river and the roofs of the sleepy city. I spied the spark of the sentry's pipe at the gate to the archbishop's gardens, where my wife was presumably flirting. A few candles shone in the bishop's house, but the rooms looked quiet. As soon as I crossed and gave another signal, Astiza would break off her conversation, walk to the Seine, fetch her basket with crossbow, and find a target to shoot at with her bolt.

We are, as I've said, a peculiar family.

Holding my newly tied rope in my teeth, I crabwalked back up the cathedral's buttress to where Harry obediently waited. "Now comes the fun part," I whispered. He held his hands out and I gathered him to me. Beneath my coat I'd put on the military cross belts that soldiers wear to carry their gear. They're a harness for humans, and now I tucked his little arms and legs inside so he was pressed with face to my chest, like a little monkey. "Hang tight." I pulled the rope until it was taut, fixed like a pendulum above a child's swimming hole. The arc, I judged, would just bridge the gap between church and palace.

I had one chance to get it right.

I gripped, pulled tight, and sprang.

We fell, swinging past the little chapel, and soared into space, Harry clutching like a kit. He gasped, making a kind of mewing sound. Momentum carried us above the canyon of air, and at the top of our arc we were weightless.

I heard a crack. The neck of the gargoyle had snapped.

We fell, me still holding the rope. There was the gray slate of the bishop's roof below. We hit and I slid, scrabbling for purchase. My legs shot out into emptiness, while the head of the broken gargoyle banged into the alley below.

There was another gutter to arrest our fall. I slammed my arms into it and stopped, trembling from strain, my legs extending into space. The rope slapped against the archbishop's balance. I heard the thud of boots as the sentry hurried back, shouting a challenge.

I hastily got my legs into the gutter, hurriedly pulled up the rope, and leaned back from the edge so we couldn't be seen. The broken demon I'd hauled in looked accusatory.

Below, the sentry stopped, peering about. Nothing amiss.

I waited an eternity. Astiza called again. The man stalked away, muttering. So I dipped my head to address my boy.

"Harry, are you all right?"

"Are we there?" His voice was very small.

"Almost." I got my knees back up on the roof and scrabbled swiftly up its slippery slate to the ridge. There I let Harry loose and waited for my sweat to cool.

Accomplishment Number One: I had not yet killed my son.

Harry looked back at Notre Dame. "That was scary, Papa."

"It's the next part that's jolly. You get to be Sinterklaas."

"Will you come, too?"

"Better. You're going to open a window, and Mama and I are going to meet you there as part of our special game. You like games, don't you?" Meanwhile, I hoped a lightning bolt wouldn't strike me dead for blasphemy.

At least it was quiet. Cardinal Belloy was an astonishingly thriving ninety-five years old who by all reports was an able administrator. I was betting the old man also needed his sleep.

"Now, let's creep along to the chimney."

Astiza had found plans for the palace in the library, and I'd picked a flue that appeared to have the necessary width and which led to the cardinal's council chamber. We sidled to it. I took the other coil of rope I'd cut from the bells and quickly lowered some crossed sticks I'd brought to make sure the chimney had no odd obstructions. The sounding went straight down, slackened in the hearth, and came up with cold ashes.

"Harry, this is the clever part. You must pretend you're Father Christmas, bringing presents down the chimney like the Dutch story I told you, but instead, you get treasure. I'm going to lower you on this rope, and you're going to get as dirty as you like." I gave him a bottle with a soft glow. "This holds fox fire, to give you a little light on the way down. When you get to the bottom, the rope will go slack. Then you're going to pull *here* to release the knot, step into the room, and look for Mama's face in a window. If you open the window latch, we can climb inside."

"What's the treasure?"

"Candy. Here are a few pieces to keep your strength up and show you what we're after." I'm so practiced telling improbable fables to nubile wenches that I can do the same with four-year-old children.

He nodded solemnly, thinking, I believe, that if such a path was good enough for Sinterklaas, it was good enough for him. He was a brave little lad, and he had his parents' curiosity. So down he went.

Harry slipped without jamming, dangling like a passive puppet as I'd instructed. The rope finally slackened and came loose. So far, so good.

Then I heard a growl, rumbling up the chimney as if it were a speaking trumpet.

Damnation! The cardinal had a dog after all. I braced for a scream and wail from my son, shouts from priests and guards, and maybe even gunshots. I froze on the roof ridge, as plain a target as the tin plate I'd used in Boulogne.

Instead, silence.

Heart hammering out of fear for my boy, I swiftly pulled the rope up, doubled it around the chimney, and dropped it down the roof to the Seine side of the palace. Then I slid along it over the side and looked for what I hoped would be there. Sure enough, a crossbow bolt was stuck in a beam on the underside of the roof eave, and from it a string led down to the ground. When I pulled on the string, I pulled up Astiza's rope. I doubled it around the beam, braced myself, and hauled my wife up. She helped by walking up the wall with her feet.

"Finally," she gasped. "I've lived an eternity. Is Harry all right?"

"I hope so. I heard a dog."

She moaned while I reeled in the rope from the chimney.

She quickly swung to the window we hoped Harry could open, climbing onto its French balcony. I followed.

"Nice that the crossbow worked," I whispered.

"I missed twice. Priests must sleep like the dead."

"Clear conscience. Women wouldn't know what that's like, would they?"

"Not funny, husband."

"You have the substitute?"

She patted a satchel at her side. "In my bag."

We tapped the window. A small face appeared on the other side and matter-of-factly climbed up on the window ledge and unfastened the leaded glass. It swung inward. That's my boy.

"You said there wouldn't be a doggie." He was accusatory.

"Just friendly ones. Where is he?"

"I gave him candy."

And indeed, a hound was snuffling at something on the carpet, growling a halfhearted warning as we dropped onto thick carpet. Some watchdog. I shook loose a curtain rope from its hook and gently approached, holding out my hand as if I had more food. The growl was a low rumble, but the beast looked warily hopeful. I gave it a pet, and then swiftly cinched its muzzle before it could do more than yelp. More rope around the thrashing legs, and I trussed the mutt like a calf.

I stood, breathing heavily. "You're a very clever boy, Harry."

"Papa said there's more candy here, Mama." Our son was covered in soot and seemed rather proud of it. I admired his mercenary instinct, which I consider common sense.

"You're a very good son and shall get some treats."

"And a bath," his mother added.

The council room had a long central table with armoires, cabinets, and bookshelves alongside. We emptied one of folded tablecloths and put the struggling dog inside, throwing the fabric on top of him to muffle any scratching. I felt sorry for the beast, but fortunes of war and all that.

Now, where to look? It was a splendid home. Clergy work is steady, clean, and with good quarters; one could do worse except for the celibacy part. Gothic arches made a fine roof overhead, stone pillars coming down like trunks in a forest. The furnishings were a little bare, the place having been ransacked in the revolution, but what had been brought back in was Italian and finer than I could afford. There were wool carpets as thick as bear pelts, fine tapestries, gloomy portraits of popes, and bright ones of the Virgin. The latter seemed to be eyeing me with particular disfavor.

Now we had to find something small enough to be cruelly jammed on our Savior's head.

I whispered to Harry to stay close and began creeping around, hating the way the board floors creaked and cabinet hinges squealed. Logically, I knew the sounds were barely audible, but when stealing Christendom's most precious relic, every peep sounds like the boom of a cannon.

I don't know how professional thieves bear the nerves.

We tried chests, armoires, shelves, mantles, and decorative boxes. Harry peered under furniture and behind curtains. Astiza had theorized that such a precious item might be hidden somewhere clever, such as a hollowed-out Bible, so she tugged open weighty-looking books. I tapped a globe, wondering if it might have a secret compartment in its hollow. We looked behind paintings in case there was a hiding spot in the walls. Each time we were disappointed. The Bishop's Chapel next door had nothing unusual on its altar or in its tabernacle. We didn't try the kitchen or cellars on the floor below, since I didn't think a prelate would put a precious relic in a pantry. We also avoided the ground-floor antechamber out of concern it might hold guards or secretaries.

"Maybe he moved it to another church for safekeeping," Astiza whispered worriedly.

"It has too much status. No churchman would willingly give it up."

"I'm tired, Papa."

"Here, I found more candy."

"Ethan, the only place left is his bedchamber."

"Our damnation if it is. What if Belloy wakes up?"

"Please be careful with your language around our boy."

"Dammit, you're right. I mean, sorry."

"Can we go home, Mama?"

"Have another piece of candy." It wasn't good parenting, but most spies don't have to bring the entire family along. He was black as a briquette and rapidly flagging.

"All right, the bedchamber if we must, but quiet as a confessional," I said. "If the cardinal suspects what we've done, the whole scheme comes to naught."

One stroke of luck was that the aged like to sleep warm. The prelate had drawn the heavy silk curtains on his sumptuous bed to make a cozy tent, and his snores were faint, which meant our burglary was also muffled. "Ethan, Harry and I are lighter and quieter," Astiza whispered. "You walk like a moose. Stand watch by the door."

"A stag, perhaps. Or a stallion."

"We'll be only a minute." My wife and son disappeared into the gloom of the bedroom. I'd given her the vial of fox fire to provide meager light, but shadows swallowed them.

I waited nervously, imagining a thousand disasters. And of course, one soon occurred. The palace was big enough to boast a corridor, and suddenly a shadow rose at its far end, where a stairway led to the ground floor.

Someone was ascending the steps.

"Astiza!" I hissed. "Hide!" But I dared not say it loud enough for her to hear. I stood in shadow by the bedroom door, trying to communicate with my family by will alone. That didn't work. She'd passed into a dressing room.

A lamp rose from the lip of the stairs like a rising sun, and with it a figure. A priest, thank goodness, not a soldier or gendarme.

He bore a pitcher of water or wine and made straight for the cardinal's room. Wash water, perhaps, for the morning? Need he bring it now? Then I remembered holy men rise at ungodly hours, as if the Almighty were on a tight schedule.

A hand touched my arm, and I jumped. It was my wife.

"All I found were miter hats and sacramental robes," she whispered. "And I've lost Harry."

"Lost him?" I was getting panicked. "It's just a bedchamber."

"He didn't come back to you, did he?"

"He's hiding, I hope, as you were supposed to. A priest is coming."

"Now?"

"Slide under the bed. I'll take care of the servant." I closed the door nearly shut and skipped to the library on the other side. When the priest came abreast of the bishop's bedroom, I spilled some books to make a thud.

"Excellency?" The priest stepped into the library, dark except for the gray rectangle that marked its window.

I put out my leg.

He tripped, grunting, and fell to the carpet, me catching the pitcher just before it shattered. Then I let it drop on his head, not enough to break but enough to stun, and taking care it didn't tip and spill its liquid. I'm fastidious in my own way. Before he could react I dragged him square with the rug and started rolling him up. In moments he was encased in a wool sandwich, his dazed cries muffled by the carpeting. I yanked down more drapery holders, letting the curtains make it even darker, and tied the rug at either end, taking care to leave just enough of a gap so he could breathe. Smothering a priest would be sure to doom our quest with divine wrath. What a bollocks our adventure had become!

I knelt and put my mouth to the hole at the end of the roll of carpet. "My apologies, Father, we'll be on our way soon." My captive shouted something, but I couldn't make out what, since it came out as a muffled whisper. I glanced toward the bedchamber. When the priest didn't return, a guard would come looking. It was past time to flee.

I went back to the cardinal's door and swung it open to look for my wife, but she was already there, holding Harry.

"He was under the bed," she explained.

"Papa, I found a nest," he said proudly.

Astiza held out a wreath of ancient brambles, as unprepossessing a crown as can be imagined. Had this "nest" of reeds really topped Jesus? Medieval fragments of the crucifixion were as plentiful as homes in which George Washington reputedly slept, so except for the periodic mummified feet or heart of a saint, all but the most devout were skeptical that anything was real. Yet I felt a chill and an odd feeling of the sacred, as if the wisps of dry vines had supernatural power. Stealing the Crown of Thorns was our maddest act yet.

If the pope lifted this Crown of Thorns in surprise as the hat for the new French emperor, the entire ceremony—and Bonaparte's campaign to win respectability—would come apart. Claiming the crown of Jesus! The subterfuge wouldn't kill Napoleon's body, but it would destroy his pretensions to being a republican and make him a laughingstock among the nobles of Europe.

"I slipped our substitute in its place," Astiza said. "It's kept in a lacquered and inlayed box. Hopefully, he won't look and, if he does, won't notice the switch."

We had chopped some brambles out of the graveyard and tied them into a circle.

Behind the bed curtains the snoring stopped with a snort, there was a shift, and we feared our unwitting host was waking up.

"Then let's descend by the rope you doubled, take it with us, and melt into the dark. We'll steal some plate and porcelain so our priest there will think we're ordinary thieves."

"But we didn't find all the candy!" Harry protested, instinctively copying our anxious whispers.

"Yes we did." I gave him another piece. "I've got it in my pocket. We'll share it all when we get home."

The cathedral bells should have rung by the time the sky lightened and we made for the rue du Bac, but the priests of Notre Dame were no doubt looking for fresh rope.

Chapter 17

"Ethan, can you help me with my petticoat?"
Catherine was calling from her bedroom.

It was a few days after our adventure in the Archbishop's Palace, and the Crown of Thorns was stored in a hatbox under my own bed. No theft had been reported, and it was unlikely that Cardinal Belloy had noticed our substitution. He was busy working with Pope Pius on the coming coronation. What he thought of finding one of his priests tied up in a carpet, his dog trussed in a cabinet, and a theft of plate and porcelain, was anybody's guess. Hopefully, he blamed the intrusion on thieves of admirable athleticism. I did notice more sentries posted when I strolled on the opposite side of the Seine the next day, no doubt instructed not to respond to the calls of passing women.

Now the comtesse Marceau wanted my aid in dressing while Astiza and Harry were out shopping. She hadn't played this game in some time.

"I'm clumsy with buttons and ribbons," I replied.

"Please, I'm having the most difficult trial. It's such a sacrifice spying without servants."

I entered her small bedchamber warily, remembering her seduction in the bath. Catherine became intimate when she was either bored or wanted something. Still, I responded. Should I be dressing a beautiful young woman who was not my wife? No. Was I flattered by this flirtation? Yes. Should I have minded my own business? Of course.

Catherine was sitting on her bed, dressed in a plain white chemise hitched high on her thighs so she could pull up white silk stockings. This gave me a good look at her lovely legs and the pink garters she was fastening there, which was undoubtedly her intention.

"I thought you wanted help with your petticoat."

"Which is beside me." She pointed with her chin at the second layer of her ensemble draped on her rumpled covers, her bed still unmade. "I'm not going to let you tie my garters, Ethan. You're a very bold fellow even to suggest it."

"I didn't suggest it, and it's inappropriate watching you do so."

She laughed. "This from a man who has seen me in my bath!"

"I didn't ask for that, either."

"That's not how I remember it. Ethan, be adult. We know we're living on top of each other like a little family, so it's hardly surprising you've seen me dishabille. It's not my fault you find the female form so troubling."

"*Troubling* is not the word I would use."

"I don't pretend to understand men at all." She twisted slightly, giving me a peek of more of her inner thigh, and then stood abruptly, her chemise slipping down over her stockings to make herself the very picture of modesty, except that her nipples poked plain through the fabric, firm as nail heads. Most of the rest of her could be guessed at, too. Her breasts were high, small, and in no need yet of a short stay for support. My mind was not in the least tempted, but I'll confess my body had a mind of its own. I believe she understood men all too well.

She stuck out her arms. "The petticoat, please. I must become decent."

I hesitated, but damnation if I wasn't already in her chamber. I lifted the sleeves onto her shoulders, turned her around to peek at the lovely nape of her neck beneath her piled hair, and studied the fastenings the way a sailor might examine the rigging of a new ship. A Parisian woman in late autumn comes in three wrappings. There's a simple chemise next to the skin that is frequently washed, a petticoat hanging to the ankles with lace fringe that will be visible when a lady lifts her dress to avoid puddles, and the outer gown of thicker fabric, its waist just below the bust. The colors this season were rose and lilac, and the material of the layers can range from gauzy to opaque. Catherine was donning a day dress, which was less sumptuous and more modest than evening wear. If you're wondering how I know all this, I am first instructed by marriage, and, second, experienced in reefing or unfurling past damsels. I also had consumed several of the romance novels when the women weren't around to tease me, not liking them of course, but still being aroused by one passage and shedding a tear at the next. No wonder they sold so well.

"There's nothing that makes less sense than women's clothing," I said. "It's buttoned, buckled, and lashed where a poor girl can't reach it. The result drags in the dirt and yet it's so trimmed on top that it leaves her freezing."

"Sense has nothing to do with it. Clothing is to decorate, elevate, and inspire. Impracticality is a small price to pay."

"Maybe women will wear trousers some day."

"What a silly thing to say!" She glanced back over the marble of her shoulder, eyes mischievous, lips curled saucily. My point is that the girl knew exactly what she was doing, and I did, too.

I fastened her as well as I could. "Silliness is why you don't like me, I suppose."

"But I do like you." She turned and grasped my hands. "I worry about you and your young family. You were gone the entire night recently, little Harry so exhausted that he fell asleep in your arms. Such labors that infant must have endured! He and I have become quite close, you know. I am like a second mother."

"I wouldn't call them labors, exactly. He got some candy."

"But I could have helped." She stepped close, breathing hard enough to have me following things up and down. "I want to help. We're allies, no? Spies against the tyrant Bonaparte? A partnership for royalist restoration? And yet you're slipping away on missions without my knowledge."

"To protect your pretty neck."

She cocked her head. "Do you think it is pretty?"

"Our missions are about the coronation, Catherine."

"Then it's about me! I'm the coronation! I mean, I'm laboring to help Josephine plan it. She cares more about the dress than the crown, and her sisters-in-law are even shallower, so all have benefitted from my advice. What jealousies I referee! Men have swords for their duels, and women, tongues."

I hesitated. Did Catherine belong in our plan? And yet, how, exactly, were we to substitute the Crown of Thorns for the one Napoleon intended to be crowned under? Now a comtesse was running her hand up my sleeve and throwing off more warmth than a Franklin stove. How women manage that on demand I don't know, but it's the rare man who doesn't want to cozy to the fire.

"I need to enlist you," I allowed. "It's terribly dangerous."

"I landed in France to embrace danger."

"We've an idea to spoil the entire coronation."

Her eyes widened.

"To embarrass Napoleon, we're considering slipping a substitute crown into whatever container the pope plans to use for the real one, meaning that someone has to risk her life by mixing things up."

"*Mon Dieu!* So daring. A substitute crown?" She looked intrigued. I hesitated to let her share our scheme—*Two can keep a secret if one of them is dead*, Franklin had said—but she was lovely as the devil. Shouldn't beauty imply character? She lifted on tiptoes, smelling of perfume, licking the air near my ear. "I love a secret."

I struggled to remember that I am married, sensible, and reformed. She was a golden-haired angel, half dressed, ripe, and adoring as a doll. Men are so used to women swerving to avoid us that it's captivating, and startling, to be paid attention by one. I swallowed. "I'll discuss it with Astiza."

"Ethan, we were partners before your wife appeared. These past months have only made us more intimate, and frankly I've trembled to resist temptation. You don't realize your virile charm."

Actually I do, and frequently overestimate it.

"Do you mind frankness?" she went on. "I confess to infatuation. Should we not consummate our alliance, just this once, while we're alone?"

By Franklin's kite, she had a charge like a battery. "We can do that with a handshake," I said uncertainly.

She laughed and kissed me instead, lips warm, hands clutching, her body squirreling against mine. "How droll you are!" I groped to get her off me, but admit I took my time about it. She rubbed long enough to be positive I was truly interested, and gave a wicked grin. "So you like me as I like you."

"Comtesse, this isn't proper."

She pouted, delectably. "You must call me Catherine. I'm only trying to be friends. Tell me our conspiracy, Ethan, and I'll leave you alone."

I didn't entirely trust her. She had the morals of a minx and, despite her royalist pretensions, had signed on to help with the usurper's coronation. But we also needed her. We were on the same side, I needed her help, and if I hesitated any more, we'd be thrashing on her bed. I took breath. "You must swear to hold the secret. We've risked our lives already to obtain the substitute, and if we're caught with it, we'll have police and priests arguing over who gets to draw and quarter us first."

"It sounds so daring!"

I allowed a dramatic pause. Then, "We have the Crown of Thorns."

She looked blank. "The what?"

"There aren't any thorns left; those were shared out centuries ago. But it's the crown forced on Jesus's head by the Romans. We stole it from Cardinal Belloy. Harry helped."

"Oh my." She blanched.

"It's been kept for centuries. Were the pope to lift that as Napoleon's intended crown on coronation day, the blasphemy would be so profound as to make him a pariah in all Christendom. He'd be mocked and scorned by every head of state. People might start muttering for the return of the Bourbons."

She blinked, shocked, and considered. Then she began to smile. "That's a magnificent idea! How clever of you to think of it."

"It was suggested by a scholar whom Astiza found. And it's clever only if it works. Can you help insert the holy relic into the coronation and take everyone by surprise, while not endangering yourself or us?"

She stood straighter. "I pledge to try. You must trust me, Ethan."

"I just have."

"Let me think how to do so. Thanks to my wit and charm, they've taken my advice at the Tuileries. They'll listen enough to make this possible, too." She pondered. "However, I'm searched when entering and leaving the royal apartments. You must bring it to the coronation, and we'll exchange it there."

"Exchange?"

"Napoleon's crown is a simple golden laurel wreath that will be kept in a ceremonial box until the critical moment so that it will evoke maximum awe when lifted and displayed. I'll find a way to insert your crown of straw and take the gold one. Stealing it would be just payment for our troubles, don't you think?"

"We'd be guillotined if we tried to sell it."

"Not if we melt it." Her face was lit with practical greed and vengeance, and I had to admire her ruthlessness. "You must bring me a loaded pistol, too. If things go awry, I may have to fight. A gun gives me a chance with a guard."

"I'm sure guests will be searched."

"Then put it in a bag with the crown. I'll furnish an imperial seal."

"The goal is to embarrass the emperor, not start a battle or make ourselves rich."

She hugged me. "The goal is to let everyone get what they deserve. I'm so happy we're partners."

I limped from our conversation with relief and regret, happy I'd stayed vaguely faithful to my vows and worried that I'd let too much slip by enlisting Catherine. I had entrusted her not just with our mission but with the fate of my family. In this final test I needed her to be the steely royalist warrior, not a flighty and flirtatious socialite.

I sat down to ponder how much of this to tell my wife.

Astiza reluctantly agreed to the inclusion of the comtesse in our plot, since getting close to the crowns of the coronation seemed impossible without Catherine. "She can finally make herself useful," my wife allowed, "though frankly I don't rely on her to manage more than a table setting."

"She's risked her life to return to France for what she believes in," I said with more hope than conviction.

"I just don't want her to risk ours. I don't trust her."

"With the Crown of Thorns?"

"With you. But let's finish what we've started and make a home far away."

"Amen," and I meant it. Astiza was justified in being suspicious. The French say one escapes temptation by succumbing to it.

And why did Napoleon, who didn't seem to believe in anything but himself, want the pope's consecration for a rule the people and Senate had already granted? Because to have Pius VII at the ceremony meant being anointed by God. It would mimic the crowning of Charlemagne. It would grant what Bonaparte craved most, legitimacy. It would reinforce his intention to pass his crown to his heir, should he father one. Thus far, Josephine had been barren since the birth of two children by her first husband. Yet Napoleon, who truly loved her, planned to crown her, too, a glory no French queen had been granted in two hundred years.

The Invalides, which had sufficed for the Legion of Honor, was too small for the coronation. Bonaparte wanted Notre Dame jammed with twenty thousand admirers. His spurs would be golden, his scepter made of unicorn horn, and his ushers would carry silver pikes. No French notable could resist such a show, and by Coronation Day, December 2, 1804, Paris was jammed with two million people—four times its normal population—and prices had soared. A simple meal cost a ridiculous three francs. I was thankful I'd been put on the French payroll, but my purse was still so light that I wondered if Catherine borrowed from it without telling me. I couldn't ask her because she spent Coronation Eve with the ladies waiting on Josephine, assuring me that the substitution would be made once we were all in the cathedral.

"I'll meet you at the pavilion entrance at nine that morning very precisely," Catherine told me before she left our apartment for the last time.

"Which means what time, again?"

"Nine, very precisely." She'd looked at me as if I were slow-witted.

So we hoped for the best. We'd arrive at Notre Dame as minor dignitaries, our rank with Napoleon gaining us modest tickets. With luck we'd watch chaos play out. Then we'd slip off in a plan I'd devised.

In considering the morrow, I took one other precaution, too.

Like all of Paris, Astiza, Harry, and I slept restlessly the night before the ceremony. The streets were noisy as carnival. Cannons thudded in celebratory salutes. Theaters had been made free and were jammed. Military bands and minstrels marched up and down the avenues, people dancing drunkenly in their wake. So many lanterns, candles, and bonfires were lit that the city glowed orange. Our coppersmith neighbors tramped home at four in the morning singing the "Marseillaise."

My wife and I discovered each other awake and made restless, rather desperate love in the middle of the night, grateful that our royalist lodger was absent. The tension gave our congress sweet urgency, but afterward we snuggled, Astiza shivering slightly from anticipation. I've felt such tension only before battle, a crucial card game, shooting matches, or boyhood athletic contests.

We groggily rose before dawn, our apartment cold and our souls restless. I opened the kitchen window and held my palm outside. Snowflakes stuck.

"Be sure to dress warmly. Whether things go badly or well, we'll likely flee Paris."

"The streets will be choked," Astiza said.

"All the easier to melt into the crowds, and why my proposed escape makes sense. I've hidden rifle, powder, food, and clothing, experienced adventurer that I am. I'm trying to think ahead for once."

"What about Catherine?"

"What about her?"

"Will she also flee with us?"

I guiltily remembered our recent encounter. "If she's willing. I don't want her to lose her nerve by plotting escape, but if she succeeds, we owe her what help we can. It also means she won't be captured and betray us under torture."

"I'd prefer she seek shelter with royalists here in Paris. She's been a trial."

"Agreed. But if we do leave France together, she'll go her own way in London." I didn't know if this was true, but it was my intention.

Astiza nodded curtly, the good soldier. "Then we should take a cloak for her, just in case. Boots as well."

"We can leave a bundle stashed somewhere. Can you pick what a woman would take? I'll finish dressing Harry."

Ten minutes later my son was ready, but my wife was not. When Astiza emerged from Catherine's chamber, she looked troubled.

"You have her things?"

"Most are missing."

"She'd take some to the Tuileries if staying over-night. And maybe she has her own plan for fleeing. She's smart in her own haughty way."

"It would be helpful if she confided such smartness."

"We didn't tell her all our preparations, either."

"We're still not a company." She bit her lip.

"Yet inextricable allies. Without Catherine, our scheme falls apart. And she can't accomplish anything unless we deliver the Crown of Thorns."

"I don't trust her."

"Women never trust women."

She glanced at our grimy windows and the gray winter light, listening to thudding guns like heralding thunder. Napoleon, the new Prometheus. "A storm is coming." She didn't mean the weather, but something vast and far off.

It was the worst time to panic. "No, it's getting light. We're going to help France regain its sanity, Astiza, and be the heralds of a new dawn."

Chapter 18

The Cathedral of Notre Dame was a brisk mile from our apartment. As we hurried and daylight grew, the snow stopped and clouds began to lift. Eight months had passed since Catherine and I had first landed on the Channel coast, and the entire world seemed to have changed. All of Paris was congregating either on the Île de la Cité, where the church was located, or along the avenues on the Right Bank where the coronation coaches would roll in procession from the Tuileries. The massive, drifting crowds reminded me of migrating buffalo I'd seen in America.

The wind bit, but the mood was festive and preparations precise. Vendors were already selling sausages and mulled wine. Cartloads of river sand had been spread for traction. Regiments of soldiers rose before dawn and marched to line the procession route three ranks deep. Ten thousand cavalry would sandwich the carriages of the elite. Power was to be confirmed by both might and God, and Bonaparte and his ministers had done all they could to avoid humiliation. It remained to us to turn coronation into fiasco.

I carried the Crown of Thorns in a bag on my shoulder, clasped with the imperial seal that would allow the baggage inside Notre Dame. Harry walked between us, scuffing happily at the light snow. He had his bag of marbles in his pocket. I knew he was likely leaving his toys behind, and those would be slight consolation.

I brooded. Would Catherine succeed? French police had followed us from the beginning. Napoleon manipulated us. I'm always nervous when things are going well.

"Whatever happens, we must stay together," I said.

Astiza squeezed my hand.

The new plazas created by demolition of the old medieval houses were already crowded—the ordinary hoping for glimpses of the famous, and the elite of Napoleonic France grumbling good-naturedly as they were forced into snaking lines to show tickets. The weather-stained cathedral was in sad disrepair. Many of its statues had been "beheaded" during the revolution because rioting peasants had mistaken saintly figures for royalty and took hammers to them in a fit of patriotic vandalism. Political fanatics had subsequently turned Notre Dame into an atheistic "Temple of Reason," a classical temple temporarily displacing the altar. Later the church served as a food warehouse. Now it was a cathedral again, but one temporarily paneled and painted on the outside with symbols of temporal glory.

The coronation committees had erected a false Gothic facade at the front of the church, covering real stones with fake ones that framed painted scenes of French heroes and battles. The temporary gallery and tent along its north side were used to muster dignitaries and keep the mob at bay. Long pennant flags flew from poles like a medieval tournament, and atop the Gothic towers of the cathedral itself, imperial banners the size of mainsails hung like gargantuan proclamations. A wooden "Roman temple" had been erected to sell snacks and souvenirs; a carousel turned in circles to amuse children; and velvet-clothed pages threaded through the crowds to give away tens of thousands of bronze coronation medallions engraved with images of Napoleon and Josephine.

Skepticism was forbidden. The playwright Marie-Joseph Chenier had opened a play called *Cyrus* in the

Opéra-Comique, but when the actors urged tyrants to be democratic, the performances were promptly shut down.

Even such attempted criticism was rare. Everyone who was anyone wanted to watch the crowning. Women in fashionably low-cut dresses shivered as they shuffled forward, pulling furs onto their shoulders but not quite ready to cover their décolletage. A lucky few dismounted from coaches near the Palais de Justice just as magistrates were marching from the Court of Cassation. The judges gave ladies shelter from the chill with their flame-colored togas, scurrying for Notre Dame like scarlet birds with chicks under one wing.

Commoners buzzed like an agitated hive. People sensed that history had turned a page and something glorious and terrible was about to be commemorated. They would tell their neighbors, in the momentous years to come, that they'd witnessed the beginning. Hawkers sold coffee and rolls. Enterprising merchants nearby charged two francs to use their privies. The most tireless prostitutes assembled, at nine in the morning under paper Chinese lanterns strung along an arcade, to advertise their wares. Farmers from the countryside gawked.

We pushed to the temporary reception tent at the rear of the church, remembering from Catherine that acting important is nearly the equivalent of being so.

There was confusion as sentries denied entry to some and pulled others forward, so I took my boy on my shoulders, wife by the arm, and squirted our way to the front. Catherine was waiting, a good sign, and waved frantically from inside. When a sentry moved to block us, she intercepted and spoke sharply. He obeyed because the comtesse wore an artificial flower dyed the French tricolor to signify her authority. She was also wearing a white silk dress I'd never seen before, making her as dazzling as a marble statue. Did the imperial household provide the gown? She ushered us into the circular tent. When she grabbed to take the bag with the crown, I found myself clutching for a moment. A guard was approaching, and Catherine tugged impatiently, her eyes flashing warning. I let it go, and she swept it up to reveal the imperial seal. It warded off the curious gendarme.

"I have only moments," she said breathlessly. "Tell me I won't be damned."

"Only if you fail. Can you get access to the crowns?"

"Presence is everything. I act important, and thus I am."

"You'd make a fine marshal for Napoleon."

"For the true monarchy, once it's restored." She leaned closer. "Did you pack the pistol as I asked?"

"Loaded and primed."

"We shouldn't need it but must brace for the worst. Now, I've tried to improve your seating—" She looked over my shoulder to someone behind me, eyes widening. "Oh!"

A hand gripped my shoulder, tight as a vise. I turned. It was the policeman Pasques, a black hangman in a sea of peacocks. Had we been caught?

No, he was only a messenger again. "The Grand Chamberlain Talleyrand requests your company, Monsieur Gage."

"Talleyrand? Today?"

"It makes no sense to me, either. Come this way, to avoid the line."

People gave my family a glance of both resentment and respect as Pasques bulled us into the church. I was apprehensive. Half the princes of Germany were here, and Talleyrand had time to see me? Pasques steered us through the throng like a barge cracking ice, and we stopped by a pillar. It was still cold enough that we could see our breath. The cathedral echoed from the theater buzz of assembling spectators and tuning instruments. The timber cribbing of temporary spectator stands broke the usual soaring sightlines of Notre Dame.

"Your wife must wait for you in the choir behind the thrones," Pasques said. He frowned. "You brought your little boy?"

"We avoid separation. They both must stay with me."

"Not to see the Grand Chamberlain. They can wait to take their seats with you together when we return. You've been moved next to great dignitaries." He shook his head.

"I fear we'll be separated in this throng."

"I'll watch them," Catherine said, pulling Astiza from my grasp. "Don't make a fuss that calls attention." Her eyes signaled warning.

I nodded. "Papa will be back in a moment," I told Harry.

"The Grand Chamberlain is waiting at a bell tower," Pasques said. He cocked his head. "Why does everyone want to talk with you, American?"

"I suppose I'm affable."

Catherine pulled Astiza and Horus into the shadows. We'd been in Notre Dame only moments and already were altering our plan. Astiza looked worried.

"Talleyrand is impatient," the policeman said.

"As am I." A quick meeting, and then reunion. "Lead on," I told Pasques.

We passed from behind the spectator stands to the central nave. Notre Dame was almost unrecognizable. A broad green carpet covered the stone floor, overlain by a narrow blue one embroidered with Napoleon's golden bees. To each side, in tiers between the nave's pillars, temporary viewing stands narrowed the church's width, giving the ceremony crowded intimacy. Each bank of benches was back-lit by stained-glass windows and curtained at the base by fabric panels painted rose and gold. Banners, flags, and white tapestries hung everywhere, turning Gothic grandeur into operatic riot, the cathedral as overwrought as a bordello. And why not? Life today is performed as if onstage: desperate conspiracies, impassioned trysts, dramatic speeches, and doomed charges. Dignity has disappeared. The church pews were gone, confessionals hidden, and the regular altar and its gate obscured.

Pope Pius, I guessed, would not be pleased.

In the transept of the cathedral's center, where the side arms join the main axis, a triumphal arch had been built out of wood. Steep steps led up to twin thrones canopied with scarlet. To one side was a temporary elevated altar with a throne for the pope.

If the hangings were grand, people's costumes were grander. Ushers wore black and green; pages purple. A choir the size of a regiment was in pious white, and a full orchestra in black glittered with polished brass instruments and lacquered violins. Officers among the assembling spectators wore the distinctive uniforms of grenadiers, fusiliers, chasseurs, dragoons, voltigeurs, tirailleurs, carabiniers, hussars, cuirassiers, and the Imperial Guard. There were turbaned Mamelukes, high-ranking gendarmes, naval marines, ladies-in-waiting, jeweled duchesses, counts, abbesses, Turkish ambassadors, a Polynesian potentate, and society matrons. No doubt they'd have thrown in some vestal virgins if they could have found any in Paris. The poles of battle flags, regimental standards, and silver pikes jostled and clinked. Swords rattled. Ten thousand female throats bore diamonds that glinted like white flames. I saw foreign uniforms of yellow, pink, orange, turquoise, and ivory. I was dressed shabbily, in clothes meant for escape, and felt as conspicuous following Pasques as a fly on a wedding cake.

The policeman led me to a door giving access to the north bell tower, guarded by a quartet of grenadiers. I hesitated. Was I going to be charged with the theft of bell rope at the scene of my crime?

"Inside, American."

No, the "limping devil" was truly waiting, his own plush coat cardinal red, his white silk sash as wide as a saddle blanket, and his silk stockings, lace cravat, and tricorne hat outdated but dignified, reflecting his affection for traditional royalist fashion. He took my cold hand with his own white-gloved one. I hesitantly half bowed, wary, curious, and calculating.

"Monsieur Gage! We're flattered by the attendance of a representative of the United States."

"Hardly that, Grand Chamberlain. A citizen of America, yes, a Franklin man for certain. But representative? No one from my country knows I'm here."

His smile was shrewd. Talleyrand, like Réal and Fouché, always gave the impression of knowing all. "But consultant to the emperor! Which is what I want to discuss. These ceremonies take aeons to unfold, and Napoleon will be late getting through the narrow streets, so come up for the view. I've also reserved you better seats inside. The whole affair will be gaudy as a circus and longer than the opera, but well worth remembering."

With surprising energy he stumped his way up the circular stone stairway. I followed, retracing my steps with Harry. I half expected the grand chamberlain to pause dramatically at the bells, point at a sliced rope, and accuse me of high treason. But no, we didn't go that high; instead, we came out on the walkway and parapet between the two Gothic towers, this grand balcony putting us directly over the main doors to the church.

The view was magnificent.

Not only had the flurries stopped, the clouds had lifted like a rising curtain. Low December sun cast

golden light across Paris. The Seine glinted, and roof-
tops sparkled from their coating of snow. There was
a haze of smoke past the Louvre, where celebratory
cannon batteries kept firing. Napoleon, the gunner,
would have a battle just to hear their music. Church
bells pealed, though not the ones directly above us yet,
and the snaking admission lines twitched as people
shuffled forward. What must it feel like to have hundreds of thousands standing in the cold merely to
glimpse your arrival? What power! What vanity!

"Paris is extraordinary, is it not?" the grand chamberlain asked.

"I'm drawn as if by a woman."

"The feminine beauty we see today is one of the joys
of life. Do you remember my theory of the feminine
and masculine cycles of history?"

"Yes. And that men and Mars are triumphant now."

"So in autumn I seek the last leaf, and in spring the
first crocus. I frequent the Louvre, Monsieur Gage, and
not just to gaze upon the wonders brought back from
Italy and Egypt." The old palace, not lived in since
the 1660s, had become Europe's first public presentation of great works of art. It was usually so jammed it
was tiresome. "I go for art, yes, but also for the visiting women. Sometimes I sit discreetly in a shadowy
corner and watch beauty circulate around the statuary.

They're as exquisite as the pieces idealizing them. It's a respite from negotiating the fate of nations."

"Then we have something in common, Grand Chamberlain."

The papal procession of coaches rolled through the square below and Pius VII emerged to walk the gallery to the waiting Cardinal Belloy. The pope looked small from this height, slightly bent, plain dressed, and yet dignified. His spiritual realm required him to deal with temporal and temperamental royals, and I suspect he saw the day's ironies more clearly than anyone. His humility made me feel guilty about our subterfuge.

Then cheers rolled toward us like waves to a shore. In the far distance there was a glint of gold from the slowly approaching coaches of the imperial family. The hedge of infantry on each side of the parade route was a silver ribbon of bayonets, quivering as the men snapped to attention. The preceding dragoons and lancers had plumed golden helmets and bobbing spears with tricolor banners. Every home on the route seemed to have hung celebratory decoration, from tapestries to evergreen boughs. From the crowds, little flags waved like leaves in a tree.

"This is power made manifest, is it not?" Talleyrand's habitual tone was cynical, but even he sounded impressed.

"This many people never turn out to see me."

"And yet you've attained a curious importance, consorting with the mighty and conferring with their ministers. Do you ever wonder at the oddness of life?"

"All the time."

Then there was a lull in the conversation, dragging on forever, which I finally broke. Silence is a weapon, and Talleyrand used it to control dialogue. "I'm flattered by your company, Grand Chamberlain, but puzzled as well. Surely you should be in the procession. Or have more significant guests than me to attend to."

"Grander, but none more important." Talleyrand could caress with flattery or bite with harsh insight. "I've no interest in being displayed for public spectacle like a guillotine victim in a rolling tumbrel. I accomplish more by waiting here. I'll talk to many important men this morning. All are rascals, highborn and low, and all potentially useful through banal self-interest."

He did not exempt me from this assessment.

"My goal is to retire."

"Yet once again you've been recruited to a mission for Bonaparte."

"I wasn't given any choice." I felt vastly outnumbered, on the wrong side of history. "He uses us all."

"Yes. Even his wife, to keep his own rapacious family at bay. Do you know the two were hurriedly remarried last night to satisfy the pope before blessings could be given at the coronation? Only a civil ceremony united them before. Josephine, the scheming widow, who by all accounts participated in orgies before fixing her talons on the rising Corsican. And Bonaparte, inexplicably in love, even while keeping a chain of mistresses he mounts like a relay of horses during his inspections of France. And simple Pius to sanction it all! No wonder a million have come to this comedy. Life is far more droll than the theater."

"We're all trying to reform." I followed the line of the river. Though I couldn't see it, I could judge where Fulton's steamboat floated half a mile away. My Jaeger rifle was hidden there.

"I'd be mystified why the police tolerate you, Monsieur Gage, if I didn't know it was on the orders of Bonaparte. Just what is your assignment again?"

"Ask him yourself."

He looked annoyed. "But of course I have, and of course he's not completely answered. He trusts no one, not me; not Fouché; not Réal; not Savary, who commands the city's military guard; nor Moncey with the gendarmerie; nor Dubois, chief of police. A dozen people spy on you, Gage, but a dozen spy on each of them as well. In a modern state, all are watched, all are rewarded, and all can fall at any moment; birth is no longer a protection, and achievement buys reward only until tomorrow. Bonaparte has made manifest what has always been unstated: daily existence is a struggle for the high as well as the low."

"Napoleon just finds me useful at times."

"Yes." He stared out over the crowds. "Suffice to say, Ethan, that I believe the mission you've been given is extraordinarily significant, and I thought I could help you."

"Grand Chamberlain, despite your rank, you know I'm not at liberty to discuss my assignments from the emperor. Again, should you not ask him yourself?"

Talleyrand ignored this. "Men like you are dangerous to political stability, unless expertly guided. Bonaparte is brilliant but lacks a certain . . . subtlety. That's what I provide. I have my own spies. So I know that your mission will take you to Bohemia and other parts of the Austrian Empire. And if you find the android that men are seeking, you must not drag it back to Paris."

I felt uneasy. Did his political omniscience make him friend or foe? "I'm ordered to bring the Brazen Head to the emperor."

"No, you're not. His armies will come to you."

"But Napoleon is marching on London." Once more I was playing the spy for the British, worming out strategic clues. But who was I, really? Why was I standing with the French Machiavelli when I should be sitting with my family? Each time I tried to provide for or avenge my wife, it seemed to result in separation.

My only salvation was my secret belief that somehow, at some time, I'd win the chance to do something truly good and make up for all my sins.

"Napoleon will march in many directions before he's finished. And he will be finished someday, as will we all. So look ahead, Gage, look ahead."

"I'm better at looking into the past. Old tombs and ancient rubbish. Often what we seek doesn't exist at all."

"This automaton does." Talleyrand still watched the golden carriages, crossing the Seine now onto the Île de la Cité, crowds roaring and rippling. "You must find the android first. At the end of the sixteenth century Rudolf II, Holy Roman emperor, established his capital in Prague. It's a learned city and a mysterious one, tucked away from the main avenues of armies and attracting alchemists, wizards, astronomers, and numerologists. Tycho Brahe and Johannes Kepler mapped the planets while at his court. Composers performed. Artists painted. Necromancers drew magic circles on cellar floors. Rudolf was mad, but he was also brilliant, and he built a wing at Prague Castle that had cabinets full of strange curiosities. They included a bowl of agate he believed to be the Holy Grail, a unicorn horn, gemstones, magical swords, clocks, astrolabes, telescopes, and stuffed exotic animals. His gardens had plants from around the world."

"My boy would like to see that." It never hurts to remind the powerful that you have a family, in order to encourage mercy should you need it.

"The cabinets have been lost, as have the laboratories where Rudolf's alchemists such as Edward Kelly and John Dee sought the Philosopher's Stone. There was parchment of indecipherable writing, peculiar art, intricate mazes, and religious trinkets from lost kingdoms."

"Now *that* my wife would like to see."

"Rudolf never married but had lovers, male and female, who held power over him. They ranged from Ottoman temptresses to a prince of Transylvania. But more than anything he was seduced by knowledge."

The wind was cold, the sky that lovely robin's-egg blue of winter, and the procession dazzling as it approached. Napoleon's golden coach had reportedly cost a million francs. It was paneled in glass to allow people to glimpse him, and was festooned with medallions, coats of arms, allegorical figurines, and enough sculpted eagles to stuff a nest. The coachman was César, who'd saved Bonaparte's life from the Infernal

Machine. Roustan the Mameluke rode protectively behind. The team was eight gray horses decorated with braided manes, bronze-colored reins, and red Moroccan harnesses.

Facing the emperor in the coach were the only two brothers who consented to attend, Joseph and Louis. Brother Lucien, the hapless politician who'd helped Napoleon seize power in 1799, was sulking in Rome because the emperor found him incompetent. Brother Jerome had joined him, smarting from Napoleon's insistence that he annul his marriage to the American beauty Betsy Patterson and disown his child by her. With them was Napoleon's shrewish mother Letizia, who'd chosen needy Lucien over hardheaded Napoleon.

How far we'd both climbed—Napoleon to royalty, which made him resented by a dependent family; me to games I wasn't prepared to play. Instinct suddenly told me to be anywhere than where I was standing.

"I always enjoy a history lesson, Grand Chamberlain, but again am surprised you've time to share it. Why are you telling me all this?"

"To guide you, because it's imperative you succeed. I'm going to suggest you look for the Brazen Head that Napoleon wants you to find amid the castles and caves of central Europe. You want to head east. I'm going to give you the hilt of a broken sword that may prove a clue. I'm doing so because I want to examine this marvel myself. Napoleon would use it for conquest, but I for peace. So I brought you up here to propose a partnership."

"East is away from England."

"Exactly. It's just as well that Sidney Smith begins to forget what you're up to. Make more money working with me."

"Money?"

"Ten thousand francs if you find a machine that foretells the future. A castle, if you want it. I suspect we'll conquer dozens in the years ahead."

Now my heart beat faster. Investments in England, a fortune from Paris, and a castle in Bohemia . . . my horizons were expanding as rapidly as Napoleon's. What was my purpose? Payback for the trials my family had endured. I was a puppet, yes, but strings could pull both ways. Perhaps it was I who was in charge! I'd manipulate these greedy, grasping men as they manipulated me, and save the world in the process. I felt a flush of confidence. I didn't need to flee, I was where destiny demanded.

"My quest seems improbable. A lost automaton?"

"That was my reaction. Napoleon meets a thousand people, of course, and more than a few get his attention by spouting nonsense. But then I remembered an old Jewish legend from my religious studies, a tale of an artificial man made from mud called a golem. It made me wonder if your quest might not have a grain of truth."

The name had an eerie sound. "A mud man?"

"A monster, answerable to a rabbi master. This golem had the power to defend the Jews of Prague if properly instructed, or so the story goes. By legend it went out of control and had to be subdued and still rests, a clay shell, in a synagogue attic in Prague. Yet isn't it intriguing how stories of Albertus Magnus, Christian Rosenkreutz, Rudolf II, and the golem of Prague all take us to the same places? If something extraordinary really exists, it's imperative I see it first. Foretelling the future! So I'm offering letters of protection if you journey to the east, money to live on, and a fortune if you succeed. Your wife is being given the necessary documents as we speak."

"And if I refuse?"

"I'll send cutthroats in competition."

So I was to be a tool of Talleyrand as well as Napoleon and Smith. If I delivered the automaton to him, he would take credit for delivering it to his own master, Napoleon. I am strangely popular. Getting caught between these men was risky, yet maybe I could use this hysteria over an android to get safely out of Paris. Ten thousand francs to find a mechanical man? If everyone in France thought I was their ally, maybe they'd leave me alone.

"I'm flattered by your confidence, Grand Chamberlain, and honored you'd share it on such a crucial day. But this could be a test, so let me say that my first loyalty is to the emperor."

"As is mine. Our friendship is for the emperor's good."

"He wouldn't be pleased if I gave this android to you instead of him."

"Nor am I asking you to. Only that I question it first. It could make me a most valuable adviser. But only an adviser."

"So valuable you can spare ten thousand francs?" I wanted to confirm this figure.

"We're going to loot Europe. Such funds will be a beggar's purse." He said it matter-of-factly.

I swallowed. "You mentioned expenses?"

He opened his cloak. There were pockets sewn inside stuffed with important-looking papers, making him a walking credenza. He fished out some gold coins. "Enough to make inquiries. And here's a stub of sword."

"What's its story?"

"Simply that its missing medieval blade might prove useful. Look for more legends in Bohemia and the lands east. So we're partners?"

What choice did I have? I was locked in orbit around powerful puppeteers. "Partners." Meanwhile, I'd entirely forgotten that I was about to corrupt the coronation and, with it, Napoleon's rule.

"Good! Let's go inside and witness the crowning. I have a feeling it will be something never quite seen before."

Chapter 19

An aide to Talleyrand replaced my yellow ticket with a gold one. I was escorted without my family to a balcony bench just to the left of the triumphal arch where Napoleon would take his throne. "Wait for your wife here." Talleyrand would attend on the cathedral floor, in a cluster of the highest ministers.

The air in the cathedral had warmed from the crush. Damp cloaks gave a wet-dog smell, mixed with incense and candles. Pigeons fluttered at the arched ceiling near holes that hadn't been repaired since the revolution.

I was lucky. Most spectators were placed so distant in the nave that they'd have to crane their necks to see. I had a direct view of the disaster I intended to cause, even while pondering this new alliance with Talleyrand. If Napoleon was confounded, would men still be bidding for the Brazen Head? Probably more so, in any scramble for power.

My ticket meant I was perched near the important, who glanced at my traveler clothing as if I'd stumbled into the wrong reception. To get to my seat I elbowed and stepped over tribunes, grand officers of the Legion, generals, admirals, procurators-general of the Imperial Courts, sea prefects, mayors of good towns, presidents of canton assemblies, and so on, each placed to make clear the Napoleonic pecking order. Across from me on another tier of benches, stacked like produce in a market stand, were princes, princesses, diplomats, famed savants, ranking police officials, and even the minister of sewers and wells. If only Ben Franklin could see me now.

I catalogued my alliances. I'd conspired with the British spymaster Sidney Smith to take revenge for the death of my wife who, as it turned out, was not dead. I'd partnered with Comtesse Catherine Marceau for a return of royalists who, as it turned out, were arrested, scattered, or repatriated. I'd allied with Réal to advise Napoleon's army officers, allied with Napoleon to find a medieval automaton I was skeptical existed, allied with odd Palatine to disrupt Napoleon's coronation with religious blasphemy, and been promised ten thousand francs by Talleyrand to let him try this "android" first. Now I was sitting in the center of an agitated porridge of two million excited Frenchmen who, if they knew what I was about, would rip me limb from limb.

For such a simple man, my life is surprisingly complicated.

Astiza's and Harry's place was empty. Their absence made me uneasy. Had she gotten the better tickets? Perhaps she was helping the comtesse make the substitution. Perhaps Talleyrand's aides were giving her further instruction on where to travel east. If chaos ensued, we should escape west as planned, but perhaps there was opportunity eastward as well. I shifted restlessly. I needed to consult with my wife.

Also conspicuously empty was a seat opposite me, intended for the emperor's domineering and everdissatisfied mother. The politically astute artist David would later paint her into the coronation, but the vacuum created by her absence reminded everyone that even absolute power is not absolute.

We waited, interminably. The pope had set off for the cathedral at nine, Napoleon at ten. The music began at half-past ten when the pope's regiment of robed clergy paraded into Notre Dame with miter hats, swinging censors, and ornate candlesticks. Cardinals and bishops from across Western Europe marched to the music of what I read in the ceremony brochure was two orchestras, four choirs, five bands, and altar boys with communion bells: about five hundred noisemakers in all. Hymns alternated with anthems followed by bands crashing into hideous military music, and then altar boys would jingle into the echoing silences. We endured, stoically.

Pius entered in a scarlet robe and weighted with a papal crown Napoleon had ordered made with a precisely reported 4,209 diamonds, rubies, and emeralds, just in case the Vatican missed the value of the bribe. The pope wore it like a yoke. Cloak and headgear were so heavy that once seated he shed them for modest white dress and simple papal cap. He blessed us, even me, turning from one group to another with fingers uplifted.

At eleven we heard the roars of adulation as Napoleon and Josephine finally arrived outside and were escorted into the Archbishop's Palace to re-dress. They required nearly an hour to exchange the morning's velvet frippery for coronation robes as bulky as bear pelts. As time crawled, Pius ran out of blessings and prayers and finally just sat with his eyes shut, praying or napping. The rest of us yawned as orchestra and choir banged back and forth. Vendors sold meat rolls that were passed hand over hand. Lords and ladies sipped from smuggled flasks.

Where was my family?

I impatiently peered into the shadows at either side of the triumphal arch, looking for Astiza and Harry. Finally, there they were, scanning the crowd to look for me! I lifted my arm, but they gave no recognition. Catherine, radiant in white, her hair gloriously set, figure sublime, whispered to this aide or that. She did glance my way, but if she saw me, she didn't share it with Astiza.

I relaxed. All was in place, and I assumed my wife and son would join me shortly. I practiced looking innocent.

The final high plenipotentiaries marched into the cathedral, the pace stately as a wedding. Cardinal Belloy looked serene for a man who has just been robbed in his own chambers, but perhaps nothing much rattles you at ninety-five. Then five long minutes of pregnant silence, except for the rustling and coughs of a huge assembly in a vast cathedral. Finally, a relieved stir when Napoleon paced into view, looking swallowed by his robes. He wore an embroidered classical tunic that fell to his ankles like a nightgown, a sash with enough fabric for a tablecloth, and a red fur-trimmed robe so heavy, and so intricately inlaid with embroidery, that he looked like he was caped in a carpet. It dragged like a cross. I knew Napoleon had battlefield courage, but it took courage of another kind for this kind of performance, where even a misstep would become the merciless gossip of Paris.

Yet Josephine was the one who entranced the crowd.

Women glow when they're in love, when they've made love, or when they are pregnant. The empress had a flush of utter triumph this day. Her smile was closed to hide her poor teeth, but what a wide smile it was, eyes damp, head high, her expression joyous from the religious recognition of her marriage the night before. And now the political legitimization of her role as empress, an opulent crowning that Marie Antoinette never enjoyed!

The Creole from Martinique was the most beautiful I ever saw her, exquisitely made up, and at forty-one—six years older than Napoleon—she looked twenty. Her gown was a spotless white and her scarlet mantle a sumptuous ten yards long, all of it embroidered, bejeweled, and lined with enough white ermine to depopulate the fur farms of Russia. Despite her mantle's size and weight, it was kept off her shoulders so that she could display elegantly puffed sleeves and a shapely bust; one end of the train was attached near her neck and the other with a strap to her waist. She seemed to be emerging from a pool of velvet and fur.

Women sighed at the sight of her.

Napoleon's sulking sisters carried Josephine's train. Yet even in their foul mood they shone from being gowned like goddesses. Each had a tiara, a long dress off the shoulders, and a necklace costly enough to buy a gun battery.

The choreography was intricate as a minuet, the panoply riotously over the top, and the drama absolutely unforgettable, as it was meant to be. Royalists might plot to assassinate a mere first consul and upstart general, but a blessed and crowned emperor? Despite what slaves once whispered into the ears of the Caesars, Napoleon was no longer a mere man. He was a political demigod.

We were transfixed, the women in the audience murmuring with envy and the men muttering excitedly about future opportunities. Napoleon's ambition fused with that of everyone in the cathedral. They would rise, and risk, with him.

And then there was a jostling of bodies, apologies of *excusez-moi*, and a man plopped exhaustedly down next to me, taking Astiza's seat.

"My pardon, monsieur, but I was told this space has become available. What a grand view we share!" I recognized the voice immediately but had trouble placing it, and then realized that by astonishing coincidence I was seated next to Marie-Etienne Nitot, the jeweler who'd first told us last year that my stolen emerald was from a legendary Aztec hoard. Before I could sell it to him, scoundrels attacked us. I'd assumed they learned of the jewel from his boasting.

"Nitot, you devil," I growled.

"Monsieur Gage, my old friend! Ah, what happenstance! I'd feared you'd come to harm, and yet here we both are, at the center of the new Europe."

If he felt guilt for the way my family was handled in his shop, he hid it well. I scowled. "You mean the harm that came our way last year?"

"But of course! We were investigating your remarkable gem, the Green Apple of the Sun, and then these rogues accost me! I found my workshop in shambles and you disappeared. I didn't know what was going on and feared scandal would damage my reputation. Then I was told you have a habit of getting mixed up with unsavory villains." He was genuinely curious. "Did you get the emerald back?"

"Eventually."

"I'd still be interested in buying it."

The gall of him to pretend innocence! But perhaps he *was* innocent, and, in any event, I'd no time for him now. "I sold it in London."

"Alas, an opportunity lost. May I ask what you got for it?"

It was none of his business, but what was the harm? "Ten thousand pounds."

"But you could have earned twice that, at least, in Paris!"

That possibility just made me grumpier, not to mention reminding me that by embroiling myself in conspiracy in France I was cut off from my funds in England. If we traveled to Bohemia, our poverty would continue. I was once again for all practical purposes poor, surrounded by rich men, and drawn in conflicting directions. "I'm impressed that you're in the stands of the highest notables," I said, implying that perhaps he didn't deserve to be here, either. Where the devil was Astiza?

"Yes. I remain a favorite of Josephine, even if Marguerite did get the commission for the crowns. But my seating is actually due to your new companion, Inspector Catherine Marceau. Such beauties you accumulate!"

"Inspector?"

"Yes, the woman in white." He pointed at my confederate, far below.

I was confused. "You know Catherine?"

"We've done business together. Rumor holds she took the place of a strangled comtesse during the Terror and has been valiantly spying on England. As brave as she is lovely! She gave me the ticket for this seat."

"She told you she's a spy?" I said stupidly. Had Catherine made up a story about herself to secure our safety?

"An agent of the police. Your wife tragically lost and this new beauty at your side: what a lucky rogue you are, American!"

He thought my wife was still lost?

"And you must be doing well the way your mistress spends your money as if plucked by the vine. What an eye for jewelry she has!"

"Spends my money?" My understanding was officially lost.

"The new French francs and old English gold sovereigns she said you brought from London! Gorgeous coins for uncertain times. Here, look at the minting." He reached in a vest pocket and brought out one that shone like the sun. Several spectators looked curiously in our direction. I was confused. Catherine had no money. What was Nitot talking about?

Gasps brought my attention back to the stage. Now Napoleon was kneeling, the pope droning on with a blessing and the emperor replying with a pledge. Censers swung on cue, incense drifting over the tableau. The substitution of the crowns would be revealed in moments. I looked down in the shadows toward Catherine and my family.

The comtesse was looking up at me, smiling as triumphantly as Josephine but with her teeth on display, ice white and perfect. A huge, looming figure had joined the group. It was Pasques, who took Astiza's arm in his firm grip and pulled her deeper into the unseen choir, Harry dragged with them.

Catherine had no money.

Unless she'd not really lost her money in the Channel surf as she claimed when we came ashore, and had been lying to me ever since.

I blinked. Without thinking of it, my hand closed over Nitot's hand and coin. Why had Catherine lied about losing her money? To selfishly keep it? Had she really been stealing from my purse in Paris, as well?

She looked up at me as if I were a joke. Was nothing true? Had the comtesse really wormed her way into Josephine's retinue? Or had she been invited there from the very beginning, as a double agent operating in London to foil the American adventurer, Ethan Gage?

Why was she watching me now, instead of the coronation?

There was a bustle at our tier of seats. Gendarmes had appeared at either end of my row, searching faces for my own.

The critical moment had come. The pope ceased speaking, and Cardinal Belloy handed him a golden box, presumably containing the imperial crown. Napoleon stood and ascended the steps to the Catholic altar. The pope turned, took the box from Belloy with slow gravity, and opened it.

Pius froze in shock. No one could see what was inside, but I knew what he was viewing: the vines that had tortured Jesus. Catherine had succeeded after all, the greedy spendthrift! My relief was intense, the world spinning, while the church was absolutely silent except for the rustlings of twenty thousand onlookers waiting impatiently for the crowning.

Now the pope would lift out the Crown of Thorns, sharing his outrage and consternation with the whole world.

Except he had no time to.

Army Marshal Joachim Murat strode forward bearing a simple crown of golden laurel leaves on an ornate pillow.

Napoleon wheeled to meet this precisely timed flanking maneuver. While Pius stood paralyzed, staring stupidly at the holiest relic in Christendom, the new French emperor calmly turned his back on the prelate, plucked the crown off Murat's pillow, and put the golden wreath on his own head, cocky as Caesar. He looked defiantly out into the crowd, ignoring the pope and daring anyone to object to his boldness.

There was an excited murmur, rising to a roar as people whispered. "Did you see? He's crowned himself!" Astonishment rushed through the cathedral like wind and wildfire.

There was a snap as the lid of the golden box that held the Crown of Thorns snapped shut. Pius stood in shock, goggle-eyed and confused.

Napoleon, meanwhile, was erect as a guardsman and as pleased as a triumphant actor. His self-crowning was audacious, unprecedented, and brilliant. The pope was on hand to provide endorsement, but he'd been adroitly prevented by the emperor's circle, including Catherine Marceau, from doing the act himself. Napoleon's new stature came not from the Catholic Church, but from the will of the French people. He'd honored a thousand years of tradition, yet surmounted it with his own. He'd maneuvered Christianity into alliance, yet owed the pope nothing. He'd been blessed, but was not a penitent to Rome.

Josephine was still kneeling, hands clasped in prayer, head humbly bowed. A second, more spectacular crown was presented. Instead of mimicking the Roman emperors, this was the medieval style with velvet, gold, and jewels, as big as a helmet. Napoleon lifted it from its pillow, smiled with his mouth but not his eyes, and crowned his own wife empress.

Another gasp rotated round the cathedral. I had lost the ability to breathe. All my mad risk, with wife and son, had served only to elevate the Corsican devil higher than ever! All that I had assumed was a lie.

Pius hurriedly slid the box with the Crown of Thorns under his chair, cast an angry, puzzled glance at Cardinal Belloy, and sat. He looked mortified. Belloy looked bewildered.

Choir and orchestra burst into song.

And I, Ethan Gage, who'd conspired with my family to humiliate this new Caesar, had instead been tricked into elevating his coronation into an assertion of secular state power.

Astiza and Harry had disappeared.

The gendarmes were closing from both sides, spectators objecting as the policemen temporarily blocked their view.

Disaster!

Napoleon was mounting the steep steps up to his new throne. He jerked to a halt at the beginning, the weight of his robes pulling him backward. Leaning into it, he trudged up the stairs to his imperial perch, dragging his mantle like a tarp.

Josephine's experience was even worse. Just as she reached the stairs the heavy train carried by Napoleon's sisters was abruptly dropped. I couldn't tell if the princesses did so out of jealousy or rehearsal, but the fabric weighed half as much as Josephine herself, and it almost toppled her. Napoleon gestured for her to keep going. She bent, surged, and staggered to the top, the clumsiness partly masked by the acreage of her mantle. A sail that big makes anything seem to ripple and flow.

A shaken Pius mounted the stairs after them, completely outmaneuvered, but, following rehearsal, he still kissed the emperor on the cheek. *"Vivat Imperator in aeternum,"* he proclaimed. A parade of beautiful maidens appeared to carry the Bible and sacramental objects from the altar up to the throne, everyone bowing, holding, thrusting, kissing, and twenty thousand viewers coming to their feet. The presidents of the Senate, Tribunate, and Corps Legislatif came forward to administer the oath. Bonaparte put his hand on the Book of Gospels and recited: "To govern only in accordance with the interests, the happiness, and the glory of the French people."

"Excusez-moi," the surrounding gendarmes said as they struggled to reach me. "Ethan Gage, remain where you are!"

Senators, princes, and soldiers roared. Music swelled, the Gothic arches making it sound as if it came from heaven. Outside, a hundred cannons bellowed, and the concussion of the report punched through the air of Notre Dame, the roosting pigeons erupting as if their wings were joining the applause.

I was trapped from the press of people around me. Nitot clasped my arm, excited as a child. "Did you see, did you see? He crowned himself!"

I knocked his hand aside. Where was my family? Catherine had played me from the very beginning. She was an imposter, taking the place of a lovely young aristocrat who had probably been strangled in her cell and truly buried. She had escaped to England with a new biography to pose as a comtesse and work as a French spy. Was the mysterious Palatine part of the plot, too? Was everyone false? I was a puppet with a block of wood for a head.

All we could do is run for the borders.

With exit through the crowd impossible, I crouched and rolled under the curtain at the base of our bench and into the timber framework that held up the viewing stands.

"Monsieur Gage, not that way!" the idiot Nitot cried.

"Halt!" policemen shouted.

It was dark, the music and cheers reverberating as if I were in a drum. People were stamping in celebration. I dropped down through the framing, hit the cathedral floor backstage, and sprinted down the side aisles to the rear of the church, looking for my family.

We must escape before our arrest for the theft of the Crown of Thorns.

We must salvage *something*, such as the Brazen Head.

Unless that was a lie, too.

Chapter 20

I kept to the edges of the cathedral, seeking shadows as I frantically looked for my wife and child. Had they already fled to our agreed rendezvous? Dignitaries were filing into the choir behind the temporary arched throne as the ceremony drew to a close. Pages and altar boys were scurrying on errands, soldiers were being organized to line the departure, and bishops and priests assembled in clusters under stained-glass windows. I wanted to shout Astiza's name, but remaining furtive was my only chance to get out of this trap.

How deep did the betrayals go? Had Catherine tipped the French as early as our Channel crossing? But why had she bothered with a wastrel like me? Had the gnomish Palatine wanted to sabotage the coronation, or been in on a clever scheme to make it even more spectacular? Did this Brazen Head really exist, or was it an invented goose chase? If Catherine were a traitor, why not murder me at the beginning?

Were we still being maneuvered? Marceau, who-ever she really was, had neatly separated me from my family, betrayed our plot with the crown to Napoleon, allowed him to use it to his own advantage, and allowed Pasques to drag off my wife and son.

I really should study insects, or take up falconry.

I couldn't depart by the main entry because I'd surely be stopped. So a quick circuit of the rear to look for my family, and then a hunt for a side door. I turned . . .

And Pasques blocked me like an obstinate bull. He was dressed in his habitual black and was homelier than usual from swelling on one side of his face. His eye was discolored and cheek bleeding.

"Your wife is a treacherous harridan, American." So at least I had the satisfaction that Astiza had slugged him and perhaps gotten away. In retaliation, he cocked his arm, his fist as big as a cannonball and signaling like a semaphore.

"Ethan, a word!" came a shout from behind. "I want to know how you did it!" It was Talleyrand, coming from the other direction. "Even if futile, it was clever!" So the foreign minister had known as well that my attempt to sabotage the coronation would become a fiasco, and yet still he had wanted the Brazen Head. So it *did* exist!

Time for payback.

I prefer to reason with people, but sometimes it's more effective to emphasize your own opinion. So I slammed my boot into Pasques's instep, making him howl, and ducked when he swung.

The wind of the blow grazed my scalp, and I heard a crack as it connected behind with Talleyrand's chin. The grand chamberlain of France went flying, skidding on the stone floor. The policeman staggered, carried by the force of his own blow.

I kicked the side of Pasques's knee. He almost buckled. *"Merde!"*

Now the man was angry as a provoked bear. He wrenched around to grapple with me, face tight with pain, and made a stumbling charge, arms out to envelop. I remembered what Talleyrand had entrusted me with and hauled out the hilt of the ancient sword with its stub of a blade. Pasques's throat ran right onto it.

The policeman's eyes went wide with shock and fear. I couldn't thrust deep enough to cut vital arteries, but iron stung and blood flooded. When he lurched back, startled, I yanked the weapon out and kicked him as hard as I could in his cockles. "I really don't need a police escort." He toppled like an oak.

I whirled, bent, and yanked at the stunned grand chamberlain, snapping the chain holding his coronation robe and tumbling him out of it like a log. I was stealing a bundle of fabric that probably cost more than I'd earn my entire life.

"We'll still be friends, I hope," I told the dazed diplomat without irony. I hate powerful enemies. Then I ran.

The sentries by the doors were shouting, and everyone in the rear of the church had turned to witness our scuffle. I dashed for an alcove at the rear of the cathedral, my goal a rainbow-glazed window that dappled massive pillars with squares of light. Pasques was crawling in pained pursuit, his look murderous.

"Ethan, wait!"

Running to intercept me was Catherine Marceau. Her arms were wide and breasts high, as fetching as she was dangerous. "You don't understand! This is our chance to work together! All must be with Bonaparte!"

I stopped, the cloak in front of me like a shield. "You work for men who strangled the comtesse you pretend to be? Betray my family? Make me a fool?"

"I work for men who will bring reform to Europe. I work so revolution need never happen again. We're idealists, you and me." Her eyes pleaded, their seduction calculated.

"Where's my wife?" Soldiers were running toward us.

"I'll help you hunt her down."

"Then escape with me, instead of my coming with you."

Her eyes looked past my shoulder, and I could hear thudding boots and the clattering belts of the sentries. She sadly shook her head and lifted the pistol I'd given her when we entered Notre Dame, pointing it at my belly. "You'll see reason from Temple Prison."

"You won't shoot me. You're in love with me." Even I knew this was ridiculous; she'd never love anyone but herself. But I was curious to see if she'd hesitate.

She pulled the trigger.

It snapped uselessly, as I knew it would.

I'm an idiot about women, but I had enough experience to never entirely trust the charms of the Comtesse Marceau, and certainly not with a loaded pistol in a crowded church. I'd substituted its powder with pepper.

Catherine sneezed.

Talleyrand's robe became a club to clout my would-be assassin out of my way, my taking satisfaction from the way she shrieked as she tumbled across an altar and fell hard on the space behind. Not gentlemanly, but then she was no lady. I leaped on top of the marble.

Muskets went off, bullets pinging off stone. One punched through a shepherd made of stained glass.

"You don't know what you truly believe!" she cried from beneath me.

"I believe in family." I held the cloak in front of me, lowered my head, and dove. Fragments flew like hurled jewels.

I tumbled down to the ground outside the cathedral and rolled to my feet. I was in the archbishop's gardens. The crowds for the coronation were to my left, escape to the right. I ran into the alley I'd vaulted across with Harry.

"Sacrilege! Blasphemer! Thief! Traitor!"

I've been called worse.

I threw on Talleyrand's robe and trotted to the gate at the alley entrance. A sentry was facing the crowd in the plaza beyond. "Quickly, you fool," I snapped in imitation of the arrogant. He swung the gate out of habit, and I was through before he had a chance to think. Beyond was a flicker at the edge of a milling mob hoping to catch a glimpse of the crowned emperor. A man had stuffed his hat in a greatcoat pocket in order to lift his daughter to his shoulders. I snatched it.

I jammed on the hat, ducked my head, and felt Talleyrand's secret papers rustle against my ribs. When I jumped into a waiting dignitary coach, where I found its driver asleep, I kicked him.

"The Tuileries, you snorer! Take the Left Bank to avoid the crowds!"

He fell out the other open door in fearful shock, glimpsing my robe more than me, and scrambled into the teamster's seat. A great shout at the horses and with a jerk we were off, spectators yelling as they jumped out of the way. I looked out the window for Astiza and Harry but saw nothing. We crossed the Petit Pont and swung downriver. At Napoleon's new iron pedestrian bridge that crossed to the Louvre I leaped without announcing my departure, leaving Talleyrand's robe inside but keeping a bundle of his papers and the hilt of the broken sword. The documents might be useful for either bargaining or fire starter. The coach rolled blithely on, the coachman hunched as if braced for his whipping.

I trotted back across the Seine and followed the Louvre downstream, out of sight of coronation audiences, coming to where the palace museum gives way to the carousel. It's a varied neighborhood with a house facing the Tuileries Palace that is entirely occupied by prostitutes. There were none in the windows to spy me because they were all working the crowds.

Floating faithfully on the river was Robert Fulton's steamboat. It was a curious craft. Jutting from its center was a cylinder two feet in diameter that rose to about the height of a man and held a piston. A box and boiler beneath made steam, a stack spewed smoke, and the piston cranked the paddlewheels with pumping arms.

Astiza and Harry weren't at this planned rendezvous.

With the gates of Paris certain to be closed against us, I'd planned another means of escape. A steamboat could chug down the open river to avoid the city walls and might even get us all the way to England.

At the very least, I bet that Fulton's contraption was so odd that it would be the last conveyance anyone thought to check.

The day before, I'd hidden rifle, firewood, and food in preparation for escape after we sabotaged the coronation. I opened the little door of its stove, started a wood blaze, and fed it coal. It would take at least half an hour to work up steam, but hopefully my enemies wouldn't connect me with one more plume of smoke among the thousands in Paris this wintry day. The coronation route on rue Saint-Honoré was on the other side of the Louvre.

Where was Astiza? Pasques's surly comment made me hopeful that she was alive and at large after striking him; the oaf was clearly having a bad day with the Ethan Gage family. Yet with authorities in pursuit I knew my bride had the kind of defiant courage to head the opposite direction to draw them off. Were we separated once more, Napoleon triumphant and I bereft? I'd also probably forsaken my ten thousand francs by stealing the coronation robe of the grand chamberlain. I needed a more lucrative career.

Best to focus on the task at hand. The fire in the boiler provided welcome heat while I studied again the instructions Fulton had left. The tedium of waiting for a fire makes steamboating an exercise in patience, but then wind doesn't always blow, either. I read which lever to thumb to check the pressure. Finally, the boiler whistled like a kettle.

Astiza, Astiza! We needed to escape, I'd been on board nearly an hour, dusk approached, and my wife and son had yet to appear at this planned rendezvous. What to do? Pulling a pin and releasing a lever would mean abandoning my family.

So I'd wait.

But then there was a shout, a stampede of soldiers on the river quay, and approaching bayonets danced up and down. A huge figure in black was leading their charge.

Pasques looked in no better mood than when I'd left him. Time to go after all. So long as I remained free there was a chance for rescue and reunification. I threw off the lines, hauled in the gangplank, swung the tiller, and let the current drift Fulton's invention out onto the Seine. More shouts as people saw the novelty move.

With pulled levers and cranked valves, the vertical rod at the top of Fulton's huge piston began pumping up and down. Smoke puffed. A crank turned gears, and the wooden blades of the paddlewheels bit water.

I looked shoreward. Pasques was running parallel to my progress, a mix of soldiers and gendarmes jogging after him. A couple of them stopped to shoot at me, one bullet hitting the hull and another kicking up a spout of water.

"No! To the bridge!" Pasques redoubled his speed to cut me off.

Ahead was the Pont Royal. If he and his men could line up before I passed, their volley would sweep the boat.

I picked up my Jaeger rifle. I had one shot for twenty men.

The bridge was only a quarter mile from where the boat had been docked, and even a battered Pasques managed to beat the slow steamboat to its span. I wouldn't have guessed such a big man to be so sprightly, but anger can do wonders. His soldiers were still running on the bank in a long string behind when he stood up on the stone balustrade of the bridge to pose astride my

path like the Colossus of Rhodes, a red-stained necker-
chief tied around his wounded throat. He was shouting
like a madman and gesturing angrily downward as if I
could somehow stop. Seeing me headed straight toward
him, the giant put his arms out and crouched, prepared
to spring. The idiot was twenty feet above the river. If
he leaped into my steamboat, he'd go straight through
and sink us both.

Maybe that was his plan.

So when I was thirty seconds from the bridge, paddlewheels churning, I fired at his foot.

The rifle was blessedly accurate, chipping the bridge
at the toe of his boot. Instinctively, he jerked his leg up,
giving me that disbelieving stare of affront that victims
must give to murderers, and then lost balance and toppled into the river with a gigantic splash.

Pasques came up with the grace of a pregnant hippo-
potamus. I steered for a gap between the bridge piers,
quickly lashed the tiller in position, and leaped over the
gearing to grab the buffalo before he was hit with the
churning paddles. "Stop kicking!" Getting him aboard
was like handling a whale, but I needed him for protection. I hauled him in as we passed under the bridge and
trussed him with a mooring line, soldiers shouting in
confusion above us. Then I slid under his squirming,
cursing bulk.

We chugged out on the downstream side. A score of muskets pointed from the bridge balustrade, but if the soldiers shot they'd kill their policeman. A captain shouted to hold their fire.

"We're both lucky they care for you," I told Pasques.

Slowly, we drew out of range. Fulton had written that his engine boasted the energy of eight horses, but I couldn't see it, given the plodding of the paddles. On the other hand, the engine never slackened. Maybe there's something to steamboats after all.

The soldiers on the bridge ran left and right, presumably scattering for horses to chase us.

I pushed out from under Pasques, reloaded the Jaeger, and manned the tiller. We slipped past the Champ de Mars, the city walls, and then as the day grew truly dim, Napoleon's suburban palace at Saint-Cloud. People stared, but nobody shot, thank goodness, since word of my escape had yet to spread. I began leafing through the papers I'd lifted from Talleyrand's coat.

Eureka! There was French strategy there, a naval plan I'd not heard before. Perhaps my luck was not entirely abominable. I'd stolen a ticket back to my spymasters in Britain.

"Don't think I won't have my revenge, Gage!" Pasques shouted from where he was trussed in the bow, on the other side of the steam engine in the boat's center. "They'll be sharpening the guillotine!"

"I saved your life," I called over the racket of the machine. "You can thank me by shutting up."

"Saved it after kicking my privates, damaging my legs, and toppling me into the freezing river! The blade is too swift for you!"

Sighing, I lashed the tiller again, grabbed my rifle, stepped over the churning gearing, and came up to him. Villains can be slow in realizing when advantage has turned. "If you're so insistent at threatening me, perhaps I should drop you back in the Seine," I said quietly. "Or simply shoot you for your foul temper and terrible manners."

"You offended God, tried to sabotage the coronation, pummeled me, disrobed the grand chamberlain, and clouted Catherine Marceau."

"It was you who assaulted me in Notre Dame. Have you no respect for a church, Inspector? And where have you put my wife and child? A simple expatriate family tries to enjoy French ceremony, and suddenly you're kidnapping, grabbing, and shooting. Guillotine, indeed."

"It was you who shot at me!"

"So you wouldn't plunge through my steamboat. No one is more peace loving than me, Ethan Gage."

He scowled, face swollen, throat red, clothes dripping. "Why do you even talk? Nothing useful comes out of that hole in your face."

"If we'd remained friends you'd be dry and happy right now." I shook my head. "Your judgment, Pasques, needs work."

He writhed in his bonds. "They'll send cavalry, Gage. The Seine winds like a serpent, and this smoking monster is slow as a nag. Your capture is inevitable."

He had a point. Far from traveling in a straight line toward the sea, we were making long, looping twists through French farmland, issuing a plume of smoke to pinpoint our position. Despite my earlier optimism, I revised my opinion again and decided Fulton's steamboat *was* a bad idea, at least for escaping spies. "True. So listen, Pasques: I've nothing to lose by murdering you. I'll let you live only if you tell me what's happened to my family."

"How do I know? That bitch of yours struck me with a bag that had something hard inside and ran. Your little tramp rolled marbles on the church floor, and two grenadiers and a priest went sprawling. Talleyrand told us not to pursue."

I sighed and aimed my rifle at his face. "Say that again."

He looked sullen. "What?"

"Call my wife and child names, so I can squeeze my trigger without regret."

From bitter experience I know gun barrels look enormous when pointed, and Pasques looked chastened. "I don't always choose words carefully when I'm angry."

"What was that? What did you call her?"

He was truculent but wary, since I looked like a madman. "We both know your wife is beautiful and wise. My apologies, monsieur."

I shifted my aim away. "You actually have manners when you need them, Policeman. And Harry rolled his marbles? He does take after his father, doesn't he?"

The Frenchman scowled. "Pity if he does."

"Why would Talleyrand tell you not to pursue my wife?"

"Because she's the one of real value."

"I beg your pardon?"

"Surely you don't think all this fuss is about you, Ethan Gage."

Again I felt off-balance. "But I do. I've consulted with Napoleon and Talleyrand. I've given advice to your army. I've written reports to England. I'm the celebrity all this has revolved around."

"Your stupidity and vanity are impenetrable!"

"What the devil are you talking about?"

He shook his head, amused that even when tied like a hog he was in a position to lecture me. "You know that the comtesse was never a comtesse?"

"I guessed that, yes." I paused before admitting it. "Today."

"It was evil to strangle the real comtesse in her cell, but at least the revolutionaries recognized an opportunity to place a young agent in England. Your 'governess' was a rising intellectual, a firebrand of reform, and she volunteered to infiltrate the corruption that is called Britain to further our great cause. There she waited for more than a decade until proper use. And now, with the invasion of England ready, it was time to bring her home and put her spying talents to new uses. Meaning, Astiza."

"Astiza? But my wife's presence on the Channel coast was a complete accident." Why did I always feel the fool?

"Word of her rescue came from the French islands in the Caribbean. Her research in Martinique was reported to the government. Here was a woman exploring the very subjects our leaders were interested in. We wanted her in France to harness her talents, but how to lure her after the tropical nightmare you conjured? Only one bait came to mind: you, hard as that was for us to believe."

I stared at him. "I'm mere bait to attract my wife?"

"And to keep Catherine informed of any secrets you held, since you will tell attractive women anything. You'd draw Astiza to France with you, and through you we'd manipulate her. It was all planned from the beginning, including allowing you to invade the cardinal's palace. Palatine we recruited, and when your wife didn't seek him at a florist we planned, we moved him to a chemist shop with a new sign decorated with a rose. It's been amusing to wind you up like mechanical toys and set you marching."

I didn't believe him, except I did. Even the gunfight in the ravine had been staged, I suspected. What was the loss of a few sentries to a man like Napoleon? The emperor had probably been briefed on the plan from the beginning, and his conversation with us at Boulogne was a nice piece of acting. Maybe the *gendarmerie* at the ravine hadn't even been killed. Maybe they were playing dead.

I slumped. The interview with Réal, the consultation with General Duhèsme, the balloon experiments with Thilorier, had it all been to keep my wife in place and researching? Why had they thwarted her in the first place? To make her later permission seem real, and to put her on their side.

Now she'd escaped. Or had she? The grand chamberlain wanted her traveling east to search for the

Brazen Head of Albertus Magnus. And she'd ultimately be more pliable, he'd assume, without her
doughty American husband at her side. If they could
capture me, I'd be hostage to ensure further cooperation. Astiza was quite capable of playing the wildcat all
by herself, the French would discover, but in the meantime Catherine's betrayal had once more broken up my
family.

What a bollocks. It turns out I'm a terrible spy,
trusting and honest to a fault. Living up to the maxims
of Franklin makes me a better man, but a terrible espionage agent.

"Everyone plays me the fool, don't they, Pasques?"

He nodded.

"Except you are tied up, and I am not."

He scowled.

Time to ponder. I could fight through all of eastern
France in hoping of catching up to Astiza and Harry.
But the British were allies of the Austrian Empire,
where Christian Rosenkreutz and Ruldolf II had
done alchemical experiments. Why not get English
help? I'd make a quick sea journey from London to
Venice, Vienna's backdoor, and dash from the Adriatic
to Bohemia and Prague. There I could rendezvous
with Astiza when she came by land from the other
direction.

Maybe my old acquaintance Admiral Horatio Nelson would give me a ride. I contemplated Pasques. It was time to play this policeman as I'd been played.

"Yes, you French have been very clever. Yet before you struck Grand Chamberlain Talleyrand with your own colossal fist, he wasn't approaching to seize me, was he? Now you must wonder: What was he trying to ask me? What did we talk about in the tower of Notre Dame? And what, exactly, does everyone want my wife to look for?"

"Monsieur Talleyrand does not confide in me."

"He wants something he offered to pay me a great deal for."

"What?"

"A secret that only I can decipher."

"You're lying."

"He thinks Astiza and I might lead him to a treasure. So why not get it for myself now, and get my wife back in the process?"

"Because you're a desperate fugitive headed in exactly the wrong direction."

"Am I? My idea is to sail around to the backdoor of the Austrian Empire via the Mediterranean and Adriatic. So yes, maybe your cavalry will catch me, and you can watch the blade drop. Or maybe you will watch as the grand chamberlain inexplicably pardons me after my arrest, while dismissing you for striking him."

"That was an accident."

"You can stake your life and career on explaining that to one of the most ruthless men in Europe. Or—and this is where you have to use your imagination, Pasques—perhaps you and I can become partners and pull the puppet strings instead of dancing to them. We can become rich together."

"Rich?"

"Think about it, Policeman. I've made you look like an incompetent by escaping the cathedral, toppling you from a bridge, and trussing you like a chicken. Your career is ruined. But I'm on the trail of something that Napoleon and Talleyrand are rivals for. So, I can kill you now; or drop you overboard; or leave you to be arrested, dismissed, and imprisoned . . . or you can help me get to England."

"You're insane!"

"Help get me to England and I'll cut you in on the deal. If Talleyrand offers me ten thousand francs of his own free will, what will he pay when we've found the prize and are holding out for real ransom?"

"Ten thousand?"

"Your career is finished; instead of capturing me, you've allowed me to capture you. Réal will laugh before he sacks you and Talleyrand will sneer before he has you assassinated as an embarrassment."

The giant glowered but knew I had a point.

"On the other hand, get me to England by telling me where police and patrols won't be, and we'll be rich as pirates, with no more answering to Réal, Talleyrand, or Napoleon. Get me to England, and you become not an agent of great men but a great man yourself. Help me find my wife, and you can enjoy the riches of a sultan."

Anger had softened to doubt, and doubt had given way to curiosity. We were a long way from trust, but I'd intrigued him. "You have to tell me what you're after."

I winked. "The means to control the world."

"How?"

"You'll learn only by throwing in with me."

"How do I know I can trust you?"

"Trust *me*? You're the one who's been arresting and pursuing and threatening."

"There's no way we can steam all the way to the Channel."

"So go back to Réal and explain how I made a fool of you."

He stared out over the dark water. "How many francs again?"

"Don't think small, Pasques. How much of the world?"

"But how do you plan to get to England? They'll block this boat at Honfleur."

"I have a confederate. But first, do you want to partner with me? I can't say it's not dangerous, but I can say I offer riches instead of demotion and arrest."

He sighed. "You're a fool, American. But you have odd luck."

"Yes."

"The British will not put me in prison?"

"Not if you're my ally. They think me clever."

"You'll treat me fairly?"

"I'll proclaim you a hero."

He shook his head, wriggling in his bonds. "Very well. I'll betray my country to join a pirate American on an insane mission that will probably get us killed."

"A wise choice. Otherwise, I'd just shoot and drown you."

He looked at me slyly. "And your secret?"

"I'll confide when we're on our way to Bohemia. First we must reach England. We'll put ashore near Argenteuil, aim the steamer downstream, tie the tiller, and let her go. Then we need to use a rose to find a red-headed Rose. And more roses, where we need to go."

Chapter 21

With the help of Rose and Pasques, I returned to England that December of 1805 to save its navy with the secret plans I'd found in Talleyrand's cloak. I expected to play the prodigal hero, while arranging transport to rescue my family.

Instead, I found myself reduced to jail, government service, penurious pay, and the disappointment of the French policeman. "You seem to be humiliated everywhere you go," Pasques told me.

My problem was once again my naive trust, this time in financial advisers. In my absence from England my bankers had knotted my fortune with loss and exorbitant management fees. Not only couldn't I afford passage to Venice, I was told, I must pay the boarding cost of feeding my new French ally during our jailing in a

British castle used as a headquarters for spies. Instead of being applauded for changing world history, I found myself discredited and dependent.

I was mad with frustration and helpless to escape. Reuniting with wife and son must wait, I was told, on the outcome of Napoleon's invasion of England.

"You're not the only one being asked to make sacrifices," Sir Sidney Smith told me when I complained. "Lord Nelson hasn't set foot on land for years."

As irksome as bad luck is getting no sympathy.

At first our escape from France went well. Pasques and I jumped off the *Vulcan* at Argenteuil and tied its tiller, sending it steaming downriver until it thrashed its way into a riverbank more than three miles away. The boat drew our pursuers to its column of smoke while I sent a flower to fetch the redheaded spy Rose, whose blue eyes appraised us skeptically before agreeing to help. She and Pasques warily combined their knowledge of French security to smuggle us to the Channel coast.

As we made our way the Frenchman began to warm toward me, as people do, and was intrigued by our comely spy. "Why is every woman you deal with as fair as a flower?" he asked as Rose led us on secret paths.

"Maybe I'm not as charmless as you think, Pasques. It was Rose who elected to deal with me."

"Every woman I get is uglier than my sisters, and you can imagine, by looking at me, how truly ugly that is." He glanced at me. "Can you help me do better?"

"You have to prove yourself dashing and exemplary."

"I'm fleeing my own country in disgrace with a scoundrel."

"But you've been in a steamboat and are after storied treasure. We'll find you better clothes, too. Catherine always said fashion makes all the difference, and she's the expert on being a poseur."

We eventually arranged to signal Tom Johnstone's smuggling sloop from the Channel coast, ran for England, and tidied ourselves for a hero's welcome after handing over the French naval plans I'd stolen. I was desperate to go after Astiza and Harry and expected enthusiastic British reward.

Instead, we were jailed adjacent to the soldier's kitchens in the bowels of Walmer Castle, a Tudor fort not far from Dover. We were being held, it was explained, as possible French saboteurs because of the likelihood I'd sold myself to the enemy due to my desperate poverty.

"What poverty?"

"You're a ruined man and apparently deserve it," our jailer said.

I hounded him with protest until I finally got to see Smith.

"We thought you'd thrown in with Boney again, Ethan," my spymaster told me when Pasques and I were escorted from our dungeon cells. "You disappeared with an English stipend, and instead of Napoleon being assassinated or overthrown, he triumphed at his coronation. In fact, it was such a smashing success that he plans to repeat it in Milan, putting on the crown of Italy. Good heavens, you've enabled bloody Julius Caesar. I'm frankly surprised you'd the nerve to return at all after such a fiasco. And with a gigantic Frenchman?" He peered at Pasques. "He's as expensive to feed as a horse."

"Then let me go, English." Pasques looked at me balefully as well, clearly disappointed with my official standing.

"And I'm offended to find myself imprisoned, Sir Sidney," I tried, deciding it was best not to reveal I'd agreed to be a double agent to save my family. I tend to edit my résumé for each employer and was a little defensive about my ability to bounce from side to side. "Always I'm the victim of misunderstandings. I wove myself into the heart of the French military establishment and reported for months on French politics and arms. My reward for such courage is rude jailing?"

"Reports? Haven't received a one. Pitt thought you were dead, but I said, No, Gage is a survivor but his alliances are one of convenience. Turncoat, I predicted. American, after all; the whole bloody country is a nest of traitors. So the man has betrayed us and is likely living in luxury in Paris, I said. The prime minister agreed, as we never expect much from foreign agents such as yourself."

I was confused. "But I risked my life and my family's life spying for England! I mailed regular as a gazette."

"Apparently, what the French say and what they do are two different things, Ethan. We haven't heard a peep from you or Comtesse Marceau since you both crossed the Channel last April."

"She *is* a traitor, and not even a comtesse. She's an imposter as secretive as a mole who betrayed me as well as you, Sir Sidney. Damned good at coronation fashion, however."

He blinked. "Catherine Marceau is an enemy? I rather enjoyed her."

"She lived with my family in Paris and broke us apart at the coronation. She's the one who worked to make Napoleon's crowning a success. I, meanwhile, told you everything I could learn about the French army."

"Your reports probably made fine fire starter in the offices of Commissioner Réal after he had a chuckle reading them." Smith cocked his head. "Unless you're posing *now* in the service of Bonaparte and lying about your every action. You can't be that clever, can you?"

I picked at some lice I'd acquired in our cell. "Certainly not. I just find myself working for everyone because I'm so popular." I sat straight to feign dignity. "We can test me, can't we?"

"How? Hot coals?" He looked sourly at Pasques, who looked sourly back.

"I've brought you a report I snatched from Talleyrand himself. It details plans to lure the British navy away from the Channel with a complex attack on Senegal, Surinam, and Saint Helena, involving dozens of ships crisscrossing the Atlantic. It's impossibly ambitious, which means it came from Napoleon instead of his admirals. He thinks you can move sailing ships like chess pieces. The British Admiralty can judge whether it reflects real French movements, and thwart it by responding prudently."

"Talleyrand? How the devil did you get that?"

"I work for him, too, or would have if Pasques here hadn't floored him with a punch. I fled Paris on a new American invention called a steamboat, enlisted this heroic if hungry Frenchman here, and avoided pursuing patrols with the aid of a beautiful redheaded spy named Rose. I assume she's yours?"

Smith blinked, skeptical but always seduced by der-ring-do. He longed to win wars with cleverness. "This Frenchman is heroic?"

"I struck the grand chamberlain only after I swung at you and missed," my new companion spoke up, which I had coached him not to do.

"Yes, we make quite a team," I put in.

Smith drummed his fingers, considering us. "Rose has helped us smuggle countless agents in and out of France, and I instructed her to contact you. An inter-esting woman with odd beliefs, she's the follower of the rosy cross, if you'd heard of that bunch. Medieval mys-tics, mostly, but she thinks there's something to it."

I filed this assessment away for my own future use. "It's not my fault the courier system you instructed me to use in Paris has been compromised." I looked stern. "Nor that I never received a word of instruction from England. Now my wife and son have fled to central Europe and I need a ship to catch up with them."

"A ship? You do have gall, Gage."

"Passage to Venice. From there I'll ride north to Bohemia. A fast frigate will do," I demanded with more confidence than I felt.

"We're going to win a huge fortune from Talleyrand and win the war single-handed," Pasques put in, with the logic of a lunatic.

Smith looked from one to the other of us. "No one is sailing anywhere until I determine what side everybody is on. We'll put this purported plan carried by Talleyrand to the test, as you've said."

"Then I must be given leave to buy my own passage. My family is in peril, and time is critical. Let me play the spy in Prague."

"Buy passage how?"

"With money. I believe that's the conventional way."

"But Ethan, you're a debtor."

"To the contrary, I've invested ambitiously and by now should have doubled my fortune," I said without any conviction.

"I'm afraid you'd better consult with your financial advisers. Since you were in our employ as a spy, I ordered an audit of your affairs and was alarmed at what we learned. It was the collapse of your fortune that made us think you'd thrown in with Bonaparte."

"But it can't have collapsed. Can it?" My voice was strained.

"Your financial advisers can explain it in some detail. You're a pauper, Gage. Our cell at Walmer here is the only thing that has kept you out of debtor's prison. The only thing you possess is the hilt of a medieval sword." He squinted. "You're a very odd man."

"I'm a collector of antiquities."

He looked at me with pity. "I'm going to provide the necessary passes for you to consult with your bankers in London while we study these naval plans, holding the Frenchman here as guarantee of your return. Get a realistic appraisal of your financial situation, and then we'll see where you stand. If you're telling the truth, maybe we can salvage a crumb of career."

A visit to London confirmed the worst. Hiram Tudwell received me in his counting house on Cornwall Street after a two-hour wait, timing it so he could plead office closing if our interview became too difficult. His bald head sprouted like a cabbage from a stiff cravat, his skin was the color of suet, and his suit was dark enough for a mortician.

"I'm afraid your holdings have become inaccessible, Mr. Gage," the senior partner of Tudwell, Rawlings, and Spence announced. He regarded me like an unwanted relative.

"You mean my money is in a particularly remote and formidable vault?" I seize every opportunity to hear the bright side.

"I mean that your account has not generated the returns expected. It was ambitiously invested as you instructed, but dogged by events. A great deal of it has been captured in the Indian Ocean and auctioned off by the perfidious French."

"Captured by the French? How could they capture ten thousand pounds from a London bank?" News of my calamity was being given in a high-ceilinged, mahogany-paneled room designed to enforce calm, but it wasn't working. I'd been offered a cup of lukewarm tea and a stale biscuit, but that didn't help, either.

"If you'll recall, you gave our firm permission to invest your holdings in aggressive vehicles to maximize potential profits while you disappeared on the Continent. I believe you said you were comfortable with calibrated risk."

"Not betting the whole table!"

"In your lengthy absence and complete lack of correspondence we diversified into coal mines, steam engines, a horse-drawn rail-wagon line to Portsmouth, and tea futures. The latter was based on delivery of a cargo on an East Indiaman, following recent victories by General Arthur Wellesley on the Indian subcontinent. We sought investments that were innovative and inclined to quick profit, our aggressiveness being the very model of bold financial stewardship. You had the potential to double your money in months. Astonishing opportunities these days, astonishing."

"And?"

"The war has caused disruption. The East Indiaman was captured, the steam engines have yet to find a market, the coal works went bankrupt, and the horses all died. It was an excellent strategy, had it worked." He pushed over a balance sheet to show me where my money went.

I struggled to understand it. "What's this one thousand, one hundred twenty-seven pounds here, then?"

"Insurance premiums. Policy not payable, alas, for acts of war. A French battleship has been prowling off Africa. Can't insure against that."

"And this fifteen hundred pounds?"

"Our management fee."

"Fifteen percent? That's usury!"

"Our fee was in the fine print of your contract."

I couldn't be bothered to read such tedious documents. "What then is the five hundred thirty-two pounds for?"

"Incidental management expenses. Postage, correspondence, resolving of claims, business meals, refreshments, stationary, and office incidentals."

"That's not included in the fifteen hundred pounds?"

"Mr. Gage, our standard fee cannot cover the unanticipated exigencies of a complex and variable portfolio like yours."

The Tripoli pirates were amateurs compared to this bunch. "And this two hundred seventy-one pounds?"

"Your losses were so severe that nothing remained in your accessible account to cover your final billing. That's how much you still owe us. You still have a balance of nearly two thousand pounds on credit, but there's a lien against it from a family called Chiswick, which claims you contracted with them to educate your son and then stole the boy away without paying in full."

"My wife didn't steal our own son!"

"They are seeking damages. I must say, your domestic affairs strike me as extremely untidy. Is that an American habit? I hope you'll settle with your litigants so we can get our money."

"My God. Are you monumentally incompetent, or simple thieves?"

"Insults will not help your situation. The decline of your portfolio results from political, financial, and competitive circumstances beyond our control. I can understand your disappointment, but I can assure you that, had we succeeded, you would have been a very wealthy man." His expression was as animated as a corpse.

I instinctively reached for my tomahawk and regretted leaving it at home. "I risked my life and that of my family for that ten thousand pounds! This is the most outrageous financial burglary I've ever heard of!"

He winced as if I'd let wind at a recital. "It's clear you don't understand the financial-services industry, Mr. Gage. I sympathize that things did not progress as you'd hoped, but I can assure you we tried our very best. Your success would have been ours, too. And should you employ Tudwell, Rawlings, and Spence in the future, we'll strive to do even better."

"I'll ruin you in the newspapers! I'll bring suit! I'll fetch my Jaeger rifle!"

Tudwell folded his hands. "Military barbarism may work on the American frontier or a Barbary pirate ship, Mr. Gage, but it has no place in the banks and courts of England. Should you seek bad publicity or legal complaint, you can rest assured of counter-litigation for defamation, late payment, and failure to respond to management inquiries while abroad in France. I could see legal proceedings extending years into the future, at a cost of several thousand pounds to us both. You will wait in a debtor's cell for final resolution. Nor does it help that you're a foreign American, with ties to the French, filing suit in England."

I calculated the odds. "Money slips from me as if oiled."

"It's often more difficult to retain a fortune than make it in the first place. Have another biscuit." His serenity was remarkable, but then he wasn't the one being robbed. Lesser thieves get carted to Fleet Prison, but the biggest bastards get a peerage. I'd trusted him with my life savings, and it had vanished like smoke.

So why didn't I throttle him? Because I feared, in my heart of hearts, that the Green Apple of the Sun had indeed been an emerald cursed by the ghost of Montezuma. Hadn't Pasha Karamanli been cursed by me, Ethan Gage, while he wore it in his turban? Hadn't Leon Martel died in pursuit of the stone? Hadn't my own wife been carried away in a storm? Hadn't it led to the kidnapping of my son? And hadn't it set in motion a chain of events that now made me spy, turncoat, and a husband who'd once more lost his family?

Why is fate cruel? Because we're meant never to get the things we think we want so we'll pursue the things we truly need, like love and responsibility. That's what I told myself, anyway. I'd always be Sisyphus on quixotic missions, trying to roll boulders uphill that cascaded endlessly down. Eve didn't sin by eating a tempting apple. She sinned because she moved the fruit out of its rightful place, as I'd moved the emerald. It's not the bite, it's the disruption of harmony.

I could escape poverty only when I finished doing whatever it was that I was supposed to do. Which was entirely unclear, of course.

Back on the London streets, I consulted solicitors about suing. They in turn talked with barristers. Was there not some legal stratagem around Fate and God? They charged money I didn't have to tell me that while I should certainly litigate, such an effort would occupy a good part of my remaining life.

"How much time again?"

"Several years. Before appeals."

"And our chances?"

"We are optimistic yet realistic, hope leavened by caution."

I forwarded their billing to Tudwell.

So I was desperate once more. I was a likely outlaw in France, separated from my fugitive wife and child by hundreds of miles, and a suspect debtor in Britain.

Fortunately, the admiralty deduced that the naval plans I'd stumbled on were confirmed by early French fleet movements, and countered accordingly. My captured information frustrated Napoleon's desire to divert the English navy long enough to stage his invasion, so the stalemate of elephant and whale continued. I'd just saved England, not that anyone gave me credit.

So Sidney Smith came to Walmer Castle to see Pasques and me once more. "Good news. We didn't take the bait, Ethan, thanks to Talleyrand's papers."

"A grateful nation might give me my fortune back."

"I've a better bargain for you and your fat French friend. You're a man of science, a Franklin protégé, and an electrician. I want you to help us pay back the frogs who outsmarted you with secret weapons."

"Secret weapons?"

"I believe you know the American inventor Robert Fulton? Like you, he's on England's side now. We're going to have the pair of you earn passage to your family by assaulting Bonaparte's Army of England and sinking his entire fleet. You'll win back our confidence by paddling into the teeth of the enemy, pledged to victory or death. You won't even miss your money when you make yourself a hero."

Chapter 22

Walmer Castle was the spy headquarters for Britain's secret struggle against Napoleon. If the French were inventing a modern national police under Napoleon, the British were inventing a modern espionage service under William Pitt, the sickly, alcoholic, and valiant prime minister. Walmer was one of his personal homes, through his family title as lord warden of the Cinque Ports. His castle looked strategically across a rocky beach at France, and so had become the wartime workplace of General Edward Smith, director of spies. This Smith was the uncle of Sir Sidney, who in turn happened to be a cousin of Pitt. On a rainy April 8, 1805, I was seated at a massive oak table in a low-ceilinged room facing not just that cozy trio but Spencer Smith, Sidney's brother who'd gathered intelligence in Germany, and Colonel Charles Smith, another brother who led a garrison nearby.

Catherine would call it breeding; Franklin, nepotism.

Sidney Smith, as was his flamboyant custom, was wearing Turkish robes and a turban he'd been given while advising the Ottomans against the French. An ostrich plume floated above, a curved dagger jutted from his waist sash, and his cavalry boots had been replaced with pointed slippers. None but Pasques and I paid this bizarre getup the slightest attention.

Joining the Smith cabal was Admiral Home Riggs Popham, another ambitious Englishman who'd organized coastal militia and a new signal system for the navy. Slim, lithe, and restless, he had the insouciant flair of an aristocrat, treating espionage as a grand game.

Smuggler Tom Johnstone was there, too, matching in height, if not in bulk, my companion Pasques. All were turned to hear three inventors, however.

One was Colonel William Congreve, who was adopting the rockets of the Maharajal armies in India as a possible new sea weapon in Europe. Like all inventors, he was happy as a hound to have a receptive audience.

A second was my old friend Fulton. Unable to win French financial backing to complete his work, he'd come to Britain to sell his ideas to the other side.

I was the third.

Fulton had greeted me warmly. We'd gone adventuring amid the Barbary pirates and used his plunging boat to rescue Astiza and Harry. "Ethan, you disappeared from France two years ago. I feared you dead!"

"I had to look for my son again, Robert. After a sojourn in the West Indies I was returning to France just as you were departing. We didn't meet because I had to sneak about. Now here we are on the same side."

"All roads lead to Walmer Castle. Tell me, did you see my boat *Vulcan* in Paris? Sweet little craft with paintbox colors that chugs on steam. I think the idea holds great promise, but the French let me try her just once before concluding she wasn't fast enough upstream. By thunder she's faster than a sailboat when wind and current are adverse!"

"I poked about."

"Is she still steamable?"

"With a little work." I kicked Pasques so he didn't reveal we'd sent Fulton's toy thrashing into a Seine riverbank. Robert might forgive me for the loss of one of his boats, but I doubt he'd be happy with two.

Congreve I didn't know. Balding and muscular, he had the rugged build of a day laborer and the peddler fire of the missionary. Like Fulton, he was a tinkerer who wanted to revolutionize warfare.

We stood when Pitt arrived.

"Sit, sit." At least there wasn't just Napoleon's one chair.

The prime minister, a decade older than Napoleon, was nonetheless "the younger" because his father had held office before him. This son had first led the nation at the astonishing age of twenty-four, a maturity at which my idea of governance didn't extend much beyond keeping my mistresses from learning of each other. Being precocious grinds on you, however, and now, at forty-five, "honest Billy" looked worn out. Two international coalitions and a royalist conspiracy against Bonaparte had all failed. Having quit in 1801 after feuding with King George over Ireland, Pitt had been called back to power shortly after I landed in France. Now he was facing England's greatest challenge since the Spanish Armada.

His nation was hysterical at the possibility of invasion; erecting semaphores; stockpiling wood for signal bonfires; building small coastal forts called Martello towers; and digging canals, trenches, and ramparts. More than thirty miles of fortifications had been started around London. Plans had been made to evacuate the government. Troops of old men drilled with pitchforks.

Nursemaids had a new ogre to frighten children with. The latest rhyme:

Baby, baby, naughty baby,
Hush you squalling thing I say;
Hush your squalling or it may be,
Bonaparte will pass this way.

Baby, baby, he's a giant,
Tall and black as Rouen steeple,
And he dines and sups, rely it,
Every day on naughty people.

So our conspiracy was to save England from that cannibal, Bonaparte. The castle itself was a fine place for intrigue. Four semicircular battlements jutted from a central keep, the edifice looking like a gigantic clover plopped into a moat. Hodgepodge additions had created sleeping quarters with modern paneling and a central sky-lit atrium. Window glass filled old gun ports, and Oriental carpeting and four-poster beds gave the bastion a homey feel. While militarily obsolescent, Walmer was a splendid hideaway for plotters, assassins, spies, and secret weapons. Rumor was that its cellars held not just agents of questionable loyalty, such as me, but trunks of gold to pay saboteurs and scoundrels. I'd wandered about to test the truth of that story, so far without success.

Now Pitt called us to order. "Gentlemen, we must defeat the French at sea, not on the farms of England. We must take the war to them, not wait for their blows to fall on us. Boney has gained thirty ships of the line through alliance with Spain. Until Austria, Russia, and Prussia march against him in a Third Coalition, we stand alone."

Sidney Smith spoke up. "The information obtained by my agents enabled us to foil the French naval trap detailed in Talleyrand's papers. That has bought us time."

I was annoyed he didn't give me credit.

"Yes, but there's a terrible new development that must be kept secret by all of you," Pitt replied. "Our spies in Paris whose reports came through instead of being confiscated"—he glanced at me—"have reported that Admiral Villeneuve's fleet slipped out of Toulon at the end of March. As we all know, the gravest threat to England is for the French Mediterranean fleet to link with the French and Spanish Atlantic fleets to achieve temporary naval superiority in the Channel. If that happens, Napoleon can invade."

"Surely Nelson is on Villeneuve's tail," General Smith said.

"So we pray, but as yet we have no word. I don't envy Nelson's task. The sea is a vast place to hide in, and the availability of Spanish ports immensely complicates his search. If he fails, we lose the war."

"Which means that was a costly four million Spanish dollars you stole back in October," I couldn't help interjecting, since I was grumpy from my troubles. The British navy had greedily intercepted a Spanish treasure convoy off Cadiz several months back when the two nations were still at peace, pushing Spain into an unhappy alliance with Napoleon.

"We're dealing with the strategic situation as it is, Ethan, not as it might be," Sidney Smith reminded, yanking my leash. "You of all people should know the futility of dwelling too long on opportunities lost. And I'll note that Commodore Moore captured one hundred fifty thousand ingots of gold and twenty-five thousand sealskins, helping balance the millions Bonaparte received from your nation for its purchase of Louisiana."

I resented the comparison. "And had to pay Spanish captain Alvear thirty thousand pounds for blowing up nine members of his innocent family on a neutral ship, the *Mercedes*." It wasn't diplomatic, but the British bullied everyone at sea. I was lonely for my wife, newly poor, and hadn't received proper thanks.

"A litigation which is none of the affair of an American agent who has debt and legal troubles of his own," Smith snapped.

I wasn't helping myself, I knew. "Sorry. I think out loud sometimes."

"You should be in Parliament," Pitt quipped, to relieve the tension. Everyone laughed.

"There are actually intriguing opportunities in South America now that we're at war with Spain," Home Popham spoke up. "The Spanish colonies are restive and might be encouraged to revolt, becoming new trade partners. I might lead an expedition there myself."

This was a larger picture than I'd contemplated. Maybe there was method to English madness after all.

"Sir Sidney recommends you as a tireless warrior when pressed," Pitt said to me with a politician's practiced charm. "And all of us regret the entry of Spanish ships into the war, Mr. Gage. The question for today is what to do about it, or, rather, how to cripple the French before they can make an effective alliance."

"The Dagos will bloody hell wish they'd never tangled with Nelson," Johnstone put in.

"Agreed, if Nelson can force battle. But can modern invention make such a clash unnecessary?" Pitt wanted to get to the point. "Colonel Congreve?"

The soldier straightened. "Prime Minister, you may recall that a quarter century ago, the Indian sultan Tippoo defeated the East India Company at the Battle of Pollilur with rockets. They hit our power stores, and our ammunition blew up. In the Indian wars as a whole, rockets have caused more British casualties than any other weapon. Their explosions kill up to three men at a time. The rockets' long bamboo tails thrash through our ranks."

I recalled Tippoo. Napoleon had planned to link up with this Indian patriot after conquering Egypt. The British killed the sultan before alliance could be made, but without Tippoo Napoleon might never have invaded Egypt, I might never have accompanied him, and Astiza might never have experienced my charm. The world is indeed small.

"Rockets were also used by the Irish rebel Robert Emmet in his failed revolt a couple of years ago," Congreve went on. "I began my own experiments at the Royal Arsenal. In effect, rockets provide an explosion without having to bother with a cannon to deliver it. They're cheap, simple, and terrifying. If launched in great numbers at the French fleet anchored at Boulogne, they could set it on fire. I've devised a black powder propellant in an iron tube with a fifteen-foot tail. Thousands of these cheap weapons might engulf the invasion fleet in chaos and havoc."

"Here, here," Sidney Smith said.

"Sounds like the devil's brew," Johnstone seconded.

"Mr. Fulton?" Pitt said.

"My inventions complement those of Colonel Congreve," my American friend said. "The French rejected them as immoral, but why blowing someone up with a torpedo is less moral than slaying them with a cannonball, I've never understood."

"Here, here," repeated Sir Sidney.

"My primary device has already seen active service against the Tripoli pirates. I call it a *torpedo*, after the Latin word for the jolt from an electric ray. A charge of gunpowder is drifted against enemy hulls and triggered by clockwork. Tide and current do most of the work. In one design, two torpedoes are attached to a rope that drifts down on an enemy mooring line. As the anchor cable catches this rope, the bombs will float past to lodge on either side of the hull of the ship. Then the explosions go off, cracking the hull like an egg. As we break the French line, more torpedoes can be floated through the gaps. The carnage should be extraordinary."

"Here, here," Smith said again.

"It sounds a trifle unfair," Popham objected. "Sinking ships without using a ship?" He was a naval officer, after all.

"Bloody brilliant," Smith rejoined. "Clandestine, silent, invisible, and deadly." His uncle and brothers nodded. I wouldn't want to face off against his clan in a vendetta.

"Setting ships on fire and letting them drift down on enemy fleets has been used since ancient times," Pitt pointed out. "This only adds technological precision to the idea. But drifting mines are hardly the most ingenious part of Fulton's scheme. Explain, Robert."

"While some of my torpedoes can be released from British warships to float with tide and current, I suggest another group be aimed precisely with what I call a *catamaran*." Fulton stood and whisked a cloth off an easel. Underneath was a diagram of an invention I hadn't seen before.

"This craft has two sealed pontoons with the torpedo suspended between. Weighted with lead, the contraption is almost entirely submerged, making it hard to see or sink. Two helmsmen steer with a paddle, aiming for specific ships and specific mooring cables. As they near the target, one yanks a lanyard to set the clockwork ticking, releases the torpedo, and they paddle the catamaran away."

"Paddle where?" Popham asked. I admired such practicality.

"To English ships waiting offshore. It will take pluck, of course, but the doughty rogues who steer this weapon might turn the tide of war."

All the Smiths turned to look at me. I hastened to speak up. "Damned clever, like all Yankee ingenuity. As an American myself, I'll direct the attack from a quarterdeck, given my knowledge of the French port. I can study the charts, observe the weather, and make calculations off the tide tables."

"Tide tables!" Sidney Smith laughed. "I know you too well to think you'd be content with that, Ethan. Nor would I trust your arithmetic. No, no, this is the perfect job for you and your giant friend, Pasques. Doughty rogues indeed! And you both speak fluent French, in case you're hailed by suspicious lookouts. By God, I'll wish I was with you, paddling toward the entire French navy and army with blackened face and dark little cap, lonely spearhead for the might of England, unleashing a positive cataclysm of rockets, mines, and cannon fire."

"You can take my place," I offered hopelessly.

"Alas, I'm chained to high command. But you can unleash a hideous new way of warfare. Not quite sporting to sneak in like that, but effective, what? Yours will become a peculiar kind of glory, but glory nonetheless."

"I'll slip you so close we'll smell their damned snails," Johnstone added.

"It is the garlic one smells," Pasques contributed.

I cleared my throat. "Sir Sidney, I thought you didn't trust me after my poor performance as a spy in France?"

"Which is why I know you're burning to prove yourself, Ethan. Sign on to make this work, and your friend Robert there gets a lucrative contract from the admiralty to build more of his devil machines."

"Bully for him."

"Sign on, and history turns a new chapter."

"History will flip its own pages without any help from me."

"Sign on," he said, looking at me intently, "and you'll win passage to Venice to find your wife and son."

Chapter 23

The French masts combed the sky like a line of dead timber, backlit by lanterns on the hills of Boulogne. The British ships were entirely dark, and we ghosted to attack on a light midnight breeze, planning to win the war not with blazing line of battle but secret weapons. The captains and sailors I met thought we inventors were eccentric at best and bound for bedlam at worst, but they were under orders to let us try.

Our mission was to set ablaze the line of ships guarding Boulogne, and then all the invasion craft inside the harbor. Our plan was to attack first with Fulton's torpedoes, and then with volleys of Congreve's rockets.

My job was to get things off to a rousing start.

It had taken nine agonizing months since returning to England to prove myself, lay new plans, and train for this mission, all the while with no word of my wife and son. I was wildly impatient to search for them, but Smith kept a close eye on me, and two warring nations stood in my way. So maybe this inventive warfare could end the conflict. My separation from Astiza had stretched to an eternity, but perhaps this night eternity would have an end.

Fulton built two pontoons connected by thwarts, with a long cylinder slung beneath that was packed with gunpowder. This was the torpedo. Each component floated, but lead sank this "catamaran" so that the top of the twin pontoons was barely above the surface of the water and the torpedo itself was entirely submerged to protect it from gunfire. Pasques and I straddled each pontoon like riders on horses, dressed in black with our faces coated with polish. Once released from our mother ship, we were to paddle with the tide to reach the anchor cable of a moored French naval vessel, tie on the torpedo, and paddle away.

"All that's required is pluck and genius to reach the anchor cable undetected and set the clock ticking under the very eyes of the enemy," Fulton told me after the catamaran was lowered over the side of the Johnstone's *Phantom*, clunking ominously against its hull. "Having first landed and then escaped from France, you've demonstrated the skulking skills necessary. And your French companion there has strength."

"I didn't accomplish a thing. Pasques is helping out of desperation."

"That's because you didn't have the aid of modern science, except for sympathetic ink. Now American ingenuity is on your side. We live in an age of invention and experimentation, and you've been chosen by fate to pioneer its wonders."

Smith, who'd been rowed over from the flagship to witness our launching, seconded this endorsement by pumping my hand. "This time you have the chance to crush the entire invasion and write Nelson about how you did it, Gage. He'll be wild with jealousy." Smith and Nelson respected each other as warriors but were inevitable rivals for public acclaim. Nelson thought Smith a flamboyant and impractical dreamer, while Smith thought Nelson vain and annoyingly lucky, even though the admiral had lost an eye, a limb, his marriage, and any ounce of fat he'd once possessed.

"And why aren't you paddling, Robert?" I asked the inventor.

"I'm the bow and you're the arrow, Ethan. The quickest way back to Astiza is through the French fleet." He pointed, as if I didn't know which direction my renewed enemy was. "Start your lethal clockwork for love."

So Pasques straddled one pontoon to prove himself to English service, and I straddled the other to end the damned war. If the invasion scheme could be foiled, Napoleon somehow toppled, Catherine captured, and peace returned, I could find my family without interference.

"Are you ready, Pasques?"

"More than you know, my friend."

Once we got under way we said not a word, knowing how sound can carry across water. I pointed at a particularly promising dark shape, Pasques nodded, and we aimed our awkward craft at the warship's anchor cable, which curved from its bow down into the dark sea. The French ships were anchored bow to stern to form a wall of cannon-studded wood. French land batteries flanked each side.

Our first problem was that the tide threatened to carry us past the intended anchor hawser, and only by digging in my paddle to pivot our ungainly craft at the last moment did I manage to snag the rope. Our stern kept swinging, so Pasques, who remained a poor swimmer, had to slide himself carefully forward to grasp the weedy cable in his big paws, holding us so we didn't drift down on the enemy ship. I glanced up at the looming bluff of its bow. There was a knob up there that might be a sentry's head, but no alarm was given. It was a cloudy night, and we were blotted out against a sea of ink. Or so I hoped.

It was eerie to rest there a moment. I could hear the creak of tackle, the mutter of French voices, and the slap of waves against hulls. I took quiet breaths as if it might make a difference. We hung just under the stern of the next ship in line, its stern windows a great bank of mullioned glass and the top of its rudder like the fin of a whale.

The rope to attach the torpedo to the ship's cable was at the front of our contraption, so Pasques tied it off while I pried off a cover and set the timer.

"Have you set the fuse?" he whispered.

"It's ticking."

We had three minutes to escape.

When we pulled the pins to release each hull from the torpedo, they squealed.

"*Qui est là?*" a lookout challenged.

Our catamaran came apart. The torpedo floated by itself. In theory, the line at its nose was just long enough to let it drift down on the ship. We backed with our paddles, my pontoon accidentally banging the explosive-filled coffer and making me wince. This was not as easy as it looked on Fulton's diagrams.

A lantern lit. *"Anglais!"*

There was a boom, and a foretop blunderbuss erupted, spraying an ark of musket balls at the shadow we made. Waterspouts sprang all around us, some bullets pinging off our lead-covered hulls.

"Merde," Pasques muttered.

Miraculously, we'd not been hit, but we were in it now. Shouts and bells sounded up and down the French line. Gunport doors lifted like lion mouths, and muzzles trundled forward to aim at British ships that couldn't be seen yet. Muskets fired blindly into the dark, the stabs of light trying to find us. I dared not shout to my companion, but he was digging his paddle into the water as furiously as I was, both of us driving our separated pontoons that were as maneuverable as soggy logs. It felt like Napoleon's entire navy and army were trying to take a bead on us.

The clockwork kept ticking.

Paddling as furiously as a Canadian voyageur, I seemed barely to budge a pontoon sheathed in metal and as easy to steer as a mule. I cursed that we hadn't time to try this in England before our attack. The tide was carrying us down the French line even as we strove to work away from it. Our saving grace was that the current was so swift that the blind shooting was throwing up spouts of water well behind us now.

For an instant, I allowed myself hope. Maybe the crazy scheme would really work! I'd be a hero, Pasques would have a new country, and the British would send us on to look for Astiza, Harry, and a medieval artifact.

And then the Frenchman looked over his shoulder.

"The torpedo is following."

I wrenched around. The bomb had somehow come loose from the anchor cable and was drifting merrily in our wake, almost keeping pace despite our furious paddling. It was only a hundred feet behind, as persistent as a duckling.

Ticking remorselessly.

"We need them to sink it!" I shouted in English. "Here! Shoot here!" I made a splash with my paddle.

"Imbecile!" my companion cried.

Cannon blasts erupted, the suck of their trajectory almost tipping me over. As a professional gambler, I was calculating that the torpedo was longer than my narrow silhouette and that such odds meant a cannonball might sink it before hitting me. There were slaps as several balls skipped off the waves. The French cannon flashes were answered by British ones. Both fleets lit up.

Sweet mother. We were caught in a crossfire.

I looked back. The torpedo was trailing as doggedly as a pet, a hundred and fifty feet back now but still drifting at a good clip. Huge plumes of water erupted around us. Lanterns and torches were being lit in the camps of Boulogne. I could hear bugles, bells, and the rumble of drums.

We'd got things off to a rousing start, but not in the way intended.

Then the torpedo blew up.

The ocean erupted. The explosion was gigantic, a geyser of water shooting upward as high as the French mastheads. The concussion sent out a clout of air that knocked both Pasques and me into the sea.

"Ethan!" The buffalo could barely float.

I could have abandoned him right then and struck out for the British, but that's not my character. I'd recruited him to this madness and felt responsible for his carcass. So I swam in the policeman's direction and found him thrashing, his pontoon lost in the dark. First Catherine Marceau, then the emperor, and now a floundering ox! I was becoming a regular Channel lifeguard. I came in behind so Pasques wouldn't drown me with his flailing, reached across his shoulder to grasp his thick chest, and pulled him to me. I shouted in his ear. "I've got you! Lie still and I'll float you!"

He kicked and thrashed instinctively. I half choked him. "Still, or you drown us both!" Finally, he quieted, floating sluggishly. Splashes continued to erupt all around us, metal screaming. Gunports flamed. Now what? The torpedo wasted, the French line intact, and the English fleet and Johnstone's mothership half a mile of cold swimming away. If steering the catamaran had been awkward, towing Pasques was like dragging a barge.

The night was growing brighter. An ominous squadron of flaming English fireships bore down to engulf the French, but we'd failed to blast the hole they were intended to drift through. Flaming chips flew off the burning vessels as French cannonballs battered them. One, then two, began to sink. Behind, a flotilla of sloops, ketches, luggers, and longboats was sending up a barrage of Congreve rockets that drew scarlet arcs across the night. They were beautiful things, climbing into the sky and then scything down toward the French fleet like meteors. Hundreds of cannons were thumping in reply from the French shore. I could feel the beat of their blasts through the water.

The pontoons we'd been straddling had disappeared.

There was nothing we could do but swim for the French side. Maybe we could somehow slip by and sneak away on shore?

As we came between bow and stern of two thundering warships, Pasques waved his arm and exhaustedly shouted for help in French.

A péniche drifted to us, its crowd of anxious soldiers pointing their guns. My French companion reached and grasped its side. An officer peered at us.

"Gage? Is that you?"

General Duhèsme stared in disbelief at my exhausted face. Pasques floated like a bloated ox behind me.

"As a good double agent I've come to give warning," I tried. "I've brought word from England that their savants are sending secret weapons against you."

"That's rather obvious, is it not?"

"Don't listen to him!" Pasques said, coughing water. "It is I, Inspector Pasques, reporting to duty after sabotaging the British attack and capturing the notorious double agent and nefarious conspirator, Ethan Gage!"

"The devil you have. I just saved you."

The policeman hung on the side of the péniche. "I cut loose the English torpedo from its attachment line while the idiot American wasn't looking. I knew its explosion would toss us into the sea, and he'd be forced to rescue me. I've been looking to trap him since he kicked my balls in Notre Dame. Now I deliver you a turncoat and saboteur."

Good heavens. The bastard switched sides as easily as I did, and looked smug about it, too. I suppose I should have been flattered by the imitation.

Duhèsme looked at us both in the water. "You've arrested Gage?"

"I brought him back from perfidious England."

"It's a sorry world when I'm more trustworthy than you," I complained. "I deserve more loyalty, Pasques."

"No, you don't. The food was awful in Walmer Castle."

The general looked from him, to me, and back again, finally shaking his head. "Excellent job, Inspector Pasques. And welcome back to France, Ethan Gage. While I enjoy your company, I suspect your treacheries have finally doomed you. You should have embraced one side, as I advised you."

Rockets were crashing all around, most into the sea. Shouting French sailors were extinguishing those that hit a vessel. Their defensive line was holding.

I could hear rising cheers up and down the French line. The British must be drawing off. Our attack had failed.

Soldiers dragged me into the French boat, and the general regarded me with disappointment. "Don't you know it is futile to oppose Bonaparte?"

"I wanted to go to Italy."

"It is too late for that now." The general glanced around as sailors beat at a score of fires. "So . . . would you rather be hanged, or shot?"

Chapter 24

What I lack in combat prowess and conspiratorial instinct I make up for in timing. I was saved from French execution by the emperor of Austria, or rather the decision by Francis II in August of 1805 to join Britain's Third Coalition, declare war on France, and march for the Rhine. In an instant I turned from condemned spy to expendable emissary.

My destiny, it seemed, was to bounce endlessly between the two sides like a tennis ball in a king's court, trusted by none and manipulated by all.

Thanks to the indecisiveness of French admiral Pierre de Villeneuve and the relentless pursuit of Villeneuve by British admiral Horatio Nelson, the last French opportunity to seize control of the Channel had been lost. Villeneuve claimed to have defeated Admiral

Robert Calder in an inconclusive and foggy skirmish near Cape Finisterre in July, but followed up his "victory" by sailing away to refuge in Spain, an act of caution that infuriated Napoleon.

News of their navy's failure, and the new Austrian threat, threw the army camps around Boulogne into frenzy. Even though Fulton's torpedoes and Congreve's rockets had not achieved any decisive result, Napoleon was forced to wheel his Army of England east to march for Germany and Austria. As his divisions departed, he got an idea to use me yet again. Instead of being shot I was being sent back to the enemy to keep England off-balance.

I was brought under guard to Bonaparte's Boulogne pavilion again, which gave panoramic confirmation that the British attackers had drawn off and the French defenses were almost fully intact. Fulton's and Congreve's torpedoes and rockets had not proved decisive.

"Your diabolical attack was a failure, and Pasques has testified to your incompetence," the emperor told me. "You're lucky you were unsuccessful, Gage. Otherwise, I might have to make an example of you by executing you as a dangerous saboteur."

"Yes, no need for that. I'm a simple sailor, fighting fair and square for passage to Venice."

360 · WILLIAM DIETRICH

"Painted black and squatting in the water, as soul-less as a snake? A sailor with no honor, I judge, with the manners of a murderer. Always I am tempted to shoot you, but your questionable character becomes useful when necessity intervenes. I need you to carry a message to the British Admiralty." He glanced out the windows at the Channel waters, gray even on this day of August 29. "Besides, I haven't forgotten you saved my life." Napoleon had turned thirty-six two weeks before, more than eight months after his coronation.

"I haven't, either," I said, ignoring his insults and exhausted but vaguely hopeful at my reprieve. I'd caught Napoleon in a charitable mood. He was actually energized by the need to abandon his invasion plans and break camp. And why not? He'd been waiting for three tedious years for a chance to land a blow at his archenemy across La Manche, and his navy had delivered only frustration. Now he could fight a land war against the Austrians, the kind of scuffle he was comfortable with. "I only tried to blow up your fleet because I'm worried about my family."

"Réal has briefed me about their escape, and how you put them in peril with your clumsy attempt to sabotage my coronation. Thanks to our double agent Catherine Marceau, we manipulated you instead of you manipulating us. Did you really think such a hare-brained scheme could befuddle all of Europe?"

"We were led astray by bad advice from all sides. Say, do you know a fellow named Palatine, an elderly gentleman who scuttles about the catacombs?"

He didn't bother to answer. Great men become accustomed to listening mostly to themselves. "Still, your temerity proved useful. My self-crowning became the talk of Europe. I've commissioned a painting of the dramatic moment. Maybe I'll have David draw you in."

"Looking resolute, I hope."

"Surprised by my mastery. The painting is about me, not you."

The fields around Boulogne were liquid with movement. The vast military camp was being dismantled, wagons loaded, arms slung, and regiment after regiment was tramping east. The terrifying threat of invasion was over! Villeneuve was hiding in the Spanish port of Cadiz, and the white cliffs of Dover remained as remote as the moon. Yet English ships dared not come closer, having been stung by the resolute French defense the night before. I'd hoped for peace, and here was stalemate. "Since I've failed so conveniently, would it be possible for you to send me in search of my family?"

"No. You can hunt for your relatives when my nation has secured a favorable cease-fire. I need a truce with Britain while I fight the Austrians, so I'm making you my special envoy. Our navies are disengaged, Nelson is reported to be sick, Villeneuve has betrayed my every plan, and no naval resolution is possible or necessary. You can save countless lives by telling England that my ambition to invade is over. Nelson can stand down. The game is a draw."

Only over for the expedient moment, of course, and England would regard any truce as tantamount to a defeat. My mission was thus hopeless, and surely Napoleon must know this. So why was he sending me back to England? To buy time to keep his combined fleet of French and Spanish ships safe from British attack until the Austrian adventure was over. I was hardly worth a bullet to shoot, and even if I tangled only a few diplomatic threads, I might keep the naval contest in confusion until winter made a major show-down unlikely. So I'd use Napoleon as he was using me. I'd deliver any message he wanted and, rather than wait for a reply, demand passage to Venice from the English as reward for my heroic torpedo attack. I would squeeze everything I could from these scoundrels, and this time stay out of the line of fire and keep my money tucked under a mattress.

I am adept at making stern resolutions.

"Agreed," I said, "but my investments have hit a rough patch. A diplomatic fee would let me better entertain key officials in London to press your case."

"Always you are asking for money."

"Your robes cost a hundred times what I need, and I did inadvertently make your coronation something of a triumph. I hope the Crown of Thorns has been put somewhere safe, by the way."

He was a hard man with a budget. "No purse until you achieve a peace I desire. Then maybe France will vote you a medal."

"I'd rather have some coins."

"Ask your rich English friends!"

"Perhaps Pasques would care to accompany me?" I'd like to drag the rascal back to England and have him thrown into the Tower.

"The policeman has rehabilitated himself. He shrewdly led you on, all the while reporting to Réal."

"Pasques is shrewd?" The possibility had never occurred to me. "Is there no one in France who can be trusted?"

"Only me, Ethan. I'm going to remake the world, elevating half of mankind and vanquishing the other. Which half will you choose?"

"The half that stays out of these quarrels entirely."

"Impossible. Come to the globe and I will explain what you must explain to the damned English."

We walked to a corner of the pavilion. A globe an impressive four feet in diameter had been installed since I last visited, broadening Bonaparte's strategic aids from maps of southern England to a view of our planet. He turned it so that the Atlantic was in view.

"My admirals have failed me, Gage. Brueys, Bruix, Decrés, Ganteaume, Villeneuve, they've all disappointed one way or another. The strategic situation has always been simple." His fingers jabbed. His hands are quite fine, and he's proud of them. "Our fleet is scattered among several ports, and inferior when divided. Each harbor is penned by the British. But if we could ever combine, France could achieve temporary superiority in the Channel. An enemy that defends everything is spread so thin that it defends nothing, and the British are trying to defend all the world's oceans. Yes, they have the better navy, but not necessarily the bigger navy in a single place at a single time. That's the only secret to warfare."

"Nelson is famous for concluding the same thing. At the Nile, he attacked just part of the French fleet so he was always outdueling your ships two to one." I'd first met Nelson when his men fished me out of the Mediterranean following the Battle of the Nile. Even back in 1798, shot and shell from earlier battles had already left a sleeve empty and an eye sightless. He was relentless in action. When ordered to break off action at the Battle of Copenhagen, Nelson lifted his telescope to his blind eye in order to ignore the signal. He was a ruthless glory hound, but also a man who endured constant pain and chronic seasickness. England used his ambition to drain him.

"Perhaps Latouche-Tréville would have had the courage to take on Nelson," Napoleon said. "He was my best ocean officer, but had the temerity to die. Now Villeneuve cowers. Two weeks' superiority! That's all I asked. But Villeneuve continually worries about what Nelson is going to do, rather than forcing Nelson to worry about what Villeneuve is going to do. This is a fatal error. By trying not to lose, you guarantee that you cannot win. Imagination deserts you. So now my men march toward Vienna instead of London. The gods of history shake their heads in disbelief."

"I'm sure your admirals did their best."

"My plan was brilliant. Villeneuve escaped Toulon when a gale drove off Nelson's blockade. He met our Spanish allies and led Nelson merrily across the Atlantic to the sugar isles of the Caribbean. We had the ships to seize British islands and outduel the English fleet! But the coward lost his nerve. So he scampered back across the Atlantic to Europe. Even then, if Villeneuve had joined Ganteaume at Brest, we could have thrown more than sixty ships of the line into La Manche, outnumbered the English two to one, and conquered London. Eighty ships, if our Dutch allies joined us. And what did Villeneuve do? Break off the action with Calder and retreat to Spain. This is why I'm not shooting you, Gage. Your petty treacheries are nothing compared to the incompetence of my admirals."

"It's good to put things in perspective."

"Villeneuve says his ships are in poor repair and his crews are tired and sick. Men are always tired and sick in war. This is why I must replace the imbecile."

"So your fleet was bottled up in southern France at Toulon and now, after thousands of miles of sea voyages and a victory over the English, it's bottled up in southwestern Spain? Just to make the problem clear."

"You're a strategist, Gage, smarter than the fool you play."

"I try to see things clearly." I was wary of giving advice, however. Sometimes it's taken. Too much responsibility.

"So bring your perspective to the British. I know they're as weary of blockading us as we're weary of being blockaded. I suggest a truce. I'll call off my invasion plans if they call off their blockade. My ships will stay in port. My invasion craft will rot in harbor. London will be saved. If they leave me to deal with the Continent, I'll leave them to deal with the sea."

I was doubtful. Once a navy assembles ships, it longs to use them. And yet, perhaps I *could* broker a truce. The war was ruinously expensive. Avoiding a climactic final battle would save thousands of lives, dozens of ships, and millions of pounds and francs. Napoleon was offering, in effect, to divide up the world. The English had feared the anarchy of the French Revolution, but this new emperor had ended it, making himself a new kind of king. Why not let him have his way on land if the British got the oceans and trade?

I gave an obedient smile, marveling at how fortune can turn. The night before I'd been cannonaded by two navies. Today I was envoy for an emperor. "I'll suggest it."

Napoleon put his hands on my shoulders, squeezing until I winced. "Convince Nelson to stand down. Balance accounts, make peace, and then go looking for this wife of yours. Serve France, and you serve yourself."

"I'll do my best. Say, if I can't get more money, would a proper suit of diplomatic clothing at least be possible?"

Chapter 25

If Napoleon had been an admiral or Nelson a general, what a battle they might have fought! Both were made by war.

They were each about five feet six, handsome, charismatic, and dagger-eyed when in battle. They differed in that Bonaparte had never been seriously wounded, while Nelson had lost an arm and an eye and lived in constant pain. But they shared energy, vanity, and ambition without limit. Their wolfish instinct was to tear the jugular until an opponent was dead. Napoleon strove not to occupy territory but to destroy enemy armies, knowing all else would follow. Nelson sought naval battles of annihilation, knowing all else would follow. They were the very personification of elephant and whale, and had they clashed in person, their thunder would have shaken the heavens.

But Napoleon turned his back on the sea. It was my job to persuade Nelson to turn his back on the French navy. This time the French sailed me out to the British ships under flag of truce. Johnstone's *Phantom* delivered me to England only after I assured a frustrated Fulton that his torpedo attack had failed because of the treachery of Pasques. It's convenient to have enemies to blame for defeat.

I brought diplomatic credentials from Napoleon, explained I was becoming astonishingly familiar with the viewpoint of all sides, and was allowed by a cautious British Admiralty to confer with their most aggressive admiral at Nelson's country estate at Merton, a 160-acre tract between London and the Channel seaport of Portsmouth. It was more house than Nelson could afford and less than his mistress, Lady Emma Hamilton, thought he, and she, deserved. Merton was a mansion in progress, constantly renovated in order to confirm the meteoric rise of a rector's son and blacksmith's daughter. More than a century old, the two-story country estate was approached on a bridge over a decorative canal. The front facade was neoclassical in design, with Greek pediment over imposing entry, while the side terrace had French doors opening onto gardens. From modern water closets to rabbit hutches and hen coops, Emma worked tirelessly to create an Eden of escape.

The rendezvous with Nelson reminded me of another similarity between Bonaparte and the admiral. Both were famous for their women. By crowning Josephine, Napoleon had cemented her reputation as the most famous wife in Europe, a Martinique creole and widow of the revolution who'd seduced a rising general and ridden him to the summit. In falling in love with Emma Hamilton and leaving his wife, Fanny, Nelson had initiated the world's most notorious love affair with a mistress who'd built a life out of worship of a one-armed, one-eyed, close-lipped hero who'd spent most of his life at sea since age twelve.

People are strange, aren't they?

Emma Hamilton's butler let me in, but the mistress herself floated down Merton's staircase in a loose gown designed to camouflage middle-age weight. She was vain, but not disciplined.

"Mr. Gage! So honored to have an American envoy from the den of the ogre Napoleon."

"The honor is mine. And I bring what I hope will be good news, Mrs. Hamilton. The ogre is marching east, and the need for a naval showdown is over. I'm an emissary of peace."

She brightened, giving me a glimpse of her former magnetism. Emma was at least forty; some whispered she'd been illegitimate, baptized late, and thus was actually forty-four. The once-renowned nymph now had a plump face and an excess of underarms that swung like suet. But she'd been blessed with looks, charisma, and cunning. In youth she rose quickly from nursemaid to shop model for a quack doctor, posing as goddesses in filmy garments to draw curious males inside. By age sixteen she was mistress to Sir Harry Fetherstonhaugh, and vaulted upward from him to nobleman Charles Greville. When this Greville became bored, she was handed off to Sir William Hamilton, envoy extraordinaire to the Court of Naples and a man more than three decades Emma's senior. Emma took the insult as opportunity. The girl landed in Naples on her twenty-first birthday, won a place in Neapolitan society, and after a five-year campaign got Hamilton to marry her when he was sixty. Her station secured, she met Captain Horatio Nelson two years later and let mutual infatuation turn to volcanic love under the shadow of Vesuvius.

The aging Hamilton agreed to the bizarre living arrangement of being cuckolded in his own house by a naval hero. Nelson, the personification of British rectitude, let Emma be his private release, caring nothing for the resulting scandal or his long-neglected wife, Fanny. Sir William had died two years before my visit. Meanwhile, Nelson was so ashamed of his treatment of his wife that he'd refused even to visit his father's deathbed, lest he meet her there. He'd given Emma the money to buy Merton, and the adulterous couple fantasized about refuge after one last great battle.

Britain's aristocracy scorned Emma not just for her low birth, her lack of formal education, and her anxious striving, but also for the very cleverness that won her the nation's best warrior. Like Nelson, Napoleon, and Josephine, she had ability without station, and thus was a rebuke to the nepotism and favoritism of European society. The harder she tried, the more she was reviled.

I'm not as judgmental and hoped the pair could find happiness, but they dragged baggage of renown and ridicule wherever they went. They pretended their daughter Horatia, who was just six months younger than Harry, wasn't really theirs. No one believed them, so in trying to live up to propriety they'd made themselves absurd.

Now "this Hamilton woman" embraced me as an envoy of hope. No battle! That meant she might actually keep what she'd won. Her dream was marriage; her fear was a hero's death that would leave her penniless. Her light blue eyes were reddened from crying.

"Ethan [her immediate adoption of the familiar was indicative of her practiced charm], we had word you were coming! I so hope you can save the love of my life. You say Napoleon has given up his schemes against England, but Captain Blackwood has brought word that the French and Spanish fleets are gathered at Cadiz. Once more Horatio is being called upon to save England."

"He's already saved it by running Villeneuve to ground in Cadiz. The French don't want a fight, they want peace on the oceans."

"Can you convince him of that?"

She was, I have said, north of forty, and a lifetime of excess had changed her from the girlish beauty painted by besotted George Romney to the voluptuous, blowsy, middle-aged matron that she was. She spent wildly, gambled more, and kept the naval hero of England in chronic debt. Many visitors wondered what he saw in her. Decades of practice had not entirely erased the edge of her commoner accent, and she had none of Astiza's intellect. I saw not a book in the house, except for books about Nelson.

But she still had large, luminous eyes that artists love, a rosebud mouth, a lustrous mane of hair, a heart-shaped face, and the remnants of an outline that had made men ache. She could speak French and Italian, evidence of good memory, and knew English society the way Napoleon knew his army lists. Emma could expertly rank the noblewomen she longed to join with the precision of a drill instructor. She also had the charm that comes from the rare talent of being able to give another person her full attention. Her gaze fell like a beam of sunlight; your cares instantly hers. She took my hand and then my arm, fingers tapping like dancing mice, and ushered me from foyer to a marble-tiled hall where a grand staircase led to the rooms above.

She lived in a shrine, her home a peculiar museum of Nelson memorabilia. Light from tall windows fell everywhere on paintings and drawings of the couple. There were Nelson mugs, Nelson plaques, Nelson souvenir medals, and oil paintings of Nelson victories. Not waiting for posterity to recognize their importance, the couple had decided to celebrate it now. I believe that philosophy eminently sensible; what good is renown when you're already dead? Better to have it when it might win a free meal or better seats to the theater.

All portraits of Emma showed her slimmer and in the pose of a Greek grace, leaning so romantically and precariously that she probably threatened to topple when she posed. These pictures were the way she still saw herself.

"There's no mistaking whose house this is," I said diplomatically.

"I fill it with him because he is so seldom here. He has given his arm, his eye, and his years to his country. As he has sacrificed his life, so have I sacrificed mine." She had the melodramatic instincts of an actress.

"Word is that Lord Nelson has been ill."

"Weary. Responsibility wears on him. He has suffered from scurvy, dysentery, seasickness, concussion, depression, heart pain, dyspepsia, constipation, gout, and rheumatism. That's why your news is so welcome."

I rotated in the hall to show my appreciation. "A fragment of one of his ships?" I looked at a timber that soared toward the ceiling.

"The topmast of *L'Orient,* the French flagship destroyed at the Nile. Its flag was attached to this fragment. Are you familiar with that battle, Mr. Gage?"

"I was in it, madam."

"Oh! Then you are a hero, too."

"Unfortunately, I was trapped on *L'Orient* and thus on the side opposite your husband, though I took no direct part in the fighting. I won't make the mistake of facing him again. He's rather terrifying."

"But the ship blew up. You represent a miracle." Her eyes were wide with wonder.

"Dumb luck, I'm afraid, and good swimming. I met the admiral after that fracas and recognized his worth. He and Napoleon have the same ability."

"But my Nelson for good, and Bonaparte for evil," she said patriotically. "I had the same flash of recognition, Mr. Gage. When the admiral stepped ashore at Naples after his Egyptian victory, grateful fishermen released hundreds of pigeons that rose in a celebratory cloud. He looked like Apollo."

"Neptune, maybe, in his naval uniform."

"I've been consumed with love ever since. How fortunate I am, and how haunted by how he puts himself in danger!"

"All the world knows of your devotion, Lady Hamilton." I personally thought doves more celebratory than pigeons, but then no one has released so much as a chicken for me.

"Call me Emma." And so we hit it off, me enjoying her instinctual seductiveness, and she sensing a receptive audience for her charms.

She also played to Nelson's vanity, earning her place in the world by fortifying the esteem of England's greatest hero. You might think the famed grow beyond the need for praise, but my experience is that renown is like money. The more you have of it, the more you want. Great men and women are driven to notoriety because compliments become a drug.

The fifteen-bedroom house had been crowded with relatives since he'd returned for shore leave in August. Merton swarmed with nine adult relatives, seven children, a dozen servants, and a constant parade of naval officers. But for this momentous business Emma invited me into a private drawing room containing Smith, frigate captain Henry Blackwood, and the famous admiral.

"Ah, Gage," Lord Nelson greeted, as if it had been days instead of years since we'd last seen each other. "We were just discussing the obliteration of the French."

I tried to hide my shock. Nelson looked as haggard as Pitt. Napoleon may not have invaded England, but his relentless pressure seemed to be aging his most vigorous opponents. The admiral looked emaciated, face drawn, hair thinning, lines etched by relentless discomfort. Being important wears on a man. Being a savior crucifies him.

Yet his eyes burned as I remembered, his lips firm, his carriage erect as a mast. There was an odd ghostliness about him, as if he already had one foot in the next world. Even while paying attention he seemed distracted, listening to voices only he could hear. Nelson was gathering himself for one last great battle.

"I put you ashore in Egypt to take word of my victory to Napoleon," the admiral said, "and figured that's the last I'd ever see of you. Yet here you are, bringing word from Bonaparte." He coughed, and as we talked I realized he was struggling with the hack as a chronic, and ominous, condition.

"I'm drier this time, Admiral. And not so deaf from cannon fire."

"Yes, you were on the receiving end of our broadsides, weren't you? And what do you think of British gunnery? Can we beat the frogs again?"

"Your crews are the best in the world, my own United States excepted, of course. I must be patriotic."

"John Paul Jones was a fighter. But he was really a Scot." They laughed.

"I bring you word, Lord Nelson, that you've already beaten the French, that Napoleon has abandoned his plans to conquer England, and that no battle need be fought at all. You are saved."

The room went still with consternation. This was the last message they expected to receive. Blackwood looked skeptical, Smith intrigued, and Nelson disapproving.

"But that is the very opposite of what we want," the admiral said.

"Peace? I thought England longed for it."

"What you suggest is not peace, but a respite while Bonaparte conquers elsewhere. Is this not true? The Combined Fleet of my enemy safe and our finely honed battle fleet laid up in port, its officers at half pay? Peace will come, Mr. Gage, only when the enemy navy is destroyed."

"Damned right," Blackwood said.

Emma closed her eyes.

"But the threat of invasion is over," I repeated.

"At the very least this is useful news," Sir Sidney told the others. "But why has Napoleon abandoned his plans?"

"He received word of the French fleet retreating to Spain at the same time Russia and Austria joined to march against him. He really had no choice. But the end result is that your long blockade has succeeded; you delayed him enough that invasion became impractical. He sent me to admit it and spare more bloodshed."

"Why you?" Nelson asked.

"I am trusted by all sides." This was a tiny exaggeration.

"Spare us until he beats the Austrians and turns again," said Blackwood.

"That may not happen," Smith said. "Our allies outnumber him."

"Yet always the threat, looming over the horizon," Nelson said. "The way to eliminate it, gentlemen, is to destroy Villeneuve directly and completely."

Nelson could be an odd man, I'd heard, prattling on about his own achievements. The British general

Arthur Wellesley had just met him for the first time in London, and Nelson had boasted like a child until learning that the officer before him was the hero of India, at which point he changed manner and became sober about strategy. That was his demeanor now. He could also be a deeply profound man, an ardent student of strategy and tactics.

Emma looked stricken. He was refusing escape.

"I endured the Battle of the Nile on *L'Orient*," I said doggedly, "and witnessed hell itself. To inflict that on men again, when the strategic situation makes it unnecessary, is a grave decision indeed."

"Your word *grave* is not inappropriate," Nelson said. "Captain Carew fished out *L'Orient*'s shattered mainmast after the battle and used the wood to make me a coffin. I've kept it since, and recently ordered it carved with reliefs and made ready."

Emma almost swooned. She was an actress, as I've said.

"No one knows the horror of war better than I, Mr. Gage. I've seen three score engagements and bear battle scars worse than Alexander the Great. I'm wracked with pain. But I also find ceaseless blockade a misery, my absence from Merton heartbreaking, and the terror that England has lived under these last three years almost unendurable. I don't want it to end on

Bonaparte's whim; I want to end it on England's terms, which is the complete destruction of the Combined Fleet. Britain must have total sea supremacy if we're ever to be safe."

Here's the truth about opportunity: people refuse it all the time. Nelson had already smashed one French fleet, destroyed a Danish one, and bottled up the survivors. Napoleon's invasion had been canceled. Yet all this meant not a whit; this admiral had already chosen his path. He thirsted for glory and closure. Death, too, I suspected. Nelson knew he was being hollowed out. Did he want to die to the whispers of gossip in bed with Emma Hamilton, or to the sound of guns on a flaming quarterdeck? The fact that he would take thousands with him never occurred. Valhalla requires a heroic demise.

"Then you'll sail regardless?"

"My orders are to return to command of our fleet off Cadiz."

Blackwood nodded approval. He was a scrapper, too. In 1802 he'd used his frigate *Euryalus* to whip French vice admiral Denis Decrés in the much bigger *Guillame Tell*. It says something of life's unfairness that Blackwood was still a captain, while the defeated Decrés had become the French minister of marine, in charge of the entire navy.

Sir Sidney summarized my failure. "You've brought us something momentous, and it changes nothing, does it?"

"Apparently not." I shrugged. "Have your decisive battle, if you will. My purpose is to reunite with my wife and son. I need a ship to get me to Venice so I can travel to Bohemia ahead of Napoleon, and as you know I haven't a penny to my name. I brought you Talleyrand's papers that foiled Bonaparte's earlier naval maneuver, Sir Sidney, joined your attack on Boulogne, suffered capture by your enemies, and came back to reveal that the French army is no longer an immediate threat. Surely I've earned simple passage by now."

My British patron considered my plea. "You also failed our torpedo experiment, let a valuable French prisoner escape back to his homeland, and brought news our admiral doesn't care for. Yes, you've accomplished something, but it only makes up for your failures in Paris, so I judge our accounts squared. There's only one more thing you must do for me, and *then* I will provide you with papers giving you passage on a naval vessel going to Italy."

"Good Lord, what now?" The more jobs you complete, the more you're given.

"I want you to do to the French and Spanish admirals in Cadiz what you've just tried to do to us. Tell them of this meeting."

"I'm to go to Cadiz now? I can't even find it on a map."

"The southwestern corner of Spain, Ethan, and we'll transport you there. It's on the way to Venice, if that makes you happier. I want you to explain that even with the immediate threat of invasion removed, the heroic Nelson will not rest until the Combined Fleet is destroyed—unless the Spanish are willing to forgo their alliance, or Villeneuve to surrender his French ships. I want you to make clear they're fighting a sea battle with no purpose, against an admiral who cannot be deterred, for a tyrant who's marched away to Germany. I want you to sap their spirit before they leave Cadiz harbor."

"But what if they then hide and don't come out?" Blackwell objected.

"Their fleet will rot and their careers end in shame. Men fear humiliation more than death, or there'd never be battles at all. So some will choose to rest at anchor and others a fight, and the result will be a muddle. Gage is perfect at making a mess of things." He turned to me. "Confuse their strategy, and *then* you are released to go find your wife."

"You'll put me ashore again in enemy hands?" *Necessity never made a good bargain*, Franklin had lectured. "I'm getting dizzy going back and forth."

"They sent you to England to confound us with Boney's preposterous proposal. I'm sending you to confound *them* with British relentlessness. And when the French kick you out, which they will, my orders will send you on to Venice from there. Dampen French ardor, Gage, and you can finish your business. It's splendid how things work out."

I was skeptical of putting myself in French hands again, but this might indeed be a way to final passage. I hardly cared what these oak-headed naval officers did to each other, and I'd consistently escaped imprisonment or execution by using my wits and indispensability. One more message and I was on my way. "If you truly promise passage afterward," I confirmed, though I wouldn't have fully trusted him if he'd dribbled blood on a contract.

"We usually have vessels going to the Adriatic on one mission or another."

Oddly, a quietly weeping Lady Hamilton had collected herself and was looking at me with new calculation.

"You'll stay with us for dinner before I take leave tomorrow?" Nelson asked politely.

"It would be an honor," I said resignedly.

And so our meeting broke up, except that Emma took me by the sleeve to whisper in my ear. "The grove of Venus behind our home," she murmured. "An hour after dinner. Please."

Chapter 26

I was confused by Emma's invitation. Was she the minx gossips described? That made no sense. I'd given no indication I was physically attracted to her, and she seemed distraught with worry about Nelson. Not only was I married, I was poor, without title or prospects. Even I didn't think I was much of a prize. Nor were there any of the covert glances, under-table foot caresses, brushing of shoulders, swirling of hair, deep breathing, raised eyebrows, exaggerated smiles, tipped tongue, curved neck, revealed ankle, sensuous sipping, laughing at jokes, or any other signs women use to signal interest.

No, Emma was clearly infatuated with a pallid admiral who struggled with a persistent cough. No wonder he'd ordered his coffin readied: if the French didn't get him, consumption might. And this was the man whose mere name panicked the French navy!

I found Nelson a charming host at dinner. He was quiet and made no reference to his exploits. But then he didn't need to; the walls had pictures of his battles and the Worchester china, a present from Lloyds, had his recently invented coat of arms. I decided he was not so much shy as the kind of man so energetic that he had to keep his enthusiasm under rein, and a fellow slightly embarrassed by Emma's worship. Nor did he need to boast; we all assured him he was the lion of England. Like all great leaders, Nelson was astute about human character. There's nothing like listening to persuade the talkative that they're the epitome of wisdom. I prattled on for a good two minutes without his interrupting me, and judged him wise as Solomon.

The admiral sat at the head, Emma's mother at the foot, and Smith and I to the right side, facing other relatives and the Danish historian J. A. Andersen. This guest was writing an account of the Battle of Copenhagen, and Nelson was already pondering his place in history. Most of us have the luxury of not having a personal biographer, but the admiral needed to edit things as much as he could. I'd already decided to write my own books.

Blackwell had already hurried back to his ship. Nelson would travel to his flagship *Victory* the next evening.

Since I was being ordered to confer with the French admiral Pierre Villeneuve, I doubted Lord Nelson would share strategy with me. But Smith remarked on Nelson's ability to wring a decisive fight, and I dared contribute. It's safer to talk about things I have no responsibility for, like naval strategy, than things I do, like retaining contact with my family.

"Napoleon believes the same thing you do, Lord Nelson. Other generals care about ground, but he cares about armies. Smash the enemy, and the political and territorial gains take care of themselves."

Nelson came alive at this statement. His blind eye wasn't patched but was vacantly unfocused. His good eye, however, fixed on me like fire, and for a moment I saw the passionate sailor Emma was hopelessly in love with.

"Damned right," he said, the sailor's profanity gaining a "tsk" from Emma's mother, Mrs. Cadogan. "Bonaparte understands that to annihilate is a mercy because it ends war quickly. We mustn't let Villeneuve slip away again. I want a battle that wipes out his fleet, and with it the danger of England ever being invaded."

"Here, here," Sir Sidney said.

"Naval warfare is simplicity itself and yet endlessly complex, Mr. Gage," he went on. "To move efficiently a ship must be long and narrow, but then its shape means it has cannon only to port and starboard, not fore and aft. Firing into the unprotected stern of the enemy is like firing into a bucket. The cannonballs rattle like marbles, bouncing, maiming, and bouncing some more, splinters flying and blood spewing. We maneuver to avoid such a fate, and lay sand to provide traction in the gore."

"Horatio," Mother Cadogan scolded. "We're having dinner."

"Quite right." He'd barely touched his food, which was leg of mutton with capers, salt fish, plum pudding, garden greens, and peaches. "So traditionally no admiral dared present his bow or stern lest he be defenseless against the enemy broadside. The solution for each fleet was to form two parallel lines and slug it out. The problem is that the fleets have gotten too big. By the time you maneuver all of your dancers into position, like some elephantine minuet, the day is almost done. That's what happened to Calder in July."

"At the Nile you got around both sides of the anchored French and pummeled them two ships to one," I summarized.

"Correct. I could outshoot the anchored Danes as well, right, Andersen?"

"We were not ready for your aggressiveness, Your Excellency. It was a fearsome display of British gunnery."

"I fought the French at night at the Nile because they were anchored to help us keep track of where they were. But on the open sea, how do you force a conclusion?"

"Perhaps by sending Ethan Gage to counsel surrender?" I said.

He laughed. "If you hand me their fleet to scuttle, I'll build you Cleopatra's Barge to get to Venice! No, not by jabber jabber, but by grabbing their testicles and squeezing so hard that they can't get away."

"Horatio!" Emma's mother scolded again.

"The traditional line of battle is too ponderous and makes it possible for the enemy to break off and escape. I want a pell-mell fight with the ships in a tangle and every captain in a death match, and a pell-mell fight is what I'm planning to achieve. Just how, Villeneuve will learn in all good time, but I'll not be another Calder. I'm going to capture or sink them all."

He displayed the relish for battle that most men reserve for a meal or a brothel. It's the small ones you want in a bad fight, I tell you: Bonaparte and Nelson were both terriers who bite and don't let go. "If you do, you'll be the savior of England," I said politely, and obviously.

"And finally get the reward you deserve," Emma said more practically.

The admiral smiled indulgently. "My dear, sweet, brave, beautiful Emma, could any reward keep up with your purchases?" He turned to the rest of us. "The latest bills from the tradesmen total a thousand pounds."

She pouted theatrically. "Only to have a decent home for the savior of the kingdom." She turned to me. "How much does Napoleon spend on his homes, Mr. Gage?"

"They seem to be running about ten million francs each."

"There, you see, Horatio? You are worth a thousand Napoleons!"

He laughed. "Good Emma! If there were more Emmas, there would be more Nelsons!"

This seemed a little self-congratulatory all around, but we were tipsy from wine; they were as smitten as when they first met; and they pawed each other while Mother Cadogan looked embarrassed, smug, and startled at her daughter's improbable rise.

I wasn't certain what the purpose of a secret rendezvous was, but an hour after we'd finished our sherry

I left the house by the terrace doors and drifted to the garden as Emma had directed. In the September moonlight I saw a statue of Venus erotically undraped and bearing a none-too-surprising resemblance to the woman I was meeting.

Emma emerged from the monument's shadow, dressed in a translucent gown that gave a good blueprint of her ample figure. "Mr. Gage, thank God you've come to our humble home. I believe you're a messenger from heaven."

"Just from Napoleon at Boulogne, I'm afraid."

"You must save my dear sweet husband from himself."

"I'm trying, but he seems quite uninterested in rescue, Mrs. Hamilton," I said, addressing her by her widow's name to reinforce propriety. Having been sent adventuring as punishment for tupping Napoleon's sister, I was wary around notorious women. "Self-confident, too. I wouldn't wish to be Villeneuve, should Nelson catch up with him. Whatever he does to bring on a pell-mell battle, I've no doubt he'll win it."

"Yes. But he thinks he won't survive." She said this solemnly.

"Every man who marches to war imagines death."

"No. And it's not just the coffin. He's put sheet music of a funeral dirge he liked into that horrid casket,

392 · WILLIAM DIETRICH

and he carries the box about like a favorite toy. Do you know he's kept the coffin in his sea cabin and sat on it to dine?"

"His profession is a risky one. Maybe it's a way of laughing at death and keeping up his courage."

"He's ill, Ethan, and plagued by fate. When he served in the Caribbean a voodoo fortune-teller foretold she saw no future for him beyond 1805."

I felt a chill. "I hadn't heard that."

"He predicts his own death if battle comes to pass."

"I thought you were both looking forward to reward from his triumph?"

"That's silly talk to buck up our spirits. I see disaster if he sails on *Victory.*"

"The commonest fear in the world. Men forecast their own death, survive, and live happily ever after, laughing at their own superstition."

"No, he's not coming back, I know he's not, unless you act." She was close to weeping, and suddenly she clutched me, her body pressed against mine. Her weight gave her quite ample architecture on top, and her breasts mashed like twin pillows.

"Me? I keep trying to, but I'm swamped by modern times, Emma." The first name seemed appropriate, considering she was draped on me like wallpaper.

"Conscripted armies, spy agencies, smoking factories, manipulated public opinion—I fear this new world we're making is damned difficult to direct. Talleyrand says the nineteenth century is a plague of democratic incivility, and a temptress named Catherine Marceau agrees. In any event, I've no power. I'm little more than a courier of unwanted information to belligerent antagonists with centuries of stored hatred, a simpleton simply trying to earn passage to look for my family." Each day was ticking remorselessly by.

"You're the only sane man here, Ethan, because you're sensibly selfish like me. Don't deny it, we're both people of low character, trying to survive in a cruel and insane world. And you're right: this battle has become unnecessary. Bonaparte has given up his plans for invasion. England already controls the seas. There's no need for annihilation because French naval will has already been annihilated." As I've said, there was shrewdness to this Borgia of a woman, who had not a thimble of Astiza's character but a mind meant for maneuvering.

"I'm flattered, but what more can I do?" I tried to step backward, but she followed like a waltz.

"Look." Emma held up her left hand, displaying a gold wedding band. "This is not from my late husband, but my one true love. Horatio donned one, too."

"When? How?" Nelson was, after all, still officially married. Bigamy would make the scandal too gigantic to ignore.

"We had a ceremony with a parson last night. We took the holy sacrament and exchanged vows under the moon, both of us weeping. It was tragically romantic, beautiful, and doomed." She was imagining a Greek tragedy of her own life.

"Like those novels women enjoy. I've studied them carefully and am thinking of writing one of my own."

"We had to solemnize our love because we know that unless a miracle happens, we'll not see each other again."

"It's not a legal marriage, is it?"

"No. Fanny is still alive and refuses divorce. But it's a marriage of the heart and soul, truer than inky documents and mumblings in church."

I was impressed. First Josephine wangles a church marriage on the eve of her coronation, and now Emma had one on the eve of Nelson's sailing. These women had their eye fixed as fiercely as Nelson scans an enemy horizon. Females have clearer strategy and firmer purpose than most generals, and more ruthlessness, too. "I offer congratulations, but this changes nothing, does it?"

"The change must come from you, Ethan. You're the miracle I've been waiting for. Who would have thought from a failed spy, a rogue, and a wastrel, defeated at Boulogne and deceived by all sides?"

I wasn't happy with this catalog, though I was impressed by her research. "Doesn't that make me a poor miracle?"

Her face tilted up, her bosom heaving with emotion and her hair lustrous under the stars. For just that moment I understood poor Nelson's hopeless love. And I also knew the pair would never be allowed to live without scandal. Once the war was won the hero worship would subside and the tongue wagging would begin. For Nelson, death was the only way out. But for Emma, his survival meant her own. Maybe even real marriage someday.

We all have our fantasies.

"Not if you persuade the French admiral the hopelessness of battle," she urged. "The English are too bull-headed and confident to listen. But France is the capital of reason. To have Sidney Smith send you to Cadiz, it's astonishing! Because you alone see truth. My love will cut Villeneuve's fleet to pieces and die in the cutting. This must not happen. The French must be persuaded to abandon all naval ambitions so we can live in happiness. Somehow you must persuade Admiral Villeneuve."

"Persuade him of what?"

"Not to fight. Lay up his ships, as you want the English to do. Offer a truce."

"But he's not emperor. He's terrified of Bonaparte."

"Then you must make Horatio an even greater terror," she pleaded, eyes wet, mouth begging. "And you must explain that if he delays long enough, the love of my life will be so sick he must retire to Merton. He's failing, Ethan. Tempt Villeneuve!" Her fingers clenched like claws. "Do not surrender to fate, Ethan Gage. Make me a miracle."

Chapter 27

I did my best by meeting with the other side in the great cabin of the French flagship *Bucentaure*, a new, eighty-gun two-decker moored in Cadiz. This port in Spain's southwest corner, guarding the approaches to Gibraltar, was where the French had retreated after the Cape Finisterre fight with British admiral Robert Calder on July 23. As the warship swung at anchor its stern windows gave a panoramic view of a secure harbor, the white city and its gray forts occupying a peninsula that gives protection from Atlantic rollers and English ships. By the same token it's a difficult pocket to work out from, since the prevailing wind is from the sea and the mouth is a tangle of shoals. This gave the French and Spanish fleet an excuse to dither. While the admirals talked I kept imagining Nelson's cannonballs smashing through all that window glass, screeching the length of the hull and bouncing like marbles.

It was October 8, 1805. The wind had shifted briefly to blow from the brown Iberian hills, and so Admiral Pierre de Villeneuve called his French and Spanish admirals to a council of war to see if they should weigh and sail. With Napoleon having abandoned his plan to invade England, Villeneuve's new orders were to proceed to the Mediterranean and harass Austrian possessions from there. The question was when, whether, or how to obey this directive. There were fourteen of us in the low-beamed cabin: seven French officers, six Spanish, and me.

I'd appeared as miracle or plague, depending on whom you asked, transferred from British frigate under flag of truce to a Spanish cutter and transported into the enemy harbor. I presented myself as diplomat, envoy, and man of peace, an American working for France and England and thus suspect but useful to all sides. I had papers from both countries and my Jaeger rifle from Napoleon to prove my bona fides, not to mention a broken sword hilt from Talleyrand and twenty pounds in English sovereigns I'd wheedled out of Smith. Indicative of the desperation and depression of the Combined Fleet commanders was that they decided to hear what I had to say. When no alternative is attractive, even Ethan Gage gets an audience.

The mood was tense. The Spanish officers were reluctant allies at best, forced by Napoleon's bullying of their nation's King Carlos to side with France. The French were no happier, frustrated that their desperate need for supplies and repairs was met with excuses and delay by the Cadiz shipyards. The Spanish merchants demanded cash, which the French captains didn't have. The French needed supplies and men for forty ships from the two nations combined, which the Spanish couldn't fulfill. Now the admirals stared balefully at me because I'd brought more unwelcome word. Nelson was returning to the blockading British fleet and bringing enough warships to allow the English to risk a full-scale battle.

"Surely the British are running low on supplies and must put into Gibraltar to get more," Villeneuve said with more hope than sense. He'd none of Nelson's dash, but instead a double chin, receding hair, and fretful hands. He seemed doggedly dutiful but a conscientious administrator instead of a warrior.

"He might send a few at a time," I said, "but he'll keep enough on station to make a fight of it. His plan is to break up your formation and create a pell-mell battle, concentrating his firepower on just part of your fleet until it's smashed. Then he'll go after the rest."

"Just as I predicted," Villeneuve told his officers. "He'll send a column to break our line like Admiral Rodney did more than two decades ago. We must maintain a tight formation to destroy him as he approaches, our broadsides against his bows."

"Yes, you'll have the advantage at the beginning, and Nelson will have his turn when his ships pierce your formation."

"If we retain formation, he will never penetrate." Again, more hope than sense.

"Or, since we've no practice maintaining such formation, we should wait in Cadiz harbor," said Spanish admiral Frederico Gravina, who looked fiercer than the commander in chief but also had a reputation for sober realism. "Let the winter storms drive the British away, and we can slip through Gibraltar in a lull. To sally out now is to play Nelson's game."

"Waiting and hiding might not work, either." I explained that Smith, Fulton, and Congreve hoped to bring their torpedoes and rockets to Cadiz. "I know it sounds unsporting, but the inventors hope to burn your entire fleet without a cannon being fired. It's deviously clever, and might have succeeded at Boulogne except for the treachery of a French policeman."

They looked at me as if I were raving, so I plunged on.

"Nelson, on the other hand, wants to gut you with cannon fire. A slugging match is far more glorious, and he's mad for fame. Even the common sailors think God is on their side over Spanish Catholics and French atheists, and the tars are as belligerent as their admiral. They're drilled tight as a drum."

Gravina looked suspicious. "Why is he telling us this?"

My best credential was honesty. "Napoleon sent me to England in hopes I could get Nelson to stand down, since the French have suspended their invasion plans. I failed. Now Sidney Smith has sent me to Cadiz to warn you of Nelson and shake your confidence. He wants to foment disunion between your two nations. But that's not why I'm really here. Emma Hamilton thinks her lover will die in any fight and wants me to forestall one."

"Emma Hamilton?"

"Nelson's mistress. She wants him home."

Now the admirals wondered if I was performing a comedy. It's not my fault I get sent on errands by eccentrics and lunatics.

"I've made something of a bollocks of being a double agent," I went on, "and having seen a lot of war, saving countless lives seems the one useful thing I might salvage out of the past year and a half that I've been tangled in great events. I'm sure every wife in Cadiz shares Emma's sentiment."

"And your reward as an emissary of peace?"

"I'm trying to get to Venice to find my family. The British promised me passage if I persuade you." I shrugged. "Nelson's arrival isn't what you wanted to hear, but is it not an excuse to hesitate?"

Villeneuve sighed. "And how do you propose we do that, Monsieur Gage? Napoleon has already expressed frustration with my prudence."

"Just admit to the British that you prefer to avoid battle and don't intend to molest England. The July battle demonstrated your mettle. Now propose a naval truce. With Bonaparte occupied in Austria and winter coming on, cooler heads can prevail. Peace has to start with someone, and why not you, Admiral? Send me back with a white flag. I negotiated Rochambeau's surrender in Saint-Domingue and helped with the sale of Louisiana. I had a modest role in the Treaty of Mortefontaine. While people are forever dissatisfied with me, I'm really simply moderate, as well as a Franklin man, an electrician, and a good father when not losing my son abroad or sending him down a chimney."

"Bah," said Admiral Magon, who remembered me from Boulogne as I remembered him. He was the one who'd dutifully given the order that led to the disastrous drownings, and had the aggressive features of a pugnacious officer in a way Villeneuve could only envy. Part of leadership depends on looks. I also noted that the officer who had followed Napoleon's foolish order of a naval exercise in a storm had been promoted, while the man who wisely refused, Bruix, had been shunted aside. "This man is a spy and a sycophant who pretended to have saved our emperor from drowning. He hangs about fleets and armies to make his fortune. Now he wants us to give up like cowards to please his British masters."

"I *did* save him, and if you want evidence of his favor, examine my Jaeger rifle. People find me indispensable, when not shooting at me. A good drinking companion, too."

"He comes with no letter from Nelson, no rank, and no retinue."

"I have a handkerchief from Lady Hamilton, a pendant from Napoleon, and common sense. War is only logical when you can win it."

"This is ridiculous," Admiral Pierre Dumanoir said. "He's here to betray us. Look at his face. There's no character there."

In a twist of fate, it was the Spanish who came to my aid.

"If what the American says is true, and Bonaparte is marching on Austria, why are we risking our nation's ships for an invasion that will never happen?" Commodore Ignacio Alava asked his colleagues. "This Gage claims to know Nelson; why not send a counter-proposal? We've nothing to lose and he can buy us time while we train and refit. We can't sail anyway. The barometer is falling. A gale is coming."

"All the more reason to get out of this trap of a harbor now," countered Dumanoir. "We've a brief window of favorable wind; let's follow orders and escape to the Mediterranean before Nelson can stop us."

"We can't escape because we don't have adequate supplies, repairs, men, or training," volleyed back Commodore Dionisio Galiano, another Spaniard. "Half our crews are soldiers with no sea experience at all. A fifth of your French sailors are sick. If the British catch us, we'll be destroyed. I think this opportunist represents opportunity. Let him talk while we train."

"Such hesitancy may be the habit of the Spanish navy, but not of the French," Magon growled. "In Spain they may count what they don't have, but in France we win by putting to use what we do have."

Galiano laughed. "When was the last time the French navy won?"

I felt like the guest at an unhappy marriage. This group had no confidence in me, or each other. "Hard to fight Nelson with unready ships," I volunteered.

"All know the courage of Spain," Villeneuve tried, "and a demonstration of that courage would be to sail now, while the wind blows fair. I know we're not ready for a final battle, but staying in this wretched port is not helping us get there." He pointed at me. "I fear infernal rockets and torpedoes. I met Fulton in Paris and consider him in league with the devil. His boats smoke like volcanoes and sneak about under the sea."

Gravina disagreed. "The barometer is falling. This east wind will soon disappear and a westerly gale could drive our fleet onto the rocks of Cape Trafalgar. Waiting isn't cowardice. It's prudence."

Villeneuve saw an opening. "Perhaps it is not the glass, but the courage of certain persons that is falling."

The Spanish admiral leaped to his feet as if on a spring, hand on sword. "Then let us test my courage!" Half the table followed, with a scrape of swords half lifted.

The French admiral stayed in his chair. "That was ill said," he said mildly. "We're talking strategy, not courage. Please, sit down."

"The Spanish navy led the way fighting Calder off Cape Finisterre," Gravina muttered. His fellow

Spaniards nodded. But then he did sit, honor restored, and I saw that Villeneuve had successfully provoked him. Maybe the French admiral was smarter than I thought. "We'll prove our valor again by leading you to sea, Admiral, Nelson be damned."

"We sail not for combat," said Villeneuve, seeking to satisfy both sides, "but to redeploy and refit in the Mediterranean. If a westerly gale is coming, we need to get to the Straits of Gibraltar so it can blow us through."

I was alarmed. Such an escape would prolong the naval campaign for months or years. It would also infuriate Nelson and put the Combined Fleet between Astiza and me. "Maybe I can negotiate your free passage under flag of truce," I stalled. "Reporting my failure if I must, but surely being on my way. I'm no coward, but as a neutral American, this isn't my fight. And fight you shall have if you try to make Gibraltar without agreement from Nelson. Thank you for listening, gentlemen, but having exhausted your hospitality, I will now return to the British."

"No," said Villeneuve, more decisive toward me than toward Nelson. "I don't trust you. This Gage will stay with us while I write Paris for instructions on what to do with him. If he's truly Napoleon's pet, let the emperor tell us so."

"But I'm a diplomat!" Such instructions could take weeks, and who knows who might dictate them? Talleyrand, seeking revenge for my stealing of his cloak? Or Réal, on advice from Pasques? "Let me report your courage to England and the world. I'm thinking of writing a book."

"Certainly not, English spy." The admiral stood, as confident of bullying me as he was bullied by the specter of Nelson. "England will see our courage soon enough. And we never intended to let you travel from our war council back to the enemy. We wanted to hear what you had to say, but you've been on far too many sides."

"That's what we concluded about Gage at Boulogne," Magon said. "Napoleon said he was a puppet, but I don't trust him."

"Then he shares our fate," said Villeneuve. "You want to help France, Monsieur Gage? Until new orders come, I hereby impress you into the French navy."

The other officers smiled at this jolly idea.

"What? I'm no sailor!"

"Neither are three quarters of the men on my ships. If we win through to the Mediterranean, we'll give you passage to Venice. Can you swim?"

"Quite well, actually. Admiral Magon may not admit it, but I did save Napoleon."

"Then we'll keep you in irons until we're out to sea, so there's no chance for you deserting overboard and betraying us."

This was disaster. In trying to foil Napoleon's coronation I'd enhanced it, and in trying to prevent a battle I'd been drafted into it. A messenger of fate? I couldn't control my own.

But my protests seemed to be the best humor they'd had in weeks.

I might have felt better about being conscripted if the relatives of the Spanish sailors and soldiers showed more confidence at the likely outcome of a battle. Instead, the final unwilling recruits were marched down the streets to the departing men-of-war dragging a train of weeping women and snot-nosed children behind. Cadiz treated what should have been a triumphal procession like a funeral. Churches were jammed with families saying prayers for loved ones. At Iglesia del Carmen, so many tried to crowd inside that people were admitted in relays. At the High Altar of the Oratorio de San Felipe Nerei, Archbishop Utrera spent an entire day on his knees. As men were rowed to their vessels, tradeswomen, laundresses, and prostitutes who'd visited the ships were transferred back ashore, and, as they passed the men, they joined the lamentation. Whores counted their money as if it might be their last.

None of this gave me confidence.

Being chained on the main gun deck, peering at the world through a gunport, gave me time to think carefully about my own wretched chances. Villeneuve seemed a decent chap, obedient but not terribly imaginative, and thus a lamb for Nelson's lion. The *Bucentaure* would be the English admiral's primary target in hopes of decapitating the command of the Combined Fleet. It was likely to be in the thick of the fighting and to take a terrible pounding.

Unless I could contrive a way to hide in the hold, I needed a safer ship.

Chapter 28

At first I had no chance. The fleet hoisted its yard-arms and unfurled topsails, laboriously hauled anchor, and worked its way out of Cadiz harbor, the ship's boats swinging sluggish bows and preventing warships from accidentally drifting down on each other. The ships crawled past the fort at Puntal to the outer Gulf of Cadiz and looked ready to break into the Atlantic. But before they could do so the wind shifted as the Spanish had predicted, and the ships were forced to reanchor, this time in uncomfortable swells. For the next ten days a gale howled from the west, exactly where the Combined Fleet needed to go. Was this a reprieve?

A British frigate tantalizingly patrolled a few miles offshore to report our movements, but my pleas for a return, or a return to land, were ignored. Day after day crawled by with me still a thousand miles from my family. Beyond on the horizon was a second English frigate to relay any signals the first might make, and then presumably a third and fourth and so on out to wherever Nelson's fleet was patrolling. Should Villeneuve ever break free, the English commander would know within two hours.

So we rocked uneasily at anchor, neither in harbor where we could resupply or at sea where we could fight. The dice of fortune finally came to rest for me as the gale began to die, Villeneuve got a shock, and I got a worse one. I was kicked awake at dawn.

"The wind is shifting," said a French ensign of fourteen who unlocked my irons, hoisted me to my feet, and pushed me toward the admiral's great cabin. "Soon we'll be too far to sea for you to swim."

"Can I stroll the deck?" I still might make a last-minute dive for shore.

"You're unchained only to see Admiral Villeneuve. He's had a letter."

"Orders from Paris?"

"Details are not shared with ensigns, monsieur."

"Might I tidy up first?"

"No need, if we're hanging you." So he pushed me again, and I was marched to the ship's great cabin, stiff, grimy, and apprehensive. French marines ushered me inside. The admiral was seated at a writing table looking pensively at correspondence marked with the broken red seals of official communication. He surprised me by looking at me not as a prisoner, but as if we were comrades.

"Mail has come for both of us, Monsieur Gage."

"A reprieve?" Might as well sound optimistic. Napoleon might free or condemn me, Nelson might bargain me loose, or I could get more bad news from the barristers I'd consulted in London.

"I'm afraid it's about your wife. Given the demands of war I was obliged to read your correspondence before sharing it with you. The letter comes from a woman whom I assume is a friend of yours, but the news is not good." Grimly, he handed it over.

"*Dearest Ethan,*" the missive began. It was on fine paper, the calligraphy elegant, and it smelled of perfume. For a moment my heart hammered, eager that it be from Astiza, but then I recognized the hand of Catherine Marceau. "*It was a pity that things turned out so awkwardly at the coronation, and a tragedy that you were separated from your family. None of that was intended; we still had use for you. But you and your wife panicked. In the long months since our parting*"—a nice euphemism for knocking her over an altar—"*I'd often wondered what became of you. The return of the policeman Pasques confirmed that you lived and were in custody, likely to be condemned. Then Talleyrand informed me that you'd once more been pressed into our own diplomatic service. How able is Bonaparte, to find a use for even the most miserably confused of his empire's minions!"*

I wish people could be more flattering in their assessments.

"I understand you're once more pressed into being a go-between and will shuttle between the French and British sides. Accordingly, I'm putting this letter in the care of Admiral Pierre Villeneuve on the chance you find yourself in his company. My purpose is to suggest that your real service is returning to me."

The cheek! But of course she missed me, too, the heart-sore girl. I read on, annoyed but curious.

"I know we have a troubled history. But we always got on well when your wife didn't insert herself, and you do exhibit a certain pluckish charm. The grand chamberlain confides he entrusted you with a mission to discover a medieval artifact in kingdoms to the east." Here it was again, the legendary Brazen Head. *"Talleyrand suggests, and I concur, that at this juncture we should combine our talents for such a quest. You may have learned something from Astiza's research you've not yet confided, and you must admit that I've*

demonstrated resourcefulness of my own. I stay several steps ahead of you."

She was as bad at modesty as I am.

"The grand chamberlain's offer of monetary reward still stands, and even Pasques is curious about continuing what he calls a treasure hunt. I'm not sure what you told the poor man. In any event, should we not forge a new partnership that saves your life, and perhaps consummate it in ways implied by your clumsy attempts to seduce me?"

She also had a tendency to rewrite history.

"I suppose you still have loyalty to your little family, a sentiment I find droll but dear. Unfortunately, hope is shrinking that you will ever be reunited. Word has come that Astiza's indiscretions have led to her imprisonment for witchcraft in a fortress somewhere in Bohemia. Presumably little Harry has been imprisoned with her, if he is alive at all. Your wife has a sharp tongue, and I think it will be impossible for her to defeat prosecution. Unless you seek my help I'm afraid she's lost, likely to be burned as a sorceress.

Burned at the stake for witchcraft? What century were we living in?

"The burghers of central Europe are more backward in their superstitions than we people of enlightenment. Astiza sealed her fate when she fled from our

care. It's too late . . . unless, dear Ethan, you return to Paris to join me. Yes, we would have you back as prodigal son! You've exhibited cleverness in searching out old secrets, and it's possible you can still be of service to the emperor and France. But only, dear Ethan, if you are also of service to me. So I'm writing to offer you opportunity. Come to Paris and surrender to my command, and perhaps we can learn something of your foolish wife together. It's her only chance. It's your only chance. I've enclosed a pass and documents with Vice Admiral Rosily to require you to do just that, under close arrest and armed guard. I'm so anxious to see you! After reunion, we can find or, more likely, avenge your family. Yours in affection and continued conspiracy, the Comtesse Marceau."

The woman was clearly balmier than Emma Hamilton. Surrender to her command? Still pretending she was a comtesse? Returned under armed guard? I'd be tortured for information I didn't have, and then disposed of.

The bigger question was whether she was telling the truth about my wife. Catherine had made a fool of me already, and I trusted nothing she said. But she gave my mission new urgency. It was even more imperative that I find and rescue Astiza and Harry on my own. Yet I was trapped in an anchored fleet. I looked wildly about, as if I might find an answer in the admiral's great cabin.

"It's distressing news, I know," Villeneuve said. "This woman Marceau, she's your lover?"

"Certainly not."

"A political ally then?"

"An enemy. She wants me at her mercy in Paris."

"Ah," he said, as if such machinations occur all the time. Which they do. "My news is just as catastrophic. Word has come that Vice Admiral François de Rosily-Mesros has arrived in Madrid from France. Do you know what that means?"

"He has been sent to make peace?" I'm always hoping.

"Hardly. There's no reason for a rival French officer to be in the middle of Spain unless he was en route to Cadiz, and no reason for Rosily, a senior and elderly admiral, to come all the way to Cadiz unless he has been ordered by Napoleon to replace the vacillating, hapless, Admiral Villeneuve—me." His tone was ironic. "The new commander is delayed in the Spanish capital by a broken carriage and the need to assemble an escort against the bandits of western Spain, but still, he was only four hundred miles away when this letter of warning was sent to me. Even now he may be approaching. Which means Villeneuve's career is over."

The admiral was referring to himself in the third person, as if already obsolete. Not encouraging. "My commiserations."

"Unless," Villeneuve said grandly, "Villeneuve sails and proves his courage."

Suddenly, I saw why the admiral thought our letters needed to be shared. We were both men in a hurry, he to salvage his reputation, me to save my wife if she could still be rescued. Honor and glory motivate the military world, and a man's rank is fixed not just by the braid on his shoulders but courage to the point of rashness. Villeneuve faced a grim choice. He could take an unready fleet out to battle and risk the lives of tens of thousands of soldiers and sailors. Or he could meekly wait to be dismissed, disgracing a thousand years of family history.

"If you remain at anchor you'll be replaced within days," I summed up.

"Exactly. And you'll be transferred in irons to Paris. But if we're at sea, the Combined Fleet is still mine, and my future is still mine. So I put it to you, Ethan Gage. Should I put you under guard for escort to this schemer of a woman? Should I wait for Rosily to take my command? Or should we both sally against Nelson and trust to God that either victory or defeat will hurry us to our goals?"

"Death or capture?"

"Be optimistic, monsieur. Victory, and a prize to sail to Venice. A long shot, yes, but when the table is almost empty, does not the gambler stake all?"

I'd no choice, nor was I being given one. I dared not put myself under the mercy of Catherine. The way to Astiza was gunfire and glory.

I stood straighter than I felt. "Agreed." Maybe I could swim to the British when our ship went down. "I'll bet on you over return to Paris."

Villeneuve seemed relieved by having his hand forced, as if a weight had been lifted. "Don't be too pessimistic, Monsieur Gage. We've more ships than the enemy, I hope, and the winds of war can blow both ways. *La fortune des armes, n'est-ce pas?* Nelson will make clever plans, but who knows which fleet will hold the weather gauge, be closest to Gibraltar, or throw the initial broadsides? A first punch can be decisive."

"I just make poor cannon fodder. I think too much."

"Yes, I've considered your utility. You can read, and swim, and thus are unlike most of your shipmates. I suspect you truly meant well by coming here, and I don't intend to keep you locked in irons as a condemned man while battle rages. I want you to fight with us with intelligence, courage, and free will."

I liked the sound of that plan, given the alternative. This Villeneuve was not a bad sort, I sensed, just the wrong man at the wrong time. "What do you propose?"

He smiled wryly. "First, to lie down on the deck when the enemy broadside comes. We officers are required to stand tall to inspire our crews, but I allow the ordinary sailors to lie low to avoid the enemy cannon balls. If I were you, I'd kiss the planking in hopes of avoiding the worst of the flying splinters."

"Thank you, but not entirely reassuring."

"On the other hand, I'm reminded of your rather remarkable rifle. Such a gift from the emperor shows your talent as well as his favor. Consider being a sharpshooter for us in the rigging."

"That sounds most dangerous of all."

"Not entirely. Our navies employ different tactics. The British who are skilled at gunnery go for the guts of a ship, shooting hull against hull."

"I saw that skill at the Battle of the Nile."

"The French and Spanish have a different philosophy, necessitated by our rustier skills. The masts and sails are a target three times as high and almost twice as broad as the hull. So, with a less experienced navy, we shoot at the English rigging. There are three reasons to do so. First, it gives us a bigger target. Second, if we can bring down enemy masts, the English will wallow helplessly and give us time, with clumsier crews, to work around to stern or bow and rake them with impunity. Third, helplessness can simply encourage an enemy to surrender, so we capture an undamaged hull we can sell for more prize money, or press into our own fleet. There are two *Swiftsures*, one on the British side and the second our own, captured from the English."

"Yes, that *Swiftsure* was with Nelson at the Nile. Now it is deployed against him."

"So here's my thinking, given your reputation as a marksman. The English will be shooting at our hulls while we are shooting at their sails. I wouldn't want to be a topman on an English ship with all that French and Spanish iron whistling about my ears. But on a French ship, going aloft may be the safest place."

I considered this charity, my mind followed the shrouds and ratlines of the rigging to the spars far, far above. There were platforms like little tree houses up there, but I don't like heights any more than I like caves or catacombs. "So long as the mast stays standing."

He shrugged. "Fortunes of war, again. But here's my suggestion. I think a man of your talents is best employed by Captain Lucas of the *Redoutable*, which is a fine two-decker ship of seventy-four guns. It may escape the center of battle, while the *Bucentaure* will certainly be in the maelstrom."

"You'd give me a better chance? I'm not used to kindness, Admiral."

He shrugged. "The plight of your wife moves me. This letter makes me sympathize with your position; it's terrible being at the mercy of a wicked woman. It's too dangerous simply to put you ashore, where you'd be hanged as a deserter or put in irons for Paris, and too risky to allow you to carry observations back to the British. But Lucas could use you. More than any other officer he's prepared to accommodate our weakness by attacking with boarders. He's just four feet and nine inches tall, and jokes that low profile is useful for keeping his head attached to his shoulders as cannon balls come whizzing by. But his size makes him aggressive and innovative. He's trained his crew in musketry and hurling grenades from the mast tops to sweep clear the enemy top deck. You could watch the battle from up high, escape the need to join his boarders, and climb back down when it's all over. It's the safest place I can think of. You may survive to seek your family."

"You are a better man than your reputation, Admiral."

"I've heard that Nelson is kind, too, constantly looking after the welfare of individual seamen. This is simple leadership. Kindness can infuse morale."

I felt faint hope. I'd no intention of shooting at the English, but I could fiddle aloft while the fleets burned. This Lucas, no bigger than a boy, might be just the kind of captain to stay on the edge of battle. When it was all over, I'd go to the winning side—almost certainly, Nelson's—and demand to be sent on my way.

It's splendid how things work out, Sidney Smith had said.

Better to have remembered Franklin: *Wise men don't need advice, fools don't take it.*

"Thank you, Admiral. I agree, sailing is the best chance for both of us now." Nelson wanted glory, Villeneuve to avoid humiliation, and I a way out of my oaken prison and a million miles from Catherine Marceau.

So battles become inevitable.

"If Captain Lucas has his way, you'll win a great prize and have money to hunt for this wife of yours." He shook my hand. "If she is not already roasted."

Chapter 29

The *Redoutable* was indeed redoubtable, with 74 guns and 643 men, but it was just 170 feet long and small enough, I hoped, to steer clear of Nelson's *Victory*, which was a deck higher, had 27 more cannon, 180 more sailors, and a tiger admiral out to finalize his place in history.

Like all warships, every corner of *Redoutable* was crowded as a hot kitchen. At night the ordinary seamen swung hip to hip in hammocks, a hive of snores and farts that made a mockery of modesty. By day they practiced the deadly battle ballet required to serve crowded guns without trampling one another. Every man had a duty he learned by rote, but every ship had more sailors than needed to fill the gaps of the coming dead.

The sensation belowdecks is of being corked in a crowded barrel. It's dim as a cave because gunports are closed against waves in most weather. The sea smell is smothered by a musk of sweat, mildewed clothing, damp hammocks, salt-stained hemp rope and sails, wine, cheese, rum, bilge water, drowned rats, the piss-dales where sailors pee, and the collected urine kept in tubs for washing clothes. A veteran connoisseur of naval imprisonment can pick out additional odors of oak, cooking coal, the ash of the ovens, tallow, tar, the heavy iron of the guns, and the pungent scent of gunpowder when that gingerly stored commodity is brought up to be fired in anger or practice. Vinegar and salt water, too, from attempts to wash things down, and vomit when the seas get rough. A call of nature is answered on the wooden seats of the head located under the bowsprit, where big swells mean a cold splashing. Sailors wipe with a tow rag, which is a rope with a ragged end that is rinsed by dragging it in the sea.

The nose mercifully becomes insensitive, eyes adjust like a cat, and a constant stooping waddle to avoid deck beams becomes second nature. I still manage to knock my head, however. Nor do I escape feeling trapped in a thick wooden box designed to absorb cannonballs weighing as much as thirty-six pounds. Such a ship is built around its guns, is run for its guns, and is jammed with guns: sailors eat on a plank suspended by ropes over the barrel of each weapon. The *Redoutable* could hurl nearly a half ton of metal at an enemy with a single broadside. If such statistics sound obsessive, understand that naval war is a merciless slamming until one side yields first, with flesh-and-blood humans sandwiched between the oak and iron. Artists paint it as epic glory, but I'd seen the belowdecks fury at the Battle of the Nile, and the result is actually perfect hell. The object is to smash, smash, and smash, in a frenzy that sustains its own mad logic.

It can be a handicap to know too much.

That's why I was grateful to have signed on with a captain shy of cannonballs, who wanted to win with sharpshooters, grenades, and a charge of boarders. Unfortunately, I learned upon transfer that Jean-Jacques-Étienne Lucas is also a bantam rooster of a man brimming with belligerency. He greeted me as if I were a knight-errant, eager for the fray.

"The American marksman! I heard talk of you even in Paris, Monsieur Gage. You are perfect for my plans!"

"My real talent is as an observer."

"The hero of Acre and Tripoli? Ha! Like all men of stoic courage, you are too modest."

"No I'm not."

"This will be a contest that will require every soul if we wish to prevail. I'll tell the marines and soldiers you've fought Red Indians. It will inspire them."

This didn't sound good at all, but I couldn't be surprised. Naval captains live their lives for a showdown such as this one, some enduring entire careers without the sting of battle to relieve the boredom. The kind of showdown looming comes once a century, and capture of an intact enemy could set up a captain up for life, once the prize was sold. Moreover, I remembered too late that men like Lucas frequently make up for shortness with ferocity. He had something to prove, whereas I had more reputation than I wanted.

The French and Spanish had a total of forty ships, thirty-three of them ships of the line, and twenty-six thousand men. This theoretically outweighed Britain's thirty-three ships, twenty-seven of them ships of the line, and seventeen thousand men. The Spanish fleet included the four-deck, 136-gun *Santisima Trinidad*, the largest warship in the world, and the Combined Fleet had six hundred more cannon than the English. Properly employed, it should win a decisive victory.

Its crews, however, were depleted by sickness and desertion. They'd been harbor-bound so long that sailors had little practice firing in the roll of the sea.

Even the simplest sailing maneuvers were exercises in confusion because there'd been no opportunity for training.

"We've one advantage, however," Lucas explained, reviewing his own tactics by reciting them to me. I'd been allowed to bunk on an "English hammock," or casket-like swinging cot near the wardroom, and wander the vessel without duties, since I was trained in nothing but shooting. As a result, as foreigner, diplomat, hanger-on, and friendless, I was the one person he could confide in without interrupting the chain of command.

"We have nine thousand more men than the British. Soldiers and landsmen, true, but why not use them as such? We'll broadside, of course, but my real strategy is to grapple, kill every Englishman on the uppermost deck, and board. We'll trap their gunners belowdecks and rain grenades on them until they surrender. This is where you excel, Ethan Gage." He clapped me on the back. "You will use your rifle to assassinate every officer in your sights."

"I admit I've been in a scrape or two," I said politely. "But I really prefer talking things out, flirting with ladies, experimenting with electricity, and gambling at cards. Accordingly, I might actually be the most help below the waterline with the surgeon. It's the safest place, I understand, and I'm clever enough to help with medical matters. If you keep me alive, I can write up your exploits in my memoirs."

"Ha! I think you like to joke, Ethan Gage! You can't describe the most glorious battle in naval history by hiding below. You'll write your book after you kill all my enemies. I think I'll send you up the mizzen, the mast closest to me and the quarterdeck, and you can shoot down the English captain. We'll win renown together, as Lafayette and Washington did at Yorktown."

Renown, as this exchange indicates, constantly gets me in trouble. "My advice is to keep a distance and save your ship for future duty. Nelson's a bit of a madman. Already has his own coffin, just to give an idea of his mood. A charmer, though." I aim to be fair.

"I'm tired of hearing about Nelson. Does he want the end of our navy? Fine. I want an end to *him*. He's haunted Villeneuve since the Nile. Shoot Nelson, Gage, and I'll put you in *my* book. And send you to Venice, too."

So I reluctantly looked after my golden weapon, giving it a fresh cleaning and reflecting that gifts come with a price, as Napoleon knew when he armed me.

Someday historians will make sense of the maneuvering that followed our lumbering exit from Cadiz, but to me we were a meandering herd of sail without clear direction, waiting to be attacked. We weighed anchor on October 19, but a light and fickle breeze meant that only Admiral Magon and six ships managed to work their way to sea that day. It took until evening of the next day to get the entirety of the Combined Fleet, twenty-five French ships and fifteen Spanish, untangled from the anchorage and out into the Atlantic. Several had to be towed by their boats. The glacial pace of the sally allowed huge crowds to line the shore of Cadiz as ship after ship slowly got under way, the wails of women carrying eerily over the water with a call as old as war itself. They feared their men doomed to slaughter by the notoriously able and ruthless English.

The east wind that had released us swung to the south, blocking our intended route to Gibraltar and forcing the Combined Fleet west toward the British who lurked over the horizon. We watched anxiously for Nelson that first day. Finally, Sunday evening, October 20, a mild wind blew out of the west and enabled the Combined Fleet to turn and begin to straggle southeasterly toward the straits and, perhaps, escape. However, as the wind picked up that night, the untested vessels struggled to reduce sail with raw crews. A topman fell from the flagship *Bucentaure*.

Our eager and sprightly Captain Lucas signaled we'd lower a boat to pick him up from the sea.

I was surprised the fellow could swim long enough to survive. Commanders discourage sailors from learning to swim because it makes them less likely to desert in port and more likely to fight heroically at sea to avoid death by drowning.

My father taught me to swim by pitching me into the Schuylkill and holding me off the dock with a pole. I didn't appreciate the lesson at the time, but it's served me since.

Redoutable's rescue gained us a crewman but put us closer to the flagship than I preferred, making me worry I'd made a mistake by accidentally picking an enthusiastic officer. What if I wound up in the center of battle? No, I must trust to fate and take comfort that I was at least headed toward Gibraltar and the Mediterranean, my route to Astiza and Harry. Just a dozen miles to the east was Cape Trafalgar. If we could get past that protuberance, maybe we could outrun the English all the way to Italy.

Evening comes early off Spain in late October, the sun setting a quarter past five. The Combined Fleet struggled to sort into assigned order as it sailed into the dark. At nine o'clock a shout came across the water that British ships had been sighted somewhere to the southwest of us. Men rushed excitedly to the rail to peer into the dark, but nothing could be seen. We'd little idea where our own ships were, let alone those of the English, and lookouts were posted to avoid collision. The wind dropped and captains struggled to keep their place in line because some ships are naturally swift or slow. There were shouts, signal shots, rockets, and lanterns. Near eleven we almost collided with an allied vessel and learned we'd lost contact with the *Bucentaure* and had fallen in with the Spanish under Admiral Gravina. Since *Redoutable* was a sprightly sailor, Lucas asked, and was given permission, to lead the Spanish half of the fleet.

I was delighted. We were now at the front of the long line of battle, closest to Gibraltar, and as far from Villeneuve's flagship and Nelson as possible. My plan was working. I went below to attempt some rest. A large swell kept the suspended coffin-like box that held my bed swinging, and it was something of a wrestling match to hoist myself into it so I could pointlessly lie swaying in the dark, anxious and sleepless like everyone else. All around me, officers shifted restlessly, muttering or praying in the dark.

The sea began to grow light at six A.M., the sky pearly from haze hanging over the ocean, which was as smooth as glass. We still had no idea where the British were, but Lucas gave the order to clear for action because the activity broke the tension. Men were grateful for something to do. Bare feet thumped, cannon rumbled, and gunports squealed as they were raised so muzzles could poke out.

Readying is the same for all navies. Hammocks were rolled into sausages and stowed into netting on the top deck as a bulwark against bullets. Nets were suspended over the top deck like an awning, to catch battle debris falling from the rigging above. The yardarms were linked to the masts with chains to keep them from being easily shot away and crushing men below. Masts, yards, rigging, blocks, and sails total 150 tons, and toppling this onto an enemy can be as devastating as a broadside to its hull.

The portable partitions that define cabins were broken down and stowed so incoming shot couldn't turn them into clouds of splinters. All tables, chairs, chests, boxes, and bags were carried to the hold below. Powder was brought up, and cannonballs racked like black melons. Sand was strewn to provide traction against the blood. A surgical table was readied on the orlop deck, the steel saws of amputation clinking as they were laid out like fine cutlery. Nelson had mentioned how cold the steel was that took off his own arm and ordered that surgical instruments in the future be heated. I saw no such care on the French ship.

The four ship's boats were lowered and towed behind so they wouldn't be shot to pieces. Their "crew" became the live chickens and goats brought on board for fresh food, and sailors joked that the condemned animals might live longer than the men hoping to dine on them. It says something of French expectations that the cattle manger was empty. This fleet didn't expect to be at sea long enough to enjoy any beef.

Muskets, pistols, pikes, and cutlasses were distributed, accentuating the seriousness of what was to come. Gunners readied scarves to pull around their ears against the cacophony of cannon fire. Shoes were stowed, trousers rolled up, and letters and mementoes entrusted to mates in the event the owners died.

I passed my long rifle around a company of curious marines.

"A gun as pretty as a woman."

"Too long and clumsy for the mizzen-top platform, though."

"And too long to load, American."

"But accurate, no?" I asked. "I'll make it work." I didn't tell them I had no intention of shooting anyone.

A last hot meal was cooked, and then the fires extinguished so that a hit on the coal stove wouldn't ignite the ship.

I wandered to the quarterdeck, where officers peered westward through telescopes. Lookouts shouted from aloft. These topmen could count English sails coming over the horizon. I checked my watch. Did we have enough wind to outpace them?

"They have the weather gauge," Lucas commented, as much to himself as me.

"What does that mean?"

"We're both sailing southeast, but because the wind is from the west where Nelson is, it reaches the English first. They can use it to run down on us, but we cannot sail against it to come up on them. That means it's their choice to fight or wait, and can time the battle to their advantage."

I looked about. To the east, an orange sun was rising over the hills of Andalusia. To the west, it lit a line of British topsails about ten miles distant, far enough away that their hulls were still below the horizon.

"*Redoutable* is a fine sailor, but we've run ahead of our station," Lucas added.

"I think it's splendid we're leading the fleet," I encouraged. "Joining with your allies and demonstrating smart sailing. It's the kind of initiative that works well for our eventual book."

The Combined Fleet trailed like a ragged group of geese. While the breeze was light there was a heavy, ominous swell on the otherwise smooth ocean, a sign of disturbance hundreds of miles away.

"Storm coming," the helmsman muttered. The barometer was falling as well.

"Maybe we should put on all sail and hurry on ahead to the Mediterranean," I suggested. "We can scout for Villeneuve by getting to Gibraltar first."

"No. We're out of position," the captain decided. "We'll tack and return to the center where we were assigned."

"What? And give up the lead?"

But he wasn't listening to me, shouting orders instead that sent seamen scurrying to halyards and sheets. We ponderously came about and ran back down the line of Gravina's ships to rejoin the French center, much closer to Villeneuve than I preferred. By the sword of Spartacus, battle seemed to suck me in like Newton's gravity! Instead of being on the edge, I was once more in the middle.

I stewed. What other ship could I escape to? The answer was none.

The British ships, meanwhile, had turned ninety degrees and were sailing directly toward us. Because we continued to drift south, by the time they intercepted us they'd collide with Dumanoir's division of ships in our rear, probably overwhelming that third of the Combined Fleet before we could turn to help.

So at eight A.M. on Monday, October 21, Villeneuve gave up our run for Gibraltar, as well as safety and sanity, and in the name of honor and courage ordered the entire fleet to turn and sail back toward Cadiz. This tactic would protect Dumanoir by putting our center abreast the oncoming British, but also make battle unavoidable. The showdown had finally come. The only good news I could see was that it would allow survivors of a defeat to seek refuge in the Spanish port. Turning around would also throw the Combined Fleet into confusion.

"Tack in this light wind? Villeneuve is no seaman," Lucas muttered.

It was so difficult to turn the ships that it took two awkward hours for all the vessels to come about. The result, despite incessant and increasingly frantic signals from Villeneuve, was a ragged crescent of a formation instead of a neat line. It was as if our line of ships had formed a shallow bowl to catch the incoming two-twined fork of British warships. What wind there was pushed the English straight at us, while we drifted leeward toward Cape Trafalgar.

Even I knew our formation was disorganized. I felt trapped, awaiting execution on a morning that crawled like syrup. Lucas's officers fell silent, unhappy but determined. Villeneuve had given up the initiative and embraced the collision that Nelson wanted.

Our entire ship was quiet. I could clearly hear the creak of tackle as *Redoutable* rolled in the swells. Officers' orders drifted up from the stillness of the gun decks to be heard on the quarter. Water sloshed and hissed. The approaching British ships loomed closer, their canvas growing in height like building thunderheads.

Battle ensigns went up on each side, flapping lazily in the hazy air.

Nelson's fleet had broken into two columns, each aimed at a different point of our struggling line. Higher and higher their masts rose, and then their bows appeared over the horizon, cannon bristling on either side like thorns. We could see the wink of red from jacketed marines. There was little sound from the British ships, either, but they were a magnificent sight. Every sail had been set to catch the whispers of wind. They were like birds stretching their wings, straining to rush down on us, and yet advancing slower than a walk. I've never known such agonizing tedium as that long morning. Two fleets waited to duel, and the wind had gone on leave. The world seemed glacial.

Yet slowly we drifted toward collision.

The sun was entirely lost now in milky overcast. At eleven thirty A.M., Villeneuve ordered French or Spanish pennants flown to identify each ship. Now there was a great rumble of drums, the soldiers aboard presenting arms. I snapped to attention without thinking about it, surprising myself, and looked about to see if anyone had noticed. None had, but I remembered Duhésme's advice to join a unit, a cause, and a country. I was trapped, yet part of something, the thrill as oddly exciting as love.

Everyone was rigid from anticipation.

On the Spanish ships, a huge wooden cross was raised to hang from the mizzen boom, the religious symbol swaying over the taffrail at the ships' rear. The French Catholics crossed themselves and kissed their own crucifixes.

On *Redoutable*, one of Napoleon's new imperial eagles was brought from the captain's cabin and presented to the crew to elicit shouts of "*Vive l'empereur.*" The standard was lashed to the mainmast.

The cheers gave spirit. The long months of chase and wait were finally over.

"You'd better take your place in the fighting top, Monsieur Gage," Lucas said quietly behind me, making me jump.

I tilted my head back. "Up there?"

"As safe a place as any. Safer, if you use your rifle to good effect. Discourage the enemy by picking off his best men."

I'd fixed a sling to my gun. Now I slung it over my shoulder, walked to the rail, and swung out over the ship's side to stand on the wooden rails called chains, the water foamy far below. The tarred ropes attached there were reassuringly sticky, angling upward in a triangle to join the mizzenmast. My rifle bumped clumsily. I wore my worldly possessions: a few coins from Smith, the broken sword stub from Talleyrand, and my tomahawk, all tightly secured beneath my clothing.

Taking a breath, I began climbing the netlike ratlines that led aloft. The swells made the mast top pivot through ten degrees, and it was unnerving as we swayed. The higher I went, the wider the pendulum. I paused, steadied, took breath, and then kept going. Dozens of sharpshooters were doing the same. Looking neither up nor down but only where my hands must grab, I slowly ascended to the lubber's hole next to the mast, clumsily squeezed through, and came up on the mizzen platform that would be my station. Ahead were similar platforms at main and foremast, crowded with soldiers. Each top extended three feet from the mast like a tree house, ratlines and rails giving security. The mast, wrapped with rope, was a comforting trunk at our back, extending far higher to more yards and sails above. A canvas screen had been lashed around the perimeter to hide us from view when we crouched to reload.

From here we would shoot to the enemy's deck.

"It's the American and his golden gun!"

"Now we'll see if you shoot as fast as you talk, Gage."

I had a splendid view of grandeur. Even Astiza, wise as she was about the insanity of war, would appreciate its beauty. I wished for the millionth time that she were beside me.

More than seventy ships were in view, sixty big enough to hammer it out in the main battle, and the fleets combined carried forty-one thousand men and thirty times the weight of artillery that would be used in a comparable land battle. We were riding the most complex, beautiful, and magnificent machines civilization had yet produced, works of art dedicated to the utter destruction of their counterpart. Each ship had acres of canvas, miles of ropes, and a city's worth of stores. The English ships were painted like wasps, their black and yellow stripes broken by the yawning red mouths of gunport lids. The Combined Fleet was black and red. The clouds of canvas were massive as icebergs, and pennants seemed to float in the light breeze with the suspension of balloons. The

Santisima Trinidad was a castle, looming over lesser ships.

The ships crawled, seeming almost frozen.

Then at last a signal ran up Villeneuve's mast. "Open fire."

A marine checked his watch. At noon, the first cannon boomed.

Chapter 30

Perched a hundred feet above the sea, I had a strange sense of detachment as the battle began. I felt wedged into a box seat, watching an elaborate stage production. The long, greasy swells kept us sharpshooters lazily rocking as if we were nested in a tree, the ships moving with the stately sway of giraffes. The quick thud of the French and Spanish guns seemed disconnected from this nautical minuet at first, too excited to fit the panorama's languorous mood. But the gunfire slowly rose in frequency to become a rolling thunder, its urgency reminding me why we were here. The ocean began to erupt from splashing cannonballs. The shooting also settled the crews of the Combined Fleet, putting them to work. They cheered each rippling broadside, gray-white clouds of gunsmoke hanging like fog because there was almost no breeze to disperse it. As a result our hulls were gradually shrouded, and the shooting became half-blind.

The British ships sailed directly toward us in ominous silence, firing not a shot. Many of the French and Spanish cannons initially missed, demonstrating their lack of practice, and the Nelson columns glided ahead in a corridor of geysers. As the distance narrowed to five hundred yards, however, accuracy grew. I began to see splinters fly, ropes snap, and holes open up in sails, perforated into lace. Seven different vessels blasted away at the lead ship of Nelson's southern column, chips spinning as if she were being whittled.

"*Royal Sovereign,*" a French marine sergeant reported after peering through his glass. "Not Nelson, but someone just as eager. Collingwood, perhaps."

"Where's Nelson then?"

He pointed to the lead ship of the northerly column, every possible sail set as it drifted downwind. "The one coming for *us.*"

Lucas had failed me, putting us in the path of the dangerous admiral instead of on the battle's periphery.

You can never find a coward when you need one.

Fifteen minutes after the opening shots to the south the *Victory* came under our own fire, our guns rippling and our ship heeling to their kick. But the English flagship sailed majestically on, utterly silent, masts scraping heaven, sails swelling like a proud chest, and its sides bulging like a bicep and studded with guns. We were frantic to stop the enemy flagship before it pierced our line, and yet it seemed impervious to anything we did. Guns roared in broadside after broadside, and the sound boomed up to us in claps of air. Sailors' ears would bleed even when wrapped in kerchiefs, and some would go deaf for days or a lifetime.

Finally, our attempt to slow and blind the enemy by blasting away at its rigging became successful. The studding sails that extended from the main yards of *Victory* were shot away, fluttering down like tumbling ducks. The foresail turned to ribbons. With stays cut, the mizzen topsail of the English ship snapped and tumbled, hanging awkwardly against lower lines and poised like an arrow at the helm below. A cannonball bounced off one of the English anchors and it sagged.

I could see the blue-coated English officers standing stiffly on their quarterdeck with little to do but demonstrate courage. The flagship's great wheel disintegrated in a cloud of splinters. They flinched and stayed standing, even as the helmsmen died. The fresh black and yellow paint was beginning to be gouged with scars of raw wood. Nonetheless, *Victory* swung to starboard, obviously steered from somewhere below, and calmly passed down our line. Damnation! The perfect place to pierce our line was between *Bucentaure*, directly ahead, and *Redoutable*. This was as bad luck as at the Nile.

Victory seemed almost impervious to the punishment it was taking, plowing ahead through a rain of cannonballs, but then a group of red-coated marines suddenly tumbled like pins in a bowl. A still-cradled ship's boat erupted into pieces, its planks whirling like scythes. I heard English screams. Surely they'd turn away? The enemy flagship was taking a terrible pounding, and maybe we could really hammer it to a halt before Nelson achieved his melee. But no, for the first time the *Victory*'s port batteries let loose in return as she cruised down our line, the wood of French ships flinching from their punch. Stout wood quivered. Masts reeled.

Redoutable had yet to receive any fire.

My mouth was dry, and I had to remember to swallow.

Then *Victory* turned again, to pierce our formation, and slid into a fog of French gunsmoke to slip at no more than walking pace between Villeneuve's flagship and our own *Redoutable*. The three-decker was only eight feet higher, but it seemed to tower over us. The English were so close that I could clearly hear the calls of the British helmsman below, a calm, "Steady! Steady as she goes!" The hats of the officers were visible through the smoke as they paced like toy soldiers in a toy courtyard. The French marines began to fire at them.

"Shoot, shoot, American!"

There, could that be Nelson? I aimed at his foot and squeezed, hoping to chase the idiot to safety below. The shot struck the planking, and the man jumped but didn't retreat. Why the pointless bravado?

To combat fear, I knew.

At the bow of the British ship I could see a crew crouched around an enormous sixty-eight-pound carronade, essentially a gigantic shotgun packed with five hundred musket balls. It was aimed not at us but at the windowed stern of *Bucentaure* on *Victory*'s other side, the mullioned glass glinting in the low, hazy sunlight of late October.

I wanted to shout warning, but it was pointless. Villeneuve knew his doom.

The English carronade fired.

The stern of *Bucentaure* dissolved into a penumbra of flying glass and window sash. The swarm of musket balls shot down the interior of the ship as if into a bag. There was an agonized bellow. The screams signaled to the lower decks of the English ship that they'd come within range, and as *Victory* slid across the stern of the French flagship, every other port gun, each loaded with two or three cannonballs, fired at point-blank range as it passed. More than a hundred round shot systematically crashed into Villeneuve's command, creating havoc I could scarcely imagine. Cannon flipped and shattered. Companionway ladders dissolved into wooden splinters. The ship's stern became a gaping cave, its interior splashed with blood like paint. Smoke rolled out from the ruins as if from a horizontal chimney.

In a single broadside, the French flagship was half-wrecked.

There was quiet as the British reloaded, enough so that I could hear the curses of French wounded floating across the water.

Then it was our turn. Captain Lucas shouted orders, the sound faint from my aerie, and we tried desperately to swing. Our bow strained to turn east so we could get our own guns parallel to the immense British flagship that was cutting our line ahead of us. But the wind remained feeble, the rudder sluggish, and we were too late. We'd punished the British ship as it had charged, and now it would have revenge.

Our bow slid into view of the cannon on *Victory*'s starboard side and once again its guns barked in turn, a steady thump like the pounding on a drum. *Redoutable* actually seemed to stutter and slow as the balls hit our prow, huge chunks of wood spiraling upward in crazy corkscrews. I saw cannonballs bounding off stout timbers and ricocheting out to splash. One of *Redoutable*'s two anchors was shot from its perch and plunged into the sea. Our foremast swayed in the storm of shot, yardarms and sails tumbling like limbs in a storm and punching through the netting to hit the deck with a crash. Sharpshooters on the foretop platform yelled as they fell, hitting the deck with a sickening thud. The mainmast swayed ominously, and the mizzen where I stood shuddered, meaning some of the cannonballs passed entirely through the *Redoutable*'s length and struck the base of our mast. I felt like a squirrel waiting while woodsmen chopped at my tree.

Better men than me report a strange coolness in battle, a sharpening of senses and attention to the business at hand that gives them robust courage.

Not today. This wasn't my fight. I felt hideously exposed, caught in a nightmare from which I could not awake, my mind whirling.

"Reload, American!" Muskets went off in my ears, smoke stinging.

I did so mechanically but with deliberate slowness, not wanting to kill either English or French. The men around me shot ever more frantically, swearing in frustration as they sought to slow the English onslaught. *Victory* had raked two French ships at once, but now it was swinging parallel to *Redoutable.*

It was time to try the French tactics. "Hoist the grapnels!" Lucas cried.

We were about to collide and tie ourselves to the huge English flagship. Madness, madness! Yet the French soldiers and marines packed around me cheered lustily, anxious to wreak revenge against cannon with cutlass and grenade. I pressed back against the mast, happy to have the other sharpshooters between English bullets and me. One of our little company grunted and fell. His comrades unceremoniously bent, hoisted, and threw him over. Another abruptly sat, wounded and coughing, blood frothing at his lips. He was allowed to stay. English marines were crouched behind bulwarks, shooting up at us as we shot down at them.

The *Victory* could have avoided our boarding challenge by standing off, but instead swung toward us so that we angled together and crashed at the front. The *Redoutable* shook with the impact, but crewmen began assembling to board. A charge was our only chance. Meanwhile, the shattered *Bucentaure* with Admiral Villeneuve was drifting slowly north from *Victory*, no longer able to control the Combined Fleet and hammered again and again as other British ships broke the

French and Spanish line and pounded it. Masts cracked and toppled. Guns disintegrated into fragments after being struck by a ball or overheating. Marines pitched from its rigging.

I looked out at the entire battle. By now it was cloaked with smoke. Clouds from sixty furiously firing ships had piled to the mast tops, so what I saw was a sea of fog lit by the flash of thousands of cannon. Metal shrieked, hissed, and flew so copiously that it occasionally rang like bells as opposing cannonballs collided in mid-air. The English seemed able to fire at demonic speed. As they out-paced the enemy more and more Combined Fleet guns fell silent, increasing Nelson's advantage. They were gnawing us to impotence.

The battle was devolving into the pell-mell pounding that the admiral had wished for, capitalizing on the superiority of British training. With yards, sails, and entire masts coming down like crumbling scaffolding, warships dragged ever more ponderously. A broadside would ripple out, pulverizing a helplessly drifting opponent, and then long agonizing minutes of quiet would pass as the guns were laboriously reloaded and one ship or the other was brought around to repeat the cannonade. Knots of two, three, and four ships formed, some shooting all the way through a riddled enemy hull and accidentally hitting an ally on the other side. The clogging dead were unceremoniously tossed overboard, forming lines of floating corpses in tidal eddies.

There was only one rule. The faster you could kill, the greater the chance of not being killed.

Grapnels lashed the *Victory* and *Redoutable* together. The two hulls ground in the sickening swell, tumble homes touching like two breasts, and yardarms reached for each other like crisscrossing fingers. The ship's rails, however, were several yards apart because of the bulge of the ships' hulls. The gap was too far to leap and this put the *Redoutable* in a dilemma. Lucas had assumed he'd be fighting another two-decker, but Nelson's path had linked him to a mighty three. That meant the British rail was a full deck above our own; the English sailors could leap down onto us but the French would have to climb up to them. Nor could Lucas's men see who might be waiting for them, unless we on the mast tops cried warning.

Meanwhile, the two ships blasted into each other's hulls. They were so close that Nelson's crew no longer bothered to run out their guns after recoil, and in fact hurled buckets of water on their French enemy right after shooting so the muzzle flashes wouldn't set both ships on fire. The gun decks were absolute pandemonium, guns leaping with each discharge, smoke so thick you couldn't see, noise so loud you couldn't hear, and comrades crushed as they fell. Some cannons were dismounted and shattered by screaming shot, setting off secondary explosions.

The only thing that kept terror at bay was the inability of any one man to see all the havoc; no one entirely knew what was happening beyond the little world of his own gun crew. I had an eagle's view but was masked by smoke, so I felt more than saw the howling shot smashing *Redoutable*'s innards. The mizzenmast kept shaking as if thrashed by bear.

"Shoot, shoot, you damned American!" The topmen were hurling grenades that exploded with a flash in the fog.

My reluctance to fire meant I had time to see things the others missed. I grabbed the sleeve of the man who'd shouted and pointed toward the bow of the British ship. "We have to warn your comrades!"

About fifty French had emerged from the chaos belowdecks with sword, pike, and pistol, and were bunching on our foredeck to scramble up to the British vessel in hopes of seizing it. What they couldn't see was that the starboard carronade, the one that hadn't been used, was being swiveled to point at Lucas's prepared attack. The massed boarders made a perfect target.

"There, there, shoot the English gunners!" the marine yelled to his fellows. "Swing down, American, and warn Captain Lucas!"

I left my rifle and slipped back through the lubber's hole to shout out the danger so the French target of men could disperse. It seemed a wonderfully neutral task between shooting my British friends and refusing to do so for the French. I did shout warning, but couldn't hear it myself in the roar of battle. I was also clumsy as the rigging swayed, and as slow descending the ratlines as I'd climbed. I felt sluggish, a fly on a sticky web.

So I was too late. Before I was halfway down the carronade fired.

The effect on *Redoutable* was as dramatic as the earlier blast into the stern of the *Bucentaure*. Again, a scythe of five hundred musket balls blasted out, this time spraying our French top deck like a gust of hail. I could actually see the shadow of the radiating cloud of lead as it kicked up a blizzard of splinters.

The gore was instantaneous. Sailors and marines were hurled like paper. Small arms went flying. Almost the entire boarding party fell dead or wounded, turning an attack into slaughter. Lucas's charge ended before it could begin.

No sooner had the carronade blasted than the French topmen got the range and peppered the British gun crew with grenades and gunfire. Several English fell and the rest ran into their forecastle for cover. Boarders and defenders were both down now, temporary stalemate ensuing. The decks of the two warships were littered with casualties.

Not wanting to join chaos below, I clambered back to the mizzen platform, noting uneasily that there was more room than when I'd left. British marines had shot several of my companions out of our perch. Our concealing canvas curtain was dotted with bullet holes.

"There! Is that Nelson?"

The marksmen peered through a momentary clearing in the smoke. A diminutive man stood on the British quarterdeck with bodies sprawled around him. He was wearing a bicorn hat of command and a coat with embroidered decorations. He almost begged to be a target.

The wearer was either insane or waiting for glory. Muskets aimed.

"Not him!" I shoved against the soldiers, making them lurch, and the muskets flashed, shots flying wide.

"You imbecile!"

"Don't cut him down like a dog." It was a plea, a gasp. "He's blessed by greatness."

"You made us miss, traitor!" A fist smashed into my face. Then a knee hit my groin. I fell onto the fighting top, and boots kicked me. I lashed back in return, tripping men, trying to save the mad admiral who strutted below.

"Take his ship and take him prisoner, dammit!" I urged. "That's the higher deed."

They ignored me. "Take Gage's rifle! It's still loaded!"

I grabbed. "No!" But they wrestled it from my grasp, my fingers slipping from its carved butt. I clawed for the sniper's legs, but I was still being pummeled. Then I heard the gun's distinctive crack.

I rose to my knees, surprised to be alive and dreading to look. Someone important had fallen and was being carried below, a concealing handkerchief draped over his face.

"We've shot the admiral!" a sergeant bellowed down to Lucas. "Their deck is clear. Now, now, board!"

Indeed, Victory's top decks looked almost deserted except for a handful of marines crouching behind their gunwale. The wheel was smashed, the boats exploded, and dead and wounded lay everywhere. The carronades were abandoned. Exploded French grenades littered the planking with fragments of metal, and a steady collapse of rigging had choked the main deck with an avalanche pan of wreckage. Far below, where the hulls ground together, I could see stabs of fire as more British and French cannon went off, tearing out the guts of the ships.

It didn't seem survival was possible for any of us.

Captain Lucas was staggering on his own quarterdeck from a wound, but now he bellowed like a bear at his men down below. "Come! They've fled their main deck! Leave the guns! We can seize them from above!"

For a seventy-six-gun two-decker to conquer the fabled *Victory* would be the proudest achievement of French arms in naval history. With Nelson down, suddenly it seemed possible. The sailors who were losing the gunnery contest below clambered up to attack across the rails. *Redoutable*'s guns fell silent as men bunched once again to rush the British marines.

"Lower the main yard to use as a ramp!" Lucas ordered. The spar holding the mainsail came down and was swung to lean like a log between the higher *Victory* and the lower *Redoutable*. It would serve as a bridge along which the boarders could scramble like monkeys.

"Midshipman Yon!"

"Aye, Captain!" A young French officer at the bow saluted and led four sailors in a daring leap across to the *Victory*'s anchor, and then up its stock to the British deck above. They disappeared a moment before his head popped up above the enemy gunwale.

"There's no one left alive! They're all hiding below!"

"Our grenades have worked!" Lucas called to his men. They cheered.

I could feel our ship quaking as the British continued to disembowel *Redoutable* with their artillery.

"Boarders ready!" The men strained like hounds on the end of their leash. If the great Nelson had been wounded or killed, the top deck swept clear, and the carronades silenced, this would be the climax of the battle. Against all odds, Lucas would sweep and conquer.

"Away boarders! Charge!"

A great shout rose up, at first warbling and then strengthening in volume. *"Vive la France! Vive l'empereur!"*

And then a new opponent loomed out of the miasma of smoke. The French and Spanish ships would not cooperate. The English did.

The British three-decker *Téméraire*, a towering monster of ninety-eight guns, bore down on our untouched starboard side like some ghastly apparition, huge and relatively unscathed. The men next to me shouted and pointed, urging their comrades below to return to the starboard cannon. But no one was paying attention; their eyes were on *Victory*. The French marines around me shot impotently at this new tormentor, hurling their last grenades. The bombs fell short into the sea, and they cursed in frustration.

The *Téméraire* sailed into point-blank range. Then it fired a thunderous broadside, every gun at once, into the other side of *Redoutable*.

It was if a volcano had erupted below. The entire starboard side of the ship caved in, cannons were upended like toys, and the would-be boarding party was lashed by iron and splinters. The decks below actually blistered and broke upward, planks raw, and the ladders leading from one deck to another disappeared like chaff. Even from a hundred feet above, the human havoc was horrific. Limbs spun off into the black pit that had become the core of my ship. Blood sprayed upward as if shot by a fountain. Torsos were cut in two.

Téméraire crashed against our starboard side, rocking us, and began hammering *Redoutable* with its guns as *Victory* was doing on the port, leaving us helplessly sandwiched between two bigger ships. Our own artillery had fallen silent because there was almost nobody left to man the cannon.

We were being pulverized. Three quarters of *Redoutable*'s men were already dead or wounded.

"*Victory* is getting away!"

The British had chopped away the grapnel lines, and Nelson's battered flagship began to drift off. The widening gap of water revealed that its hull was pock-marked with shot holes and that our own hull was little more than ravaged ribbing. So much wood had been shot away that iron nails jutted like coat hooks. Dead and wounded tumbled into the growing crevasse between the two ships, vanishing in the ocean. As *Victory* got some sea room the rhythm of its guns actually increased, hammering with vicious determination. Shrouds, stays, and halyards snapped; lines scythed; and yardarms crashed down. The protective netting had long since collapsed, and the spars bounced as they hit the main deck with great crashes. The broken French deck was a tangle of sails, rope, and bodies.

We'd lost. My surviving topmen turned on me. "The damned American has been a coward the entire battle!"

"Not a coward, but an ambassador," I gasped. "I tried to stop this."

"Hang him!"

"From what, François? Our rigging is tumbling. I'm going to shoot him before we go over ourselves."

"Lucas wants me alive," I tried. "He'll need a negotiator."

There was no reasoning. They were in a rage of despair, deafened from the fighting, their friends dead.

I represented bad luck. Two held my arms while a third pressed a musket muzzle against my head.

I closed my eyes.

Then *Téméraire* broadsided again, and the mizzen shook as if every cannonball was aimed at its base. Everyone on our platform jerked and fell, the musket's blast going off by my cheek and giving me a painful powder burn. The world pitched and rolled. The mizzen cracked somewhere below, cut like a great tree, and we all yelled and screamed as it leaned, men plunging. With majestic momentum, it fell toward *Victory.*

I instinctively clung to a ratline as the French mast pivoted, watching time again slow to molasses. A few surviving British marines and sailors shouted soundlessly, looking upward at this tower falling toward them. The shattered English rigging loomed like a tangled forest canopy. The gun smoke thickened as we descended into it, as if I was falling into an alien atmosphere of poisonous clouds. A wrack of canvas and broken tackle rushed up.

Harry! came into my mind. Not just my wife, but my poor dear son.

And that was the end.

Chapter 31

I awoke in hell.

The underworld was murkily lit by an amber lantern, and my body was held down on a satanic altar. My tormentors were a coven of demons, their hands and forearms red with blood. I could hear screams and groans of the damned. Some kind of primary devil leaned over me with a shiny saw, ready to begin an eternity of torment.

I should have paid more attention to the maxims of Franklin.

Then the devil frowned.

"What's wrong with this one?" Satan demanded at his minions.

"Brought down insensible and gory. Dead, for all we know."

"Look at him blink. Which limb needs to come off?"

"Blood everywhere, Dr. Beatty. We ain't quite sure."

Grateful heavens, I wasn't damned, but simply in the cockpit in the bowels of the *Victory:* stunned, carried, and now about to be amputated if I didn't testify to my own health. I opened my mouth and a bubble of blood and saliva formed. I gaped like a fish, trying to summon speech.

Surgeon Beatty yanked impatiently at my arms and legs. "Good God, the admiral's dying, and you bother me with an intact lump like this? Get the useless bugger off the table so we can do some real work."

And the demons, or rather seamen, threw me against a bulkhead. Salvation!

I slowly comprehended that I was still alive, and in the British flagship where I'd fallen. It *was* hellish in *Victory's* cockpit, a grim preview of the afterlife. There were at least forty wounded crammed into a space little larger than a kitchen, some bleeding their life away, others sobbing from the agony of quick amputation, and still others lying stunned like poleaxed cattle. Everything was sticky with blood. Lanterns danced eerily, offal slid on the floor, and even here below the cannon, acrid gunsmoke made a thin fog in the air. The beams quaked from the continued roar of massive thirty-six-pounders overhead, the guns leaping and then slamming down with each discharge. The battle was still going on.

My fall had carried me onto the British flagship. By peculiar damnation, I managed to change sides even when unconscious.

I blearily peered about. There was a cluster of men opposite me, attending anxiously to someone important who was propped up against a timber on the larboard side of the flagship. The victim's face was pale and sweating, his features twisted with great pain.

It was Nelson.

So the man I'd seen shot down by the French from the mizzen platform had truly been the commander of the British fleet. Could the Combined Fleet actually win the battle over the English because of this calamity?

But *Redoutable* was being torn apart, wasn't it?

Cheers rumbled from the *Victory*'s crew above.

"What's that? What's that?" I heard Nelson's distinctive nasal voice. He coughed, the sound wet and dire.

"Another one of the enemy must have struck its flag, your lordship," a wounded lieutenant replied.

The admiral lay back. "Good. Good."

Did these officers know I'd just been on the fighting platforms that had mortally wounded their commander?

What had become of my Bonaparte rifle? Would I be remembered as a confidant of Nelson at Merton, or his would-be assassin from the *Redoutable*? I fumbled to check for belongings or wounds. None of the latter, but I was still wearing my Napoleonic pendant. I needed to put distance between this bunch and me until battle emotions cooled.

I shifted slightly, shying toward the cockpit entry, trying hard not to be noticed. A midshipman was screaming and kicking on the surgery table as Beatty sawed, the boy's teeth clamped on a soggy hank of rope. His leg fell away like a hank of beef. The boy gasped, giving great shuddering sobs as his stump was doused with vinegar, bound, and he was shifted to lie like cordwood with the others. There he could contemplate his future as a cripple.

"This next one's already dead," a seaman reported.

"We've no room," Beatty snapped. "Throw him overboard."

I inched farther away. As my vision cleared I saw more than I wanted to. Cracked bone jutting from broken flesh. Skin roasted from flash or fire. Discarded legs and arms piled like pallid sausage. An eye gone, a foot crushed, and a man sucking breath with a three-foot wood splinter impaled between his ribs like a spear. A mouth opened to groan that had no teeth.

A boy no more than twelve sobbed, looking at a wrist that no longer was attached to a hand.

All this glory I had failed to prevent.

There was a bustle of men stiffening to brief attention and a new officer came bent into the cockpit to confer with Nelson. This was Thomas Hardy, I recognized, having seen him after the Battle of the Nile. His uniform was tattered, slivers of wood hanging in fabric that was spattered with blood, but he otherwise seemed to be unhurt. He knelt next to the admiral. Nelson's eyes focused for a moment in recognition, and he reached with his one remaining arm to clasp Hardy's, left to left. You could see his body shaking as he gathered strength to talk. Thank God Emma couldn't watch.

"Well, Hardy, how goes the battle?" It was a croak. "How goes the day with us?"

"Very well, my lord. We've twelve or fourteen of the enemy's ships in our possession, but five of their van have tacked and show an intention of bearing down upon the *Victory*. I've therefore called two or three of our fresh ships round us, and have no doubt of giving them a drubbing."

Nelson managed a weak smile. "I hope none of our ships have struck, Hardy."

"No, my lord, no fear of that."

His head rolled back. "I'm a dead man. I'm going fast; it will all be over with me soon. Come nearer to me."

The captain leaned in.

"Pray let my dear Lady Hamilton have my hair, and all other things belonging to me."

"I hope that Dr. Beatty can hold out some prospect of life." The captain's voice shook with emotion. He glanced at the surgeon.

"Oh, no, it's impossible! My back is shot through. Beatty will tell you so."

The hero was drowning in his own blood. You could hear his struggle for breath. In a melee slaughtering thousands, here was the pathos summed up in one man, one life, and one death. We were all weeping, and I realized I was witnessing something as historic as Napoleon's coronation. We'd never see Nelson's like again.

Beatty came over to probe the admiral's legs. The admiral reported no feeling. "My lord, unhappily for our country, nothing can be done for you."

"I know it. God be praised, I've done my duty."

Duty! It was what General Duhésme called me to as well in the Boulogne camp. But duty to which side? Duty to slaughter, endlessly repeated through history? I shifted and dragged myself a good foot toward the exit.

"Fourteen or fifteen enemy ships surrendered," Nelson muttered. "I'd bargained for twenty."

I didn't see the admiral die. Witnessing history is all very fine, but not if it risks your own survival. I kept creeping. Another bustle and a bosun burst in, one ear trickling blood from the concussions, face black from powder, eyes wide and straining. He looked anxiously about and then pointed at me. "There's the one! That's the frog bastard!"

A dozen heads swiveled. I gasped my protest. "I'm no Frenchman," I said in quite fluent English. I dragged myself by my arms half outside the chamber. My hospital stay was over.

The bosun followed me out. "He came over with the *Redoutable*'s mainmast, carrying a pretty gun from Boney hisself! Could'a been 'im who fired the fatal shot!"

"I'm sure you're confused . . ."

"Let's hang him!"

"Come, Jack," a saner seaman said, "the poor sod's just another prisoner."

"We've no masts or yards left to hang anybody from anyway."

"Bloody hell, then I'll rig one meself!"

"Aye. I won't have a damned jack traitor lying near our saintly admiral!"

"I'm trying to leave . . ." I wheezed.

"Maybe we should just shoot him with his own damned rifle."

I was the only man in a dozen miles to try to keep out of this battle and now was being proposed for execution by both sides. By the devil's horns, why are my accusers so unjust, and so enthusiastic? I'd promoted myself from spy to diplomat, but I was the only person who recognized my high station.

I'd also been stunned, as if taking a blow from a hammer, and I struggled to think fast. These sailors still had their blood up from the battle, and I couldn't wait for sense to return. I had to use trickery.

"Just don't drown me!" I suddenly cried.

They paused. "As if you have a choice, assassin."

"I'm fearful of water, lads. Hang or shoot this misunderstood American if you must, but don't put me overboard and watch the sharks. Oh, I hate the cold sea! Anything but that!"

"Hate the sea? Can't swim, I suppose."

"Not a stroke. Lord, I'll sink into the black depths and be eaten by fishes. That's a preview of hell, that is. Nelson dreads it, too. Yes, hemp around my neck would be a mercy. There's a good fellow, give me a proper hanging. With ceremony and a Bible, if you don't mind."

The sailors looked at each other and grunted. "That's it then, lads. Sometimes simplest is best." One bent. "Say hello to Davy Jones, assassin."

"But I can't swim, I told you! Surely you won't let me drown!"

They laughed, grabbed, lurched me upright, and glared like a mob rousting a heretic. Hands tore at my wretched clothing, and one came away with the pendant.

"Look here then, a medal from Napoleon!"

"And a savage tomahawk!"

"Bloody hell, he's a filthy spy. Or worse."

"What's worse than that?"

"I'm just an American tourist," I protested feebly. The broken sword I'd strapped to my inner thigh, and they didn't snatch that.

"Yes, the sea for him."

Sometimes I make my own luck.

They hustled me up to the lowest gun deck and gave an angry shove toward a shot-smashed gunport. It reminded me somewhat of being pitched from a gambling salon or brothel, but I was usually fortified with alcohol when that occurred.

The last glimpse I had of the lower gun deck of *Victory* was as ghastly as the medical cockpit below. Several cannon had been dismounted by French shot, their barrels tilted like sprawled logs. Bodies were being picked over to find the rare wounded, with one corpse shoved out a gunport even as I watched. Smoke smeared the horror with greasy gauze, and new beams of light poked from shot holes to highlight cones of carnage. Splinters had turned the deck into a bed of wooden spikes, wet with puddles of blood. Blobs of flesh were lodged against framing like hurled pudding. Disconnected fingers lay like worms.

The entire cavity had been newly painted with blood, so heavy that it literally dripped from overhead beams in places. Some French cannonballs were embedded to jut like iron breasts. Loose balls rolled to the pitch of waves. I could hear the desultory clanging of a pump below, and the slosh of seawater as the ship groaned.

"Here's what your frog friends did, bloody spy."

"I've been trying to halt this slaughter."

"Rob us of victory, you mean."

"You probably shot poor Nelson with that fancy gun of yours."

"No, I tried to save him. I'm his friend." I waved feebly. "If you'll just ask . . ."

"Pitch him, Jack. The French are bearing down again."

"Bloody right. No more time for this nonsense."

"Don't drown me! I'm a British agent for Sir Sidney Smith!"

"You're a spy, a turncoat, and a Yankee dog. I can see it in your eyes."

I shut them. "I've got intelligence of the French fleet . . ."

They stuffed me through the ragged gunport as if they were grinding sausage. "There you go!" I dropped into the sea.

My rifle, and tomahawk, they kept.

The lower gun deck isn't far above the water. I rolled off the curved hull, cutting myself on the ragged edges of fresh shot holes and barnacles, and hit the cold Atlantic with a splash.

The water was a shock, but the plunge flushed my thinking. My head stung, and I surmised I'd cut it on the long fall on the mizzen. I'd no idea how I'd survived at all, but as I kicked away from the *Victory* I saw the flagship had lost all its masts and the deck was a tangle of fallen timber. Sails dragged in the ocean.

I must have fallen into a web of wreckage when the *Redoutable*'s mizzen came down, the tangle breaking the fall just enough to save my life.

Now I backstroked away. The sailors stared at me with consternation.

"Look at that. I thought the bugger couldn't swim!"

"He's paddling like a damn duck. Say, Jack, I believe he lied to us."

"That ain't fair. Come back and be hanged, you!"

I waved.

"Bloody damnation, let's just shoot him. You there, marine! Your musket loaded?"

So I rolled and struck out for all I was worth, and when a bullet plunked nearby I dove and swam underwater for a spell. Thank the Lord for idiots.

When I surfaced, I looked back. One man shook his fist, but the wind was blowing *Victory* away. The others had lost interest or been ordered to other tasks. A swell lifted me and set me down again. The wind was picking up as the battle went from a boil to a simmer, and the black sky to the west foretold coming fury.

I set off swimming toward *Redoutable.*

It was drifting down on me even as *Victory* drifted away. For a mile in each direction battered battleships wandered, rigging trashed, guns thumping, men staggering. Everyone was exhausted. Firing cannon is bloody hard work.

One ship, presumably French, was burning like a bonfire. Many of the French and Spanish vessels had already surrendered, including the gigantic *Santisima Trinidad. Redoutable* had struck to the *Téméraire.* The two ships, still locked together, floated about a hundred yards from where I'd been flung. I swam to the vessel I'd started on fairly easily, initially hoping for more of a hero's welcome from the French. But wait, those soldiers had wanted to shoot me, too, hadn't they? And the British prize crew that had clambered aboard might be even less friendly if they got word of my exit from the *Victory*.

So I treaded water, thinking. For the first time I was in the neutral ocean, not attached to either side. No one was trying to enlist me, no one was trying to extinguish me. I was without any cause but my own, exempt from imperial passion, floating between both fleets. And somewhere my family waited, possibly in prison.

The French vessel was an even greater wreck than the British, the main and mizzen entirely gone and foremast shorn short. The stubs gaped with yellow shards of wood erupted like prickly flowers. Cannon tilted at crazy angles. Its perforated hull was draped in shot-off sails like the skirts of a forlorn bride.

The sea was a mess of floating spars, smashed boats, and bobbing bodies. Eddies were still tinted pink from the downspouts of blood. Remembering the threat of sharks, I needed to make a decision. I could hear English shouts and cheers across the water as enemy after enemy lowered their colors.

All that regal beauty destroyed in an afternoon. The destruction, of course, made the splendor more poignant.

How we love war! People will elect men who promise it. Napoleon understood this, and had his crown.

No one tried to help me back aboard the *Redoutable*. Casualties were so heavy that she drifted like a ghost ship. Smoke steamed from her shot holes. Cries for help echoed from her ports. Shrouds and halyards hung into the heaving sea like lifelines, but warships no longer tempted me. I speculatively floated along the hull of the captured French warship to its stern and beyond, to the towrope holding the ship's boats. I could hear the "crews" aboard, chickens clucking and sheep bleating.

I rotated in the water. Captain Lucas had surrendered to some British officers who were pointing to a longboat to take him off. A new ship, the *Swiftsure*, was hove to off *Redoutable*'s stern, and lines were being rowed to take the prize in tow. The freshening wind made cat's paws on the sea, and what would happen to these battered fleets when the storm fully struck? The clouds were getting blacker.

I was tired of waiting for passage to Venice. It was time to pirate a boat of my own. One of the craft being towed behind *Redoutable* would do just fine.

Chapter 32

I swam along the line of boats and hauled myself into the captain's gig, the smartest sailor of the lot. I moved aside two hen coops and used a boat's knife tethered on a cord to cut the towline, slipping away from the rest of the chain of small craft. I tensed for an angry shot from *Redoutable* but didn't get one; its marines were occupied with greater tragedies than the loss of a captain's gig. Or the loss of Ethan Gage. Far from being missed, I'd likely be counted as dead, I realized. I could later resurrect myself, at least briefly, as whomever I chose.

I drifted, coming to grips with the beauty and horror of the day. Nelson dead, England triumphant, the Combined Fleet destroyed. Napoleon would never seriously threaten England with invasion again.

The admiral's victory against the Combined Fleet was even more decisive than at the Nile. I would eventually learn that seventeen French and Spanish ships had been captured. One had blown up. Britain didn't lose a single ship. England's greatest naval victory had been accompanied by the death of its greatest naval hero, and was about to be followed by one of history's most terrible storms.

Swiftsure had taken its prize under tow, but *Redoutable* was settling. Across the water, I could hear the creak of pumps.

Dripping and shivering from my dunking, I took inventory of my new flagship, a sixteen-footer I christened *Astiza*. The fleets were scattering, the wind building. Of the seventeen captured prizes, fifteen were so wrecked by gunfire that they were being towed. Five damaged British ships had to be towed as well, and dismasted warships like *Victory* were barely under control. The storm was pushing the hulks toward the lee shore of Spain.

Was the emerald I'd pawned in London still exerting its Aztec curse? I'd tried to become rich and failed, tried to prevent war and failed, tried to save Nelson for his mistress Emma and failed, and tried to stay close to my wife and failed.

In each case I'd been dependent on others for any success.

Perhaps it was time to depend on myself.

Redoutable was slowly sinking by the stern, while tied to the laboring *Swiftsure* two hundred yards ahead. With the wind rising, waves dashed against the beak of the French ship as if against rocks on a shore. Men were chopping away wrecked rigging to try to save her. Two great hawsers led from bits on the foredeck to the English man-of-war. The ropes would slacken when the roll of swells briefly lessened the distance between the ships, and then snap taut when the rhythm went the other way, humming like harpsichord wire. At some point they'd snap.

It was time to cut my own puppet strings.

Since escaping the Caribbean and arriving to avenge the wife I thought dead, I'd ricocheted from one side to another, the spy and diplomat of both English and French. I'd been hired and used several times over, betrayed by Catherine Marceau whom I'd saved, sacrificed the safety of my family, and been nearly killed.

I'd also come away with a quest involving a fabled Brazen Head, with Catherine, Talleyrand, and Pasques after it, too, for their master, Napoleon.

How easy to avoid the traps of the present if you knew the future! Had Albertus Magnus crafted that power into an "android"? And had it been destroyed as evil, or hidden for rediscovery?

If my wife and son were still alive, the Brazen Head might lead me to them, or them to the Brazen Head.

I was done working my way for passage, done relying on London financial brokers, and done allowing policemen to separate me from my family.

As self-appointed captain, I took inventory. There were emergency stores of water, wine, and biscuit on the boat, plus a musket, two pistols, a cutlass, and two cloaks thrown in by French officers in hopes they'd be saved from bullet holes. I poked slits in one and lashed it to cover the front of the gig and help keep out spray in the coming storm. Then I erected the boat's mast and tied on its sail, reefing it to not much more than a handkerchief.

I settled by the tiller, snugged in the second cloak, trimmed my scrap of canvas, and began to move, bubbles swirling in my wake. I sailed around the shattered stern of *Redoutable*, looking into a maw in which just a few survivors crept. A British officer who'd taken charge of the smashed prize finally challenged me from the battered taffrail on the poop. "You there! You can't take that boat!"

"But I have." The wind snatched my reply across the water.

"Are you mad? A storm is coming. You won't get fifty yards!"

"More like five hundred. You can watch me flip and say, 'I told you so.'"

He shook his head. We were all half-mad with sorrow and weariness.

As I steered onto a broad reach running south-southeast and the rudder bit, the little gig took off like a Congreve rocket. My hope was to run before the blow and make harbor near Gibraltar, bargaining for a bigger ship to Venice. When we'd left Cadiz, I'd felt imprisoned. Now, alone on a wild ocean, I was free.

I leaned against one side of the hull to keep the gig in balance, feeling the tiller dance like a live thing as the boat climbed one side of the swells and then sledded down the other. The wind was brisk but fair. If I could keep from broaching and turning over it would be a sleigh ride to Gibraltar.

There was a crack. I looked back. The lines holding *Redoutable* to *Swiftsure* had snapped, and the French vessel's stern was submerging in the waves, its shot-pocked bow rising. I could hear the last faint screams of terror from those still on board. A final British long-boat was taking off its own prize crew and however many French could fit. The rest were doomed.

I made a broader survey. As far as the eye could see, the dismasted hulls of warships tossed on a gray horizon, some nearing the dangerous shore.

I learned from newspaper accounts months later that nine captured ships were wrecked in the storm, drowning 2,700 men. Five ships were burned and scuttled because they couldn't be saved. Four more French ships would be captured by the British in the coming weeks, completing the Combined Fleet's annihilation. Total French and Spanish dead and wounded were eight thousand, justifying the premonitory wails of the women of Cadiz.

Villeneuve's attempt at personal honor had been purchased at high cost indeed. He'd retained command and led it to disaster. To survive this life, you have to understand that all men and women are fundamentally mad.

Eventually, the captured admiral would be exchanged for other prisoners and would then commit suicide in France, stabbing himself several times in a locked room rather than face Napoleon.

Lucas was also captured, but he survived imprisonment as a naval hero.

Those great events were a universe away. My world was a small stolen boat, the surrounding swells of an angry ocean, and a wind that blew me toward Astiza.

I felt danger, but also strange calm. I had a fundamental conviction that I was at last steering where I was supposed to steer and that Astiza and Harry were alive and waiting, whatever Catherine claimed. The storm was wicked, but hadn't I already threaded the rocky fangs of a reef with Johnstone? I was sailing to reunite with my loved ones and perhaps find the best treasure of all: a machine that could foretell the future.

As the last light faded on that storm day, a swell lifted me high on the undulating dunes of the sea. Faraway lanterns shone on imperiled ships, signaling futilely for rescue. Cape Trafalgar looked like a smudge of smoke on my port side. Somewhere directly ahead was the great mass of Africa. Spray blew off wave tops like whipping streamers of gray.

I settled back with bread and wine, toasting escape and determination.

Somehow I knew my family was waiting.

The puppet had cut his strings.

Historical Note

H istory is life: complex, confusing, and inconclusive. Problems drag, personalities linger, careers meander, and love sometimes goes unconsummated.

The British naval victory at the Battle of Trafalgar is so celebrated because it is so different. England's greatest sea victory was accompanied by the death of its greatest naval hero. Triumph and tragedy in a single afternoon! The twin events hit Britain like a thunderbolt and have inspired poets and painters ever since. While reminiscences of the battle differ in detail, its course has been tracked almost minute by minute, blow by blow, and ship by ship. The combat of *Redoutable* and *Victory* described here is based on the historical record, with the exception that the French ship's mizzen did not fall on the English flagship, delivering an American with it. Nelson's dying words in this novel are an abbreviation of what he actually said. Such perfect drama seldom occurs.

Ethan Gage is not alone in his awe of the drama that was Trafalgar. Survivors testified to the grand majesty of the approaching fleets and the horrific slaughter that followed. Perfect grace produced hideous destruction.

It's ironic, then, that historians can (and occasionally do) argue that the battle need not have been fought at all. Napoleon had abandoned his plan to invade England, and the French and Spanish fleets were deteriorating because Nelson's quest for sea superiority had already been achieved by tedious blockade. After weeks of hesitation, Admiral Villeneuve led his unready ships to sea only because he'd been warned of his own replacement. Risking catastrophe became a matter of honor. Napoleon had goaded his commander to self-destruction.

Nelson's victory at the earlier Battle of Copenhagen may also have been unnecessary since the murder of the Russian czar ended the coalition in which the Danish fleet might have been used against England.

But battles are harder to stop than start, and Trafalgar ensured that Bonaparte would never directly threaten Britain again. England's domination of the sea would not be challenged until World War I.

Whether a physically deteriorating Horatio Nelson had a death wish—when he wore embroidered replicas of his medals while strutting exposed on his quarterdeck—is a psychological mystery that can never be resolved. He was killed from the mizzenmast platform of *Redoutable* as described in this novel, but a specific claim by French sergeant Robert Guillemard to have fired the fatal shot, made a quarter century after the fact, is considered a likely fabrication by most historians. There was so much battle smoke that it is possible, and even likely, that the fatal shot was blind.

Certainly Nelson's quest for glory was a more rational calculation than it would be in today's grimmer and robotic age. He was a rector's son who rose to lordship and wealth through his prowess in battle. Sacrificing his arm and eye won him adulation, gifts, and Emma Hamilton. Admirals didn't accumulate fame for avoiding battle, they got it by seeking victory, and Nelson stands upon his column in London's Trafalgar Square precisely because he sought a battle of annihilation. He and Napoleon were not just heroes to their respective nations, but celebrities. Both commented that they recognized the extraordinary drama of their own lives. They were actors in a play they both suspected would have a tragic ending.

The history behind this novel is true. There were royalist conspiracies to overthrow Napoleon, an increasingly efficient French secret police to counter them, an increasingly ambitious British spy service, and imaginative schemes on all sides to win. French ideas for crossing the Channel included balloons, tunnels, and yes, dolphins. Robert Fulton and William Congreve did invent torpedoes and rockets and these new weapons were tried several times, anticipating modern war.

Napoleon's coronation went as described, except for the role played by the Crown of Thorns in this novel. That crown is real, stored in the Treasury of Notre Dame and still displayed monthly, but exactly why and how Bonaparte ignored rehearsed protocol and crowned his wife's head and his own has never been adequately explained. Is it possible a renegade American played a mysterious role? For readers who doubt, go to the Louvre and study David's painting of Napoleon's crowning of Josephine at the coronation. If you look in the painted crowd to the left you will see the surprised face of an onlooker. He looks very much like Ethan Gage.

As in the other novels of this series, most of the characters in this book were real people, including the military officers and police officials (I have taken liberties with Pasques), smuggler Tom Johnstone, royalist conspirators such as Georges Cadoudal, and coronation participants such as Talleyrand and Cardinal Belloy. Catherine Marceau is fiction, but the agent Rose is inspired by a real-life Channel spy of that name. I've described events at Boulogne as they happened. Napoleon did foolishly order a naval exercise in the face of a gale and did try to save some of the men who drowned, his boat swamping in the process. He did lose his hat, which later washed ashore.

Legends of a Brazen Head or "android" are true. The Paris catacombs are real and can be visited today, if you want to keep company with six million dead. The details of Parisian life in that period are as accurate as I can make them, including anecdotes about personalities such as Talleyrand or Juliette Récamier.

Similarly, one can tour Walmer Castle, although its true Napoleonic-era role as spy headquarters goes unmentioned in the audio commentary. Nelson's home at Merton no longer exists, but the description of its being crammed with his memorabilia is based on history. Nelson did order a coffin made from the mast of the French flagship *L'Orient* (after a battle Ethan describes in *Napoleon's Pyramids*), did store the casket in his cabin at times, did supply it with funeral sheet music, and did relate that a Caribbean fortune-teller

488 · **Historical Note**

had told him in his youth that she saw no future for him beyond 1805. The children's poem warning of a cannibalistic Napoleon was really recited as England braced for invasion.

It was common practice after sea battles to unceremoniously dump the dead overboard because there was no way to embalm them. Nelson anxiously asked that his body be preserved so Dr. Beatty put him in a barrel of brandy. The admiral was eventually buried with great ceremony in London's St. Paul's Cathedral.

Horatio and Emma never married, but did exchange rings before his departure for Trafalgar. Their secret ceremony was never recognized. His wife, Fanny, and Nelson's relatives received pensions from the British government eventually totaling £200,000, but Emma was ignored, and she squandered what Nelson had left her. She died a lonely alcoholic at the port of Calais in France in January of 1815, between Napoleon's first abdication and his final defeat at Waterloo. Horatia, increasingly estranged from her mother, married a vicar, gave birth to ten children, and lived to age eighty.

Because this novel follows carefully recorded historical events, I'm in debt to contemporary accounts and modern historians. At the necessity of leaving many out, I must acknowledge my regular reference to such scholars as Mark Adkin, Roy Adkins, John

Elting, Christopher Hibbert, Christopher Lee, Tom Pocock, Jean Robiquet, and Napoleonic biographers such as Robert Asprey, Proctor Patterson Jones, Frank McLynn, and Alan Schom, all of whom help bring Bonaparte to life. Two valuable works from the early twentieth century are the 1906 *The Enemy at Trafalgar* by Edward Fraser, which assembles narratives from the French and Spanish participants, and John Masefield's *Sea Life in Nelson's Time*, published in 1905. A number of even earlier historical works on such subjects as the Boulogne Camp, the royalist conspiracy, the French police, and Napoleon's coronation have become more readily available as reprints in recent years. We even have *Indiscretions of a Prefect of Police* by Réal himself, though it is more a compilation of period gossip than a confession by the inspector. Recognizing what an extraordinary period they had lived through, many participants wrote memoirs, including Napoleon. All must be taken with a grain of salt. Memories are selective and calculating, and psychologists have found the more we remember something, the more we embroider it. But what tumultuous times their recollections record!

Acknowledgments

The continuation of the Ethan Gage series is made possible by the enthusiasm and support of my editor, Maya Ziv; publisher Jonathan Burnham of HarperCollins; and agent Andrew Stuart. Maya is my new muse in guiding Astiza and pondering the ways of women of the early nineteenth century, Jonathan has a native Brit's enthusiasm for an American rascal, and Andrew keeps the contracts coming. What a team! Others at HarperCollins I'm indebted to include publicist Heather Drucker; production editor David Koral; designer Richard Ljoenes, who gave a new look to the Ethan books; artist Seb Jarnot, who decided what he might look like; foreign rights marketer Carolyn Bodkin; online marketing manager Mark Ferguson; and many more. HarperCollins is not just a conglomerate, it's a home.

I benefited from many museums, both French and English, but am particularly thankful for the National Museum of the Royal Navy in Portsmouth, England. It is remarkable that you can tour *Victory* as Nelson sailed her, and see where he died. There's even a shot-torn sail on display that survived the battle.

My wife, Holly, was once more navigator and helpmate in researching this novel, my muse for Ethan's relationships, and first reader. She endured the tedious line to visit the Paris Catacombs, spending part of our visit with the dead. She enjoyed it, just as balmy Astiza would.

About the Author

William Dietrich is the author of twelve novels, including five previous Ethan Gage titles—*Napoleon's Pyramids*, *The Rosetta Key*, *The Dakota Cipher*, *The Barbary Pirates*, and *The Emerald Storm*. Dietrich is also a Pulitzer Prize–winning journalist, historian, and naturalist. A winner of the PNBA Award for Nonfiction, he lives in Washington State.

THE NEW LUXURY IN READING

We hope you enjoyed reading
our new, comfortable print size and found it
an experience you would like to repeat.

Well – you're in luck!

HarperLuxe offers the finest in fiction and
nonfiction books in this same larger print size and
paperback format. Light and easy to read, HarperLuxe
paperbacks are for book lovers who want to see
what they are reading without the strain.

For a full listing of titles and
new releases to come, please visit our website:
www.HarperLuxe.com